WANDERLUST

"Fast-paced and thrilling, *Wanderlust* is pure adrenaline. Sirantha Jax is an unforgettable character, and I can't wait to find out what happens to her next. The world Ann Aguirre has created is a roller-coaster ride to remember."
—Christine Feehan, #1 *New York Times* bestselling author of *Dark Predator*

"The details of communication, travel, politics, and power in a greedy, lively universe have been devised to the last degree but are presented effortlessly. Aguirre has the mastery and vision which come from critical expertise: She is unmistakably a true science fiction fan, writing in the genre she loves."
—*The Independent* (London)

"A thoroughly enjoyable blend of science fiction, romance, and action, with a little something for everyone, and a great deal of fun. It's down and dirty, unafraid to show some attitude."
—*SF Site*

GRIMSPACE

"A terrific first novel full of page-turning action, delightful characters, and a wry twist of humor. Romance may be in the air. Bullets, ugly beasties, and really nasty bad guys definitely are."
—Mike Shepherd, national bestselling author of the Kris Longknife series

"An irresistible blend of action and attitude. Sirantha Jax doesn't just leap off the page—she storms out, kicking, cursing, and mouthing off. No wonder her pilot falls in love with her; readers will, too."
—Sharon Shinn, national bestselling author of *Troubled Waters*

"A tightly written, edge-of-your-seat read."
—Linnea Sinclair, RITA Award–winning author of *Rebels and Lovers*

Also by Ann Aguirre

Sirantha Jax Series

GRIMSPACE
WANDERLUST
DOUBLEBLIND
KILLBOX
AFTERMATH

Corine Solomon Series

BLUE DIABLO
HELL FIRE
SHADY LADY

AFTERMATH

ANN AGUIRRE

ACE BOOKS, NEW YORK

THE BERKLEY PUBLISHING GROUP
Published by the Penguin Group
Penguin Group (USA) Inc.
375 Hudson Street, New York, New York 10014, USA
Penguin Group (Canada), 90 Eglinton Avenue East, Suite 700, Toronto, Ontario M4P 2Y3, Canada
(a division of Pearson Penguin Canada Inc.)
Penguin Books Ltd., 80 Strand, London WC2R 0RL, England
Penguin Group Ireland, 25 St. Stephen's Green, Dublin 2, Ireland (a division of Penguin Books Ltd.)
Penguin Group (Australia), 250 Camberwell Road, Camberwell, Victoria 3124, Australia
(a division of Pearson Australia Group Pty. Ltd.)
Penguin Books India Pvt. Ltd., 11 Community Centre, Panchsheel Park, New Delhi—110 017, India
Penguin Group (NZ), 67 Apollo Drive, Rosedale, Auckland 0632, New Zealand
(a division of Pearson New Zealand Ltd.)
Penguin Books (South Africa) (Pty.) Ltd., 24 Sturdee Avenue, Rosebank, Johannesburg 2196,
South Africa

Penguin Books Ltd., Registered Offices: 80 Strand, London WC2R 0RL, England

This is a work of fiction. Names, characters, places, and incidents either are the product of the author's imagination or are used fictitiously, and any resemblance to actual persons, living or dead, business establishments, events, or locales is entirely coincidental. The publisher does not have any control over and does not assume any responsibility for author or third-party websites or their content.

AFTERMATH

An Ace Book / published by arrangement with the author

PRINTING HISTORY
Ace mass-market edition / September 2011

Copyright © 2011 by Ann Aguirre.
Cover art by Scott M. Fischer.
Cover design by Lesley Worrell.

ISBN: 978-0-441-02078-2

ACE
Ace Books are published by The Berkley Publishing Group,
a division of Penguin Group (USA) Inc.,
375 Hudson Street, New York, New York 10014.
ACE and the "A" design are trademarks of Penguin Group (USA) Inc.

PRINTED IN THE UNITED STATES OF AMERICA

10 9 8 7 6 5 4 3 2 1

For Liam

ACKNOWLEDGMENTS

As ever, I start with my agent, Laura Bradford. We're both busier than we used to be, but that means we can have a meaningful conversation in a few words. She still handles all my concerns with her customary aplomb, ever a source of reassurance, good sense, and valuable advice.

Next, I salute Anne Sowards, who saw Jax's potential . . . and who usually doesn't like first-person, present tense. I'm glad you made an exception. Our heroine's come a long way with your hand on the rudder, so thank you for your expertise. There's only one book left, and I'm proud of what we've accomplished. Thank you. And it's about time Jax got her happy ending, isn't it?

Thanks to my copy editors, the Schwagers. In fact, much appreciation to the whole Penguin team. Your work makes mine possible.

I must also express admiration and awe for the beautiful art that graces my covers. Scott Fischer doesn't even need a whisper from me because he sees Jax's world with an artist's eyes, and he's depicted her beautifully from the very beginning.

My friends are ever patient and supportive. Big thanks go to Bree Bridges, Donna Herren, Lauren Dane, Larissa Ione, Jaye Wells, Louisa Edwards, and Candace Havens. This magical crew keeps me positive, motivated, and ready to tackle my goals, day after day. They do this through their own tireless work ethic and because they are consummate professionals who lead by example. I'm so lucky to have friends like them.

I need to give a special shout-out to Suzanne McLeod. I sent *Aftermath* to her, and her words of encouragement made me feel like a million bucks, but more than that? At the eleventh hour, as I was peering at my manuscript, wondering what else it needed, she was kind enough to make some notes, and they were brilliant. Everything she said, I was like, *Yes, why didn't I see that?!* So if you love the book more than you expected to, the credit belongs to Suzanne.

Major thanks to my family. Andres, Alek, and Andrea are wonderful. They know how important my writing is to me, and they are patient and flexible with my schedule. You all enrich my life and make it possible for me to dream as big as I do.

Finally, I send profound appreciation to my readers. You're the reason this works. I cherish each e-mail, so please send them to ann.aguirre@gmail.com. I value you all and thank you for buying my books.

CHAPTER I

Dying isn't like living; it requires no effort at all.

I just have to sit quiet and let it happen. But I can't. Like a fish with a barbed hook caught in its mouth, I twist and pull, desperately fighting my way back to the anguished meat I left in the cockpit with Hit. She has no way home without me, and if I don't succeed in this, the consequences will be far worse than two lost females. Despite the siren call of grimspace and the scintillant colors, I *must* live; it's never mattered so much before.

I have to get back. I have to warn them, or every ship that tries to jump will never come out again.

Since the Conglomerate doesn't have an armada to match the size of the Morgut fleet, I had to reprogram the beacons; it was the only way to slow them down. Otherwise, so many lives might have been lost. But no impulsive act, however well intended, comes without consequence. I know that better than most.

As I draw closer, the pain ramps up. At least I have the assurance that the nanites will repair the damage, so whatever I've done to myself, I won't wind up trapped in my own body. If March were here, he'd help anchor me, but Hit lacks his Psi ability, which means I'm on my own. Instead of the door in the far horizon—that place of passing through—I focus on my body. Past the silent screaming, I can hear my heartbeat, faint and sluggish, right now no more than a reflexive physical response. Yet it might be enough.

With each thud, I pull myself closer, as if that tenuous thread is a rope I can grasp with ghostly hands. Each pound of my pulse brings me a little closer, then, with a wrench almost as agonizing as the one that tore me loose, I fall back in. My hands move, and I feel Hit beside me, questioning. *You back, Jax?*

Sickness boils in my veins. I don't feel right in my own head, as if I've come back smaller somehow, but I block it off from her. She's done enough. The consequences from this point on are mine alone.

Yeah, I reply, *time to go home.*

I don't know whether I've been gone minutes or hours, but we've tarried too long regardless. Grimspace is a bitch mistress, who will drain you dry and leave the husk without a second glance—and without my implants, this suicide run would've killed me, no question. Weakness wracks me, but I can get us out; I have that much left. Though it might break me, I'm determined to bring my pilot home safely. The colors glow brighter as grimspace swells within me, and it feels as if a door opens in my head. Thanks to the neural blockers, I can't feel the associated pain; the ship shudders and sails through.

We emerge in straight space, high over Venice Minor. Such a long, impossible journey, when we didn't go any-where at all. Not really. Not in the sense of distance, but this is the nature of paradox. My hands tremble as I unplug, then the scene unfolds before me.

Lights twinkle in the dark, but they are not stars. *Mary, no.* We weren't fast enough. So many Morgut ships made it through; they dim the constellations. Their shapes are alien to my eyes, like creatures that came out of the sea, finned and spined, with odd appendages and stranger designs. Because we're so small—a two-person vessel—we haven't registered on their sensors yet; there are too many energy signatures clustered in a small area for our numbers to leap out at anyone. But it's only a matter of time, and we have no weapons.

The Morgut have left their homeworld and are seeking to colonize other planets, most of which are Conglomerate held. They treat us as livestock, food for the feast, and it's all I can do to contain my fear. My mother, Ramona, sacrificed herself, dying on the dreadnaught hull, to give us a chance, and bought time before the rest of the Morgut fleet could arrive at Venice Minor.

But they're here now. Not the whole force, certainly. I accomplished what I set out to do—I diminished their numbers. Mary only knows if it will be enough.

Sweat cools on my forehead as I study the scene. With some relief, I note there are no more dreadnaughts. If we can get ships up here, we have a chance in this final battle. It looks as if they're positioning to bombard the planet. The flagship is enormous, with jutting guns powerful enough to take out entire city quadrants. As yet, I don't see any movement from the armada; they must still be forming up and performing repairs down below.

I hope they weren't sending reinforcements here when I changed the beacons. The changes I wrought in grimspace will affect jumpers universally; the Morgut can't navigate, but neither can the Conglomerate—or any other ships for that matter. I've done a dire thing, but I refuse to let fear govern my actions. That's not me, and it never will be. First off, I must bounce a warning, but we're close enough to the Morgut fleet that they'll catch the transmission, then blow us to hell. I weigh the risks and decide the message can wait until we land; if I die here, then I've set humanity back a hundred turns in terms of using the beacons to navigate. Still, I don't feel good about the call. At this point, every second counts.

"Do we make a run for the surface?" Hit asks.

"We can't do anything up here."

No weapons, no shields. So that's the answer. She offers a brief nod in reply, and we start the insane journey home. As we approach the atmosphere, the enemy fleet notices us, and Hit dodges shots coming in hot on our stern. One successful strike, and we're done. But she flies like other people dance, and even negotiating the burn as we fall planetside, she manages to skew us away from the incoming barrage. I can only watch; I've done my part, and the rest is up to Hit. Her constant maneuvering makes for a rocky reentry; she can't calculate the best angle and take care with the ship hardware, so I watch the ground sail toward me at insane speed and fight the urge to close my eyes. The flagship shoots wide, its missiles zooming past us toward the ground. *Ha. Missed.*

The clouds whip past, and the tiny dots on the ground resolve into lines, then trees; the green-and-brown patchwork sharpens into the lines of my mother's garden. In the distance I glimpse the blue shine of the sea, but several alarms flash red, and a low whine fills the cockpit. The small ship rattles as if it might break apart entirely. I do shut my eyes then.

Our vessel goes into a low roll as we near the ground; impact flings me forward, but the harness catches me. I'll have bruises to show for this most recent bit of insanity, but that doesn't seem like enough damage. I should have new scars. I risk a look and find we're upside down, but more or less in one piece, outside the hangar. I don't know who's more surprised, Hit or me. She flashes me a triumphant grin and a high sign.

"Pretty fragging good, right?"

"Maybe the best I've ever seen," I admit.

She winks. "I won't tell March."

We've burned out the stabilizers, but otherwise, we did remarkably well. Maybe *only* a tiny ship like this one could've gotten past the vanguard of the Morgut fleet. I imagine the rest of them lost in grimspace, trying to interpret the new signal and failing. They'll die there, no matter how powerful they are or how indestructible their dread-naughts.

"Does the comm still work?"

"It should."

I set it to Tarn's personal code and bounce a message at the highest priority. "Don't let any Conglomerate ships jump. They won't be able to interpret the new beacon frequency without instruction. Give coordinates for a central meeting point and instruct them to make their way via long haul. Doesn't matter how long it takes . . . It's better than being lost. I'll explain everything fully when I see you."

Not content with toppling the closest thing we had to a stable government, I've now crippled interstellar travel. But it was for a good cause. I'm still positive I did the right thing, no matter what they do to me later. If it means prison time or execution, I'm not sorry. Someone had to make the tough call, and I was there.

The doors are jammed from the rough landing and don't respond to the computerized controls, so Hit and I kick our way out. Before I exit, I snag the small survival pack that's included in ships like this one. My limbs still feel weak as I pull myself up; I'm not prepared for the wreckage that greets us. Oh, not from our ship. All around us, the jungle burns, black smoke swirling toward the sky. Stone rubble constitutes all that's left of the villa, just a bombed-out shell with broken walls rising no more than two meters any-where. Cracks web the foundation, charred black, and I can smell death in the air. It's not a scent you forget.

"They weren't shooting at us," I realize aloud.

Hit shakes her head. "I should have realized. Those weren't ship-to-ship weapons . . . though if we'd been hit, they would've vaporized us just the same."

As we rocketed toward the ground, the bombardment began. What I'd taken for lasers being fired at our stern had been photon missiles from the flagship, aimed at decimat-ing the ground. The wrongness hits me then—because we left, we lived. Survival feels like cowardice.

I can't see the point in destroying such a beautiful,

defenseless place, but I'm not Morgut. Maybe this devastation serves their master plan, or it's simple retaliation for
our defiance. Millions of innocent civilians will die on
Venice Minor, innocuously enjoying their vacations; they
might've saved for the trip their whole lives, as such consummate luxury doesn't come cheap.

The smoldering wreck of the *Triumph* catches my eye,
recognizable only from the charred metal piece bearing its
Conglomerate registration number, and the rest lies scattered around the hangar in bits no bigger than the span of
my arms. God help any crewmen who were still aboard,
working on repairs. My heart feels like lead in my chest.
Beside me, Hit curls her hands into fists.

"We should look for survivors," I say at last.

We ready our weapons in case the Morgut sent a ground
team—yet why would they? They can continue the blitz
from above. The missiles aren't toxic, so the natural beauty
will rebound in time—and by then, they will have claimed
the lush, tropical paradise, a replacement for their own
dying world. Once they establish a foothold on Venice
Minor, fighting them will be more difficult. For all I know,
they might breed fast enough to compensate for the troops
lost in grimspace, and then we'll be back where we
started—with no solution in sight.

Still, I power up my laser pistol, wanting it charged and
ready in case we run into trouble. Silently, Hit does the
same. We move through the burning graveyard with the
scent of smoke and scorched metal in our nostrils, compounded with a chemical burn that makes breathing difficult. There's no telling what might be in the air, but I don't
have any air scrubbers handy. The little ship we departed
in offered no special equipment, and there's nothing left
intact here on the ground.

"Any movement?"

Grimly, Hit shakes her head, continuing to pick a path
through the wreckage. It looks as if we've lost all our ships.
How many dead? So far, we see no signs that anybody survived the attack. As far as I know, my mother didn't have

an emergency bunker. Nobody would reckon that a necessity on Venice Minor.

My timing was off. I didn't get there fast enough. *They'll find some way to blame you for this,* a cynical little voice says.

I shake my head, trying to silence it. The Conglomerate isn't like Farwan, I tell myself. *If I'd been here, I only would've died with them. No help in that.* But maybe it would've been better for me. More than most, I know the pain of surviving.

There is an awful gravitas in standing at ceremony after ceremony, listening to a holy man intone words that are supposed be comforting but instead merely remind you that you've been left behind.

Not this time, I tell myself. *You'll find them.*

In slow, stealthy movement, we complete our circuit of the perimeter. No bodies, but I recognize the stench of burned meat. It lingers in the air; people become ash in a white-hot instant. They rain down on us in the aftermath, clinging to our skin and hair, the dust of the ones we loved drifting in ladders of light. This is a wound too grave for weeping, a silence of the soul burned black as a night without stars.

.CLASSIFIED-TRANSMISSION.
.SUCCESS.
.FROM-EDUN_LEVITER.
.TO-SUNI_TARN.
.ENCRYPT-DESTRUCT-ENABLED.

From the tone of your last communiqué, I believe you have become anxious about my safety. That is . . . unusual for me. I am not accustomed to anyone noticing whether I disappear or run silent, as is sometimes necessary. Tarn, my work is, as they say, often best done in the dark.

At any rate, I am pleased to report success at last. It took nearly all my guile and expertise to interest the gray men in a mutually beneficial arrangement, as they had found much to occupy them since Farwan's fall. They required convincing that it was not less complicated to hunt whomever they choose—with little or no authority to stop them. But at length, I reminded them that hunts sanctioned by an operational governing body carry no repercussions. They do miss that autonomy, and they are willing to talk terms with the Conglomerate. With judicious financial finagling, you can afford them.

Attached, please find the coordinates for a meeting that will permit the gray men to commence seek-and-destroy on those Morgut vessels that survived the carnage above Venice Minor, and the subsequent grimspace disaster.

For your other remarks, I respect a man who is capable of owning his moments of self-doubt. Mary knows, we've all had them, questioned our course, or whether we deserve the boons life has bestowed upon us. I think no one could have steered this ship better than you, not under the prevailing circumstances. You have stepped up to the mark during a difficult time, and you will be remembered for that courage, not for your imperfections. I will make sure of that myself.

Do you find the political life a difficult one? From my vantage, it seems so akin to living always in the public eye. Does that suit you? I would find it vexatious in the extreme, I believe.

And . . . thank you for caring.

Yours,
Edun


```
.ATTACHMENT-MEETING_COORDINATES-FOLLOWS.
.END-TRANSMISSION.

.COPY-ATTACHMENT.
.FILES-DOWNLOADED.
.ACTIVATE-WORM: Y/N?

.Y.
.TRANSMISSION-DESTROYED.
```

CHAPTER 2

"Where's the Dauntless?" Hit asks.

The question gives me pause because I didn't I notice it as we scouted the area. With the others, I saw enough fragments to identify the wreckage. So maybe they got away. I cling to that hope anyway. They might have been flying up to fight even as Hit and I raced down. *Please, please let that be true.*

"I'm not sure."

"That might be a good thing."

"Our ship won't fly, but it has the only working comm in the area." I name our biggest challenge as we head back to the tiny vessel.

"We could try hiking out of here in hope the rest of planet has fared better."

As if in answer, the horizon lights up with the impact of more missiles—an awful red glow that burns like twin desert suns, deeper than Gehenna's permanent sunset and far more sinister. They're going to kill everyone on the surface. Complete extermination, as if we're merely pests that prevent them taking possession. I suppose I should be grateful they aren't eating us; maybe we've taught them at last we're an enemy to be reckoned with, not mindless meat, but that elevation of status comes at a high cost. They'll assume this area has been saturated sufficiently unless they learn otherwise, so we don't have to worry about renewed bombardment here.

"They're still bombing," I say needlessly.

Even if they weren't, I'm not up to a long walk just yet. The nanites haven't had a chance to finish repairing all the damage I did during the long immersion in grimspace while I reprogrammed the beacons. So I merely shake my head. Hit seems to understand my limitations, as she drops the suggestion without argument.

"If I rest some, I can keep up with you later," I add.

"That leaves the problem of food and water."

Fortunately, we're on a hospitable planet, not like Lachion or Ithiss-Tor. We can find fruit and freshwater nearby. The insects and hungry indigenous life will make survival a challenge, but it's not insurmountable. The Morgut ships overhead, on the other hand, trouble me, but I've told our allies not to risk jump-travel, which means Venice Minor won't be seeing Conglomerate reinforcements—and maybe that's for the best. In wartime, they talk of acceptable loss; from my training, I know that commanders are prepared to lose up to 33 percent of their troops, and when the representatives present this as a victory, that's how they'll describe the people who died here; but right now, it doesn't feel tolerable to me at all.

There hasn't been time for my message to reach Tarn or for him to respond. Which means Hit and I must focus on finding shelter and staying alive until the Morgut finish the eradication of our species here. After that, I don't know what the hell we'll do—steal a ship, maybe. At least with my implants, I have the advantage of understanding Morgut speech and some of their technology. I might be able to explain to Hit how to fly one of their scout ships, assuming we aren't caught and eaten first.

"It's gonna be a rocky few days," Hit says.

"I'm aware."

"The jungle's not secure with the fires still burning." Her dark gaze roves around the rubble, looking for safe harbor.

We both know we can't roam too far from the ship. At this point, stealing a Morgut scout vessel and rendezvousing with the rest of the Conglomerate fleet offers our best chance for survival. I can't feel March, but this time, it's because of the physical distance between us. That's what I tell myself anyway. *It doesn't mean he's dead. He's probably on the* Dauntless *with Hon and Loras.*

You better hope they don't jump. If they do, you'll lose everyone on board.

Icy terror crawls down my spine. *Please, please let them be in orbit, fighting the good fight. If they are, maybe . . .*

"Do you remember the *Dauntless* comm code?" I ask Hit.

Regret colors her expression as she shakes her head. Damn. I don't either. If Rose were here, she could tell me, I have no doubt. She was a good comm officer, but we lost her even before we landed on Venice Minor. I remember Doc's grief, and sorrow steals through me. War has no regard for love.

"Maybe we can find part of the *Triumph*'s ship's computer and link it to ours," she suggests. "It should have records of past communications."

I hope her technical expertise surpasses mine because I can't do that. But spending as much time with Dina as she does, it's not surprising some of the knowledge has sunk in. For all I know, she helps the mechanic with repairs between the nuzzling and softly whispered words.

"Let's look."

The *Triumph* wreckage lies nearby, and we creep toward it in silence. Together, Hit and I sort through the metal and burnt components. I try not to think of Kai; he died long ago, yet he haunts me still. I imagine the ones we've lost as ghosts who prowl about the edges of the light, waiting for us to join them. Sometimes that's terrifying, and sometimes it's reassuring, a promise of homecoming.

At length, she produces a chunk of the computer's trailing wires, and says, "I think this is it."

More explosions light that bloody glow in the distance. We're too far from ground zero to hear the booms or feel the earth shake; the Morgut are moving off now, systematically destroying the defenseless resorts and private homes. I wonder if the civilians had any real warning, or if they went from relaxing massage to dying in abject terror. There are no RDIs—Residential Defense Installations— here, no ground resistance at all, apart from Hit and me. Right now that seems like an impossibly tall order; we're not shock troops trained in terrestrial guerilla warfare.

"Do you feel like we saved the Conglomerate only to lose everything that matters?" I ask her quietly, as we pick a path toward the downed skiff.

"Only if Dina died here," Hit answers. "*If* she did, then I'll find a way to eradicate the Morgut. I will hunt them to extinction, then delete all their records, all their writings. They will pass unremembered." Her coldness gives me chills.

But I feel more or less the same way; I'm just less articulate about it. "If I've lost March, then I'll help you."

She doesn't answer as she drops down through the open door to the cockpit. I come in on the other side and squat on the ceiling, watching as she snips and entwines the wires. Sparks fill the air, simmering white-hot, then dying with a hiss as connection begins.

"Got it. Cycling through old logs now."

Through crackles of static, I listen as Rose sends the calls through. Her voice echoes from beyond the grave, more memories I cannot shake. "You have Hon from the *Dauntless* requesting a connection."

"Patch him through," March says.

Mary, how it hurts to hear his voice, even blurred with electronic interference. It makes me feel as if he's one of my ghosts, and I can't give in to grief before I find the answers. Hit plays the log until she successfully extrapolates the comm code, a matter of some urgency, as there's no telling how much longer this wreck will have sufficient power to send—or receive—messages. Hit cues me with the go-ahead, and I angle my head as best I can toward the comm array. The video's not working, but as long as we have audio, it should suffice.

"Hit and I have returned to Venice Minor. We encountered no survivors. Our ship's disabled, but we don't see the *Dauntless* amid the wreckage so we hope you survived the initial bombing. If you're still in direct comm range, we implore you not to jump as your navigator won't be able to interpret the signals. At best, you'll wind up far from your intended destination. At worst, you'll be lost for good. Until we hear back, we'll be waiting on the surface, so please advise with intel and our new orders."

Unless they court-martial us for going AWOL. But it isn't time for disciplinary action; we're in the middle of a war, for Mary's sake. Once the dust settles, then I'll take my punishment, but I'm not letting them touch Hit. I'll lie if I must.

After a nod from her indicating she has nothing to add, I say, "Send."

A ping from the comm indicates it's resolved the link, which indicates they're up there, somewhere. Who's on the *Dauntless*, we cannot know. Then from the damaged console comes an alarming beep, accelerating in speed. Even I know what that means. Frantic, I scramble out of the cockpit, cutting my palms on metal shards as I pull myself out. Hit grabs my hand and we sprint full out away from the skiff.

"Jax!"

At first, I think I'm imagining the call, but I look over my shoulder and spot Doc crossing the hangar yard, Evelyn not far behind him. *No. No, no, no, no.* Looking backward, I stumble, and Hit pulls me on, not looking back. She didn't hear. Better if I hadn't, then I wouldn't know the collateral damage.

"Run!" I scream, but it's too late. "Saul, *run!*"

They're almost to the skiff now. Doc glances up, then

takes Evelyn's hand. Even from this distance, I can see his resolve. Tears stream down my face; I suspect I'm to blame. The light expands, swallowing the ground, leaving me with a picture of their last moments in my mind's eye. We reach the outer edges of the burning trees as the explosion rocks the hangar yard. I don't see them die, but I feel it in my bones. Even at this distance, the impact sends us flying head over ass toward the fires deeper in the jungle. I land in the shallows of the river that feeds my mother's water stores and lie there for a moment, my blood washing out into the current. I flex my fingers in the water, stunned, and watching the ribbons of red trail away. An orphaned quote stirs in my mind—*wars, terrible wars, and the Tiber foaming with so much blood*. I can't remember where I read it or who wrote it first, but it seems apropos.

"The Morgut caught our signal this time," Hit guesses, pushing upright.

"Doc and Evie were back there. I think our message drew them out of hiding." There's no way to be sure, of course, but nothing else makes sense. Afterward, I wish I hadn't said anything.

Pain and grief dawns in her dark eyes; I can tell she gets it. Our survival came at the cost of theirs, and they possessed brilliant, inimitable scientific minds. I consider now the cost to future progress, and the promise I made to Loras going unfulfilled. I shake my head, but I can't change this. I can only bear the scars, as I have always done, as I ever do.

Doc saved my life so many times over the turns. He comforted me, and he gave me the strength to go on when I faltered. In some ways, he was like a friend and father combined. And the loss of his calm logic and his kind heart might beggar me. Evie, I hadn't known as well, but she had the good sense to love him. She had been brave and stoic, a worthy companion, if only he'd had time to get over Rose's death.

But neither has any time now. Pain wells up in a crimson rush.

"We didn't know," she says softly, and I take her hand as we kneel in the river, our tears spilling with the fast-flowing water.

Those brief moments are the only ones we can allow for grief; mourning must come later. For we're cut off, no way to know if our warnings have been heeded or if the rest of our loved ones survive. *Now* we're completely alone.

CHAPTER 3

"I wish we knew what's going on up there." Despite the smoke, I don't break from the cover of the trees in case the Morgut send armed drone ships for recon.

"Me, too."

Hit stands with a hand shading her eyes, peering up through the blackened canopy as if she can pierce the foliage, the cloud cover, and the barrier of the atmosphere to see the battle overhead with the naked eye. I sympathize with her desperation; like me, she doesn't know if her lover survived the battle, and we both carry the knowledge that we lived when Doc and Evelyn did not. It's absurd and senseless. Silently, we push deeper into the jungle and look for a place to hide.

Rescue will come, I tell myself. We're not simply waiting for the Morgut to finish conquering Venice Minor.

"Here," I say eventually.

Though covered in moss and vines, the shelter looks like an old groundskeeper's hut. At first, I wonder if there's a comm panel in there, but we shouldn't risk another message, even if there is. We don't want them blowing up this location, too. Humidity makes the door stick, swollen from the dampness in the air, but with some effort, Hit shoves it open. Inside, it's dim and hot, moist with mildew.

"Think there are any spores in here?" she asks.

"Hope not." If they take root in our lungs, we could be in deep trouble without proper medical facilities and no idea when—or if—help is coming. Bluerot is one of the many strains of fungus that can thrive in the human body; I'd rather not test the nanites to that degree.

Even the faint light can't disguise the derelict nature of the place. Spiders have long since laid claim, and the hammock has been chewed to strings, which now hang in forlorn rags. Otherwise, nothing lives here but dirt and mold, certainly no comm. I imagined a hero's welcome when we returned from grimspace. There would be furious screaming first, of course, followed by obligatory punishment. And then everyone would cheer . . . because what we did, nobody's ever done before. Yet here we are, hiding from the battle. There are no ships to steal, no help to summon. From Hit's expression, that doesn't sit any better with her.

"As soon as you feel up to it, we're getting out of here."

I nod. Wearily, I sink down onto the floor and lean my head back against the wall; I can't feel the rumble of the bombs anymore. On the surface, that seems like it's a good thing, but I imagine them raining down on innocent tourists. Their dying screams fill my head, and I feel raw, as if I'm at fault for them, too. So many restless ghosts. When I close my eyes, I see Doc and Evelyn, joining hands at the last. They seemed so small against the destruction raining down upon them—two souls, surrounded by burnt metal and flaming wreckage. They had no chance. No chance at happiness. It's beyond wrong that a man of peace should become a casualty of war.

"I should've found some way to stop this."

"Yeah? How?" Her tone is kind enough, but her expression reveals impatience. "I know we're not as close as you and Dina, but I figure there will never be a better time for some straight talk.

"You've let March get inside your head so you don't see things like a normal person anymore. He has this epic sense of personal responsibility, and you've let that become your code as well. Honest to Mary, I don't see how you could've done more. This guilt is a joke, and it's exhausting to watch you martyr yourself. Now shut the frag up and get some rest, so we can hike out of here."

"Yes, ma'am."

I'm too weary and heartsick to sleep, but I don't burden Hit. She's right; it's tremendous ego to think I could've prevented this. And for the first time, I accept that maybe war was coming even if I hadn't toppled the Corp. It might just be Farwan fighting the Morgut now, instead of the Conglomerate.

But Doc and Evie? I am all but positive that was me. I sent that second signal because I wanted March to be safe so much that I didn't contemplate the risk. I was afraid he'd jump before the message I bounced to Tarn went out as general orders, so I acted to save the *Dauntless*. I don't know for sure that Doc heard our message, but I can't imagine what else drew them out at precisely that time. I don't believe in coincidence, which means I'm guilty.

I wish it wasn't true. They're too smart, too vital, to be gone. Part of me hopes beyond reason that this is a dreadful mix-up. Eventually we'll find out that they're not lost, vaporized beneath the infernal heat of Morgut weapons— that Doc found somewhere to hide, where the bombs couldn't touch him—but I know what I saw in those last moments. There is no mistake, and denial solves nothing.

On the *Triumph*, just before I left, he was red-eyed, eyes burning with pain. Doc's raw grief when he lost Rose, the woman who had loved him all their lives, threatened to make him do something stupid. I had feared enough for his life that I put the AI on watch. My only consolation in this fragged-up mess is that Evelyn loved Saul, no matter the ambivalence of his own heart, so at least they were together at the end, and he did not die alone.

Despite my sad spirit, I try to get some rest, and as we sit

in silence, rain drums on the roof. By nightfall, I'm ready to
move, but it's going to be a miserable march. At least I studied maps of the immediate area, the last time we were here;
before coming up with the plan to steal the shuttle, we
debated hiking out on foot, despite the dangerous fauna.

"There's a city fifty-five kilometers northeast of here."

My mother never traveled there, of course. Not when
she had a villa with her own private hangar. There was no
reason. Remembering Ramona gives me a little pang, as I
must count her among the heroic dead. She surprised me at
the end. Surprised the whole galaxy, I guess. She would be
so furious right now to see what the Morgut have done to
the place. I can almost hear her saying, *And that's the trouble with foreigners, Sirantha*.

"By the time we get there, the Morgut may have reduced
it to rubble."

Yeah, I'm aware. But I don't know what else to do. Our
personal comms don't have the range to signal far enough
to do us any good. I'm not even sure if Tarn got my message or if the whole fleet has been lost. Mary, I hope not. In
that scenario, killing would be too good for me.

"But there's a better chance of us finding functioning
equipment there."

Hit consults her handheld and gets us started in the right
direction. With nothing more to say, we stick to the cover of
the jungle. Animals snarl in the darkness, calls and cries that
raise gooseflesh on my arms. At least the rain has put out the
fires, though damaged branches come crashing down with
the weight of the water. I learn to stay light on my feet, avoiding the deadfall as it drops from the canopy. The downpour
doesn't let up, so before long, we're both soaked to the skin.

"In this weather," Hit said, "we could be walking most
of the night."

"No shortage of water, at least."

She flashes me a fleeting, rueful smile. The night passes
in a tangle of dark leaves, near misses with the native
fauna, and sheer exhaustion. It's not cold, but the wet sinks
into my bones, making me feel as though I'll never remem-

ber what it's like to be comfortable again. Still we keep moving, and at daybreak, the rain stops.

Hit shoots a furred thing with too many eyes and teeth as it leaps toward us from the branches above. The animal falls with a thud, revealing green-spotted fur. I've never seen anything like it, but she kneels, slices it open, and checks the meat.

"We can eat it," she says. "If we must."

Dear Mary. I've never eaten fresh flesh.

"Wouldn't we need to cook it? That would slow us down."

She nods. "Point."

I'm just as glad it worked out this way. I don't want to see how things get turned into food, even if this beast tried to eat us first. We walk on and leave it behind for some other creature to feast on.

Eventually, we come to a point where we can't continue, and we rest, rolled up in giant leaves. Insects bite me as I try to sleep, tortured by images of Doc and Evelyn. Worry over March haunts me, but I force myself to relax, one muscle at a time. Hit takes the first watch.

Creatures prowl around our campsite, some smaller than the one we killed. Others sound bigger, but they won't close as long as we can find dry wood for a fire. I don't rest well, even when I'm not on guard duty. The need to locate freshwater and forage slows our travel; but as we can, Hit and I keep moving toward Castello, the capital of Venice Minor.

She falls sick on the third day. I don't even know she's feeling poorly until her knees buckle. Whether it's something she ate, or a tropical fever, the outcome remains the same. I have to take care of her. Her skin is hot, her eyes sunken in her head. I set up camp near the river, which we've followed as much as we can.

The night is endless as I bathe her forehead and try to get her to take some water. There might be medicinal plants nearby, but I can't identify them. If I could use my handheld to bounce a connection to a satellite, I could scan and identify them, but I'm completely cut off from the amenities of the modern world, and my ignorance has never been more terrifying.

Helpless, I care for Hit as best I can, but the hours drag interminably. More than once, she reaches for me, whispering, "Dina," through cracked lips, and I let her put my palms to her cheeks as if I am the woman she loves above all others. My heart breaks a hundred times before her fever does.

Day three of her illness. Sometime in the night, she sweated out the bug. I've been making a broth out of grass I know is harmless, but we're both suffering from malnutrition. We should have reached Castello by now. The fact that we haven't doesn't bode well for rescue attempts—or the overall welfare of the Conglomerate. Surely, if they could, they would have sent a ground team by now.

A little voice whispers, *Maybe we lost. Maybe you did this for nothing.*

I can't let despair take root. I can't.

"What happened?" Hit asks groggily, her hand on mine as I hold the collapsible flask for her to drink.

"You've been sick."

"Feel like hell."

"I'm not surprised. But you're on the mend now."

I hope.

On the fourth day after Hit fell ill, I forget my scruples. I can't choose to starve down here any more than I could stay in grimspace. I have work to do yet. So I build a fire and go hunting. I provide Hit with a laser pistol, but it hasn't been charged in days, and she won't have many shots before the gun dies.

Leaving us defenseless.

The weapon in my hand doesn't have much juice either. I find a likely blind and hunker down, listening to the jungle around me. I've grown accustomed to the insect noises over the past few days, so I tune them out. Other sounds capture my attention, and I lie in wait until something gets my scent. From the sound of it creeping toward me, it's the same type of creature that tried to eat us once before. It thinks I'm dinner.

They're not picky about their own food, and I feel less guilty about eating something that tried to devour me first.

When the beast bursts from the undergrowth, jaws wide and slavering, I shoot it. Killing is nothing new to me; I've actually gotten pretty good at it. But this is the first time I've ever slain something with the intent to eat it. I get out my small survival knife, courtesy of the skiff we crashed. It takes me ages to skin and gut the thing, and I'm nervous the whole time. The blood will draw predators if I'm not fast enough. My hands shake, and my stomach churns as I deal with the carcass.

At last, I have good chunks of meat, suitable for roasting. Hit needs the protein to recover fully and continue our march. When I return, I find her propped against a tree where I left her, laser pistol still in her hands. But she's sound asleep, and I send up a silent thank-you to Mary that the fire kept the animals away.

I don't wake her as I cook, but she rouses to the smell. I get that. The scent of roasting meat reminds me of the *Sargasso*, so I have to hold my nose in order to force down the charred flesh. *It's just nutrition,* I tell myself. *Protein, just like the paste.* Not too long ago, this protein was running around the jungle. *Gross.* My stomach threatens to rebel, and Hit quells me with a sharp look.

"Keep it down. No telling when we'll eat again." Even in infirmity, she has more determination than I do. I admire the hell out of this woman.

We're both lean as blades now; I could cut myself on her collarbones, but someone will come soon. The battle has to be over by now. They must know we're on Venice Minor, somewhere. *If they got our message. If anyone survived to hear it.*

Someone will come. I repeat that refrain for the next two days. By this time, Hit is strong enough to move again. I use my handheld to check our course—maps are on the drive already, no need for uplink—and we set out toward Castello once more. I won't be sorry to leave this jungle behind.

In another day, my feet are raw from wearing the same socks without washing them, the salt of my sweat eating into my skin. I'd kill to be clean. Wrong thought. There's been too much death.

I tap my comm, which gets enough light in between the canopy and the intermittent showers to hold at nearly half a charge. Our personal units are equipped with small solar panels in the event we're stranded on a class-P world. At this point, I'm wondering if we'll ever see civilization again.

Just before nightfall, my comm beeps, which means someone's out there, somebody who knows my personal code. Euphoria lights me up like the bright morning sky, clouds shot with pink and gold, and that's how I feel, despite my mud-encrusted boots and my sodden clothes.

I fumble with the buttons to answer fast enough. "Jax here."

"Glad to hear it, Sirantha." Even before his face flickers onto the small screen, I'd recognize Vel's voice anywhere. "I hoped you would come into comm range."

"I don't think I've ever been so glad to see you." Relief leaves me shaky. Beside me, Hit punches the air in triumph. "Can you give me a sitrep?"

The situation report will be bad, no doubt. It only remains to be seen just how dire our circumstance. At least I can rely on Vel to give it to me straight.

"I think it best if we rendezvous first, then I can bring you up to speed."

"Can you pick us up?"

He shakes his head. "We managed to get inside their line after your first message went out, but we cannot move until you get here. I prefer not to increase our chances of detection. Scout ships are still buzzing the surface, and it would be unfortunate if they found you first. I do not imagine you are in any condition to fight."

Talk about a gift for understatement.

"So where are you?"

"On the other side of the ruins."

Ruins? He must mean the city. *Shit. The Morgut leveled it, just like Hit predicted.* It occurs to me then that their attitude reflects ours with their La'heng. I remember Loras saying, *When humanity first visited La'heng, we did not greet them warmly. We killed all of their delegations, rebuffed all attempts to establish contact. They correctly adjudged us a hostile alien race and took steps to civilize us. They seeded our atmosphere with a chemical that dampened our ability to fight.*

And then Doc had added, *RC-12. It's generally only used to sedate violent criminals. It had never been used on a global scale before.*

He's gone now. I'll never hear him explain in that pedantic tone again. He never judged my overspecialization, my ignorance of larger galactic events. Now it's up to me to remedy my lack of knowledge.

Loras concluded, *They took La'heng bloodlessly and fed us more drugs to keep us compliant. They didn't take into account our physiology. We adapt quickly, integrate changes. The RC-12 produced a new generation of La'heng young incapable of fighting, even to defend their own lives. We're helpless.*

The Morgut look on us as we did the La'heng. They don't see us as capable of making our own decisions, just as we didn't respect the La'heng desire to protect their insular culture. It seemed incomprehensible to us that they would fight us for no reason, so we *changed* them. I imagine the Morgut finding a way to render humanity docile, uncomplaining meat, and a shudder runs through me, chased by shame. Sometimes I don't like what it means, being human. We are an ambitious, driven people, but sometimes the dark side spills out, and we're like selfish children, unable to see beyond our own desires.

Heartsick, I realize I've been quiet too long, check our position, then reply, "We're not far. Just sit tight and give us an hour. We'll get there."

"I will come to meet you at the city center and guide you to the ship."

"Can't wait to see you. Jax out." I hit the button to terminate the connection. "Looks like we have an exit."

"Let's move," Hit says.

"Double time."

Buoyed by hope, I speed into a jog. The day is bright and new as we break from the jungle, feet pounding over mud and fallen leaves. Droplets splash up, spattering my knees, but I can hardly get dirtier than I already am. There's no benefit in slowing down, but I do pace myself, so I can manage the last kilometers as quick as humanly possible.

Flat farms occupy the no-man's-land between jungle and city, but even those fields have been scorched. Blackened patches radiate outward, crops destroyed, homes decimated. We move past the destruction, but it doesn't get better. As I jog toward what used to be the largest city on Venice Minor, even at this distance, horror steals my breath. No buildings stand; they've been reduced to chunks of stone and ash. Great pits have opened in the streets, a web of cracks raying outward. It makes our passage precarious, and more than once, Hit and I save each other from a painful fall.

The silence is oppressive. No birds. No people. I have never stood in ruins like these. Never. On Dobrinya Asteroid, where my fellow soldiers fought the Morgut and died beside me, I thought I knew the face of war. But this is a monstrous visage, the magnitude of which I could never have imagined. In time, the grasses will grow up through the rock, moss will soften the loss, and animals will nest here. If permitted, Venice Minor will erase all signs of human passage, and that would be better than the alternative, for when they're done raining death from above, the Morgut will come down and build.

We can't let that happen. They will not have this world; my mother gave her life to save it, and I will yield them nothing more. It ends here. Somehow. They will not take the war to New Terra.

Mary herself must have been instrumental in your timely reply. Between the Ithtorians who arrived at Venice Minor just before the two-fold catastrophe and the gray men hunting the Morgut in other systems, this war may be won, and at a lesser cost than I feared, all told.

Yet the lives were lost in such a way that it doesn't feel like a regular battle, and there will be inquiries. Indeed, my comm is already alight with demands for information. I hardly know what I will say. I am ambivalent about the outcome. I have no doubt that Ms. Jax did what she thought best, but she is notorious for her lack of regard for authority. My constituents will wonder—and perhaps rightly so—whether there was a cleaner alternative.

I have reviewed the circumstances, and she did save lives on a grand scale, provided we can manage the prohibition on interstellar travel in the interim. That will prove no small feat, and will cost billions of credits as trade is restricted. But I would be a heartless man if I cared only for that aspect. I'm also concerned about the colonies that will suffer from a dearth of supplies, but they would be far worse off if they had Morgut dreadnaughts on the horizon. I am loath to punish a brave soldier for acting in such a fashion, but the public will accept no other outcome. So I fear I have no choice but to step back and permit the legal process to take place. Ms. Jax will take this for spineless disavowal, I have no doubt; she does not tend to see the world in subtle shadings. Sometimes I wish I didn't, and that I had gone into my father's business instead of pursuing a career in politics.

It will take the Conglomerate a long time to recover from all this. I hope I have the fortitude to steer the ship, as you put it, for so long. The government would not benefit from a change at this juncture, but I am tired. To address your question, at last, yes, it is hard. I am always on my guard. I trust precious few with any fullness. I suppose you could say the right hand seldom knows what the left is doing. None of my closest advisors know about you, dear Leviter.

But instead of higher rank, I do dream, now, of days in retirement, where I will have earned my peace. What do you dream? Such an odd thing to ask of a man who can make the impossible come to pass. And yet, I ask.

Yours,
Suni

.END-TRANSMISSION.

.ACTIVATE-WORM: Y/N?

.Y.
.TRANSMISSION-DESTROYED.

CHAPTER 4

Jaw clenched, I lead the way through the wasteland. The impact site still steams heat, though the days of sporadic rain have cooled it enough to make it safe for human passage. Small remnants of normal life leap out at me—part of a sign advertising fresh seafood, a child's toy partly charred and now discarded. The red polymer of the hat has melted across the doll's face, so it looks like fresh blood.

I pick my way around fallen metal shards, six meters across, and Hit shakes her head as we pass. "This was a ship."

Though I never visited Castello, I've seen vids. This street used to be green with tropical trees, spiky plants grown in their shade. Flame-hued flowers bloomed in profusion on the ivory walls, and children ran ahead of their parents to splash in the fountains; unlike most cities, they didn't mind such behavior here. Beautiful caramel-skinned men sold iced drinks from cafés lining the public promenade.

They're gone now.

I remember teasing March with thoughts about how I

intended to retire here, but Venice Minor will do a different kind of tourism henceforth. Too many died here for it to be believable as an unspoiled paradise any longer. Someday, there may be monuments and commemorative plaques, so people don't forget. Mary knows, I never will. I feel their ghosts watching us as we move through in respectful silence toward the city center, where Vel will be waiting. Adele—my spiritual mentor on Gehenna—would doubtless offer a prayer for these lost souls. I don't know any sacred words, but I offer some heartfelt ones in their place.

"Find peace," I whisper to the ashes and the dust, to the broken stones and the soot-stained fountain. I bow my head for a moment.

Hit pauses beside me and offers a longer, more eloquent prayer. "Holy Mary, have mercy on these, your lost lambs. For those who remain, enkindle in us the fire of your love. Send forth your spirit, that our hands perform your work, and together, we may renew the face of the world. Amen."

"Damn."

The taller woman shrugs. "Madame Kang was a devout woman in her way. She asked forgiveness each time she sent us out on a job."

There's a certain twisted logic in that.

Here at the fountain, the heat must have been so profound as to evaporate the water, melt the pipes beneath the ground, and fracture the basin; at least that's the evidence left behind. I see the overwhelming damage and once more picture Doc and Evelyn, standing hand in hand. The hurt swells; he was my friend, and I killed him. Even if I never know for sure, I'll still carry the burden of his loss.

We walk on. In places, shop windows melted rather than shattered, clinging to the remnants of the structures in glittering, uneven waves. Sorrow weights my steps, but with each one, I move closer to Vel—to hope—and soon I'm running again, as much away from these memories as toward the promise of rescue.

Hit keeps pace beside me. I don't worry about being spotted by the Morgut anymore. So far, we've heard no sign of recon drones, and they've shut down the planetary communication network with sheer destruction. Vel mentioned scout ships, but unless we power up some impressive machinery, they're not going to notice us.

I hope.

Ten minutes later, we arrive at the city center, what used to be a civic administrative complex. Now there's only wreckage and the scent of dust lingering in the air. We climb the steps and wait beside a fallen monument; this used to be a statue of Padric Jocasta, the general who fought in the Axis Wars. His family has been famous for generations, and his descendant Miriam, the diplomat, died in no less spectacular a fashion than her forefather. Now he's toppled from his pedestal, the bronze melted and disfigured.

"Think he'll make it?" she asks.

At first, I think she's talking about Padric, whose monument is clearly cast down, then I realize she means Vel. Before I can answer, I spot movement in the distance. *He never lets me down.* I break into a run, going down the stairs as fast as I can manage in my mud-caked boots.

I'd recognize him anywhere; the commander of the Ithtorian fleet has come to rescue me alone. Somehow I'm not surprised at all. Instead of a hug, I greet him with a heartfelt *wa. Dearest white wave, you come for me even to the breaking place . . . and brown bird waits in despair.*

He returns the salutation. *Always, brown bird. The tides are locked.* And then he takes me in his arms. Huddled against his cold chitin, I should be more conscious of his otherness, cradled by claws that could disembowel me, and yet he is dearer to me than my own heart. He is not the same person as when we met, but . . . neither am I. Time has refined us, but instead of pushing us apart, we're closer than ever.

"Come," he says. "Let us return to the ship. There, it will be safe to talk."

Though it's another four kilometers, the journey passes in a blur of dizzying relief. Neither Hit nor I have eaten much in the last twenty-four, but it doesn't matter. Determination will carry us as far as we must go. I move in silence, avoiding the worst of the wreckage.

As Vel told us, their ship—a skiff with a skeleton crew—put down on the other side of Castello. This private estate fared slightly better than my mother's villa, and there's no further hell falling from the blue sky. This is a small, light vessel, sleek and aerodynamic. Interestingly, it's crafted of a dark alloy, probably nearly invisible to the naked eye at night. Hit and I board, grateful to be out of the elements; I'm sunburned, chafed, and covered in bug bites, but I'm alive.

Unlike Doc and Evie.

With effort I put the guilt aside. There will be a time for me to let it excoriate me. *Just not now.* So I take stock.

This ship reminds me of the one Dina won from Surge, at least in terms of size. It's newer, of course, just built in the revitalized shipyards on Ithiss-Tor. The hub has eight seats and two corridors heading off in opposite directions. One must lead to the cockpit, as we came down the other from the boarding area. A couple of Ithtorians linger here, working on the equipment, but they give me the impression they want to listen in. I wonder if that means they have translation chips. Tiredly, I drop down onto the nearest seat, appointed for Ithtorian comfort, which means the backs are longer and the seats are lower to the floor.

As I strap in, Vel hands me a packet of paste. Grimacing, I tear it open with my teeth and squeeze a glob into my mouth. "I thought you couldn't abide this stuff—that you'd rather die than eat it."

"Perhaps," he admits. "But I would not choose that option for you."

His words fill me with warmth, despite the situation.

"Catch us up," I invite.

"Shortly after you disappeared"—his vocalizer offers no judgment on the decision—"March commandeered the *Dauntless*, along with the crew who were fit to fly, and went back up to join the fight."

Frag. I understand his state of mind better than I want

to. I can imagine what he thought, how he felt, all too well, when he played what might've been my final message. He may never speak to me again. This time, I went so far outside the chain of command that I'll be lucky if they just boot me out of the Armada."

"When did you get here?" Hit asks.

"You were fortunate," Vel says. "The Ithtorian fleet arrived before you changed the beacons. When we joined the battle, it was only the *Dauntless*, against the whole Morgut vanguard."

Shit. I could've killed them all. The idea that my impetuous behavior might have hurt my best friend makes me ill. Big-picture thinking has never been my strong suit, but I've never been quite so sick over it before. I still stand by my decision, but I am beginning to believe I didn't consider it from all angles. Instead, I led with my heart and just jumped, which is my greatest strength and my biggest fault.

Despite my dread, I manage a smile. "You saved their butts, huh?"

"I did."

"Go on," Hit prompts.

Yeah, tell us what we need to know. Who survived? Who's on the Dauntless?

"A large number of the Morgut ships were lost in grimspace," Vel answers. "You timed that gambit well. They had just begun jumps to strike other targets."

But not New Terra. Those bastards didn't touch our homeworld.

I nod. "Conglomerate losses?"

"Yes."

I imagined as much, but it's hard as hell to hear it. "Because of me?"

He declines to reply, which offers its own answer, but I have to know the worst. I persist, "Vel, tell me. How many lost?"

"Three ships."

"How *many*?" I repeat hoarsely.

"Each carried a full crew, Sirantha. Two hundred souls."

Dear Mary. I killed six hundred people. And that's not counting any private vessels that may have been traveling. The math at how many family members will be grieving because of me becomes impossible, astronomical. If I thought the universe hated me after the *Sargasso*, well, I suspect I haven't seen anything yet. The public will scream for my blood.

And they're right. They are *so* right. The tally's too high. This time, it's no misunderstanding. I'm not the victim of somebody else's scheme. It's all me. I steady myself with some effort, repeating my prior conviction. *Someone had to make the tough call. It's regrettable, but you saved lives. You did.*

While I wrestle with the sickness in my stomach, he goes on, "I arrived with twenty ships, and we aided the *Dauntless*. When only a few Morgut vessels remained, I broke from the battle to head the extraction team."

"So there are still a few up there?" Hit finally sits down herself.

"Scout ships mostly, but I did not wish to risk your safety further."

Typical Vel. He's put in charge of the entire Ithtorian fleet, but when push comes to shove, he's on the ground looking for me. Nobody ever had a better friend.

A third Ithtorian—this one almost as tall as Vel, honor marks on his carapace—comes down the hall from the cockpit. He holds his claws in what I recognize as a salute. "We have the all clear, General."

"Then take us up."

"What's going on?" Hit asks.

Ah. I forget not everyone understands Ithtorian.

"We can fly now," I tell her.

Hit straps in. Even though we're not jumping, it's never a bad idea to refrain from splitting your head on a bulkhead thanks to turbulence. The two crewmen secure themselves opposite us, and Vel takes his place next to me, smoothly fastening his harness. Maybe it's because he's lived so long, but he exudes the most reassuring aura of unflappable calm.

"I know you have bad news," I say softly. "I'm ready for it."

But that's not true. One is never ready. You just lie and say you are and hope you can take the hit on the chin without going down.

"Is Dina all right?" Hit asks, a catch in her voice.

The ship rumbles, and I feel the pilot working with the thrusters to bring us off the ground. As such liftoffs go, it's fairly smooth, unlike the chaos exploding inside me. *Not Dina,* I tell myself. Hit takes my hand in a grip that hurts as we wait to hear the best news . . . or the worst.

"She is well enough," Vel answers. "A few burns."

Thank Mary.

He continues, "It would be most efficient if I simply break the news. Doctors Dasad and Solaith are missing."

I swallow hard. "They're not, actually. We saw them die."

CHAPTER 5

*Vel asks a number of questions about what we saw. I out-*line the circumstances, and he inclines his head, making some notes on his handheld. "I will file the report, then."

So that's it. Official news. I promised Mac on Perlas that I would look out for Evie—that I was saving her by taking her away. Hurt jabs my stomach in shrapnel shards, splinters of failure. Mary, he'll want to shoot me when he hears, but he'll have to get in line.

The ship goes up and up while Vel tells us of other losses—Torrance, the scout, and Drake, the medic. So many clansmen followed March into the stars to die, but I didn't know them well. Their losses feel different; I have some distance from them. No losses hit so close to home as the two scientists.

They say funerals are not for the dead but for the living. Those rites are what permit you to move on, so if you don't deal with the remains, you can never deal with the memories. That might be true; we may have walked in their dust down on Venice Minor, but it's not the same as a proper good-bye.

"How many survivors down there?" Hit asks.

"Less than thirty percent," he answers. "It took us too long to destroy their flagship."

That would be the enormous ship we saw as we came back, leading the Morgut vanguard. Right now, I should feel elated and grateful, but the losses are just too profound; this doesn't feel like victory. I can only summon a weary numbness. I try to tell myself that it worked out for the best, but I'm not a military officer at heart. No amount of innocent blood spilled feels acceptable.

"Thank you for coming for us."

"I would leave it to no one else," Vel says.

March is still fighting, I have no doubt, still chasing the stragglers and obliterating the last of the scout ships. He won't sleep until they're all erased from this part of the galaxy; that's his particular curse. He can't be the first to lay his weapons down, and he doesn't know how to walk away from a fight.

Hit sits back and closes her eyes, head tilted against the back of her seat. Her whole body relaxes visibly. Since she knows Dina is all right, and Vel has answered most of our questions, she seems content to let me do the talking.

"How long before we reach the ship?"

"Half an hour."

I have the unmistakable feeling there's something he's not telling me, and my foreboding mounts. "Okay, out with it."

"Admirable though your intentions were, the cost to your standing was . . . considerable." He pauses, as if he doesn't want to continue.

This so isn't like Vel that I'm starting to worry; I didn't think about the consequences beforehand because, honestly, I didn't imagine I'd be around to face them. Then, afterward, I realized I had to come back to warn everyone—that my farewell message to March wasn't specific enough to explain the danger.

So here I am. It sucks when your blaze of glory turns into a small sputter.

Hit cracks an eye open, her muscles coiled with the lovely danger she can bring with the flick of a fingernail. Literally. "If we hadn't gone, they'd be counting their casualties in planets instead of ships."

"I am aware," he says to Hit, then addresses me. "But your reputation precedes you, Sirantha."

"I don't like the sound of that." A sigh escapes me.

"Since you made this decision on your own, it has been determined you must account for these lost lives."

The hub seems too small, not enough air, and the foreign design only amplifies my sense of alienation. I'd known when I chose to act on my own that it might come to this. I swallow, my throat tight. Seems like I'm right back where I started, only this time it's my fault. I did it. I made the choice, and soldiers died. There are no excuses that can whitewash the truth, though there is merit in what Hit said. Sometimes, though, they need someone to shoulder the blame. For obvious reasons, the families who lost sons and daughters want to know why—this is the worst disaster to occur in grimspace in more than a hundred turns. It's supposed to be a safe way to travel now; we're a century beyond the terrible mishaps that marked our interstellar learning curve.

I take a deep breath to steady myself against the sudden fear I'll die, not in grimspace, but in a prison cell, and this time, there can be no daring rescue, no righteous flight against the oppressive authorities. "So I'll be taken into custody when we reach the *Dauntless*. What are the charges?"

"Dereliction of duty, desertion, mass murder, and high treason."

That hits me like a brick in the head. My vision goes spotty, and I lean forward in the harness, battling nausea. Hit touches me lightly on the shoulder, but she doesn't try to reassure me. I'm in deep trouble, and there may not be any dodging this shot. Furthermore, I'm not sure I deserve to be exonerated. It occurs to me that this could be construed as capture on Vel's part—the second time he's hunted and caught me—and not a rescue at all. This time, though, I won't try to elude him.

"Will there be a trial?" Hit asks.

"Certainly. Commander March has instructions to deliver Jax to New Terra, so formal hearings can begin."

"Do they realize they need me to train the jumpers on the new beacons?" At least that means they shouldn't execute me on the spot. In fact, I have to deliver myself for criminal proceedings to begin, if I want to move forward in teaching the rest of the navigators how to interpret what I did to the beacons.

"Chancellor Tarn made it clear you are not to be harmed," Vel says.

I fall quiet then, weighing what kind of greeting I'll receive from March. Those thoughts carry me through the atmosphere and out into the stars; they expand endlessly around us. Docking procedure doesn't take long, and Vel leads us back down the corridor toward the hatch. The Ithtorian skiff is small enough to fit inside the *Dauntless*, though it's larger than a shuttle, and I emerge in the cargo area.

It's cold in here in contrast to the tropical climate of Venice Minor. The Ithtorians form up around Hit and me like a squadron of guards. They don't know me at all if they think I'll run. Not from something I did. While it might be a nightmare of a choice and have left me in the worst mess of my life, I did what I thought best. *Too bad I survived it.* Dead women get monuments; live ones get trials.

But I couldn't choose the easy road when that would've meant even more collateral damage. March taught me the importance of doing the right thing, even when it lands me neck deep in hot water. Sometimes I miss the old me.

Inside the ship, a number of Lachion crewmen have assembled. As one, they salute me. They don't blame me for what I did; but then, the clansmen have long defied authority and marched to their own drummer, so they understand better than anyone else in the galaxy. Others will find my decision inexplicable and inexcusable. Good soldiers follow orders; they don't make their own judgments.

Frag it. I guess it's obvious I'm not a good soldier.

Argus steps forward to clasp my shoulder with comforting

warmth. I'm happier to see him than I expected . . . mostly because he can carry on for me, if the worst comes to pass. In fact, maybe I can train him on the way to New Terra. He can start teaching the others while I'm incarcerated, assuming they're willing to trust my protégé, the only jumper from outside a Farwan academy since before the Axis Wars.

Under watchful Ithtorian eyes, Argus gives me a quick hug. "Lachion's behind you, all the way."

The guard behind me nudges me forward, past the well-wishers, and toward what used to be my cabin. Long after we turn the corner, I can still hear them cheering me on. I must seem like the ultimate authority in self-determination, but that's not always a good thing. I wanted to save lives—and I did—but there were consequences, too. The prosecution will talk about how with prior notification and coordination, these losses could've been avoided entirely. But I didn't plan this in advance, and the clock was ticking. At the time, it felt like my only option. Overall, I'm just glad they're not leading me away in shackles.

At the first intersection, Hit says, "I'll see you soon, Jax."

I wave as she goes; I know she's eager to see Dina and hold her in her arms. For me, such reunions have to wait on March's discretion and desire. He may not want to see me right now, as I did the one thing I'd promised him not to— go over his head and disrespect his command. Added to that will be his sense of devastation and abandonment—I grasp the gravity of my actions and what they may cost me.

They escort me to my room, and I go inside, weary to the bone. There's a tray waiting since these quarters lack a kitchen-mate. Apparently I won't be permitted to visit the dining hall, understandable under the circumstances. They can't take the chance that I intend to break out, steal a ship, and run. Let's face it—it wouldn't be the first time. But on this occasion, March is my captor, not my liberator.

Vel comes in with me, but his officers remain outside the doors. I just want to get cleaned up, and sleep, but I know he won't leave me alone, just as I put the AI on watch for Doc. Vel's the best friend I've ever had, bar none. So without protesting his presence, I locate a clean uniform and try not to think about what the future holds.

"Give me a few," I say, and he inclines his head.

In the bathroom, I lean my head against the wall, fighting tears. If this is victory, why do I feel as if I've lost everything? After several moments, I strip out of my muddy clothes, but nothing can scrub away what I've done. I'd like to wreck the place, but it's a utilitarian space, nothing I can break or throw. So, denied that, I clean up quickly and join Vel. After I pull my damp hair back, I step back in my cabin, marginally more prepared for bad news, if there's more of it. Mary, how could there be? I sit down and go to work on my food while Vel watches me, his head canted in concern.

"How bad is this going to be?" I ask eventually.

"The trial will be a nightmare." Vel doesn't pull his punches. "You will, most likely, be isolated for your own protection."

"People want me dead, then."

"Some."

How many is some? So the tide of public opinion has turned. Good to know. Before I can think what else to ask, the door swishes open. Seems like so much longer since I've seen March. I left him in our bed, but he doesn't resemble my lover now. His face is hard and wary, eyes like slivers of ancient amber.

"Thanks for staying," he says to Vel.

It's clearly a dismissal, and the former bounty hunter departs with an inclination of the head.

CHAPTER 6

March wears a uniform well, even when he's wishing me to perdition. I drink him in, as I'm glad to see him regardless of his mood. We stand in a silent tableau for endless moments; he doesn't come toward me, and there's no welcome in his eyes. Instead, he laces his hands behind him, a military stance.

So that's how we're playing it. I'm nothing if not adaptable, a Jax for every occasion. Most people would say that makes me crazy. Maybe they'd be right. I come to my feet, no longer at ease, but I stop shy of a salute. "Hit knew nothing about the mission beforehand. I want her exonerated."

March nods, agreeing to my terms of surrender. "I'm sure Vel apprised you of the situation."

"We're heading for Ocklind, I gather."

"I have permission for you to get a night's sleep before you jump us there."

Right now, I'm the only one who can. "I appreciate that."

"It was Tarn's idea."

Ouch. Now there's no question where I stand with him. I've never seen the man so coldly angry. At this point, I could offer excuses for my behavior, but at base, I would make the same choice again. I feel sick and terrible; I may never shake the weight. But even knowing the consequences, I would sacrifice those three ships for the sake of billions. I carry the guilt for those we lost in grimspace as well, but it was the right choice. I'm sure of it.

But I understand the Conglomerate's difficulty, as well. I put them in a bad position. If the ships had been destroyed in battle with the Morgut, we wouldn't be having this conversation. But since I took matters into my own hands, the circumstances are different.

Yet I didn't know if my idea would work; it wasn't something for which I could've sent warnings ahead. By the time they received them, more ships—and maybe worlds, too— would've been lost to the red cloud. I did what I had time to do, what the crisis demanded.

"Are we finished?"

In those three words, I ask about a hundred questions, but I don't sense him in my head. Probably, it's better if March keeps his distance. He doesn't need my shit to splatter all over his pristine uniform.

"I don't know," he says softly. "Certainly your military career is over. You may end up with a dishonorable discharge even if you avoid a criminal sentence."

"That's not what I was asking."

"It's all I feel equipped to answer right now. As your commanding officer, your decision reflects on me."

"I know. I'm sorry."

"Instead of trusting me to make the best strategic decision, you went around my authority." He pauses, his mouth tightening with visible anguish. It's the first emotion he's shown, a break from the perfect soldier. "Why didn't you let me protect you?"

"I didn't think you'd let me go when there was a good chance I might not come back."

March pauses, studying me for a moment as if I'm an incomprehensible alien species. "Because we broke regs right before you left?"

Broke regs. Such an impersonal way to describe the

way we made love. His touch has always made me catch my breath; he's capable of phenomenal passion and tenderness, but right now, I'm entitled to neither. March can also be the coldest bastard in the world.

"Partly. I was afraid you wouldn't be thinking like my commander right then."

"So you feared I'd make an emotional decision and not a tactical one."

"I guess I did."

Though I'm better than most at compartmentalizing my life, before I left, I didn't look at him in my bed, tousled with pleasure, and see him as my superior officer. I saw him as the man I loved, the one I left behind for the best and most inevitable of reasons. But maybe it was cowardice, too. So I wouldn't have to face him and speak that good-bye in person. It's true what they say about the road to hell and good intentions.

"You underestimated me," he says softly. "To our detriment. If you'd outlined your plan, and I ordered you to do it, then we'd be covered. Instead, you're twisting in the wind, and I'm faced with the charge that I can't control my people."

Oh, Mary. What a muddle I've made of things. Another apology seems futile, so I hunch my shoulders, misery draping me like a shroud. Okay, so maybe I would do things a little different. Given a second chance, I'd trust March to let me go, no matter his personal feelings. He's always been stronger than I gave him credit for.

"If I could go back—"

"Your escort will expect you to be ready at 0700." He cuts me off, likely knowing my regrets are pointless.

"Could you have Argus join us in the cockpit?"

"Why?" Yeah, he doesn't trust me a millimeter anymore.

I explain my desire to attempt to train Argus on the new signals before I go into custody. He listens with a half frown, then nods. "I'll see to it that he's there. Teach him what you can. It will help your case if we can prove you do not, in fact, intend to hold the galaxy hostage unless your demands are met."

"That's what they're saying?"

He shrugs. "It's not the first time you've been called a terrorist, is it?"

No. But last time it was the Corp's spin machine.

But it matters he's letting me take us back to New Terra instead of insisting on a long haul in straight space. That has to mean something—a flicker of faith remains.

"You trust me not to run?" I'm glad he doesn't think I'll make a bad jump and attempt to escape justice.

"It wouldn't serve. You wouldn't be permitted to get off this ship."

I find his response chilling, coupled with his dead eyes. "Would you order my execution, Commander?"

"Don't put me in that position, Jax."

So that's a yes. He'd order his troops to kill me rather than let me go. I don't know if we can come back from this, but I put all the balls in play. He's only fielding what I've set in motion; I'd be surprised with anything else. I always knew how much a soldier he is. After all, he was a merc for more than half his life, where following orders meant the difference between life and death.

"I won't."

His eyes ice over. "As I recall, you also promised to respect the chain of command. So I already know what your word is worth. A sentry will be stationed outside your quarters until morning."

No parting words as he turns, his motion sharp as only a military man's can be. He stalks from my quarters without looking back. I would've given anything for a mental touch, some hint that our relationship isn't broken beyond repair.

For love to flourish, Kai whispers in my ear, *there has to be trust, Siri. Promises don't matter as much as personal choice.* I know he's right—and I screwed this up. I'm tempted to reply, but it's not my dead lover, just my memory of him.

I'm lonelier now than I've been in a long time. Though I don't want the rest of my food, I eat it mechanically, knowing I'll need strength in the days to come. Sleep comes slowly, and I dream of my trial, where dead men sit in judgment, and their families wait beyond the doors, endlessly sharpening their knives.

At 0600, the AI rings me awake, and I dress in a clean uniform. Likely, I don't have the right to wear it anymore, but I don't have anything else, so they can take it from me after I'm court-martialed. I pull my wild, damp hair back, so I'm ready when the guard signals; it's a clansman I don't know by name, though I've seen him around. He snaps a salute as if I haven't, in fact, betrayed them all.

"Hell of a thing," he says, shaking his head. "You saved so many lives, and they're taking you to task for it. That's the sort of thing we wanted to get away from. It's why we colonized Lachion."

But I'm not a victim. I went into this with my eyes open, so I answer, "I went about it the wrong way. Shall we?"

It's early enough in the shift that there aren't tons of soldiers standing around. I don't think I could stand that. My progress to the cockpit passes unremarked, and there, I find March waiting for us to make the jump that will deliver me to New Terra.

He doesn't look like he slept, though. Dark shadows frame his eyes, and his jaw bristles. So maintaining that icy distance wasn't easy, and he paid for it. That offers me some comfort as I sit down to check the nav chair. I half expect to find Hon supervising our use of his ship, but I guess he doesn't want to be a part of this. Or it might just be the hour.

Hon's an old rival of March's; we first ran afoul of him on Emry Station, where Hon tried to establish his own space station. Farwan took care of his pretensions to grandeur, and he went back to raiding. Later, he took March up on his offer of amnesty and went to work as an Armada officer for the Conglomerate. I wasn't too sure how that would work out at first, but he's been steady, as far as I can tell. It's a mark of his smuggler's luck that his ship—the *Dauntless*—is the one that survived the blitz at Venice Minor. March, on the other hand, has a history of wrecking his vessels, though not through any fault in his piloting.

Silently, we prep for jump. I check the star charts, though it doesn't matter where we are. Combined with my implants, my natural ability, and the tweak to the phase drive, I can jump from anywhere. It's a huge stride forward, and it came as a result of numerous factors. Nothing will ever be the same again.

I jack in, and the world winks out. For the first time, blindness is a comfort. I don't have to see that beside me, March is grieving. His mind touches mine in the nav computer, and only here does he let me see the full scope of it. I appreciate that he doesn't block me; he has the skill. There are stolen, precious moments, where he's decided to allow himself this secret intimacy.

I thought I'd lost you. That's not my commander. That thought belongs to my anguished lover, who believed I was gone for good.

In this neutral space, I admit, *I wasn't sure I could come back. I fought for it, though. For us. For you. And to carry word of the shift in grimspace, so I could save as many lives as possible.*

Silence, but warmth purls through me. His love doesn't waver, regardless of what I put him through this past week. Then he replies, *I'll be waiting.*

At last, here's the answer to the question I asked last night. Knowing helps, even if he can't speak of his feelings out loud. It'll help me deal with the difficult days to come. And there's no question it will be tough, maybe the worst thing I've ever faced.

Argus arrives shortly thereafter, and he jacks in using a patch cord. It's not a suitable solution for training, but it will be enough for me to show him what I need to. The rumble of the phase drive tells me we're almost ready, and rising heat spills through me. That's the cations kindling for the jump. The corridor opens; the ship spirals through, then my mind's full of grimspace. Even to me, the beacons feel strange, and full of unusual echoes.

My apprentice reacts, testing the new signals. In the space of seconds, I show him what I did and how to read it. Realization sparkles through him. Despite the circumstances, he loves the job, and he loves learning new tricks. He's going to adore playing hero on New Terra.

It takes me longer to feel out the proper course, then move us there. But March isn't surprised when we slide out of the jump with New Terra spread before us, glimmering with its aquamarine waters. I unplug and sit quiet, waiting for the landing while he negotiates with the docking authority. Before long, the *Dauntless* receives a priority landing clearance, and we make our approach.

"Dismissed," March says to Argus.

The kid leaves without another word, doubtless knowing we need a moment. March handles the landing with his usual skill; though with each kilometer, it takes me closer to captivity. Once we put down in the hangar set aside for diplomats and other important personages, he turns to me.

"This is the last time I'm going to see you alone for a while. I've already been advised that you will be permitted no visitors apart from counsel, not even me."

That's an unexpected blow, but I should have been prepared. The charges levied against me are heinous, and from this point forward, it becomes a media event and a public circus. But I survived incarceration once before— and at least this time I won't have anyone trying to drive me crazy with dream therapy.

I hope.

To my surprise, he bends and kisses me on the mouth. His lips taste of strong *kaf* and infinite sweetness. March nuzzles his stubbled jaw against my throat; the scrape feels divine, and that, too, I will carry with me. Lifting his head, he traces the curve of my cheek as if striving to memorize my features. I have no idea what he sees.

"I still love you."

Thank Mary. I can survive, as long as I know he's there for me. "And I, you. I'm sorry—"

"No." He presses a finger to my mouth. "I have my own regrets, you know. Since I got your message, I've wondered if there was something I could do differently, some way to make you trust me."

"I do," I whisper.

But that's not the whole truth.

Even if I'd believed he could make an impartial decision regarding my sacrifice in grimspace, it's not in me to turn to someone else at such times. I refused to put the decision on March and leave him shouldering the weight. By the grim look in his golden eyes, he hears the unspoken reply. I feel him, tender warmth in my head, and I don't want to be without him.

But I must be.

The chime rings on the door, and March kisses me again, again, as if he can wipe this all away with the heat of his mouth. I cling to him for a moment, before making myself step back. It's time to let go.

"Vel's outside," he says.

He came. Of course he did. I draw in a breath that hurts in the exhalation. "Then let him in."

When the door to the cockpit swishes open, there is nothing personal between the commander and me. We stand a professional distance apart, as if I can't feel his pain screaming in my head. Mine amplifies his; they share a joint sound—that of glass breaking—until they swell to a crescendo that deafens.

I want to scream, March whispers. *I want to take you away from here.*

I know, love. I know.

It requires superhuman effort for me to step into the hall, going away from the man I love and toward uncertain future. Vel knows, I think. He always does. With his unpainted carapace and his near-human mannerisms, he looks nothing like the Ithorian officers waiting behind him; the Conglom-

erate has chosen an Ithtorian guard to prevent any accusa-
tions of preferential treatment. Vel touches a talon to my
cheek and we exchange a *wa* that says everything.

March signals with a resigned gesture. "Prisoner ready
for transport."

This time, I'm not spared the shackles. I get the full-on
treatment, bound at wrists and ankles, with a loose chain
connecting the two. There's no point in protesting; the Conglomerate wants to make it clear they take my trial seriously. I get no special handling. I'm just another criminal.

Each step takes me farther from March; he fades to an
echo my head. Our connection grows quieter and quieter
with the distance, until the connection snaps, and I take his
loss like a knife in the heart.

.CLASSIFIED-TRANSMISSION.
.RE: AFTERMATH.
.FROM-EDUN_LEVITER.
.TO-SUNI_TARN.
.ENCRYPT-DESTRUCT-ENABLED.

Those who never lift a weapon are oft quickest to stand in judgment over those who act in accordance with their consciences. It is not a great thing to achieve renown, for the public is notorious in its refusal to permit one to change, and it takes no small effort to alter such public opinions, once formed.

You seem to have some fondness for Ms. Jax. Would you like me to intervene? I could find some method of corrupting the jury or ensuring that a sympathetic judge receives the case on his docket. Though this is not my normal sphere of influence, I am not without my resources, even here.

As to what I dream . . . in all honesty, dear Tarn, I dream of nothing these days. My sleep is black and empty. But in my waking hours, I think it would be very pleasant to meet you when you have put aside your purple robes, and I am, once more, only a quiet weaver in the shadows.

Yours,
Edun

.END-TRANSMISSION.

.ACTIVATE-WORM: Y/N?

.Y.
.TRANSMISSION-DESTROYED.

.CLASSIFIED-TRANSMISSION.
.RE: AFTERMATH.
.FROM-SUNI_TARN.
.TO-EDUN_LEVITER.
.ENCRYPT-DESTRUCT-ENABLED.

No. In the interest of fairness to the people whose interests I represent, do not tamper with her trial. She may use all resources at her command, however, to actualize a positive outcome on her own. To that end, please recommend a good barrister, and I will see that this best-qualified person takes up her defense. The Conglomerate needs its heroes, even if they emerge from the fires of war a bit blackened about the edges.

Dear Leviter, this will be my last message for some time. Our work together is at an end, but I, too, would enjoy a personal meeting. In due course, we may arrange it, and I look forward to that day more than you might imagine.

Yours,
Suni

.END-TRANSMISSION.

.ACTIVATE-WORM: Y/N?

.Y.
.TRANSMISSION-DESTROYED.

.CLASSIFIED-TRANSMISSION.
.RE: AFTERMATH.
.FROM-EDUN_LEVITER.
.TO-SUNI_TARN.
.ENCRYPT-DESTRUCT-ENABLED.

I shall miss you, perhaps more than I expected. See that Ms. Jax receives Nola Hale for her defense. She is the best.

Yours,
Edun

.END-TRANSMISSION.

.ACTIVATE-WORM: Y/N?

.Y.
.TRANSMISSION-DESTROYED.
.CORE-DELETE-SCRUB-ALL.

CHAPTER 7

*We make the exchange in the dock, where local authori-*ties take me from the Ithtorian guards. As they drag me off, Vel says, "I will see you soon, Sirantha."

I know him. And that's a promise.

The transfer goes smoothly up until we leave the immigration area, as there's no choice but to cross into the public part of the spaceport. Phenomenal crowds nearly overwhelm my security detail. Bright lights blind me, vids with spotlights aimed in my direction. Various paparazzi—some old acquaintances—shout questions.

"Do you have any words for the bereaved families, Jax?"

"Is it true Chancellor Tarn directed your actions as part of a top secret government initiative? Can you comment?"

"Jax, we heard you were working for the gray men. What's your current involvement with the Farwan loyalists?"

"There's been a complete embargo on all interstellar travel. Do you, in fact, intend to hold the galaxy hostage?"

People with furious, avid faces push toward me, and in my shackles, I can't fight back. I stumble against one of my captors and nearly go down. Roughly, the guard jerks me to my feet and tries to forge a path through the mob. They refuse to give way, and now they're just screaming, not questions, but curses and condemnations. If anybody's on my side here, I can't make out their words of encouragement. They wouldn't ordinarily be present in the VIP hangar, but they've slipped security somehow—or maybe this is an intentional snafu, so the general public can see that the Conglomerate takes my crimes seriously. If a PR rep planned this, I give him credit. It's a hell of a photo op.

"We need two Peacemaker units, ASAP," a local guard says to his comm.

Someone lobs a bottle at my head, but it's empty, and the impact isn't as bad as other hits I've taken. The glass shatters at my feet, and the noise incites the crowd to greater violence. But before it can escalate to stampeding levels, a distant door opens, and two enormous bots wheel out. Both bear cannons in their chests and heavy laser rifles on each limb. They're not sophisticated in terms of programming; they don't need to be. Instead, they carry the kind of ordnance people would be crazy to fight. Matched with their thick plate armor, they're almost impossible to handle, short of heavy weapons.

"This scene will be pacified. To avoid bodily harm, desist from civil disobedience and vacate the area."

The Peacemaker units only make the announcement twice before the crowd loses steam and disperses enough for my guards to shove me through. Over my shoulder, I glimpse a young man with a sign that reads FREE JAX. My escort jerks me out the doors and into a waiting vehicle; it carries me to the jurisprudence center, where they keep criminals who aren't permitted bond. In some cases, that's because they're too dangerous to cut loose for any number of credits; in others, it's because they're deemed a flight risk. I wonder which it is for me.

I've been to the center before, but never in this capacity. Instead of going in the front, the penitentiary transport flies around back and deposits me at the processing entrance. The gunmetal gray door opens to a white hallway going in two directions. The universal sign for the female marks the right; the left bears the male symbol . . . and a couple of men, shackled as I am, come in ahead of me.

My escort tows me down the hall to a service window protected with three different layers of security. The woman behind it scans the proffered datapad and buzzes me through. Guards shove me, as if I'm likely to resist, even though I haven't so far. Maybe they think this makes it more real, but for me, it was real from the moment Vel told me this would happen. He's never lied to me.

"Did she give you any trouble?" the clerk asks.

The first guard shakes his head. "Just a big fragging mess at the spaceport, that's all."

"We'll have to do better with the crowd control," his partner adds. "Are we done here, Carlotta?"

With a nod, she dismisses them, then turns to me. "Do you swear on your citizenship that you are, in fact, Sirantha Jax?"

I hold up my right hand, and say, "I do."

In the next hour, in her office lab, she strips away most of my humanity and all of my dignity. The ordeal starts with a battery of tests, some more invasive than others. She ret-scans me, tests my blood and DNA. She's quick and competent, at least, comparing the processed samples with what they already have on file. I don't see the point.

At my look, Carlotta explains, "It's to make sure you're Sirantha Jax. Sometimes wealthy defendants hire a stand-in willing to do their time in exchange for a payout."

Now, there's an idea. If only I'd thought to have a double waiting in the wings. But I'm grateful she explained the situation to me; the guards treated me like I'm less than self-willed, a package to deliver. After she finishes, she scans me thoroughly, then a frown builds between her brows, and she isn't a pretty woman to start with. Her protuberant forehead hangs heavy over deep-set eyes, giving her a primitive look.

"You have a lot of implants."

I shrug. That's not illegal unless I use them to avoid incarceration.

She hands me a datapad. "Please describe the nature and purpose of each."

As requested, I take it and tap in the information. She skims, then asks, "Two pieces of experimental tech? How can we validate the truth of your claims?"

"Commander March can verify."

Right now, she only knows about the regulatory implant and my language chip. For obvious reasons, I didn't mention the nanites. Those don't show up on routine checks, and I can only imagine what she'd say if she found out.

"Pardon me," she says.

A privacy partition goes up around her desk, and the rest of her office goes into lockdown, just in case I take the notion to try to go back out the way I came. Because leaving would be that simple. With my nerves becoming more ragged with each moment, I wait for the verdict. When she finishes, she doesn't tell me what he said, but she does approve my implants and move forward.

"I'd like to hire counsel now," I say.

"Not my department. We're finished."

Then Carlotta turns me over to a team in masks and white coveralls. I tell myself this is part of the process, meant to break me down and change my perception of myself as a free being. Knowing that doesn't help fight their practiced strategies, though; fear prickles through me, past my resolve. I thought I'd faced every horrible thing the universe had to offer. Yet right now, I don't feel prepared for this.

"Strip," orders a disembodied voice. "And put your clothing in the chute."

I obey. It's cold in the white room, so my skin pimples, my scars purpling beneath the harsh overhead lights. The team in white watches me through the glastique from the other side of the wall; I presume it's standard decon procedure in case someone finds a way to breach the chamber. Robotic brushes drop from the ceiling and scour me from head to toe. Sometimes the pressure hurts, but the shame is worse. Water sprays from everywhere, blinding me. Then they treat me with chemical sanitizer; I recognize the lemony scent. I'm sure it's become SOP because they drag some fugitives out of truly foul and hellish hiding places. So everyone has to be clean before they come in. That, and it hammers home how completely you've lost control of everything. Hope leaves me then; it's a pale, fluttering thing against the far wall. I watch it go through the stinging of my eyes.

"Proceed."

The door opens at the far end, and I stumble, naked and bleary-eyed, into another area, where I find prison garb waiting—gray pants and shirt, dingy underwear. They've given me slippers, too, and there are no ties or fasteners that I could use to hurt myself . . . or anyone else.

"You have two minutes to dress."

Frag. This place makes Perlas Station look like a bowl of choclaste cream. I scramble into my new togs, realizing they've effectively isolated me from my old life in a surprisingly short time. A woman dressed as a guard enters then; she's the oldest person I've seen in the facility, with a face hard as hewn rock.

"Bend forward and lift your hair."

A sharp pinch steals my breath. "What did you do?"

"Imprinted your identification number. It comes with a tracking chip, so don't even think about running. This way now."

Without another word, she leads me down a grim hallway. Overhead, the indestructible glastique covers the lights, nothing a prisoner could break for use as a weapon. There are no cracks or seams in the walls either; they've been poured in one slab out of a cement polymer that can't be broken with less than ten thousand pounds of pressure. Glowing arrows on the floor light our path.

The guard stops outside a plain white door. "When it opens, step inside. Failure to comply with any commands given by jurisprudence personnel will result in behavioral correction."

That sounds worse than dream therapy. I acknowledge her words with a weary nod and do as I'm told. Inside my cell, it's just as bleak: gray walls, a bunk, and that's all. I assume I'll be taken to meals and to use the facilities, but when I ask, the woman just grunts at me.

"I wish to hire a barrister," I repeat, this time to my guard, as she's leaving.

"I'll pass that along," she says in the same tone as *frag off.*

The door closes, lock engaged, alarm armed. No way out. This has to be a violation of my rights; I should be permitted to consult with legal counsel before being locked away. Yet based on the scene at the spaceport, I can't deny the situation is volatile. It's possible they've put me here for my protection. Since there's nothing else to do, I lie down on the bunk and stare up at the ceiling.

Hours pass in this fashion, or at least I think they do. Eventually, I sleep, and awaken to a polite, AI voice. "Please stand back from the door, prisoner 838."

I have a number now; she imprinted it on the back of my neck. As instructed, I remain where I am.

It's a different guard this time, also female. She appears to be in late middle age without any signs of Rejuvenex treatments. Her body is heavy and strong, more than a match for me, should I get any ideas.

"The jurisprudence center employs a large human work-force," I note.

"Bots can be hacked and reprogrammed. People can't."
But they can be bribed. Wisely, I don't say this aloud.

She goes on, "Follow me."

I see no point in asking where we're going; it isn't like I have any choice over my movements henceforth. Resistance will just earn me behavioral correction. So I follow her down the bleak gray hall. At the four-way, she makes a left turn and leads me to a set of security doors. The locks in place require a code, her pass card, and a ret-scan. Once she finishes, we pass through and into what looks like a visiting center.

For the first time, I see other prisoners in stalls made of more unbreakable glastique, where they can be supervised at all times.

"Hold out your hands," the guard orders. When I comply, she shackles them at the wrists. "You will be permitted fifteen minutes for legal consultation. Second booth to the left."

Puzzled, I head toward the stall she indicated, and the door pops open at my approach. So everything is automated. I don't recognize the woman waiting for me; she's sharply tailored in black with her brown hair pinned up in a complicated arrangement. Impossible to say how old she is, but she bears the smooth, ageless look I associate with Ramona, which means she's had top-notch Rejuvenex treatments. If nothing else, it says she's a capable barrister because she can afford them.

Her clothes are real fabric, another mark that she's high-priced, and they've been hand-altered to fit her perfectly—nothing straight out of a wardrober for this woman. I admit it adds to her aura of perfect confidence. She stands as she notices me but doesn't offer a hand to shake. Instead, she turns her face up to the ceiling.

"Please turn off all monitoring software at this time. I'm invoking counsel-client privilege."

"Acknowledged," replies the imperturbable AI. "Switching to visual human surveillance only."

I step into the stall and take a seat opposite her at the table that has been formed out of glastique. There are no loose parts in here, either, just as in the halls and in the cell, nothing that could instigate an escape—a well-designed prison, this one. She consults her handheld.

"Thanks for joining me, Ms. Jax. I'm Nola Hale, and I've been hired to defend you against all criminal charges."

"By who?"

"Irrelevant. As we have only a short time, I'd prefer to be efficient."

I nod. "What do you need to know?"

"Everything. But we don't have time for that today. I intend to defend you pursuant to Title 19."

"What does that mean?"

"That everything you did, you did with executive authority. Did Tarn tell you that your mission was of the utmost importance?"

"He may have." Honestly, at this moment, I can't remember.

"Under Title 19, in times of war, the chancellor may commission an agent to act on behalf of the Conglomerate in its best interests, disregarding all other legislation and jurisdictions in order to act for the greater good. Such an agent cannot be held accountable for lesser crimes, if the discharged duty was, in fact, imperative for the Conglomerate's survival."

"So you intend to argue that I was so commissioned."

"It will be enough if I can convince the tribunal that *you* believed you were acting with executive authority."

"Do you believe that?"

"It doesn't matter what I believe," Ms. Hale says briskly. "But I will ask this: Did you believe you were preserving the Conglomerate's interests?"

I consider the bombing on Venice Minor and imagine the consequences if the Morgut had reached New Terra. "Absolutely."

"Good. My job is easier. I only have to create doubt, whereas the prosecution must prove guilt."

"That doesn't sound simple."

"Don't worry about that. Just let me do my job. Now, I need you to tell me about every conversation you can remember with Chancellor Tarn, and, after that, I need to hear about your mission to change the beacons."

That's a lot of talking, and before I'm halfway done relating everything I can recall about Tarn and his various orders, a buzzer goes off.

The barrister stands. "Our time's up. I'll be back to hear the rest, and then we'll talk again once I lay the foundation for your defense."

"How long before my trial?"

"Ordinarily, it could take months, even turns, but they need to process you quickly. They're rioting outside already . . . It will be madness if it's permitted to escalate."

"Rioting?" I pause on my way out. "Why?"

"Some want the death penalty. Others want you freed. It's a polarizing case."

"Can you win?"

"If anyone can," she answers without false modesty. "See you soon, Ms. Jax."

Jax,

I didn't know whether you'll get this, but they said they would let you read low-tech correspondence. I'm a little out of practice with this kind of thing, so bear with me. I'm not sure if I've ever written a letter before. Everything's via vid or voice to text, you know?

I think about you all the time. Watch the nightly bounce for news, along with everyone else. Dina and Hit have been mixing it up with the protestors, and I'm worried they'll get themselves arrested. They're hoping to get put in the same cell block as you. So far, nobody's pressed charges, much to their dismay.

Vel came up with a plan to break you out, just to see if he could. I hear they have you in solitary, and they aren't permitting visitors, especially not me. But then, we knew that going in. They have a record of the way I stole you from Farwan on Perlas, and the Conglomerate seems to think I might try a similar maneuver here on New Terra. I would, too, if I thought you wanted that. It's just as well they won't let me in because seeing you like that would be more than I could take. I'd have to get you out of there or die trying.

But you made your choice, and I respect that, even if I don't understand it. I can love you without always getting how your mind works. At one point, I would've said I knew you better than anyone, but even you—when I've been inside so deep I couldn't tell where you stopped and I began—retain secret depths and hidden spaces. I suspect I'd adore that mystery if I didn't wind up coldcocked by it so often.

I can't take sitting here, Jax. Doing nothing. I'm drinking too much, and I don't sleep. While I worry about you, I also can't stop thinking about my nephew, whether he's safe, healthy, or happy. He might be in good hands in that state home, but he needs to know he has other options. Family. I've weighed this, wrestled with it. And I can't think what else to do.

So I'm going to Nicu Tertius to look for him. Before the war ended, I promised myself I'd do whatever it took to save him. I won't fail him like I failed my sister; I'll be there for him.

I'll write when I can with my comm code, so you can bounce me when you get out, as I know you will. They won't be stupid enough to hurt you; they just need to put on a show for the grieving families. I'm sorry I'm not there with you, but they won't let me be. I would be, if I could . . . You know that. But I can't sit and do nothing for however long your trial takes, and this child needs me.

It kills me that I don't even know his name.

Love you always.
March

[Handwritten reply, sent via Nola Hale]

March,

I'm not good at writing about how I feel, but I guess we have no choice. On the other hand, maybe it's easier this way. I can talk to this paper because it won't judge me. Not that you do.

Oh, Mary, I love you. And I'm so sorry for everything.

The guard's staring, as if I might stab myself in the neck with this writing device. Prison isn't like it is on the vids. At least, this one isn't. I'm sure there are whitefish holes where you never see daylight, and it's all tooth and nail, but this place is painfully civilized, white, and silent. Except for exercise periods, I never see anyone but my guards, and they take great care of me. By which I mean they hate my guts and would love to kill me but are legally responsible for my safety.

Some days I don't even see the point in getting out of my bunk because I'm not going anywhere. That's when I close my eyes and think of you. I've made so many mistakes, but you are not one of them. Even though my heart's breaking right now for both of us, even though I want you so bad I hurt with it, I'm not sorry for that pain because it lingers like no ache I've ever had. There's a sweetness to it because I know it's ending, and when I see you, everything will be all right again. Because you love me, even if I'm a monster. Six hundred soldiers, March. How can I live with that? Sometimes I ask myself this question, knowing my barrister is preparing my defense.

I won't pretend it doesn't hurt—the thought of you going. It makes me feel like I'm losing you, but you need something to do. And your nephew needs you. I get it.

My time's almost up. Guard's coming to take me back to my cell. I'm not allowed to take this device with me. So let me say that I miss you and I hope your search goes well.

Jax

CHAPTER 8

The female guard escorts me back to my cell, where a meal is waiting for me. "So how's prison working out for you? Three squares a day," she says. "Exercise with the other cellies. I hope you like your own company."

Then she locks me in again. A hum and a buzz—that's all it takes to drive home an immutable sense of isolation. At least I still have March's letter; I read it a hundred times more, and I miss him so much it hurts. But he's right—I don't want to be rescued. I understand why he's not sitting around Ocklind. He has a personal mission right now . . . but I treasure that letter like nothing I ever owned.

I didn't put down my true feelings—that I do feel like he's abandoning me. But what could he do if he stayed? It could be months before we go to trial, and I can't see him even in the courtroom as the proceedings will be closed. There's nothing he can do here for me, but I *hate* that he left.

Thereafter, the days pass in a monotonous nightmare. I once saw an old vid where convicts adopted rats and cockroaches to stave off loneliness, but my cell is clean, no cracks where anything can crawl in.

Except despair. There's plenty of room for that.

To drive off the madness, I cast back to my combat training and run through the drills, practicing forms and fighting an imaginary opponent. From there, I move to stretches against the wall, crunches, push-ups. After a while, I stop counting; I just work until sweat streams off me, my muscles feel like water, and I cannot do another rep. At that point I stagger to my bunk and lie there in a daze. Rinse, repeat. As time passes, I notice a difference in my body, what they call prison fit.

Ms. Hale comes by regularly to pick my brain as she shapes my defense. Otherwise, I sit in my cell alone, poking at my food and waiting for the bright spot that is exercise time. There are five other female prisoners in my block, but they don't speak to me. For obvious reasons, the guards don't encourage fraternization.

On my tenth day in custody, things change. The old guard lady comes to fetch me earlier than usual, before I've had my first meal.

"Your barrister's here."

Mary, I hope it's good news. Without letting my hopes spike too sharply, I follow the old screw down the hall to the visiting chambers. Ms. Hale is as polished and coiffed as ever. Not for the first time, I wonder about her fees; but she refuses to discuss that with me, as I am her client but not her employer.

"You have news?" I say in greeting.

"Good morning to you as well, Ms. Jax. You're looking thin."

My cheeks heat. "Sorry. It's hard to remember my manners in here."

"I understand. I *do* have news. Your trial starts next week."

A pleasurable shock—she'd mentioned they needed to expedite the process, but that's fast by any standards. *If only March had waited. I could have gone with him, maybe.* The dart of anger sparks and fades, leaving me wrestling with guilt. I made the choices that landed me here . . . and I don't expect him to suborn his life into mine any more than I would change my dreams for him. We're not one soul, one being, however much we love each other.

I fix my mind on business, crushing my wounded feelings. "Can you check into some things for me?"

"Certainly."

"Find out whether Commander March has left New Terra . . ." I'm sure he has. He wrote days ago that he was heading out to look for his nephew. *Don't hope.* ". . . and if Argus has started training the other navigators yet."

"I'll put my assistant on it as soon as I return to the office."

"Thank you. What do you need from me for the trial?"

Ms. Hale spends a considerable amount of time briefing me on how to comport myself in court, how to elicit sympathy, and how to avoid alienating the jury of my peers with my attitude. From there, we proceed to fashion tips and other crucial trivia that will allegedly make the difference between success and failure. I listen with full attention, as I don't want to spend the rest of my life locked up.

"Any questions?" she asks, once she finishes.

"I think I got it."

"The guard will bring your court clothes the day before."

That gives me almost a whole week to think about the ordeal to come, so I'm preoccupied during the exercise period, usually my favorite time of day, because at least people surround me, even if they don't talk to me. But on the fourth day after the barrister's visit, one of the other prisoners takes the machine next to mine. She's young and covered in ink. Blue whorls twist up her arms and beneath the plain gray of her prison garb. Red spirals crawl down the back of her neck. The girl, for she's hardly more than that, has dark hair that looks as though she trimmed it in the dark with a razor blade.

"You're Jax, right?"

I offer a cautious nod, not pausing in my reps. "Can I help you?"

"Maybe," she says. "The girls figure there's no way in hell you're staying here. Not *you*. So when you run, we want in."

The other women watch us from the corners of their eyes, as if they expect drama. I'm not giving it to them. "I'm sorry to disappoint you, but I'm going to serve my time and stand trial."

Her face falls. "You didn't before."

"That was different." But I can see from her expression, she doesn't see the distinction. "What'd you do anyway?"

"I killed a guy," she answers flatly.

"I guess you had a good reason."

"He wouldn't take no for an answer. Turns out he had credits and a powerful family. Bad luck for me. I shoulda just let him stick his thing in me. Not like it'd be the first time." But beneath the bravado, she's nursing a grave wound.

This girl did what she had to defend herself, and now she's rotting in here because some bastard's family has connections. For the first time, a spark of the old Jax comes to life. Maybe I've done terrible things, and maybe I deserve to be in here. If I'm past saving, it doesn't mean I can't help somebody else.

"You did the right thing," I tell her. "What's your name?"

"Pandora."

Of course it is. As I recall, Pandora had a knack for trouble, but I can't blame this girl for her situation.

"When's your trial?"

"Dunno. I think they're trying to make sure I die in here without ever getting a fair shake."

"How long have you been in?"

"Eight months."

Frag. That sounds like a hellishly long time for jurisprudence to take its course, even if the wheels of justice do turn slow. That's glacial.

"Do you have a barrister?"

"Can't afford one."

Which means she'll have to take court-appointed counsel if they ever call her number in the system. Thinking about her problem gives me something to do, at least. I'm not positive how much I can help her from in here, but I'll try.

"I'll see what I can do."

"Are you really staying?"

"Running would just make it worse," I say quietly.

"That's what they tell me." She continues her workout, eyes downcast. "But I'm not sure I believe it."

Considering the mess I'm in, maybe I shouldn't be giving advice. I finish my exercise in silence, then the guards come to escort us back to our cells. This isn't a high-end prison. I've heard about places where you live just like on the outside with access to the comm network and vids. Here, they make sure you have plenty of time to think. That's not a good thing.

Lately, I've been dreaming of Doc and Evelyn. Of everyone who died in the Battle of Venice Minor, they haunt me.

Tonight is no exception, but the nightmare takes on a different shape this time. It's strange because I know I'm asleep, but that doesn't alter the shock of seeing Saul in my cell. He paces the small room, then faces me.

"I should've known you'd be the death of me," he says conversationally.

"I'm so sorry." The apology is pointless because I'm begging my own subconscious for forgiveness, and that Jax is a hard, merciless bitch. I ought to know.

"You realize you're fragged."

"In what way?" There are so many.

"There's nobody who can monitor your nanites anymore. Or your regulatory implant, for that matter."

Frag me. With everything else, I never thought of this. That's probably to my credit, as it's a selfish concern, but a valid one nonetheless.

"Maybe another scientist can reverse engineer the technology," I offer, "based on your notes."

He laughs. In my dreams, he's always happy, which makes them something other than nightmares. "A good idea, except Evie was paranoid about data theft. All her work was on the *Triumph*."

Which is now in pieces. "No backups?"

"Sorry."

So am I. The only two people who understood what they did to me are now dead. "What does this mean?"

"Hard to say. But you'll have a hell of time finding out, won't you?"

I wake then to an impersonal flicker of light above my bunk. To kill the time until the guard comes for me, I pace, counting each step. I'm on my thousandth when the door opens. It's the middle-aged guard this time. She tosses me a packet.

"You have five minutes to make yourself presentable."
This is it.

Quickly, I don the dark blue suit. My barrister has selected an elegant cut that makes me look fragile and refined. No black, as that would make me look sallow and sinister. Instead, we're going for ladylike sorrow and regret. Mary only knows if I can pull it off. Last, I pull my hair back away from my face and use the tie they've given me to bind it in place. Ms. Hale will make up my face, nothing heavy, just enough to make me mediagenic; she intends to play to the jury.

True to her word, the guard returns for me shortly, and I follow her down the hall. She doesn't shackle me for transport, unexpected but welcome.

We pass a series of security doors and into the main government center, where spectators and paparazzi swarm toward the courtroom. They catch sight of me, but the officials did a better job predicting the traffic volume this time, so the area's already cordoned off, and they content themselves with shouting at me. The guard shoves me past—not that I wanted to speak with any press—and turns me over to Nola Hale, who's waiting outside the doors.

"Showtime," she says.

"What did you discover about—"

"Commander March has taken a leave of absence. Personal business. Nothing more was available."

Personal business . . . so he's already gone. After his note, I'm not surprised, but a sliver of hurt works its way beneath my skin. Deep down, I wanted him to stay and watch the trial on the bounce, so I could imagine him nearby for moral support. But I'm glad he isn't facing criminal charges as a result of my actions and our relationship. The fact that they've let him go about his business is a good thing. It *is*.

"And the other matter?"

"Argus Dahlgren has, indeed, begun retraining all Conglomerate navigators how to read the new beacon signals." Her tone sounds odd.

"That's good, right?"

"For the Conglomerate. Two nontier worlds have already applied to join the Conglomerate, so their navigators can receive training."

So I increased their powerbase, as unintentionally, I've created a benefit to signing the agreement that didn't exist before. "So what's wrong?"

"It limits our leverage in pushing for an acquittal. If they had a strong reason to free you, it would accelerate the trial . . . but I may be able to spin that to our benefit. 'Heroine jumper so dedicated that she took steps to serve the galaxy, even on her way to trial.' That'll make a great sound bite."

It's funny how she can take anything and make it sound self-serving. Except it's not, because for Mary knows how long, I have to listen to strangers vilifying my behavior and my past—that's going to be painful—but it might be worse to hear Nola Hale trying to sanctify every stupid, thoughtless thing I've ever done.

"If you say so."

"I do. Come on. Let's go fix your face."

As I follow her, with the paparazzi howling behind us, I think, *Welcome to the cinema of shame.*

CHAPTER 9

The hearing room is smaller than I expected, with two smooth alloy tables for defense and prosecution, a jury box, and the judge's desk. Such an insignificant space wherein to decide my fate. The jury members have computer panels on the arms of their chairs, where they can take notes, confer with one another, and eventually vote on the verdict. I half expected there to be a spectator's gallery, where people could stare at me and make book on my odds of survival.

Bright lights hurt my eyes after the dim isolation of my cell, but it's better than the cacophony outside. Before the bot-bailiff activates the soundproofing, I still hear them screaming even after I take my seat. Repeated thumps against the door make the jury shift worriedly in their seats, then the bot raises the field, blocking external stimuli. It's important that these people focus on what's going on in here to the exclusion of everything else.

According to Ms. Hale, presentation matters. She gives me a last-minute check to make sure I'm not smudged, then briskly nods her approval.

"Remember," she says, low. "I expect you to stay focused. No daydreaming, no napping."

"People actually *do* that?"

"You'd be surprised."

Shaking my head, I glance around. It's a blessing there are no spectators permitted in the courtroom, though interested parties can watch on the bounce. Drone-cams hover near the ceiling, bearing the logos of four different news services. Yeah, I'm big news again, and how I wish I weren't.

The ONN drone-cam whirs toward me, then zooms for a close-up. So badly, I want to make an obscene gesture, but I restrain myself in compliance with my instructions. I've no idea whether I succeed in creating a soulful, sympathetic expression, but I give it my best shot. During the trial, I can't be scornful, scathing, or sarcastic; in other words, not myself at all. Sober, thoughtful Jax wears a navy suit and keeps her hair in a neat upsweep; she doesn't look like a mass murderer.

Judge Wentworth is an older gent with iron gray hair and a heavy mustache that wraps around his mouth. He already looks tired, so I suspect he didn't volunteer for this assignment. While I sat in solitary, they likely debated whether I would be tried in a civilian or military court. Fortunately for me, they decided on the former.

I scan the faces of those who will decide my fate—evenly split, male to female—some young, some old, and the rest in between. After the long days of my incarceration, I thought I was prepared for the worst, but somehow hearing the charges against me read aloud drives a fresh spike through my heart.

"Sirantha Jax, you stand accused of dereliction of duty, desertion, mass murder, and high treason. How do you plead?"

My barrister rises; Nola Hale makes a pretty picture, the epitome of a composed professional. "Not guilty, Your Honor, by virtue of Title 19."

A rumble goes through the jury; I wonder how many of them know what Title 19 is at this juncture. Before Ms. Hale explained it to me, *I* didn't, and I'm still not sure I had executive authority. Tarn's the only one who could say for sure whether I did, and he's divorced himself from the proceedings.

"How will you prove this?" I whisper to her, as she sits down beside me.

"Let me worry about that."

The opposing counsel takes the floor. Latimer is tall, slim, and well-groomed; he doesn't look like he'd stab somebody in the neck, but he sure goes for the jugular in the courtroom. "Sirantha Jax has a history of causing chaos. Her service with Farwan shows she has a long and storied record of conflicts with authority, borderline anarchist behavior, difficulty complying with chain of command, and no ability to act with any concept of future consequences."

He points at me, and I work not to shrink in my chair. "You wouldn't know by looking at her, of course, but don't let my esteemed colleague blind you to the facts. Six hundred men died because of Sirantha Jax, and those deaths *were* avoidable. They were *not* casualties of war. These sons and daughters should be home with their families, celebrating our victory over the Morgut, but instead, through Ms. Jax's dangerous, reckless disregard for other sentient beings, they are forever lost."

The prosecutor shakes his head in grave sorrow. "But I will not appeal to your emotions." *Bullshit, you just did.* "Instead, I will walk you step-by-step through the events leading up to one of the most horrific events in our history, the day six hundred brave soldiers paid the ultimate price for one woman's hubris."

His gaze is firm and uncompromising; he gives every impression that he believes what he's saying, and it hurts to hear. With some effort, I maintain the posture that Ms. Hale recommended. I don't want to come off as cold or indifferent. So I make no effort to hide my pain. I don't *ever* put it all on display like this—but for today and all the rest of the days of the trial, I must. My every flinch, every flicker of pain, will be magnified a hundred times over, then dissected by the pundits and talking heads. But I'm told it's necessary; the world needs to see me vulnerable and wounded. I cannot appear not to care or to lack remorse, but that removes a crucial component of my self-defense mechanism and leaves me bleeding for all the world to see. I suppose that's rather the point.

"They will attempt to persuade you that she acted in the Conglomerate's interests, but I promise that before I conclude my arguments, you will understand that she committed this heinous crime to serve no one's needs but her own. Sirantha Jax is a vainglorious narcissist. There were other ways that would not have cost so many innocent lives. She simply chose for the sake of her own self-aggrandizement without regard for the welfare of others—and that is typical of her, as you will see in days to come. I will not rest until she pays for what she's done, and I hope in the interest of justice, you will not betray the bereaved families who depend on your clear thought and rightful ruling. Thank you."

Nobody stirs as he resumes his seat. Nola Hale touches me reassuringly on the shoulder, no doubt intended to convey to the jury that I am no monster—that the horrible things Latimer just said about me have the power to cut me to the bone. She steps away from the table and strides toward the jury; her gaze touches on each member.

"I intend to prove beyond a shadow of a doubt that Ms. Jax acted in the interests of the Conglomerate, and indeed, had she not undertaken this course, we would all be food for the Morgut. Furthermore, I will also establish that Chancellor Tarn gave her executive authority."

She leans forward, adopting a confidential posture. "He used her as a tool in a gray-op situation, and when the political blowback became too intense, he disavowed her. What happened to those Conglomerate soldiers was tragic, but if Ms. Jax had not acted, we would, at this moment, be fighting a war on six fronts against an unstoppable dreadnaught army."

The mention of dreadnaughts sends a ripple of fear through the room; they must've seen footage from the battle above Venice Minor. Remembering the losses from that day, pain spikes through me. *Doc and Evie*—somehow I manage to pull myself back from the brink. Counsel expects me to stay alert.

Nola continues, "I would like you to consider, for a moment, the fate of New Terra if the Morgut ships had completed their jumps. In times of war, extreme sacrifices must be made. Each and every soldier volunteered for combat, knowing it might mean his or her life. They died as heroes, and you belittle their valor by questioning the necessity of their deaths. Sirantha Jax had just lost her mother when she took that small craft out into the great unknown. She asked no help. She was prepared to give her life, every bit as fully as those who perished for your freedoms." The barrister paces, making eye contact with the jurors and taking their measure.

Nola Hale is, quite simply, spectacular in her chosen venue. Her gestures are perfect, impassioned restraint; she's taken classes in body language. She continues, "When I first heard of the charges against my client, I was astonished that any honorable government could seek to prosecute its own heroes. If the Conglomerate succeeds in their attempt to scapegoat Ms. Jax for the loss of those ships, then they are no better than Farwan Corporation."

Oh, well played. Bring the bogeyman right into the room. Even I can see the revulsion in their expressions. They don't want to think they've exchanged one corrupt master for another. If she succeeds in forging a link between what the Conglomerate is trying to do now and what the Corp did to me after the crash of the *Sargasso*, then I have a shot at walking out of here a free woman. I'm afraid to hope; I don't even know if I *should* be exonerated.

"Over the course of the next few weeks, the prosecution will attempt to blacken Ms. Jax's name. Mr. Latimer will paint her actions in the darkest possible light, but I want you to remember as you listen that this woman was prepared to die for each and every one of you, so that you might live in peace. Thank you."

Judge Wentworth inclines his head, clearly wanting to get this over with. "If both defense and prosecution are prepared, let us begin."

CHAPTER 10

The trial has been going on for thirteen days. We've heard from character witnesses and people I don't even remember meeting. Tarn himself has been subpoenaed and is scheduled to appear in the witness box. I show none of my nerves as the opposing counsel gets to his feet. I've been grilled for the last two hours, and my testimony may be the one thing Nola can't defend.

Today, the prosecution ends with a punch to the face. "Were you, at any time, ordered to make the jump that ultimately destroyed interstellar travel as we know it?"

"No, but—"

"That's all," Latimer says.

"Witness is yours to cross-examine," the judge tells my barrister.

Ms. Hale rises gracefully. "Sirantha, did Chancellor Tarn speak with you about the significance of your mission?"

"Yes, he did." I've been coached to answer only the questions as she asks them and to let her build the momentum.

"And what did he say, to the best of your recollection?"

"He said, 'Your mission is of the utmost importance. If you fail, all is lost.'"

There are no more questions, so I return to the defense table. More people take the stand; some have good things to say about me. Others are not so complimentary. Through it all, I try to wear the expression she prescribed—sympathetic and remorseful. It doesn't take much; I will always be sorry for the loss of those six hundred soldiers. If I could go back and fix it, I would . . . but I wouldn't change what I've done. The Morgut have been permanently weakened, and I can't think that's a bad thing, after what I've seen.

Finally, they call Chancellor Tarn himself. His testimony might bury me. He enters the courtroom with six armed guards, and they escort him to the witness box. The bot makes him promise to tell the truth, and his guards step to the side.

Latimer starts the process. "How well do you know Sirantha Jax?"

"We have enjoyed a working relationship since just after the fall of Farwan Corporation."

"And what is your impression of her?"

"Objection," my barrister says. "Impressions are opinion, nothing more."

"Withdrawn. Let me rephrase: As substantiated by her record, does Ms. Jax have a reputation for thoughtful, careful behavior?"

"No, she does not."

"Then what made you ask her to become the ambassador to Ithiss-Tor?"

I see regret in Tarn's eyes. He knows his answers will hurt me. "Expedience. She had formed a close friendship with Velith Il-Nok, and he would not work with anyone else. I felt the mission stood a low enough chance of success without him that any other option would prove utterly ruinous to our efforts to forge an alliance."

"Did you have confidence in Ms. Jax's abilities to make logical decisions and restrain her temper?"

"No, I did not."

"But you lacked any viable alternative at that time?"

"Correct. Catrin Jocasta was still mourning her mother's death, and none of the other trained diplomats could've coped without a native guide to Ithtorian culture and politics."

Latimer turns to the jury then. "That's how Ms. Jax lucked into her cushy assignment on Ithiss-Tor. Connections. She had only basic diplomatic training, that which any jumper gets in the academy to help her handle first contact, and it had been turns since she'd practiced any of those techniques. From there, she was promoted in the Armada, based on her sexual relationship with Commander March."

Ms. Hale calls, "Objection! My client's scores in the combat jumper training program are part of the court record. She took first or second in all trials, and no other jumper possessed her combination of real-world skills. Point in fact, she earned that rank. They had severed their sexual relationship by the time he became her commanding officer."

Wentworth levels a cold look on the prosecutor. "Sustained. Please cleave to the facts, Mr. Prosecutor. I will not have a smear campaign in my courtroom."

"My apologies, Your Honor." By Latimer's expression, that little slap on the wrist doesn't matter because he's about to bring out the big guns. "At any time, Chancellor Tarn, did you give First Lieutenant Jax authority to make such an enormous decision, either tacitly or by express statement?"

I see regret in Tarn's eyes, just before he says, "No, I did not."

"Your witness, Ms. Hale."

She doesn't look worried as she approaches. "You said earlier that you enjoyed a professional relationship with Ms. Jax, is that correct?"

"It is."

"Would you say you are intimately familiar with the way her mind works?"

Tarn looks uneasy, as if he suspects my barrister of hiding barracuda teeth behind her friendly smile. He's not wrong about that. "I'm not sure I would use the word 'intimate.'"

"Then you can't be sure what meaning Ms. Jax may have extrapolated from your instructions?"

"I suppose not."

"Therefore, if you're admitting reasonable doubt about what significance she took from your communications, then you must also concede reasonable doubt about her execution of said instructions."

"Yes," Tarn admits, wearing a look of relief.

I guess he didn't want to see me spaced. Part of me thinks I deserve to be. I have a lot of blood on my hands, so much that I don't know if I'll ever feel clean. It doesn't matter what I intended, only what I did. I remind myself of the lives I saved, but they're intangible. There's no roster anywhere of *People Jax Saved*, unlike the list of the dead on those lost ships.

"And did you, at any point, tell her, 'If we fail here, all is lost'?"

"Yes. Those are my words. About—"

"Can you say with complete certainty that she didn't have those words in mind when she acted to defend Venice Minor?"

Tarn shakes his head. "I cannot."

"That's all."

"The witness may step down."

His six guards come to escort him from the room. Vid-cams whir, trying to get a shot of the departing chancellor's expression. People will be speculating about his opinion of the cross-examination, but I already know he's glad she cast some doubt on his denial. He likes me well enough; he thinks I served to the best of my ability—and the sad part is . . . I *did*.

I drift during the prosecution's closing arguments. According to Latimer, I'm the worst butcher who ever jumped; small children ought to run in fear of my shadow. It's odd to hear myself painted this way. I used to be the party girl everyone loved to hate, and now my reputation's even worse. I don't kid myself—even if I walk out of here, I won't be free. This will follow me.

Then it's my barrister's turn to try to make the jury look somewhat less judgmental. The older woman on the end looks like she'd happily space me herself.

Ms. Hale turns to the judge. "Your Honor, in closing, I wish to call on precedent. In the case of Conglomerate v. Kernak, it has been found that an agent of the government, acting on behalf of said government, can be judged an autonomous authority in certain extreme situations. As with Jacob Kernak, I present that Sirantha Jax found herself in a circumstance where there was no alternative and as an agent for her government, she took action to minimize the loss of life."

"Objection. Ms. Jax—"

The judge interrupts, "I will allow mention of the precedent in the trial records. But make a convincing connection, Ms. Hale, or the reference will be stricken."

"Thank you, Your Honor."

She turns to the jury; the remote drone-cam zooms over to capture her every expression. So strange to think people are watching this all over the galaxy—laughing, jeering, and taking bets on my chances. I hear there's a fairly sizable pool among the well-to-do . . . Of course, they're wagering on whether I get executed.

"How many of you are familiar with Conglomerate v. Kernak?"

Not a single hand goes up among the jury. That's just as well because my barrister wants to sway public opinion, as well as the panel of my peers, so she'll play to the drone-cams as well. She nods, putting on her teaching face.

"Jacob Kernak was an operative, just after the Axis Wars. The galaxy was chaotic, and it was before Farwan stepped into the breach left by the Conglomerate, who had authority, at least in theory. Enforcing the laws was often difficult. Captain Kernak had a choice between blowing up a ship that was being hijacked and permitting those hijackers to go free and perhaps kill thousands of more civilians. He only had a short time to make his decision, and no superior officers in the field with him. No time to ask via bounce."

She offers a half smile. "Sound familiar? It should. My client found herself in the same situation during the destruction of Venice Minor. Kernak sacrificed the passengers of that ship to make sure those hijackers never hurt anyone else. Was it a tough decision? Absolutely. And I'm sure it haunted him, long after his trial, at which he was acquitted of wrongdoing. But ultimately, his choice saved lives, and it stemmed the tide of pirate activity in any sector patrolled by Kernak thereafter. Sometimes, difficult decisions are necessary, and you must be grateful to Captain Kernak—and First Lieutenant Sirantha Jax—for taking on that burden."

Opposing counsel looks as though he would love to object, but he can't think of any grounds since there is, definitely, a correlation between the cases. Ms. Hale did her homework. I owe whoever hired her for me a drink and a big thank-you.

"She mourns the loss of her fellow soldiers, but the reality is, soldiers die in wartime. Though we all grieve their loss, do you think such heroes would begrudge their lives so that billions might live? No, and I think they would be shocked and saddened to see a fellow officer persecuted. If Ms. Jax had not acted when—and precisely as—she did— we would now be overrun with *ten thousand* Morgut vessels, and each carried five hundred hungry monsters. Can you even comprehend those numbers against our fledgling Armada?"

The jury shifts uneasily, their imaginations filling in the rest. The eating swarms and the bloody, endless death, the bombardment from above if our ground troops offered resistance—it would've all come to pass. I saved New Terra and countless other worlds at the cost of six hundred lives. Three ships lost. And when I get out of here, I will sit with the roster and I will memorize all the names. I won't forget those I killed. I'll build a monument with my mother's ill-gotten money, and it still won't help dull the ache.

What they don't know is, no matter how they decide, they can't penalize me more than I'm already punishing myself.

Jax,

I got your note. Nola scanned and bounced it to me. I don't think I've ever seen your handwriting before. It's an oddly personal thing, isn't it? I keep your letter folded up in my shirt pocket, close to my heart. That sounds ridiculous, but I read it at night before I go to bed.

What you said about the sweetest pain? That fits us. I guess you already knew this, but I've never been in love before. That's why I'm clumsy, and I don't always know what I should do or say. I hate thinking of you there, but at least I know you're safe. I miss you. Love you, too. The ache never stops.

It's taking forever to reach Nicu Tertius. There are no jumpers willing to risk the beacons, and I wouldn't want them to. Which means we're doing a haul through straight space. People haven't traveled like this in a hundred turns—and I understand why. Remember how tough Emry was from New Terra?

This is actually worse. The crew is angry all the time and spoiling for a fight. If they served under anybody but Hon, they would've already mutinied. But his reputation deters all serious rebellion, as he doesn't deal kindly with traitors. It's going to be six more months before we get there, and the constant refueling is expensive. I don't know how our ancestors ever got out of the home solar system at this speed.

We get only old news on the bounce, but I'm watching as much of your trial as I can. I'm proud of how you're bearing up; though every time that prosecutor opens his mouth, I want to stab him in the neck. Yet you sit there, taking every hit, then your barrister does her thing. She's good. Drawn blood more than once. I'm glad she's fighting for you since I can't. And that bothers me, too. I feel like I'm failing you.

I thought it was bad when we were on the same ship but we couldn't touch. Thought it was bad when I was on Lachion, fighting in the clan wars, but I was constantly moving then, constantly fighting. Here on the *Dauntless*, this is the worst separation because I have nothing to do but think. I'm always replaying moments with you, wondering if there was another path I could've taken that would end with us together.

I hate being without you. My arms are empty, and I miss your laugh. The way you throw back your head, and your hair flips out, bristles, because it's electric, like you are. I'm not putting this well at all, so I should probably stop talking to the machine and just say send.

[message ends]

[Handwritten reply, sent via Nola Hale]

March,

You're not failing me. There are too many reasons why you can't be involved in this. If I'd wanted this shit to spatter on you or Hit, I wouldn't have chosen my course as I did. This way, I alone am responsible. That's how it has to be.

Though I miss you, I'm also glad you're out looking for your nephew instead of caught up in this shipwreck. It gives me strength knowing you're doing something good. I mean, if a man like you still cares about me, even after all that I've done, then I'm not a lost cause, right?

We should see a verdict fairly soon. The witnesses have been endless, people I don't remember, but who sure have a lot to say about me. But you're right . . . my barrister's doing a good job. I think she sees my case as a challenge, the ultimate win.

And, of course, I remember that long haul to Emry. Sorry to hear you're doing the slow ship to Nicuan, but I imagine you didn't feel like you had much choice. It's not your way to sit around waiting for someone else to solve your problems. We have that in common. I'm glad you're with Loras and Hon. Makes me feel better knowing you're among friends. More or less.

I wish I had more to say, but nothing goes on in here. The only life I have happens behind my eyes, and those are mostly memories I'm replaying. We've lost so many people . . . I don't think I could stand it if I lost you, too.

Mary, I'm in a mood today, aren't I? I'm going to call the guard and give her this message. I know she reads them, so I'll also say what a fine, upstanding human she is, and that I love her hair.

Hoping to be free soon.

Love,
Jax

CHAPTER 11

"Have you reached a verdict?"

"We have, Your Honor."

This is it. Nola Hale doesn't glance my way or give me any reassurance; she's convinced we've already won. I wish I shared her confidence. But for the last three weeks, I've been alone at night, wondering if it's like Latimer said, and I just wanted the glory for myself. I'm buffer than I've ever been, arms tight, six-pack abs. Prison will do that to you because there's not a lot else to do, especially when you're in max-solitary for your own protection.

"We find Sirantha Jax not guilty by virtue of Conglomerate v. Kernak."

Yeah, I killed to save lives. Not even intentionally, as Kernak did, so there's now another legal precedent. Maybe someday, someone else will find herself in a mess and get out of it because of Conglomerate v. Jax. Somehow the idea doesn't give me much comfort.

"So recorded," the bot says.

And that's all. I feel the sense of anticlimax now. I can walk right out of here into the face of screaming enemies and fangirls, paparazzi who want to take my picture and hope I'll be the old defiant Jax, but she's gone forever. Some fissures go deeper than superficial scars, all the way down to my soul.

"Thank you," I say to Nola Hale. "A lesser barrister would've gotten me life in prison instead of an execution."

"I play to win. Are you ready to face them?"

"Almost. Will you tell me who hired you now?"

"It was Velith Il-Nok," she says, as if I ought to have known.

That's true, as March can't get involved with my defense for obvious reasons. His personal and/or professional involvement would only give the prosecution cause to call for a mistrial. I can see the vids now, whispering of corruption at the highest levels of government and how the Conglomerate is, at base, no different from Farwan at all. They'd lose all the progress they've made.

"You did a splendid job."

"It's the star in my crown to date. So thank *you*. I'll be able to write my own ticket henceforth." She glances toward the doors; I've only come through the prisoners' entrance before. "We should face them before you lose your nerve."

Yeah, she does understand. I steel myself as we move toward the exit. Beyond the doors, I hear screaming and catcalls, but once they open, the scene facing us surpasses my wildest fancies. People clog the corridor until it's impossible to move. They're red-faced and outraged; others are drunk. One man carries a sign that reads SHOW US YOUR TITS, LOVE, like that's the only part of my past that matters. But even he's better than the furious woman in black who is howling, "Kill the bitch!" Audible even over the other shouts.

Kill the bitch. The words echo in my head, in my ears, even after the shots ring out. The crowd tries to scatter, but they're packed too tight, and people trample one another. Nola Hale pulls me back against the doors. Everything seems too slow and too bright as pain blossoms through me.

I'm hit. I don't know how bad it is, but from the white-hot burn, I guess it must've been a laser pistol. They deploy a Peacemaker unit along with ten guards to clear the hallway so that medical personnel can reach me. Everything goes black and spotty, then the world falls sideways.

Hours later, I wake in a private clinic. There's a bandage directly over my heart, and at first, I don't understand the placement. That's a kill shot. By rights, I ought to be dead, unless I was wearing body armor when I took the hit. And I wasn't; I was in my street clothes. *So what the hell?*

"You're a lucky woman, Ms. Jax."

The prosecution called me that so much that I tense at hearing it, and I don't relax until the doctor moves into my field of vision. With silver hair and a lined face, he's an older gentleman who has clearly forgone use of Rejuvenex completely. He has a slight hunch to his back, as if he spends long hours reading test results or studying specimens.

"In what way?"

"That assassination attempt would've killed anyone else. But your nanites kept you alive long enough for us to perform a heart transplant. Fascinating technology, though I can't imagine implanting them before they'd gone through turns of testing."

"I used an alternate medical program." Remembering Doc and Evie gives me a painful twinge, deeper than the ache in my chest.

"You'll have a scar," he tells me, "but it should be thin and minimal."

"Thank you for saving my life."

"That's my job." From his expression, he's not thrilled about having me in his hospital, so things must still be messy out there.

"Is it bad outside?"

"Constant marine presence keeps the violent protestors away," he answers, "but your sojourn here has not been enjoyable for the staff."

"I imagine not."

"I'll send in your first visitor." The doctor heads out, and I hear the murmur of voices in the hallway, but I can't tell the gender of the other.

Let it be March.

It isn't. Nola Hale steps through my door. Then I remember he's off looking for his nephew on a slow ship to Nicuan, no telling how long that will take. I curl my hands into fists and repeat in my head how much I don't mind. After all, I'm a grown woman, not a helpless child, and I've never leaned. I don't need someone at my bedside, but I'm glad to see the barrister nonetheless.

"I'm glad you plan to live," she says. "I'd be annoyed at winning for you, only to have the story end like that."

. I have to laugh. "Yeah, my dying would really wreck things for you. It's not a good anecdote for prospective clients."

She grins at me. "Exactly."

"I'm glad you came by. I'd like to hire you."

Nola raises a brow. "For what? I don't do civil suits."

Frag. If the bereaved family members sue me, I won't fight. I'll settle with them, even if it takes all my mother's money. I've been poor before; I know the drill. After Simon—my ex-husband—cleared out my savings, I lived on clan kindness.

"I met a girl inside." I explain the situation. "I think her case might be almost as unwinnable as mine, but I want you to try for her. I'll foot the bill . . . If you have a hand-held on you, I'll make the transfer now, before I lose everything."

She considers for a moment in silence. "Fine, I'll do it. The high-profile stuff is good for keeping my name on the nightly bounce."

"You get more clients that way, I guess?" .

"Absolutely." She hands me her unit, and I input the codes.

"How much?"

The price she names makes me a little woozy—or maybe that's the pain meds—but I know from personal experience, she's worth it. So I request the transfer, while still marveling at all the zeroes.

"At any rate, I just came by to make sure you're going to

live. Pandora's case is a bonus prize. I'll enjoy convincing the jury the son of a bitch deserved to die."

"From what she said, he did. But I expect you'll dig into the particulars before you go talk to her." I hand the device back.

This is the best I can do for Pandora. I hope Nola gets her a happy ending. For me, this is more of a respite between disasters. From this point on, I must watch for angry people with guns, as they won't be content with the verdict. They won't be satisfied until I stop breathing, if the nanites will even let me.

Nola glances up from her handheld. "I've already put my team on it. I have to get going, as I have work to do. Good luck, Jax." Her manner isn't as formal, now that we're no longer client and barrister. In other circumstances we might've been friends. But now she's just a woman in an expensive suit, waving as she goes.

Hospitals are boring. It's even more so when your visitors are screened within an inch of their lives. Lots of people come to the waiting area, but few are permitted through the doors, mostly because the searches and scans reveal weapons on their persons. I catch snippets of the chaos outside my isle of quiet, and I start to dread the day when they release me, and I have to face it all for myself.

Right now, they're watching me to make sure the new heart doesn't cause me any problems. Since it was speed-cloned from my old one—an expensive procedure—while a mechanical one pumped my blood, there shouldn't be any problems, but given my notoriety, they aren't taking any chances. If I die under their care, there's a chance people will assume they did it on purpose. In fact, I worry about the food I'm served for exactly that reason, but the nurse takes care to test it in front of me for foreign contaminants. Though I've survived some tragic events, this is certainly the darkest time of my life . . . and I feel more alone than I ever have. Kai's loss was painful, but it wasn't my fault. I have to live with knowing I caused this.

And if I'm alone, it's because I deserve to be.

CHAPTER 12

A few days later, the doctors let Vel in. Relief streams through me at sight of a familiar face. He sits down at my bedside with a worried flare of his mandible.

"This is becoming far too familiar," he tells me.

I manage a smile. "I'll try to cut back."

"They intend to release you today."

Thank Mary.

"How's Hit? None of this blew back on her, did it?"

"No. Since she only piloted the skiff, in the initial hearing, she was judged not liable for the deaths that resulted from your shifting the beacons." Then my deal with March held.

"I'm so glad to hear that. And Dina's all right?"

"They are happy to be together."

Shortly thereafter, the doctor comes with my release documentation, and I'm permitted to dress in the fresh street clothes Vel brought with him, as the suit I wore in the courtroom has a big singed hole in the chest. I can tell that the medical staff will be glad to see the back of me; they all wear identical expressions of muted tension and dislike,

whether for what I did in grimspace or for the mess I made
of their hospital, I can't say for sure.

"Where to now?" I ask, after I've been discharged and
am ready to go.

"I have been asked to convey you to a ceremony formally relieving you of rank in the Conglomerate Armada."

Smart. That way, any mess I get into from this point on,
they've officially cut ties with me. I understand it, even as I
feel a little betrayed by it. I wonder now what happened to
Jacob Kernak, if he was murdered in his bed or if he ate his
gun after turns of living with the memory. But either way,
I just know his story doesn't have a happy ending. For the
moment, I decide not to ask Vel to look it up.

"Am I getting a DD?" *Dishonorable discharge.*

"Since you were cleared of all criminal charges levied,
you will receive all regard for your rank and thanks for
service rendered."

I nod. "I'm ready to go if you are."

"This way, Jax. I cleared a path out the back. The front
is rather a mess."

That's an understatement, I suspect. Before the press
and the protestors realize I've left, Vel spirits me away
through service tunnels, out to a waiting vehicle. Wearing
dark glasses and a hat over my distinctive hair, I feel like a
vid actress who specializes in dirty scripts. Some people
love you; some hate you; but everyone knows who you are.
It's way less delightful than the fame hounds imagine.

The hovercar lifts us out of the madding crowd, hurtling
toward the hall at the government center, where the armada
can wash its hands of me. Vel rests a claw on my hand,
silently telling me he knows how bad it is, and he's still
here. Some of the tension drains out of me. For me, a normal life won't be possible for quite a while, if it ever is, but
there are still people who care.

At the government center, we take the back hallways
again because the front of the building is jammed with people. More signs. More screaming. It's not quite as crowded

as it was at jurisprudence, mostly because people are already starting to forget. Scandal has a short life span, and only those who were personally injured remember past the next shocking event.

Inside, I spot Hit and Dina, who both stand to salute me. *Mary*, I thought I was beyond any emotional reaction, but that chokes me up. Fighting tears, I follow Vel up to the front of the chamber, where Chancellor Tarn waits. Really, as my superior officer, March should conduct the ceremony, but he's on indefinite leave.

Tarn greets me with an uncertain expression and a two-handed handshake. "I want you to know I understand what this cost you . . . and I will be forever grateful. We wouldn't have won this without you."

But he couldn't come out and say so, against popular opinion. He had to hedge his bets and work with the prosecution because people always need a scapegoat when things go wrong. In that, the Conglomerate is not so different from Farwan after all—and for that reason, I'll never work for them again. From this day forth, I am a private citizen, and I will do as I think best.

"I understand your position," I say coolly. Though he may be a fairly honest politician, he's still a politician, and I am done with them.

"We're ready to begin." He can likely tell I want to get this over with.

The ceremony is quick; it involves long-winded thanks and the playing of music. I don't really pay attention until Tarn speaks the words I have been waiting for:

"From this day forward, First Lieutenant Sirantha Jax, you are relieved of duty and obligation to the Conglomerate. Thank you for your service."

More salutes, more music. I let it wash over me, and it's like freedom, only heavier. Dina and Hit push through the crowd to my side, and they both hug me. As always, the blond mechanic smells of flowers, a minor tweak to her apocrine glands, as I recall. Hit is smiling, though I glimpse residual guilt in her eyes. She knew what I was planning to do before we left, but I let the tribunal think I didn't tell her. No need for her to get the negative press, too.

"I should've been right there with you," she says then. "In prison and on trial."

I shake my head. "It would've been worse for me, knowing I'd pulled you into my mess."

"*Our* mess. I didn't make my choice blind."

But she acknowledges I had the right to make the call. I was her superior officer, after all, and maybe the Armada would disagree, but I feel like I need to shield my people whenever I can; the blame stops with me. Listen to me— *my people*. Thank Mary, I don't have subordinates anymore. I'm just Jax, whatever that means.

Dina says, "You should get over to the training facility. I know Argus could use your help . . . It's slow going with him working alone."

I'm not eager, but it's my responsibility—one more step toward the time when I can keep my promises, first to myself about Baby-Z, the Mareq newborn I failed to protect, then to Loras, whose homeworld has been occupied for as long as anyone can remember. Maybe that's not my fight, but I will make it so, the last thing I do, before I take off for the great unknown. I keep a mental checklist in my head, and once I've satisfied all those obligations, then I'm adrift from my moorings—free to explore the universe and chart new beacons. I dream of that like some people do of finding the perfect lover. I hoped March would be my partner in that adventure, but now I'm not sure. He will likely come to the end of his quest with obligations, and I can't search for him before I clean up my mess.

Fortunately, Vel plans things down to the millimeter, and he has a private hovercar waiting outside. The back entrance to the jurisprudence center hasn't been completely overwhelmed, so with Hit and Dina helping to clear a path, we manage to get inside the vehicle with a minimum of trouble. Of course, the press still scream their questions. I try to ignore them, but this one burrows into my brain:

"What are you going to do, now that you've gotten away with murder?"

"Ignore them," Dina says quietly. "They're assholes. They have no idea what you did for them. Not really."

It means a lot to have her support, but I must look terrible if she's abandoned our normal mode of interaction, which is pure sarcasm. I know prison honed me, leaving me thinner and more muscular. The death toll probably shows in my eyes as well. They will ever remain on my conscience, those six hundred.

"I need their names," I tell Vel. "Could you please pull up a list?"

"Are you sure that is wise, Sirantha?"

"No, but it's necessary."

He complies then. And soon, I'm staring at the long, long roster of people who died because of me. This will be my bedtime reading for turns to come. Hit and Dina exchange a look, like I can't interpret their silent concern, but neither of them argues with me, a fact for which I'm grateful.

"Thanks for standing by me," I say to both of them.

Hit nods. "Thanks for protecting me."

Really, it could've gone much worse for me if I'd had a less talented barrister. I hope Nola can do as much for Pandora. *Speaking of which . . .*

"Vel, I don't know where you found Nola, but—"

"Chancellor Tarn recommended her," he interrupts. "And he transferred the funds from his own accounts for me to cover her fees."

Huh. So the Conglomerate prosecuted me, but Tarn paid to get me acquitted. I like him a little better right now. It's not the credits; I could have afforded to pay for my own defense, but this makes me feel less like they used me and cut me loose when I became inconvenient. I understand why he couldn't take a public stance supporting my actions, but deep down, he's an honest man. He knows I did what I had to, no matter how ugly it looks on the outside.

I fall quiet, pensive, watching the buildings blur into lines of color as we travel away from the city center. Ocklind is a beautiful city, temperate weather, semitropical beaches. If I hadn't acted as I did, New Terra might, even now, be swarming with Morgut. I see scenes superimposed from Emry Station. So much blood. I squeeze my eyes shut, but it doesn't help because these images are memories.

Vel touches my arm lightly, grounding me, and by the time we land, I have it under control again. The Morgut won't be landing here. Between the standing Armada, the Ithtorian fleet, and the fact that there's a shipyard producing more vessels as we speak on Nicu Tertius, the Conglomerate will never let itself be caught off guard again. We will defend our territories to the death . . . and our enemies will have to parlay with us to learn the new secrets of grimspace.

The new training facility is a building comprised of a series of interlocking domes, visually interesting, but I wonder if it's tough to navigate. The bot puts us down outside, where there are no crowds at all. I don't delude myself that I will never see the media again, but they haven't anticipated my movements to this point. It makes for a welcome break from all the shouting.

"Comm if you need us," Dina says.

Right. There's no reason for everyone to come inside; there's no work for them to do here. Lifting a hand in farewell, I go into the complex and am impressed when they test me for contaminants at the entryway. This is nothing like the Farwan academy where I studied; it has a more ominous feel. But since they converted a former asylum in short order to establish this training program—which is more apropos than they realize—it's not surprising. Once they determine I carry nothing that will harm the students within, the doors unlock, and I am permitted my first glimpse of the complex.

Halls lead out from the main hub in six different directions. Luckily, there's also a map on the wall, identifying who has offices in the building. I find Argus's name near the center. He's been appointed as director, despite his relative lack of experience, by virtue of his crash-course training before I turned myself in. I hope he's glad to see me.

I navigate the corridors alone, trying not to attract attention. A couple of the students give me a second look, then shake their heads, as if to say, *Nah, couldn't be.* I'm grateful for the rare anonymity as long as it lasts.

Argus answers my knock, wearing a harried look, and an expression of profound relief dawns on his young face. Despite my dark mood, I can't help but smile. He looks like he's in over his head.

"Oh, thank Mary they didn't kill you," he breathes. "Maybe I'll survive this job after all."

CHAPTER 13

"What's wrong?" I ask.

We've stepped into his office, the door closed behind us. He takes a seat at his large desk, and I sit opposite. It's so funny to see him on the other side of authority, the director of this place. To me, he'll always be my apprentice jumper; maybe this is similar to having children.

A long, frustrated breath escapes him. "I can't teach it. I can navigate the new signals, but I can't show anyone else like you showed me. I've just been buying time with bullshit exercises to 'prepare their minds,' hoping they'd cut you loose. But it's been so long now that I think they suspect something's wrong."

Frag me. There might be some truth to the accusation that I held the whole galaxy hostage. If they'd executed me, it would've crippled grimspace travel for turns to come. But I can show them all how to read the way the beacons pulse now, just like I did Argus. It will be time-consuming, but it's doable, and maybe along the way, I'll come across a jumper who can teach it alongside me. Unfortunately, I know of no test to identify that capacity.

"All right," I say, switching to work mode. "How many jumpers are here for training?"

"Over five hundred, but more arrive every day."

"Then strictly speaking, from a facilities standpoint, how many jumpers can jack into a training chair with me at one time?"

"No more than five."

I tap the comm. "Dina, are you still in range?"

"Dammit," she replies. "I knew it was too good to be true. I'm not getting a vacation, am I?"

"I'd appreciate your help here. I need you to figure out a way to patch twenty training chairs into one nav chair, and all processed through the same console."

"Like I did on the *Triumph*, times twenty?"

"Pretty much."

"You don't want much, do you?"

"I would love you forever if you could swing it."

"You'll love me forever anyway." I hear her giving instructions to the drive-bot, then she adds to me, "I'll be there in fifteen. Need to grab my tools first."

"I would be glad to assist," Vel adds. "I have some mechanical aptitude."

To say the least. He knows more about gadgets and gizmos than anyone I've ever met, save Dina. And when they work in concert, there's nothing they can't accomplish. I'm feeling better about this already.

"This is doable?" Argus asks.

"Very. Here's what I need you to do now. Tell the students to take the rest of the day off because tomorrow, they start wrapping up their training."

"Are you sure about that?"

"Absolutely. We'll work through the night to make all the necessary adjustments." I do a little math in my head. "I can probably do five classes a day, which means it'll take me a bit less than a week to handle the ones already on hand. I'll need your help prioritizing by those who arrived first. I trust you took notes?"

"Yes, I have plenty of records. I just didn't know what to

do with them after I failed my first attempts to show them the difference."

I laugh softly. "You get high marks for stalling."

He shrugs. "I really just want to jump."

"You'll be in demand, don't worry. There will be shipping companies that'll pay you a *fortune* at this point to get their goods moving again."

"I'm ready for a job like that," Argus says. "Relatively low pressure."

"Had enough of the thrills, chills, and death-defying?"

His young face grows somber. "Esme died in the attack on Venice Minor."

I remember her; she was the young blonde with whom he celebrated his first solo jump. Though I don't say so aloud, he now knows what it's like to be a jumper. Death stalks us through our days, taking those we love as if in warning not to forget how great a hold it has on us. Loss rides us from birth to grave, endless shadow cast over the euphoria that burns in grimspace.

"I'm sorry," I say quietly.

"It stopped being a game then." He's older now. I should've noticed at once, but I was focused on sorting the training situation here.

"Did you love her?"

He gives the question thoughtful consideration, then shakes his head. "I didn't bother getting to know her enough to say. I was just having fun."

"And now you'll never know if it might've been something."

"Exactly."

"We all lost people we loved on Venice Minor, and we can only go on as they would've wanted. Suffer the aftermath. War is bloody and awful . . . It leaves terrible wreckage to clear away. There are no heroes, only survivors."

"That's not what they believe on Lachion," he says. "They sing of great battles and people who died well for their clan."

"Do you still believe that's true?"

"No. After what I've seen, I don't see how it could be good or glorious."

I feel sad for him, as he's grown too much, and he can never return home. He cannot believe in their stories. But maybe a better life awaits Argus elsewhere, after a long career as a jumper. I can hope for that, even if I do not believe. Navigators like us don't wind up surrounded by our grandchildren, full of satisfaction at a life well lived. Like most, he will die in the nav chair, unable to speak a farewell to those who love him.

A small part of me pricks up in protest. Times, they are changing, and that may alter his end, too. Despite Doc's death, his gene therapy lives on. Unlike Evie, he wasn't paranoid about theft, and I know where he backed up his data. We can use his science to save jumpers from burnout. Maybe one day, there will be no dire tales about what happens to navigators who give too much to grimspace.

But first things first. I've got to prepare this facility for training in volume, then run the classes. Gene therapy can wait until after there's FTL movement on the Star Road again. I give Argus a list of things he needs to requisition, and he's happy to have a job he can do while he's on the ground. The stress flows away from him as I take charge; I can only imagine how tough it's been for him to pretend he could do what they demanded of him.

Half an hour later, Vel and Dina show up, tools in hand, ready to begin revamping the existing equipment. By this point, I've learned the school layout, so I lead the way to the training room, which is inadequately equipped for the number of experienced navigators who need to be retrained. If I can't find someone who can teach the new signals alongside me, then I'll be stuck here for the foreseeable future. That would be just as bad as prison.

"Thanks for coming," I say, as they set up.

Dina dismisses it with a wave of her spanner. "No problem. The sooner we finish here, the sooner we can move on."

We. She might not realize it, but that word means everything to me. It means I have friends who will stick by me, no matter how rocky it gets. I know better than to mention it, though, or she would rib me unmercifully. She hasn't changed *that* much.

Soon, workmen deliver chairs and cables, stacking the crates three deep against the far wall. While Dina and Vel go to work, I unpack, sorting the gear as best I can. If I were better with my hands, I'd help them with installation, but I suspect I'd just end up creating more things for them to fix. So it's better I just facilitate setup.

As it turns out, I wasn't kidding when I told Argus we'd work through the night, but by morning, we have twenty training seats successfully patched into one nav chair. With Vel's help, I tweak the programming to reflect the new pulses. That takes several more hours as I tinker, looking for precisely the right pitch. It's a lot of trial and error, until I find the correct setting.

After that, I wake Argus to test them, and he tries them one at a time while I sit in the center. Each time he joins me, I sense his tension easing a little more. He knows I'll handle the situation; I'm humbled to realize the depth of his faith, even after the mess I've made.

"It looks good," he says, after we complete the testing. "Are you going to be up to doing the first classes today?"

"Probably not," I admit. "I'm pretty tired, and I don't want to start off on the wrong foot."

"Another day won't kill them. I suspected you wouldn't want to start so soon, so I gave them two days off instead of one."

I give him a tired, admiring smile. "You're not just another pretty face. Well played. But I'll definitely take the first class tomorrow morning."

"Will it be as fast as it was for me?"

"I have no idea. We're breaking new ground, here. Some may not be able to learn at all, for all I know. If they've been jumping too long, their brains may not be able to hold the new patterns."

"So you think the fact that I'm relatively new helped me?"

"Maybe. I won't be able to extrapolate until I see more."

To my surprise, Argus hugs me. "Thanks for saving my ass."

"I'm the one who put you in this situation. It's the least I can do."

He shakes his head. "The least you could do is run. But you wouldn't."

No. That's not me. Not anymore.

CHAPTER 14

The system works.

Today I train twenty students at a time, and some of them learn faster than others. Turns out I was right—the young ones learn like Argus, but the older jumpers take longer, and a couple of them can't seem to grasp the shift, even after hours in the simulator with me. A veteran jumper named Ashley seems broken with disappointment.

"I know it's different," she says tearfully. "But I don't understand how."

I'll keep working with her over the next few days, but I suspect she's never going to get this. Her career as a jumper is done. I'm sorry as hell to have done this to her, but maybe I did her a favor. People rarely quit our profession voluntarily, so maybe now she has a chance at a normal life. Given the addictive nature of the job, she'll probably turn to chem and burn her mind out that way. But she has a chance, however slim, at something else.

She storms out of the session angrily, muttering curses, as I welcome the next batch of students. It will be my last of the day because I'm finding this more tiring than I expected, especially with the veteran jumpers. Some of them mutter at having to deal with me; I hear whispers of *murderess* and *vile bitch*. I pretend I don't hear it.

Just got to stick with this for a few weeks, and you can cut them loose.

I fire up the nav chair and the console, waiting for them to join me inside. They do so with varying levels of eagerness. Most of them erect partitions so I don't glimpse their emotions, but others take pleasure in showing me their scorn. I ignore them and focus on the colors streaming in my mind.

Clear your thoughts, I instruct the group. And then, as I showed Argus, I demonstrate how things have changed, the paths subtly altered. A couple of young jumpers catch on right away, and of those two, a girl flashes the same message I did. *Perfect duplication.* After her display, glimmers of understanding echo through the web. *She can teach.* We run the drill several more times until well over half the jumpers jacked in understand the difference.

Find Gehenna for me. Volunteers?

Not surprisingly, it's the girl who caught on first. She's eager to test herself, and she performs the jump flawlessly.

Does everyone see how that varies from the old way?

A general sense of assent, underscored with a hint of confusion and resentment. The old Farwan jumpers aren't happy with change, and even less so at my hands. I was the one who destroyed their world the first time, after all.

We drill until I sense that their exhaustion outstrips their ability to focus. At that point, I dismiss the class and jack out. But I ask my prodigy to stay behind.

"What's your name?" I ask.

"Faye." She's shy, unable to make eye contact. Or maybe she's afraid of me. I have a reputation these days.

"You have a talent for pattern duplication. How would you like to teach?"

She shakes her head. "I want to jump. Just as soon as I can get back out there."

"You can go back to jumping after we get the rest of the

navigators back up to speed," I say persuasively. "It could mean the difference between life and death for some of those colonies waiting on supplies."

Yeah, that struck the right note. She pales. "I guess I could stay a couple of weeks and help out."

"I need you," I tell her bluntly. "We're facing a challenge unlike anything that's happened in all the turns since we discovered phase-drive technology."

She nods. "I'm in. Just tell me what I need to do."

Over the course of the month, Faye and I train the classes together. In time, she becomes skilled enough to handle the younger, fast-adapting jumpers on her own. We develop a testing system to make sure the navigators who leave the program are competent enough to handle jumps, and gradually, interstellar travel resumes.

But more and more jumpers turn up; it seems like the job is endless.

Luckily, we find a few old-school folks who can teach the new beacons but are too set in their ways to want to use them to travel. So they're content taking jobs passing along patterns they will never use themselves. These days, I rarely have a moment to myself, running from class to class, or supervising a test. That's just as well, because as long as I'm secluded here, I don't have to think about what's going on in the greater world.

I slam into Vel on my way to an exam; it seems like ages since I've seen him. Honestly, I have no sense for how long it's been because I'm running on a twenty-four-hour schedule. I sleep little, and thanks to the nanites, I can get away with it for longer than most humans without going crazy. They take up the slack, sharpening my mind.

"You are pushing yourself too hard," he tells me.

"I broke it. I have to try to fix it."

"You bear too much guilt." Hit said it first—in a different way—but coming from Vel, who knows me better, it carries more weight.

"I blame March." It's not wholly a joke. Before loving

him, it never would've occurred to me to take on so much. I lived party to party, jump to jump. Most would argue he made a better person of me, but I'm not as happy as I used to be.

"Come. I have something to show you." Without asking my permission, he calls another teacher and instructs him to take over.

I raise a brow but don't protest. This is unlike Vel enough that I'm curious what he has in store. So I follow him through the school halls, down to the comm center. He commandeers the controls from the man working there, and tells him, "I believe it is time for your break."

It would take more bravery than most can muster to tell an Ithtorian no, so the guy scarpers, leaving Vel in charge of the various screens. He tunes them to public bounce channels without another word. With growing puzzlement, I watch.

Five minutes in, I understand. There's no news about Sirantha Jax or the six hundred soldiers. The public is now focused on a representative from a world that just joined the Conglomerate, who apparently has seven wives, though that's against the laws on New Terra. There's a big debate about whether his whole family—legal on his colony—can accompany him to sessions in Ocklind without facing social censure. Though the Conglomerate promises to uphold all religious and political freedoms, they cannot mandate that the natives behave in a friendly fashion. The representative is crying prejudice and discrimination in his interview; he's the new nine-day wonder.

"It's not news anymore," I admit. "That doesn't mean they've forgotten . . . or forgiven. Nor should they."

With his customary bluntness, he says, "It is more to the point to ask whether you have forgiven yourself."

I'm sure he knows I haven't. It's a steel shard, lodged in my heart, not because I feel I made a mistake but because so many paid for my decision with their lives. I never wanted that kind of power. I only ever wanted to jump.

"Sirantha," he says gently, "you may work yourself to death, and it will not bring those soldiers back. You try to atone, but you do not mourn. You must cede their loss and give them over to the Iglogth."

He's wise—and he's right.

"I don't know if I can," I whisper. "I've seen some tough times, but this is the worst because I can't get their families out of my head. I must be such a monster in their eyes."

In a lightning gesture, he lashes out with a claw, drawing a shallow X over my heart. The blood wells through my sliced shirt, and for a moment I am too shocked to move. I can't believe Vel hurt me. I would've sworn he never, ever would. I guess this means he hates me, too. The agony sears way more than it should for the size of the wound, burning from the betrayal, and tears spring up in my eyes.

When I see my pain reflected in his side-set eyes, I know why he did. So I can cry. Even though it hurt him, too, he gave me the wound that permits me to let go. It's a selfless thing, because I can see by the twitch of his mandible that it injured him, too. He has a friend's blood on his bare claws, a horrendous thing—and lovely, too.

My sobs, when they tear free, wrack me from head to toe. He draws me to him, all smooth chitin, cool and hard to the touch. There should be no solace in it, but there is because he's Vel, and he took my pain for his own. Now he must live with the knowledge he harmed someone he cares about—and that's not lightly done for one who lives as long as he. I respect his bravery and fortitude more than ever.

For I need this scar over my heart to remind me. Crazy as it sounds, if I can bear the wound on my body, it lessens what I must carry on my soul. How he knew that about me, I cannot fathom.

But he did, and it helped, and I weep in his arms, as though all the light in the world has died.

[Grainy vid-mail from March, arrived on the four-day bounce]

I saw that you're a free woman now. I'd congratulate you, but I expected this outcome, or I'd have never left, not even for my nephew.

Tomorrow we arrive at Nicu Tertius, but that's only the beginning. There are seven state homes, and four are designated for Psi training. They're all in different cities, and my problem is compounded by not knowing the boy's name. If they left Svetlana attached to his file as birth mother, that will simplify matters, but Farwan is notorious for excising such information to prevent Psi from wondering about their pasts. I can ask for a genetic search, as his markers should be fairly similar to mine, but that will take time, and it's hard to restrain my patience, particularly after this long haul.

I wouldn't admit this to anyone but you, but I'm afraid of what will happen to me when we land on Nicu. It's illogical, but I fear an instant regression to the monster I was before. The jungles on this world hold more ghosts than anyone could imagine; I killed so many men here, and they didn't even get a proper service. We left them wherever they fell, so their bones just worked their way down into the mud.

Right now, I wish I'd stayed because I want you at my side. That sounds pretty selfish, but I don't mean it that way. You just never needed me that way; I said it to you once as I was leaving—that you love me, but you don't need me. You don't lean. But I admire that about you, and I could use some of your strength right now.

Thinking of you. Love you still and always.

[message ends]

[Vid-mail reply from Jax, sent on the four-day bounce]

Free is a relative term. I'm no longer incarcerated, but I'm not my own woman, either. I'm obligated to set things right before I go. I mean, it's not a sentence or anything; though it might have been if I hadn't volunteered. I've been at the training academy in Ocklind for months now. This is the longest I've ever been dirtside, and it's hellish.

I used to dream of Doc and Evie, and how they died down on Venice Minor, but now I dream of grimspace. There's an ache in my bones as if I'm dying by millimeters each day I spend on this planet. I don't know how people live like this. I met a girl once who didn't attend school; she spent her whole life on ships. She was educated by AIs like Constance, and that sounded like the best thing in the universe to me. Imagine the wonders she saw, every single day. But she told me she just felt trapped on that ship and unable to form lasting relationships. It's so strange how one person's heaven is another's hell.

Things are progressing well enough here. Soon I'll have a complete team of teachers, and I can go on my way. Our graduates are already making their way onto the Star Road to get the shipping lanes moving at normal speed again. I feel for the colonies that are withering because of the slow supply shipments. I did that. But I can't help wondering when it all ends. You said I'm strong, and that I don't lean, but if you were here, I'd tip my head against your chest. How much must I give before we can be together? I live for the day when we can fly away into uncharted space, away from the paparazzi and the rumors and speculation. I don't want to be famous—or maybe that should be infamous—anymore.

Mary, I miss you. And don't worry, you're not going to fall back into old patterns. I can say that with complete certainty because you'd never do anything to hurt your nephew. You'll do whatever it takes to find him and see him safe. I know you.

Love and miss you always.

[message ends]

CHAPTER 15

Six months along, and we've trained the backlog of jumpers. Now we just have raw recruits coming in from the new tier worlds. But I've put a crew of teachers in place, and they know what they're doing. It's almost time for me to move along.

Thank Mary. I don't want to be doing this, but I believe in cleaning up my own messes, and this one is colossal.

I've agonized over my decision. Part of me wants to see March more than anything, but we have separate purposes. He doesn't need me hanging around while he searches for his nephew, and I have my own agenda. So with profound regret, I decide I need to take care of my business while he does the same. Hopefully, our paths will realign soon.

To my great satisfaction, the training facility runs smoothly these days, and I don't need to stick around forever. Ships are jumping again, which is the most important thing. I just have one more thing to do; that's why I'm heading for a panel of doctors and scientists, none of whom I know personally, but they all have a reputation for cutting-edge developments. The room is already full when I arrive, and a sea of expectant faces turn toward me. Some are old, others young, but all bear a fascinated expression as I launch into my explanation of why we're here.

"How many of you are familiar with NBS?"

Navigator Burnout Syndrome—the number one reason why my job is so dangerous. But it's not a problem for me anymore. Seventy-five percent of them raise their hands, which means I have to explain for those who don't. That takes five minutes. Once I'm sure they're all with me, I continue, "Before his death, Dr. Solaith devised a gene-therapy treatment that eradicates the danger of NBS. I realize you'll want to study his method and his results before you begin trials, so I am forwarding all of his research to your handhelds . . . right now."

As one, they turn to their devices, skimming through what Doc did to me. A murmur goes through the collected scientists as they realize I've been injected without all the preliminary studies. I can tell they don't approve of his methods; they think he was something of a barbarian for taking such chances. Since he's not around to defend himself, however, they don't speak the condemnations aloud. Just as well for them because I'd take them all off at the knees if they dared.

"There will be Conglomerate grants for research in this area . . . and I suspect I don't need to tell you how much money would be involved for the team that patents the NBS vaccine. Shipping companies alone would pay millions of credits for better longevity in their jumpers. Any questions?"

For ten more minutes, I field some basic queries before the scientists stream out, most eager to begin digging into Doc's fieldwork. The knowledge is all there, waiting for the right team to develop into a universal vaccine. Right now, the only handicap is that each treatment must be tailored to the patient's unique genetic code, which worked for Argus and me in small scale but would be utterly inefficient for every jumper in the universe. They need to refine it some-how, so that it works on whoever takes it, but I've given them the tools to figure it out, and in my lifetime, I fully believe we will see a cure for NBS.

"That went well," Vel says.

I meet him in the hallway. I'm tired of this place. But by the cant of his head, I know he doesn't bear good tidings. "What's up?"

"The civil suits have begun."

I can't say I'm surprised. Ramona left me a fortune, and the families who lost children because of me want some form of recompense. They'll ask some incredible amount, and the judges will likely pare it down before demanding I pay up. It's not that I mind giving them the credits, but on some level, I feel as though they're cheapening their loss. I shouldn't be able to buy expiation as though it were an indulgence sold by a corrupt priest. They can take everything I inherited, and it won't touch the stain on my conscience.

"How much?"

He names a sum that would've made me dizzy once. But since I received Ramona's empire, my sense of scale has ratcheted up. I nod. "I don't want to contest. Just settle with them."

"That will encourage the others to apply for their shares."

"I don't care," I say simply. "I never wanted her credits, knowing how she earned them. If I run cash poor, there are assets we can sell off."

Vel has been acting as my business manager. Given his long life span, he has a personal fortune that rivals my mother's, so if anyone knows what to do with extra credits, it's him. He's managed to squirrel away certain of my dividends into untouchable, interest-bearing accounts, so I'll never be completely destitute even if I give away most of my wealth.

"What would you like to liquidate first?"

Right now nobody will buy the devastated land on Venice Minor, which leaves the mining colony on the asteroid Dobrinya, and part of a moon. I don't know what mineral resources the moon might possess; as yet, it's undeveloped.

"Dobrinya," I decide aloud. "Uranium is worth a good deal in today's market."

"Noted. I'll start seeking offers."

By the time it's necessary, he will have identified the most advantageous deal.

As we walk, he taps on his handheld, authorizing the civil settlement. I chafe at the obligation to wrap up all the loose ends here, but I have five more meetings today, setting up a hierarchy in the training program. Someone has to take responsibility after I'm gone, as I am damn sure not spending my life *here*.

"Have you found a ship?"

We plan to leave for Gehenna as soon as possible. Realistically speaking, it will be another week before I can break away, but I want all the pieces in place before I make my escape.

"Dina found one that the owner was ready to scrap, so we got it for a bargain."

I nod. "She prefers to do all her own maintenance anyway."

It's not like she would trust a brand-new ship. She would still go over every millimeter of it, and replace half the parts with her own mods. I must admit, I rather love seeing what she can do with a vessel everyone else has given up on. In fact, maybe that's why she sticks by me.

"I would not fly on it were anyone else doing the restoration." He bestows the highest of compliments, there.

"How big is it?"

"It will take eight people, comfortably. Not including pilot and jumper."

"Small crew quarters, I take it?"

"Miniscule."

"Then it's just as well we won't be on it long."

Mary, but I'm dying to jump. It feels like I've been grounded forever, and I am losing my mind slowly. It was bad in prison, but there, I knew I had no choice. So I sublimated my need in constant exercise. Here, I function as the school administrator, and I have no outlet for the junkie cravings boiling in my brain. I long to travel to Marakeq and try to make right the damage I've done. Perhaps I never can, but I will think less of myself if I don't try, and I need every scrap of self-esteem these days.

Every day, waking up feels like I'm strapping on lead boots and daring myself not to sink beneath the dark, dark water. I run in place, and I pretend, but it's not getting better. Only time will do that, at least according to Vel. He says it like a promise, so I live for the day, maybe fifty turns from now, when I don't feel sick over what I've done.

Gehenna first, though. Vel and I have unfinished business there. He will want to visit Adele—as the last time, she said he'd see her again—and I need to hire Doc's old friend, Ordo Carvati. There's a certain symmetry in that. While we tend to those matters, Hit and Dina can go for the open markets and the leashed wildness of life inside the dome. Gehenna was the only place where I ever lived for myself, like a normal person, and therefore, it will always hold a special spot in my heart.

"I will see you later, Sirantha. I have many irons in the fire."

I have to chuckle at Vel's attempt to speak colloquially; he always does so with such formality. After watching him go, I rush through the rest of my meetings, and at night, I run instead of sleep, but the memories are always nipping at my heels. In the silence, I wonder how much longer I can continue without breaking. But escape will help; grimspace will welcome me home, no matter what.

A week later, I resign my place at the training facility and turn it over, gladly, to my successor. There is no fanfare when I walk away from New Terra, when I climb the ramp and run toward the cockpit. The stars await me with their cool auras and their nonjudgmental light. As the world falls away behind me, I settle into the nav chair, with Hit beside me. Since we have flown together before, I have no fear of her.

This feels like coming home.

CHAPTER 16

This world fades into beautiful darkness, just nothing and more nothing.

I welcome the black because it means I'm only a whisper away from my first jump in long, long months. Hit jacks in beside me, and she's mentally disciplined as only a trained killer can be. A whisper of respect filters from her, but that's all she gives me; everything else belongs to Dina—and that's how it ought to be.

The phase drive powers up smoothly, hardly shaking the ship at all despite its small size, which means Dina has been hard at work. I gather she's already installed the mod that permits direct jumps because I feel the cations firing in my veins in response to the ones in the nav com. The ship mind is brand-new, nascent and curious. I let it get to know me as we prepare to make the leap.

With a small shiver, we pass from straight space into the maelstrom. Grimspace blazes in my mind, full of lovely, chaotic colors. The stars have gone, but the ancients left beacons in their place, the ones I reprogrammed at such great cost. They echo with me now, giving a whisper of Jax to eternity, and that knowledge humbles me. Countless eons from now, I will remain, my heartbeat as part of the navigation system for societies I cannot conceive.

Here, I feel whole. But I cannot stay; I would die. As with any living creature, grimspace would drain me and cast me adrift as one of its infinite ghosts. I care too much about those I carry on this ship to let that happen, though I imagine making the jump alone someday . . . and never coming back. I used to dream of retiring on Venice Minor, but I am far past such innocent hopes. The best I can imagine now is dying here, where none can know to mourn me.

Hit gives no sign she's aware of these thoughts as we prep for the return. I use the new pulses to find Gehenna, then make the fold that permits us to pass through. Hit responds to my mental directions, following with seamless skill. We return smoothly, emerging a few thousand klicks from Gehenna.

Even at this remove, I see the streaks of gold and orange, flashes of red that make it so spectacular from the ground. I can't imagine what led them to build here, where there isn't even a breathable atmosphere, but it's a rich man's paradise, artificial and full of glamour. They say you can buy any extravagance on Gehenna, provided you have the contacts and the credits. I know from my time with Adele that there are lords of vice who have built their kingdoms on the sins of strangers.

Adele gave me shelter when I needed it most. She awakened a hint of spirituality in a soul that had previously lived only for pleasure. In short, she was the mother I always wanted, and I treasure my memory of my short time with her. I learned so much about human kindness.

Hit taps the comm. "Gehenna authority, this is the *Big Bad Sue*, requesting clearance and coordinates."

I grin and mouth at her, *The* Big Bad Sue?

She shrugs and mutes the mic for a second. "It came with the moniker, and Dina liked it. Like *I'm* gonna tell her no."

"I like it, too." It just strikes me as funny because this little ship clearly isn't a big bad anything. Sounds to me like the prior owner had a sense of humor.

"*Big Bad Sue*, what's your purpose in port?"

"We plan to visit friends and relatives, enjoy your fine hospitality, and spend a few credits."

"*Big Bad Sue*, you said the magic words. Are you carrying cargo today?"

Hit shakes her head though only I can see her, as they haven't engaged the vid—no need and it distracts the pilot. Too many crash landings by those of lesser skill, and they learned better. "Negative, authority. Personnel only."

"Stand by for docking bay number and trajectory for your arrival. We will, of course, need to scan for contraband."

"And then tax us on it," Hit mutters.

I stifle a laugh because that's so true. They don't much care what you bring into the dome, unless it's Morgut, but you damn well better expect to pay the powers that be a cut of the profits. They won't find anything interesting on us, however; we truly are here to see old friends . . . and trade in information.

Hit takes us in smoothly though she does calculate to make sure they've given us the correct trajectory. I haven't trusted docking personnel since they killed my lover, seventy-five Conglomerate diplomats, and nearly ended my life as well. But the port authority here has no reason to want us dead; they want us to land, clear customs, and spend our credits inside the dome. After landing, it doesn't take long to pass through the red tape. A routine scan, and we're on our way.

Gehenna is a wonderland. Even in these difficult times, when interstellar travel is only beginning to recover from the blow I dealt it, the spaceport bustles with activity. Cargo ships from the outskirts whose tired crews look as though they hauled straight space to get here unload crates of raw herbs that will be processed and used to create kosh—one of the more expensive designer drugs, available only under the dome. It's madly addictive, but it provides penultimate euphoria, or so I hear. I never did kosh; liquor was my drug of choice.

On my way out of the spaceport, I pat my pocket to ensure I have the two data spikes, different information, but destined for the same principal. The slight bulge beneath my fingertips reassures me. If I lost this data, it would mean profound failure, and right now, these missions give me a reason to push forward. I need to finish what I started.

Vel touches my arm to get my attention. "Could we call on Adele before our other business?"

"Of course." She's the woman who valued him enough to set him free. Back on Ithiss-Tor, I remember he mentioned a human lover, and it hadn't taken much for me to connect the dots, given her odd words to him when he came for me clad in Doc's skin. "Would you prefer to see her alone?"

I don't want to intrude on a private moment.

But he curls his claws in obvious distress. "No, I would like you to go with me. It will be . . . difficult to see her. It was, when I came hunting you. She had changed so much, even then. It will be worse now."

"Then I'll go. I do want to see her . . . She was good to me."

"That is her way," he says softly. "So full of kindness."

"I never knew how you ended up with her." It's a leading statement because I want to put it in the form of a question, but I shouldn't pry.

He thinks a moment, head canted. In many months, I have not seen him in faux-skin. These days, he shows his chitin, if not proudly, then with a certain acceptance. But he is the general of the Ithtorian forces . . . or at least, he was. Vel resigned his commission around the time they booted me politely from the Armada. We're both free agents now.

"You know everything else," he answers at last. "I will share this as well if you would listen. But it is a story worth telling properly, not in bits and fragments. Would you have all my words, then, at a time of my choosing?"

"Please."

The tale will be told with all ceremony and formality because of the great regard he bears for Adele even now. It's hard for me to resign the image of the older, coffee-skinned woman with someone who would take Vel as a lover, but I can't wait to hear their story. I know this much, though; he'll share it at the right time and place.

Once we leave the spaceport, Hit and Dina find a romantic lodging house, all pale stone given a sweet, rosy glimmer by the shadows above the dome. Vel and I continue on, closer to Adele's neighborhood. I know she will permit me to stay in the garret with its glastique walls, but I'm not sure if Vel would be comfortable there. I don't ask because his body language reveals clear distress, the closer we get.

The crowd parts around us, giving him a wide berth. Even with the increased Ithtorian galactic presence, people still stop and stare. Women pull their children away from him, and I hear whispers about how Sliders steal little children. Because I know him, their behavior infuriates me, and Vel snags my hand to keep me from popping one especially rude female in the face.

"It does not matter," he says, spreading his claw in an open gesture.

My chip tells me that signifies letting go, how it all flows away. But anything that hurts him sets my teeth on edge, and it's been a long time since I cut loose. If they keep this up, I'll wind up in a Gehenna jail. There are few people I'd fight for these days, but Vel is one of them.

He selects a quiet café a few blocks from Adele's building, and we take a seat inside, where it is all soft shadows. The servo-bot takes our order, something simple that will not distract me from his secrets. I want them because I have none from him. Not now. He's seen too much of my past while I know so little of his.

"Here. I will speak here."

And I sit quiet, rapt with the emotion radiating from him.

I have no mate.

I have no house.

I have no young to guarantee my immortality.

When I die, there will be no one to lay out my body or log the colors of my deeds in the ancient way. I have no colors.

Once, I thought it best that way. I saw my opportunity and took it. The life the stars gave strangled me, and so I ran. I called it by another name, but so many turns distant from the choice, I can name it what it was: cowardice. Shame finds me bare among my own kind, and they know me for what I am. Exile. Outcast. It does not matter that I chose it.

And yet . . .

And yet . . .

For a time, I was happy.

Not in the service of the legendary bounty hunter, Trapper, for all he was a fair man. Without his offices, I would not have survived. That one discovered me quicker than anyone since. He had a knowing to him that I miss to this day. He could look at a thing and tell you its nature. I have never experienced the like.

He alone knew that my name, to my people, means "white wave." And so, I stayed with him because it was the closest I had to home, though I had left mine of my own free will. An artist may starve in uncertain times, so I laid aside those dreams as the price of freedom. Thus, I learned to stalk and track my prey. I learned to be ruthless. I learned never to back away from a deal once I gave my word. All that and more I learned from Trapper.

Over the turns, I became a legend. I do not say this lightly, but doubtless you have heard the stories. In colonies all over the galaxy, mothers tell their children: "You had better be good, or the Sliders will get you."

That is not strictly accurate. Since the Axis Wars, I am the only one to break the isolation. I alone turn our native camouflage into something else, passing among humans undetected. Thus, the stories they tell?

They are all of me.

The time I spent with Trapper did not seem long, but he aged like a husk before my eyes. It almost seemed a flicker; humanity flares so bright that it cannot sustain the flame. I find the process fascinating but alarming. So I stayed with him until the end. I was there when he passed. Only I appreciated the irony of being named his heir. He called me son toward the end, and that, too, was a bitter irony.

But I did learn then that credits were power, and that within the guild, wealth might be all that kept me safe if my secret became known.

But that—that is another story.

Without Trapper, I was rudderless, a bounty hunter stripped of any real desire to hunt. I had spent too many turns taking orders from that old man to know what to do with myself once he was gone. And so, as is my custom, I ran.

In time, I found myself on Gehenna, with no quarry in sight. I had wanted a place where one could get lost, outside laws and boundaries. I think I also wanted to be something other than what I was, a pretender in human skin, so I went away from the guild and everything I knew. There, I made myself over.

I do not know if there has ever been such a lost creature as I, standing in that bustling market. Nobody thought to offer a wa, and they seemed blind to body language. To my inexperienced eyes, it seemed a vast carnival of a world, with titian skies that never shift outside the dome and life at all hours. The cacophony rendered me quite mad, even through the false skin that dulled my senses. Roasting meat and spilled blood, molten ore and silicon dust, incense and scented candles, herbal remedies and rare poisons—these scents combined to overwhelm me.

To this day, I think she took me for one who had lost his wits. But there was sweetness in her dark eyes as she touched my arm. Everyone else had passed me by, jostling in their haste. I saw everything and nothing, but the world skimmed down to her face when she touched me. I could not feel it, truly, but I understood what it meant. It was compassion.

"Have you lost your way?" she asked kindly.

I had long ago received an implant, making it possible for me to communicate. Otherwise, I would have been a mute as well an exile. She waited for a response. I am certain if I had not been so shocked, I would have offered something less candid.

"I have nowhere to go."

"Come." She smiled up at me, laugh lines crinkling the corners of her eyes.

It should not have been that easy. With the added benefit of turns and experience, I am angry with her now. Her faith in the decency of other sentient beings stood in the face of everything I have come to learn about the universe.

I can still see her in my mind's eyes as she was then. She came to my shoulder, and she had a softness to her, though her hands were firm.

In the shape I had taken to best cover my true form, I was tall and thin, shaping the camouflage to what was already there. I did not like it when I had to pretend to be more compact. At length it would become painful—and since I had chosen this physical representation to suit myself, it was as close to nature as I could permit. My hair was brown, I think, and my eyes, likewise.

To my surprise, she took me to her dwelling. Only a crazy woman would do that, so I readied myself for some outburst or incipient threat. Instead, she made a drink of boiling leaves, which I was afraid to touch. I had learned there were certain human foods and beverages that I must avoid on pain of death.

"I'm Adele," she said. "And in Mary's name, you'll be in need of work. What can you do?"

It was a fair question. But instead of answering it, I repaid her kindness with scorn. "Is this Mary the god of fools?"

Her wit was quick. "Rather the goddess of rude and rootless men, I think."

"It was unwise of you to take me up," I said. "Put me back where you found me."

"I will not. If kindness is unwise, then perhaps I do worship the goddess of fools. Answer the question." In her smile lay pure gentleness. At that time, I had not much skill in interpreting human faces, but I did not read her wrong.

So I told her I had some ability to draw and paint, and that I could repair certain machines. Of my darker skills, I did not speak, as that was the least of my secrets.

Later, when she returned to the room from which she'd brought the drinks, I quickly analyzed the contents of the cup and found it was safe. In fact, by some odd coincidence, she'd chosen beneficial herbs. I should have realized then that something guided Adele's steps. My people would call her Beloved of Iglogth; however great their pragmatism, Ithtorians lack nothing in the way of mysteries.

As she returned, she saw me sipping from the cup. There is a trick to it, one it took me turns to perfect, so the fluid finds its way truly through the camouflage and into my own body where it can do some good. She seemed pleased by my trust, though why she should want it I would not understand until much later.

"I have a friend who runs a shop off the market," she told me. "He takes in broken things and makes them new again."

As do you, I thought.

"I would like to meet him."

In that way, I came to be apprenticed to Franco Schmidt, who, shortly after I met him, bade me call him Smitty, then to get to work. Like Trapper, he cared nothing for licenses or work permits. He was akin to the acerbic old man I'd lost, and I found myself at home. Perhaps I could only find myself when I served others.

Smitty offered me a room above his shop. In his early days, he had used it himself, but now he did well enough with the repair of broken things that he could afford a better dwelling. As it offered plenty of privacy, it suited my needs, as I regularly regenerated the camouflage that safeguarded me from those who would call me monster.

In that way, I learned another trade. Days turned to weeks, weeks to months, and months to turns. It was not the place I'd wanted when I set out to start anew, but it was a place nonetheless. I was safe.

When things changed again, it had been three turns since Adele found me in the marketplace. Oh, she had checked on me from time to time, but this visit would alter my circumstances in ways I could never have imagined.

She came into the shop, smelling of hyacinths. I had altered my design slightly, so my olfactory sense was not dulled as it had been. The light perfume could not cover the faint smell of morbidity, but I have learned to overlook that. Your kind cannot help that your cells are constantly dying and flaking away; you leave bits of yourselves everywhere you go. At first I found it grotesque and distracting, but it is no worse than what I must do with the camouflage to walk among you.

Of course, my tactile senses were muted, so I felt nothing but pressure when she shook my hand, but I could do nothing about that. Smitty had gone home early, as he often did by that point, leaving me to tend the latecomers and lock up before I went upstairs.

Her smile still held kindness. "Are you settling in, Vel?"

The familiarity surprised me, though I had told her it was my name, turns past. It was rare enough that anyone spoke it. Half the patrons of the repair bay called me Young Smitty, either in jest or lack of interest. I did not object; it had been so long since I spoke with anyone who cared about the truth of my naming, or who knew how to make a proper wa, that I sometimes felt like a spirit forgotten by the Iglogth. It is a hard thing to cast your shadow on alien earth, far from that which sheltered your ancestors. And yet . . .

And yet, I chose it.

"Yes," I said. "I am happy here."

"Are you?" she asked.

Such a question. Even now, I ask myself why she cared. But that was her way, looking after such strays the universe brought to her. Adele thought it Mary's will.

I regarded her, puzzled.

"You don't seem happy. Smitty tells me you have made no friends, and you seek no new companions. All you do is work."

"What more is there?" It was a naïve question, based on inhuman values. Even social intercourse between Ithtorians is fueled by what may be accomplished by it.

I should have said something else; I should have kept silent. But for all my turns among them, I had not lived as a human, merely passed. I had never come to understand you, nor had I tried. Humans seemed soft and fragile, bursting with irrational impulses that drove them to excess. I might as well attempt to comprehend that which spins or creeps or lairs in dark, damp places as to unravel the human condition. I could only mimic it.

"Oh, Vel," she murmured. "What have they done to you? Were you raised in a labor crèche in the far colonies? I've heard they don't let those children play at all."

I do not remember what I said—some noncommittal response—for I had only a rudimentary idea what she meant. Human young were noisy and undisciplined, messy and full of mischief. If there was a place raising them to be more sober and industrious, I could only consider that a good thing.

But in that moment, the damage was done. She decided to save me from myself. Despite my lack of hospitality, she stayed until I finished all my work for the day. She stayed until I locked up the store, and I did not know what to do with her. My room upstairs was small and sparse, and I had nothing to offer.

We stood gazing at each other across a counter strewn with electronic components and bits of wire. I raked them into a box, and said uneasily, "I do not know what you want."

She laughed then. "I know you don't. Come on."

I looked at her outstretched hand for a moment. Then I did something for which I have no explanation. I took it.

Adele led me out of the shop, waited while I set the security code, then dragged me toward the marketplace. Despite the late hour, the sky held the same fire. Nothing changed, nothing except the faces. At that hour, a man juggled flaming rods in the center of the plaza. Musicians had come out to beg their livelihood with melodies haunting-sweet. I saw a man bend and dip his credit spike into the small wireless terminal set out for that purpose.

"Where are we going?" I asked.

"To eat. And talk. You're alone too much," she told me. "Smitty was right."

After that night, she came for me often. I do not know why I acceded, but again and again, I let her lead me out, where she showed me what it is to be human. We ate in open-air stalls, food I never would have touched on my own. I grew adept at scanning the ingredients to make sure they would not send me into convulsions.

Once, she caught me at it, and I had to lie: "I have many allergies. I must be cautious."

Sadly, she had such an honest soul that she accepted it without question.

This became our pattern once a week, then twice. I found myself seeing her nearly every night. I had no idea what she wanted with me. It was strange, but not unwelcome, to have a companion who knew the city. Unlike most, she had been born within the dome, and she knew the hidden ways, where old men sold songbirds from gilded cages, and old women sat in doorways smoking pipes that sent blue smoke curling up toward the sky.

It was not until Smitty made an offhand remark that I realized the significance.

"Good to see you found someone," the old man wheezed. "You don't want to end up like me, no sir. And you can't do better than Adele. That girl has a heart of gold."

"Do better for what?" It was another of my blunders. I could tell by the way Smitty's white, bristling brows shot up.

"You mean . . ." He peered at me over the kitchen-mate I was repairing. The circuits were scrambled, so the orders placed came out wrong; it was my job to fix it, so we could sell it at a higher price than we paid for it. "I guess you believe in moving slow, don't you, boy?"

It took me a moment to work out his implication. Humans often shared sexual contact for recreational purposes, but I knew nothing of that drive.

I tried to think of a response. "I have no reason to believe she would welcome such an overture," I said at last.

Smitty laughed and shook his head. "Adele's a good girl, not a saint. Grab her and kiss her, son. You'll find out soon enough there's a reason she spends all her free time with you."

Pretending to heed his counsel, I went back to work. What he suggested, I would never do. Touch meant nothing to me, offered through two centimeters of camouflage. But I had come to enjoy her company, and I hoped she did not find mine burdensome.

Despite the old man's interference, things continued as they were for several more months until Adele proved him right. We had eaten in the marketplace and were walking from stall to stall as she admired the various goods. She paused where a vendor had various lengths of cloth that sparkled in the light. I did not know their purpose until she wound one round her shoulders.

"Does it suit me?" she asked, smiling up at me.

"Yes," I said, because a more detailed answer was beyond me.

Her face fell. I think I was meant to praise her appearance, but I had missed another cue. In all honesty, I did not find her beautiful. Her skin was too smooth, her eyes sunken in her skull instead of proudly outthrust. A monstrous animal lurked in the shape of her lips against her teeth, but something shifted in me that day.

"You don't think I'm pretty." Her gaze dropped. "You probably prefer pale women with their delicate figures. Is that why you've never kissed me?"

No. That certainly was not true. Dark or fair, lean or large, I wanted no human female with dying skin and spongy flesh. But it mattered more to make her happy than be truthful. So I bought the cloth with my credit spike and gave it to her. I shaped my mouth into a semblance of a smile, and said, "You are lovely even without this, but I would like you to have it if you will accept such a gift from me."

Her dark eyes sparkled, and it was she who first kissed me. At first I thought it was an attack, and I braced myself for worse, but her mouth merely moved against mine. It was not repugnant; I felt nothing but the pressure against my mandible. Like most human customs, it was easy enough to learn, and she seemed pleased when she pulled back.

After that she touched me more, which meant I had to take care that the camouflage was fresh. I used one night every two weeks to regenerate, which she found mysterious, as I would not tell her what I was doing. In retrospect, I should simply have lied.

This was my first relationship of any length. I marvel now that she did not guess my strangeness from the first, as Trapper had, but she claimed to find my differences adorable. After a time, I realized I liked making her happy—enough to put up with whatever strangeness our association demanded.

Which brings me to our first mating. I knew she wanted it; such was the normal progression. It bothered me that she might one day expect me to sire her young, but I had come to rely upon her presence by that time. I no longer enjoyed being alone; I no longer enjoyed the silence. I tried to put sexual congress off, knowing it would be awkward. I watched vids to give me some idea what to expect, but it was hard to know which ones represented the median experience, and I had no one to advise me.

Regardless, the moment arrived unexpectedly, as did most events with Adele. It was nothing she planned, I am sure, but we had dined at her dwelling and were sitting close, as she liked, sharing warmth. For a while we spoke of nothing in particular, but then her mood turned from words to kisses and from kisses to deeper things.

In the end, it was not as complex as I feared. I think on some level she sensed my inexperience and talked me through it, whispering what I should do—and what she wanted most. Of that night I can say, I did not mind it. Even in this, I am an adroit mimic. Her pleasure pleased me. I also liked the human way, for it did not leave me vulnerable and fearing madness might overtake my mate. There was no release in it, but it was another sort of gratification—that of making Adele happy, which had become important to me.

We went on this way for two more turns. Smitty passed, and he left to me his shop. Now I had a place of my own. I need not hunt the dregs of the galaxy if I chose otherwise. I could pretend to age and stay with Adele until she died. Then I would have to "die" myself and start all over again. The prospect left me feeling so bleak that I withdrew from her.

At this point, you probably believe you can guess what happened next. But I think it will surprise you.

Yes, she came to me one night when I had no human skin to hide behind. She knew the codes and let herself in. On quiet feet, she came up to my room, expecting to find me with someone else. The truth shocked her more.

She stepped into my room from the stairs, and I spun, exposed as I had never been.

To my astonishment, Adele did not flee or scream, though she could never have seen anything like me. Instead, she came toward me and touched the chitin of my thorax where it met the hinged plates of my lower limbs. A gap lies there; it is sensitive and only meant for mated pairs. I cannot imagine how she knew.

"So this is your secret. I must admit, I'm relieved. It could've been worse."

"It could?"

She smiled then. "It explains a lot, too."

"I am sorry," I said formally. "I have stolen away your chance at bearing young."

"I'm not so old as that," she told me. "But it's good to understand the why of it. I'd gone to see a doctor, you know."

"I am sorry for that, too. I never meant—"

At that she shook her head. "I started this, not you. Don't speak of regrets unless you're sorry for the time we spent together."

I could not read her face and did not know what she meant. But in this, I could be wholly honest. "No."

"But it was never real, was it?" She shook her head sadly. "It was only you pretending to be what I wanted."

Part of that was true. In some regards I did have to pretend. The camouflage made it impossible for it to be otherwise.

"It was not all false," I said. "It gave me great contentment to make you happy."

"Did it?" Her face lit, as it had when I bought her that length of cloth. Such simple things gave her joy. She carried the loveliest heart in her soft, ungainly body. "Then it is my turn, surely? If you trust me, I would know you, the truth of you; and then we shall see what I may do for you."

So we lay in my bed that night, and I talked. No one has ever heard my story so fully since, nor known me inside my skin as she did then. She lay beside me with sweetness and wonder, listening rapt to the chronicle that brought me to Gehenna. For the first time, I spoke of Ithiss-Tor and the life I had left behind. Her acceptance remade me into something I did not loathe.

Afterward, she touched me as only mates do, and we discovered that there was something we could share. I learned the purpose of pleasure for its own sake. I gave back to her, such as I could. It was a crossways fit, not natural design, but there was rightness in it.

After that, she did not argue my need to wear camouflage to avoid trouble on Gehenna, but on regen-nights, she seemed happiest because it was real then.

And I was happy. Can you quantify such moments? Can you catalogue them by intensity and say, This is the best of times. I cannot. I can only say that those turns with her were good.

I did not leave her by choice. I did not return to hunting because I wanted to. Given the opportunity, I would have stayed with her until she died. I altered my outward appearance appropriately, aging as she did. I was content with that life.

But as all things do, they came to an end. She saw it more clearly than I. At that point, we had been some twenty turns together by my reckoning.

One night, after sharing in our way, she lay with me, running her fingers along my mandible. She had learned the flesh was sensitive where it joined my throat. No Ithtorian mate would do so, for it offered no measure of rank or dominance. It was not done to prove her superiority, and for that reason alone I would have knelt to her where I would acknowledge no other female so.

"It's time for you to go," she said quietly.

At first I did not understand. I rose and regarded her; many-faceted images of her came back to me since I looked through my own eyes, and I relished every one.

"Go where?"

"Away."

"Why?" It was a pointless question, but I hoped she would answer it.

"I will not see you bound to me," Adele said. "While I grow old and weak and eventually you are my nurse, not my lover. In thirty turns more, that is where we shall be. Already I find it hard to speak these words, so I need you to go and carry the memory of me. In you I will live on, always."

"Since I cannot give you young," I said bitterly.

That is our way, our immortality. We are long-lived, compared to humans. We breed less often, but we create a new generation at a time. And I could give her nothing of it.

"You have given me the universe," she responded, smiling.

That she could smile while I hurt in ways I could not understand— it broke something in me. I did not understand the heart of her, then. She is made of brightness, too much for sorrow. Such a glad spirit— I am humbled now that she shared it with me.

And so, I went from Gehenna, went back to building my own legend, with a hole in me that would take longer to fill than I knew. But that, too, is another story.

CHAPTER 17

Twenty turns, such a long time. The weight of the story bears on me, making me understand why it's hard for him to see her like this, now. Because of his life span, their time together doesn't feel like an affair that ended long ago; in Vel's terms, theirs is a fairly recent breakup, strange as that might seem to me.

"You love her still."

"I do not know," Vel answers. "I have never been sure if I have the capacity. It is not an Ithtorian emotion."

Maybe not love, then. But caring. Affection. Whatever word he chooses, it applies to what he shared with Adele. I finish my drink and clear our tab with the servo-bot, then it's time to move along. We step back onto the public walk, only a short distance from Adele's flat now. Given what he told me, I can't imagine what this is like for him, but he's determined. I follow in his wake as the crowd eddies around him. The stares still bother me, but I don't start anything. On Gehenna, people don't remember my face like they do on New Terra. It would be a mistake to make myself notorious here as well.

Then I'm standing outside, gazing up. Unerringly, I find the row of glastique windows along the top. Mary, I was so happy there; sleeping right up against the windowpanes reminded me of flying. It was the only time I've ever been content when I wasn't jumping. The rest of the building is an artistic nightmare, and as I recall, the lifts don't work. There's no security to speak of, so we pass inside unquestioned and walk up the flights to her apartment.

Vel touches the panel beside her door, but instead of asking who it is, she buzzes us in. She always had a whisper of prescience about her—and I hope it's kicking in now. Otherwise, she's too trusting for her own good. I step into the flat, which smells of tea and good fruit marmalade. She has a tray waiting on the table in her salon, but she does not get up. As I step closer, I see the lap robe tucked across her legs. She has aged visibly since the last time I saw her, more gray in her hair, and her skin has gone sallow.

"Forgive me for not greeting you properly," she says warmly. "But I'm not getting around as well as I once did."

"Were you expecting us?" Vel asks.

"I said I'd see you again, didn't I? I'm never wrong about these things."

He crosses to press the side of his face to her cheek. The chip recognizes the gesture as akin to a kiss, at least in Ithtorian terms. She touches the hinge of his mandible with familiar tenderness, her milky eyes lit with such joy that it hurts me to look at them. I sit down and take a cup to give my hands something to do, doctoring it with sweetener to avoid violating their privacy.

Vel clicks to her, and the translation software can't process it, but even without interpretation, I sense it's a sound of deep and abiding affection.

"Will we meet again?" he asks.

Adele shakes her head. "At last the time has come to say good-bye, my dear."

"How can you *know* that?" I don't mean to interrupt, but the question stands.

"That is my gift—and my curse. The knowing."

"Are you saying you're Psi?" That would explain a lot.

"I'd never say that because it would mean I broke the law by not turning myself over to Psi-Corp for indoctrination and training. But *if* I were, well, it's such a tiny little talent. I can't foretell the fate of random strangers, only those I love."

I smile. "I won't tell, I promise."

Vel takes a seat opposite me, visibly disturbed by talk of permanent farewell. To see her withered with age like this, it has to be awful for him. She was right to send him away, even if he was lonely, because he would've hated seeing her grow old, up close and personal. From the poetry of the story he shared earlier, he remembers the vibrant young woman she was instead of the dying flower she's become. His claws flex against the arm of the chair, leaving jagged scratches in the polymer.

Adele pretends she doesn't notice. "Come over here, Jax, and give me a kiss."

Since she's the mother I always wanted, I oblige. She hugs me, and her frailty sends a shock of horror through me. Beneath her loose robe, I can feel her bones. She's brittle like a bird, as if precious little ties her to this life.

"Are you eating enough?" I ask, stepping back.

"Food doesn't taste good anymore."

That's when I know for sure she's dying. I've seen it before, and that's the unwavering symptom. It hurts me even to think it, but she'll be gone soon. Vel sits very still, his claws cutting deep into the arms of his chair. But it's not in me to let people go without a fight.

"You have to try. I could fix you something." I half rise to go check out her kitchen-mate, but she waves me down.

"No, I've seen the end. I'm just happy you came to see me off."

We should offer to stand deathwatch, but before I can, Vel rises. "We should conclude our business with Dr. Carvati. Then we can return and do whatever is needed here."

"If you need to go," I tell Vel softly, "I understand. But I'm going to stay here for a little while."

He offers a jerky nod. "I will catch up with you later, then."

Vel springs for the door. When he moves quickly like that, it highlights his alien qualities. But I understand what drives him now. He needs to escape, so I just watch him leave, and when I turn back to her, there are tears in Adele's eyes.

Heart twisting, I pour the tea and make some toast with her good marmalade. "Do you need anything?"

"I'm fine, child." Not true, obviously. She's dying. And she hates that Vel is hurting.

"Did you suspect?"

"That there was something different about him?"

I nod.

"I knew he wasn't like other men. I had no notion just how special he was."

"He told me your story. It's . . . beautiful." I take a sip of the tea, conscious of how brave and selfless she was to send him away. While they would have had more time together, I don't know how he could have survived her loss if he'd stayed. Even now, after so many turns, it seems like it's killing him.

"He's easy to love," she replies. "As I think you know."

Oh, Mary. Does she think I'm trying to replace her? Pain tightens my chest.

"I'm not—I could never—"

"Love him?" For the first time, she frowns at me. "I thought better of you."

"No, I meant I could never take your place."

Adele laughs softly. "Oh, you foolish girl. Did you feel March was trying to take Kai's place?"

"A little. Sometimes." It's hard for me to remember the way I fought loving March because I thought it meant disloyalty or betrayal or I don't know what. I was a mess.

"It doesn't work that way. Each love is unique. Special. Giving to one never takes away from another." Those might be the wisest words I've ever heard.

I don't know her as well as Vel does, but when I focus on losing her, I could cry. Because I know she doesn't want me to be sad, I fight back the tears and finish my snack. This afternoon tea reminds me of the happy times I spent here on Gehenna with her.

"Would you like me to stay with you? Until . . ." There's no reason for her to be alone at the end. Our business on Gehenna will keep.

"It's enough you came at all." She radiates peace now. I feel it flowing from her, as though she has no more unfinished business. If she has pain, it doesn't touch her any longer, either. "I'd rather be alone, if you don't mind."

It's a dismissal, so I stand, but I don't want to leave her. "Is your kitchen-mate fully stocked?"

"I'm provided for, and the chair gets me around. Don't you worry." Her easy smile absolves me of guilt.

Finally, I have no reason to stay. I can't insist she let me stand deathwatch for her. "See you soon, Adele."

On the street, I find him waiting. Pacing. Vel wheels to face me, and the flare of his mandible, the spread of his claws, communicate his tremendous disquiet.

"Vel."

"Human death is terrible," he says in a neutral tone. "Your bodies break down like machines inadequately maintained."

"It's not like that for your people?"

"No. Since we have three hearts, when one wears out, the others compensate. When the last beats its final time, life simply stops. But there is no external deterioration."

"No brittle chitin, then? No crippling of limbs?"

"Our aging process does not work in that fashion."

At least I've distracted him. So as we move down the walk away from her building, I continue with the questions. "How many do you have left?"

"I have two functioning hearts, Sirantha."

Relief flickers through me. Though I don't know what that means in practical terms, it should mean he has plenty of turns left. I know he's already old by human standards, but I'm nowhere near ready to say good-bye.

I hail a hover cab because we're in the wrong part of the city entirely to call on Ordo Carvati. It would take us all

day to walk across the city, and I do want to get back to
Adele as soon as possible. Vel slides in beside me, quiet
now, and I respect his need to process the impending loss in
his own fashion. Death isn't like separation, after all. With
the latter, you have some hope of seeing the person again,
which is why I try not to think about March too often. I tell
myself we'll be together again; I just don't know when.

"I will not be coming in with you," he tells me, as the
hover cab slows. "I need some time."

"It's not a problem. I can handle this."

What seems such a long time ago now, I first met Ordo
Carvati through Doc. What I intend to do strikes me as
unbearably presumptuous. First I'll inform him of his loss,
then I'll try to hire him. Mary, I'm such a dumb-ass. I stew
over the unlikelihood of success as we fly toward Carvati's
private clinic. You can't even reach the place from the
ground; it perches high atop one of the top-security aeries,
so if you can't afford the emergency skywagon or a hover
cab, then you're out of luck.

I alight on the platform, but Vel does not. I lift my hand as
the vehicle carries him away, then turn toward the hospital.
It's an exclusive, expensive haven built of ultrachrome and
diamante with a marquee that reads, WE BUILD A BETTER
YOU and a second one that flashes WHERE THE STARS COME
WHEN THEY FALL. Inside, it is bright and clean. They've
changed the chairs in the foyer since I was here last—no
more bright orange. Instead, it's a tasteful ecru edged in silver. The plants are new, too; these bear lightly scented blossoms with delicate crimson petals. Overhead, the skylight
remains, bedazzling me with titian-tinged glamour.

The Pretty Robotics receptionist asks, "How may I help
you today?"

I've no doubt I ought to have an appointment, but maybe
connections will help. "Could you tell Dr. Carvati that Sirantha Jax is here to see him? I have news about Dr. Solaith."

Her face shapes the facsimile of a smile. "I will pass along
the message. Please have a seat and avail yourself of the entertainment package on the vid. Shall I order refreshments?"

"No, thank you."

No more than a quarter hour passes before Carvati joins me. He's a slim, silver-haired man with a smoothly cultured voice and an artificial tan. Yet one cannot help but like him, though he's the consummate illusionist. From what I gather, he attended school with Doc, and they remained friends.

"How is Saul?" he asks, ushering me back to a private consultation room.

Sickness roils in my stomach, but I cannot dance around these tidings. I wait until the door swishes shut before replying. "He died as a hero during the bombardment of Venice Minor. I'm sorry."

Carvati's smile fades, his color dropping beneath the warm, false hue. "No. Saul wouldn't have fought. That can't be right."

"He was a noncombatant," I agree. "Providing medical support to the troops."

I've no idea what he was doing on the ground, but the truth is complicated and hard to explain. Better to let the matter rest like this. People prefer concrete answers, comprehensible reasons why, and I need to secure his support.

His hands tremble as he orders a drink. Carvati sits down at the conference table, flattening his palms against the cool alloy surface as if that can assuage the loss. "Mortality packs a hell of a punch." The bot brings the tray faster than I would've believed possible, and the room is silent as the doctor drains his glass. When he glances up at me, I see speculation. "You didn't have to carry this news in person. Therefore, I collect you have some additional purpose."

He's smart. I decide not to stretch this out. Carvati is busy, and he has others to attend. Taking a seat across from him, I say, "I want to hire you."

"Not for organ transplant or cosmetic procedures?" Those are his specialties, but this clinic does unbelievably advanced work. The organ transplant business is booming; Carvati can clone a healthy organ to replace a diseased one. And that's significant, given what I want him to do.

"I have a small tissue sample . . . and I'd like to hire you for a clone job."

"Not Saul?" His face reflects true horror.

"No. It's a Mareq hatchling who died in my care. I would like to return the clone to his mother's clutch. I'm not sure if she'll think of him as her child, but I can't return to make amends empty-handed."

"Identical DNA creates the same individual," Carvati says. "The only difference arises from nature versus nurture. So I think she'd be pleased to see him."

I nod. That's the prevailing school of thought on clones. They're the same person, essentially, but if they're raised in different environment, then disparity emerges. Since Baby-Z didn't live long enough for anyone to get to know him, his personality is yet unformed, and his mother should be glad of his return. Cloning doesn't make sense to replace a loved one because it's a lengthy process with humans, so if I'd cloned Kai, I would've been old enough to be his mother by the time he reached maturity. Most people don't go that route with lovers, though I've heard of a few wealthy families doing so to replace kids lost to misadventure. Science hasn't shown much success with accelerated development; the Breed experiments were an expensive disaster with only a handful of viable subjects.

"A Mareq hatchling would be fairly simple," he goes on, thoughtful.

"Will you do it?"

He makes up his mind quickly. "Certainly. It will pose no problem for my labs, though you'll need to take great care with a Mareq so young."

"I'm familiar with their needs. If you could also synthesize a protein mixture, I'd be grateful." I'll be wearing Baby-Z, mark two, all by myself this time. A little pang goes through me at the memory of March with the hatchling on his chest.

He pushes to his feet. "Thank you for telling me about Saul in person. Was there anything else?"

"Actually," I say, "there is. I have some notes here on

Doc's last project. It would mean everything to me to see the work completed."

"What was it?" Carvati is wary, but interested.

"Devising a cure for the La'heng."

He whistles low. "That's a tall order. They need a treatment that counteracts the prior damage to brain chemistry without creating any new side effects."

"I know. And that's tough because of their hyperadaptive physiology. I'd like you to assemble a team, the best people you can find. I'll pay . . . Price is no object." Vel told me he'd help foot the bill for this endeavor, even if the civil suits deplete my fortune entirely. He said it's a worthy goal—and I couldn't agree more.

Carvati offers a half smile. "I intended to pass until you spoke that last sentence. I'll see what I can do."

"Excellent. Now, for the third and final order of business, I'd like to schedule an elective surgery."

He sweeps me from head to toe with an assessing glance, as if he can predict what I want. "Breast work?"

I flush. "No. I want a vocalizer installed that will permit me to articulate in nonhuman languages."

"Like Ithtorian and Mareq," he guesses.

There's a reason he gets the big bucks.

"Precisely."

"Speak to the receptionist. For obvious reasons, I can't take walk-ins for nonvital procedures, not even if you came by way of Saul. Tell her you're a priority one patient, though, so she doesn't make you wait months."

"Understood."

Out in the foyer, I convey the message and receive an appointment for next week. Then the Pretty Robotics model summons a vehicle for me, and I step onto the platform to wait. There is no view like this anywhere in Gehenna, so close to the dome, with the world spread out below like a miniscule model. And somewhere in this blood orange glow, Vel is alone and grieving.

CHAPTER 18

Since I don't know where to find Vel, I return to Adele's and walk up the flights to her flat. Her door recognizes me, after all this time, and I'm touched anew by her kindness. I remember how I used to come down from the garret to use her san-shower, and we'd eat breakfast together. That was a long time ago, before everything changed, even before Farwan's fall.

I come into the sitting room where we left her . . . and find her quiet in her chair. Her eyes are closed. I tell myself that she's sleeping; any second she will open them and greet me and offer me some tea. But even after I reach her side and touch her arm, she remains motionless. Her skin is warm, but not the heat of a living person anymore, more that energy that lingers long into the night on a sun-warmed walkway. Once the stored warmth drains away, there will be no more. I touch my fingertips to her wrist, then her throat, just to be sure. There's no doubt.

Adele is gone.

This is not the first time I've been confronted with death. NBS leaves a very quiet corpse, who happens to be capable of breathing. If that jumper has any true loved ones, then they do a merciful injection and handle the details. Though Adele only needs the latter, not the former, that's the least I can do for her, this woman who was like a mother to me while I lived on Gehenna.

I drop to my knees, but no tears come. This feels more like a pilgrimage than true grief. If anyone can find immortality, it is Adele. Perhaps she has gone, now, to Mary's arms or into the great Iglogth. There are mysteries whose answers we can never know, until our time comes to tread that road behind those we loved. An ache springs up in my throat, but I push it back.

"You would've left instructions," I say aloud, through the clot of sadness.

It's impossible that she, with her whispers of foretelling, didn't see this coming. So I search her apartment and find a new message on the console. I sit down, elbows on my knees, and listen to her last wishes.

"Jax," she says—and of course she knew it would be me, somehow, "you will play a daughter's role at the end. I saw that when I first found you at Hidden Rue. Please notify Domina, as she was good to me. The dancers will want to come, too. I prefer a simple service and molecular dispersion afterward. It's enough to know you will remember me. As for Vel, he's going to take my death hard, and he'll need you in days to come. Farewell, dear Sirantha."

The vid ends then. I don't realize I'm crying until the first warm tear splashes onto the back of my hand. Wiping my eyes, I activate the comm and enter the code for funeral services. A bot answers, the same one they use as receptionists and admin all over the galaxy, plain and efficient. Dr. Carvati has a similar model.

"Gehenna Mortality Center, how many I direct your call?"

I explain who Adele is and what she wanted, then the bot connects me to the correct party. Fortunately, she forwards my information, so I don't have to repeat the explanation. A human answers this time, middle-aged, but well preserved thanks to targeted Rejuvenex treatments. He wears a patient, understanding look that grates on me straightaway, or maybe it's his waxed eyebrows.

"I'm so sorry to hear of your loss. I'll send a technician to assist you right away. If you could provide your direction?"

I do. The actual conversation doesn't take long. He just needs some banking information to be sure I can afford his help. When he realizes who I am and whose fortune I inherited, his manner shifts toward the obsequious. Yeah, my instinctive antipathy was spot on . . . but then, it usually is. Thinking and planning may not be my strong suit, but I have reflex down to a fine art. He doesn't care about the trial or what I've done; he only cares that I have a big bank balance. The mortality manager tries to sell me bells and whistles: a host of mourners to add consequence, a choir of angelic children, and a night black hovercar to convey us to the ceremony. Stubbornly, I refuse it all because Adele asked for simplicity, and I will do as she requested. He's annoyed when he cuts the call.

The technicians come and go, removing the body with utmost discretion, then they leave a bot to scrub away every last trace that someone died here. That seems wrong somehow, so soon, but I don't protest. Better to have it done.

Hours pass as I use her contacts to notify people as she requested. By the time Vel returns, it's nearly evening, though on Gehenna, the sky always looks the same. One can only mark passage of time by artificial means, by the way the seconds tick away. I'm standing at the window, gazing up at a tangerine dream of a sky, when I hear his steps outside. The door recognizes him, too, even after all these turns. That twists me up inside.

Oh, Adele. You never really said good-bye to him, did you? Not in your heart.

"Where is she?" he asks, but as I turn, I see he already knows.

He saw the whisper of death in her tired eyes and her sallow skin, the hands that trembled in her lap. And so he ran from it. He told me that was what he did best; he ran from Ithiss-Tor, and his life with Trapper permitted him to hunt as he ran. He only ever stayed once—with Adele—until she *told* him to go. I make up my mind, here and now, that I never will. That's the one thing I'll never ask him to do.

"At the center, being prepped."

"There will be a ritual?"

I suppose he's attended a few such services, Trapper and Smitty, at least. Before now, I never considered what it meant for him, living among us. He must be so tired of losing people, and yet he goes on. He does not return to his own people because he cannot. He is a changed being, not wholly Ithtorian in spirit, and their ways chafe him now.

"Yes, tomorrow. I handled all the arrangements according to the vid she left. Would you like to watch it?"

"No, I think not. When I see her like this, it is harder for me to remember her as she was, before."

Before she got old.

"That's why she sent you away, you know. Not because she didn't love you. Because she did."

Vel stands so very still, but such pain lives in that stillness. "It should not be so sharp after all this time. I should have reached some acceptance."

This is an area in which I have some experience. "I'd like to say you forget the pain, that it fades, and you only remember the sweet moments, but that would be a lie. Sometimes, with Kai, I go along without thinking of him for days or weeks at a time, then something sets it off—a smell, a man's laugh—and then the knowledge drowns me. That he's gone. I'll never see or touch him again. And it is brand-new, all over again."

"How do you bear it?"

"Because they're worth it. So you ride out the rough days."

"I . . . loved her, for all I said we do not bond as humans do. She taught me."

"Love," I correct gently. "And you always will."

He turns away to gaze out her window, as he must've done with her at his side, so often before. And then he strides into her bedroom, which he might have shared, turns past. At first, I think there's nothing here of him to speak of their time together, then he picks up a framed image. It's not a simple still. This is Adele with a tall, thin, and average-looking man. Brown hair, brown eyes. Not special, except it's Vel. It *is*. They're at the market—she's bright with joy—and some random art photographer has captured these ten seconds, where she gazes up at him, and then he leans down to rub his cheek against hers.

Adele knows, I realize. This was taken after he told her the truth, and so he's offering affection in the Ithtorian way. And her reaction is . . . luminous. Vel watches that perfect moment loop endlessly. His claws tighten on the frame, and a small sound escapes him. Nothing I ever heard from him before, but I don't need the chip to tell me it's born of raw anguish.

"Would you leave me for a time?" he asks quietly.

"How long?"

"The night should be sufficient. I will see you in the morning, Sirantha."

On some level, I understand what he intends—a final, solitary good-bye, where the dust of her skin lingers. Vel can detect it on a level humans cannot. It must feel, to him, as if her death surrounds him even now. He said to me once, *My people can communicate with pheromones, so our olfactory sense is more refined.*

"Will it bother you if I spend the night upstairs?" I want to stay nearby in case he needs me; I don't trust his composure. An outward show of grief would reassure me, but that's not his way.

"Of course not."

I pass the night in the flat where I once spent six glorious weeks, the only path I've ever chosen for myself. Until now. So it's only right that the circle carried me back to her, even if I grieve in the unchanging light, gazing out over the city that never seems to sleep. Here Gehenna offers vice-never-ending.

I stand and remember Adele.

She rented me a room in her building; the word "garret" seems to apply. My flat used to be storage space before someone took the bright idea to replace half the walls with beveled glastique. Consequently, my ceilings slant beneath the line of the roof. She told me it used to be an artist's studio; nobody's ever actually lived up here before. But I don't mind; the open vista and the altitude make me feel like I'm flying, which might make a mudsider uneasy, but I've spent so much of my life on ships, this place feels perfect. It feels like home.

When she brings a bowl of soup up for my lunch, I just have to ask, "Why are you being so nice to me?"

She gives me a Madonna's smile. "Mary teaches us that's how you change the world, one soul at a time, one kindness at a time. That's the only way it'll ever take root."

"Didn't they kill her for that doctrine?" I ask, taking the dish from her.

Adele shakes her head. "No, that was her son. They knew better than to martyr her. It was meant as an object lesson from the authorities, but it didn't shut her mouth. She went on to live a good life."

I've never been religious, never thought much on the oaths I swear, but I pause in spooning up a bite of soup. "That's why she's revered? For living a good life?"

I don't mean to minimize its importance, but I can tell my tone struck a chord because she drops down on the battered old sofa that came with my apartment. "Isn't that more than it sounds like, Sirantha? It's easy to do right when everything goes right. But let everything go wrong, and see how difficult it becomes."

Now with some turns distance from that statement and the benefit of greater heartbreak than I thought I could ever bear, I acknowledge the rightness of those words until Vel comes to tell me it is time to go.

CHAPTER 19

The service is lovely. All the girls from Hidden Rue attend, and Domina closes the club in honor of the occasion.
Afterward, we drink together, raising endless glasses to Adele,
and I wonder if they know that my silent Ithtorian companion
was her lover. None of them gives any sign, and since pain
radiates from Vel's quiet space, I don't invite them in.

But I wish they did realize he has the right to mourn her
as a partner.

Before long, they're all sloppy-drunk, but the nanites
won't let me overindulge. As I've known for sometime, I'm
not human. Not anymore. I'm something else, something
different, and I hate it, but life has pushed me to this point.
Oh, I don't disavow my complicity in the process. I made
the choices every step of the way because the consequences
would have been worse if I hadn't. But I miss the woman I
was, even as I learn to accept the new creature I've become.

"Are we done here?" Vel asks, watching the others tell
anecdotes about Adele. "Have we been respectful?"

"I think we can go."

As if in answer to my thoughts, my comm sounds. "I have

to take this," I say to the group, and I push away from the
table and head outside to the bustling pedestrian walk. I smell
distant airs from the market, sweet and savory, copper kiln
smells and the spicy scent of kosh. A woman sits on a bench
across the way, wearing a smoker's dreamy-eyed smile.

"Jax?" It's Dr. Carvati. "I have your Mareq hatchling ready
for transport, along with the synthesized protein you requested."

"Thanks. I'm on my way."

Popping my head back in, I signal Vel that we're heading
out. He does not take his leave of anyone gathered, and
they're all too numb to notice. Probably best this way. Domina
will wrap up Adele's business affairs; she only asked that I
stand by Vel—and I would've done that anyway.

A hover cab takes us to the clinic. This time, the
reception-bot sends us straight back, but not to Carvati's
office. Instead, we hang a right and head to the in-house labs.
Though I know what's coming, I'm not emotionally prepared
for my first glimpse of Baby-Z mark two. He looks exactly
the same with his webbed toes and translucent skin, so tiny
and fragile. I see the first clinging to March's chest, clinging
to life with such tenacity, even though we had no fragging
idea how to care for him. In the end, I killed him, and with
this hatching, I must try to make amends.

I greet Carvati with a handshake and a nod of thanks.
"Your team did great work, but I suspect I shouldn't let him
imprint on me until I've had the procedure."

The doctor agrees. "It should only take an hour or so. I
can bump you up if you promise not to tell my waiting list."

I smile. "Deal. I'd also like you to upgrade the processing option on my linguistic chip if you can."

"Not a problem."

Carvati doesn't put me under completely. Drugs send
me to a halfway place, where it's warm and hazy, streams
of light that likely come from his equipment. A local anes-
thetic numbs the area, so I don't feel any of the pain, only
pressure as he works. Eventually, the lights flow into darkness, and when I awaken, I hear:

"Are you with me, Ms. Jax?"

"Yeah."

Carvati goes on, "You may notice some residual soreness and you'll need to apply Nu-Skin to the incision twice daily until it heals."

"I understand."

"The vocalizer works on neural command. You tell it to switch languages, then speak. Now try to say something in Ithtorian for me."

I glance around for Vel and find him within arm's reach. His posture still radiates deep mourning, but he remains steadfast as ever. Honest to Mary, I don't know how Adele found the strength to let him go. When my fingers flex, he covers my hand with one claw.

Ithtorian, I think. *This gizmo doesn't have an on-off switch, so . . . Speak Ithtorian,* I tell the vocalizer. And then I say, "Thank you for being here."

But it comes out in clicks, chitters, and whistles. Vel's mandible flares in instinctive response; I can only imagine how strange it is for him, hearing me speak his native tongue. Well, with technical assistance, but still.

Also in Ithtorian, he replies, "It is my pleasure."

"By my reckoning," Carvati says, "the operation was a success. Another hour in recovery, and you should be ready to go."

The residual soreness he mentioned before tingles in my throat, creeping about the numb edges. "Will I be able to jump today?"

"Give it eight hours," the doctor advises me.

So a night's sleep, then, basically. Medi-bots move me into the recovery room, and I doze through my waiting period. Vel wakes me when I can leave with a touch on the shoulder. Nodding, I slide off the bed and get dressed. After what we shared on Ithiss-Tor, there is no reason for modesty between us, and the human body offers him nothing in the way of visual interest or titillation.

From there, we head for the labs again, where they're readying Baby-Z for transport. This version is feisty, too, legs kicking as they lift him out of his incubator. Remembering how it's done, I open my shirt, slick my chest with the synthesized protein gel, and take the hatchling, who unerringly hones in on my heartbeat. He attaches just below the protein slick on my sternum, and his tiny tongue licks out to explore the taste. I sense the precise moment when he decides I'll do and snuggles in, reassured by my warmth, my heartbeat, and the fact that I can feed him.

I'll do better this time, I vow silently. *I will protect you.*

Tears sting in my eyes, but I don't let them spill over. Vel watches me with grave concern, but his silence offers no clue as to his thoughts. With equal reticence, I wish Dr. Carvati well, and add, "Don't forget to ping me when your team finds something for the La'heng."

He nods. "You realize it will take turns."

"I know. But it's worth doing."

"Agreed. And your credits make it possible."

Outside the clinic, on the platform, waiting for the hover cab to take us back to the spaceport, Vel says, "There have been two more requests for settlements, Sirantha."

Not unexpected, after I agreed on the first. "Pay them both."

"I have an offer for Dobrinya, but I believe you can do better."

"Then decline. Accept whatever you think is fair." I don't know enough about this shit to manage my mother's fortune, and really, Vel is just the trustee, until the bereaved families take it, bit by bit.

"Very well."

Every meter this aircar flies takes me closer to the end of my obligations. As yet, I have two quests to complete, and I don't kid myself—they'll each require a lot of time and effort, but my conscience won't let me rest until I keep my promises, both to myself and to Loras. Only then can I live the life I've always dreamed of, devoid of duty or obligation. Just me, my crew, and the silent stars, free to leap anytime I want and follow the beacons anywhere at all. That is my paradise, and a dream I must defer. For now. Where March fits into this future, I can't say. He made his choice when he went after his nephew.

Though I couldn't have admitted it, a kernel of bitterness lodges in my heart. It's always him leaving me, isn't it? First, it was Keri, and Lachion. Now it's for the nephew who needs him. His reasons are sound, and he's a good man who loves me, but I just don't know if he's the one with whom I can spend my life. I won't change my dreams to fit his needs, nor do I think he should do so for me. If we can't find a median that makes us both happy, then—

Well. Until I hear from him, it will keep. He left. And even in his good-bye letter, he offered his comm code, not an invitation. I've been long enough dirtside. I need to travel. Joining his quest on Nicuan would be just as bad as my time on New Terra, training endless waves of jumpers.

I sleep on the ship. As Vel warned, the quarters on the *Big Bad Sue* are miniscule, but Baby-Z and I don't need much room. I lie on my back, feeling his tiny movements under my shirt. This time, I'm not full of horrified amusement as I was when the hatchling imprinted on March.

After the span Carvati prescribed, I head to the cockpit, where Hit is already waiting. She grins at the tiny lizard-baby lump on my chest, and I brace myself.

"You and Vel, huh? I'd have thought it would be more insect than reptile, but love works in mysterious ways. But you gotta tell me, how—"

"Okay, seriously."

I just lost Adele, not that she knows, and I'm feeling oddly sensitive about any mockery directed at Vel, particularly in that way. No, looking at him doesn't get me hot because he's so far beyond my type as to be absurd—and yet . . . I love him. I do. It's a thing beyond explaining, beyond sex, and beyond all customary definitions. Not the way I love March, but I don't love March the same as I love Vel, either. The human heart defies such boundaries sometimes. It just does what it's meant to do, and gives love where it receives it. Sometimes it can be blind in the best of ways.

Hit stops smiling when she sees my expression. Nobody ever said she wasn't sensitive . . . for a killer. "Marakeq, then?"

"Get us above the dome and out of the atmosphere, please. I'll take it from there."

CHAPTER 20

Hit handles the departure with the docking authority and receives our clearance to depart. Smoothly, she powers up the ship, and the *Sue* responds with a little hum. That smoothness is Dina's handiwork. From the exterior, you'd never guess how well this ship runs—in that, she's like the *Folly*, the first ship I flew on with her.

And March.

But I'm not thinking about him.

That way, this ache I feel won't get worse. I won't wonder whether he's safe or if Nicuan is driving him nuts. At this point, I have to trust he knows what he's doing, and he won't make any terrible decisions on world, but the truth of the matter is, he'd do anything for Svetlana's son, no matter the cost to himself. So I put him from my mind; he's beyond my reach for now. Choices were made; paths diverged, and only Mary knows if they'll ever intersect again. I hope so. I'm not ready to say good-bye to him, not with Vel's story about Adele so fresh in my mind.

But he chose his course, as I have. I have no business on Nicuan. Maybe it's cold, but I cherish no attachment to his sister's child. I would never ask him to pick between his family and me, but he must realize I'm not the settling-down type. Ever since I heard about the kid, I've had a bitter, stark feeling, and it's not getting better. During the war, it didn't matter as much. None of us could do as we wished.

It matters now.

Gas streaks the world red behind us, blood-tears to mark the loss of a beloved soul. The rest of Gehenna burns orange inside the dome, reflections cast in glastique that protects the city from the killing air. There was a breach, once, in the early days; I saw pictures in school of the bodies, asphyxiated where they fell. That was before they installed all the locks and seals. Even inside the dome, the idea of absolute safety is more illusion than reality. Death hovers just outside the glimmering barrier, swirling at the edges.

Hit flies with the same grace that marks her combat style, and soon we're through the locks and chambers, rising into the atmosphere. Even now, the knowledge I'm about to jump sends a thrill of pleasure through me. Deep down, I'm still a junkie. The rush still calls to me more than anything else in this life; for me, being trapped dirtside would be the worst punishment imaginable, so I'm glad as hell that Nola got me out of prison.

Wonder how Pandora's doing.

While I'm thinking about it, I bounce a message to New Terra, asking for a status update. I figure since I'm footing the bill, I'm entitled to that much information. Hit glances at me as I record and send, but she doesn't ask.

Instead, she says, "We're out of range of the planet's gravitational pull."

Which means I'm on.

Sheer joy as I plug in. Blackout comes on cue, then Hit joins me in the nav com, contained as always. On a ship this size, the phase drive shakes all the way into your bones, a unique vibration that says *I'm getting ready to take you into the unknown*. The cations in my veins seem to rub against those flowing through the modified phase drive, throwing sparks in my mind. Neural blockers take any associated pain, then Hit pushes us through the corridor spiraling before us.

Then I'm home. Grimspace rushes in my head as if I've flown into a cyclone, spinning me in all directions, and yet it's perfect, inexpressibly right. I open myself to the shimmering colors and the echo of the beacons. So strange to have fragments of me reflected in each pulse. I imagine this is what it's like to have children you haven't seen in turns; they resemble you in ways you've almost forgotten because you aren't that person anymore.

And that's just about the perfect analogy, for these beacons I've attuned to my DNA signature are the closest I'll ever come to offspring of my own. This is my genetic legacy, my message to future jumpers. *Hello,* they say with each pulse. *Sirantha Jax was here.* And maybe that's all that needs to be said.

Without further luxuriation, though I take great pleasure in being here, I cast out for the Marakeq beacon. They all feel different to me now in minute gradations, and so it takes a little longer to find it. *There.*

Hit follows my directions, and the phase drive pulls through me. It's a peculiar symbiosis, using the beacons themselves to jump, but I think this is what the ancients intended all along. I suspect we've only unlocked a portion of their capabilities. In a thousand turns, jumpers may be traveling in ways that I can't conceive right now.

The ship responds with an eager leap, pushing through to straight space, and I unplug. Next, I check on Baby-Z2. There's no gear small enough to protect him, and I examine him to see if he's taken any harm from the jump. His vitals are good, and he doesn't appear changed in any fashion I can see, still alert, still interested in lights and sounds, with his neck craning around so he can peer out of my shirt.

"The Mareq okay?" she asks.

"Seems to be."

I assess our location on the star charts. "Not bad. Four thousand klicks off."

Direct jumps aren't foolproof, I haven't done enough of them to guarantee my accuracy, and I'm a little out of practice, what with my trial and incarceration. So I'll take this.

"Won't be a long haul," Hit says. "I was meaning to ask . . . do you want us to come with you?"

"The better question is, do you want to?"

The small bundle beneath my shirt twitches. It's time to bathe him, clean my chest, and freshen the protein gel. But I can wrap up this conversation first. Baby-Z2 clings to life as fiercely as his sibling did, determined to take his place among his people. And I'm doing my damnedest to get it done.

Her strong face turns thoughtful. "While it'd be fascinating to be part of a first-contact encounter, I'm afraid too large a party might spook the natives."

I consider that. "There's that chance. We might also need you and Dina as backup if the mission goes bad."

"My thoughts exactly."

The *Big Bad Sue* is too small to have a shuttle, so we'll all go down on planet.

That's not optional. But we don't all have to hike out to the settlement. I'm running scans as we speak, pinpointing the place where we put down here. I have the eerie feeling of retracing my steps, but I'm so fragging different now that it's like seeing the same things through new eyes. And I've lost *so many* people that I care about. The old Jax thought she knew pain, but the universe had an ocean of lessons to teach her about grief. I guess it's made me stronger, or at least more dogged, because I don't think about how I'm going to die so much anymore. I mostly think about how to keep my promises, one step at a time, one minute at a time.

"Then why don't you remain on the ship. Can you take us down without crashing?" I ask, remembering the last time.

March is a good pilot, and between the atmosphere, the

utter lack of ground support, the jungle, and the deceptive readings, we were lucky to get the *Folly* down in one piece. As I recall, that was when everything changed between us. I see his face now, so dark and ugly-beautiful with his broken nose and too-strong jaw, smeared with mud, rain spiking his lashes. There's that damn ache again.

Oh, Mary, keep him safe. Watch over him until I see him again.

Hit glares. "I can't even believe you just asked me that. Damn. Do you think this is my first low-tech landing?"

Despite my fear about things to come, I grin. "Sorry. Put us down right here."

I slide the coordinates her way, and she studies the terrain, weather conditions, and the trajectory before giving a sharp nod. "This is gonna be fun."

CHAPTER 21

Hit takes her own scans after I do, compiling data. It would be just our luck to arrive during hibernation season again. I'd come in trying to bring a hatchling home, and wind up waking another one. But no. That can't happen, not without March. I won't touch any birthing mounds as he did, nor will I sing the Coming-Forth song. Things will be different this time. I'll make it better.

So I ask, "Do you see any life signs down there?"

"Thousands."

Thank Mary. Unlike last time, the ship sails through the atmosphere smoothly. I stare out at the tangles of green jungle flashing past the hull. It's raining, but on Marakeq that's nothing new. If the Mareq are active, then it's a warm shower.

Either Hit's a better pilot than March—and to be fair, he was out of practice when we put down here the first time—or this ship's more maneuverable. It might be a combination of the two. Either way, within moments, we set down gently in a muddy clearing less than a klick from the river. No damage that I can see.

"Really well-done."

She flashes me a cocky grin. "Like you expected any-thing else."

"True enough."

I check the small bundle beneath my shirt, and Baby-Z2 seems content enough, plenty warm and lapping at the pro-tein on my chest. If things go well, I won't be wearing him for long. I'll give him back to his mother to assuage my sore conscience. Leaving the cockpit, I head for the hub to look for Vel.

Not surprisingly, he's already waiting with his ubiqui-tous bounty-hunter pack, weatherproof gear in hand. We can't afford to let the hatchling get cold or to have the rain wash his food supply off my skin. It's a couple of kilome-ters to the settlement from here. While Hit might have been able to take us in closer, I was afraid of frightening them. I want to ensure a peaceable exchange.

In transit, I downloaded all the sounds Fugitive scien-tists have recorded, and my chip has been working on pro-cessing them. Nonhuman languages are more difficult to decipher because sometimes the sounds don't have equiva-lent word meanings; they're more nuances, intimations, and hints. But the Mareq tongue appears to be fairly com-plex, and my chip now has some idea how to decode them, which means my vocalizer can attempt a reply.

After checking Baby-Z2 one final time, I shrug into the slicker and take my pack from Vel. "Ready?"

"I am."

"We're gone," I call, without touching the comm since it's a small ship. "I'll signal when and if it's safe for you to join us."

"Because I can't wait to take my own walk in the mud," Dina grumbles.

But she smacks me on the back as a measure of her affection when I go past her toward the exit ramp. I lead the way with Vel at my back, the way it should always be. He's been quiet since we left Gehenna, but I'm hoping this mis-sion will distract him from his loss. Deep down I know one person can't replace another, but at least he's not alone.

"Do you need scrubbers?" I'm already fitting mine in place.

The last time, Doc reminded me to wear them, but he's gone, and I have Vel at my side instead of March. Everything changed once on this planet. I think this is where I started to love him, no matter how much I didn't want to. I can't shake the feeling that everything is about to change again.

"Yes. The atmosphere has spores and pollens that make raw inhalation a risky proposition."

It also contains trace elements of chlorine, hence the scrubbers. Vel fits himself with compact breathing apparatus, slightly different from my nasal plugs, but they function in the same fashion. Once we're ready, we step off the ship and into the muck. The planet is every bit as dismal as I remember, algae growing in the mud sucking around our feet. All around us, the jungle breathes, leaves rustling, rain spattering on the sodden trunks. But even the plants have a secondary layer of green growing over the top of them, moss or mold in swirling patterns.

Before we move away from the ship, he scans the area with his handheld. "No large predators."

"The Mareq hunt to keep the territory surrounding their settlements safe."

That's all I remember from Canton Farr, other than the fact that he was a terrifying lunatic. As far as I know, none of the Fugitive scientists who studied the Mareq ever made contact, which means this is a historic moment, and it should be recorded for posterity.

"Turn on your ocular cam?"

"Already done," Vel answers.

"Then let's move out."

The air is hot and sticky, even beyond the rain. There's a heaviness to it that weighs on a warm-blooded creature, though I imagine it's quite comfortable for the Mareq, who depend on the weather to regulate their body temperature. It must be simple and peaceful to live according to the changing seasons.

Vel follows a path down to the river, no more than an area where the vegetation has thinned from frequent passage. Rain sluices down his back; he isn't wearing protective gear. No need when you're already armored. Beneath my shirt and slicker, Baby-Z2 wriggles around, a testament to his fortitude.

Almost there, little guy.

The hike is miserable. Neither of us complains, however. At the swollen stream, Vel reaches for my hand, and we cross together, fighting the current. It rushes at my legs, trying to topple me, but with his help, I push onto the other shore. He stands for a moment in the rain, face upturned.

"Did you know, Sirantha, that my people cannot weep?"

I didn't, actually.

He continues, "We have no tear ducts. Instead, on Ithiss-Tor, there is a mourning song, uttered by every surviving member of the clutch."

"Do you only sing for clutchmates?"

"Or progenitors."

"Never for friends or partners?"

He shakes his head, water dripping from his mandible. "It is not done. But here, it is as if the whole world weeps."

"Teach me," I say impulsively. "Teach me, and I'll sing with you. For Adele."

"Now?"

"Yes. Please."

And so I learn the mourning song. It is full of clicks and hisses and long-held low notes, sounds I could never make without my vocalizer. Though I know it's imprecise at best, the chip in my head translates it thus:

Oh, though you are gone beyond all knowing
We will join you one day
Many become one
In the wholeness of the Iglogth
Away, away, far you are becoming
We are less with your loss
Away, away, our song sends you safely

But we keep you always in our minds.
Away, away,
Away.

The last note stretches for an unbearably long time. I'm
sure I would find it painful, were my throat doing the work.
All around us, the jungle falls quiet. And then the most
extraordinary thing occurs. The insects in the wetlands
echo the sounds back to us, imperfect, but mimicked, as if
they recognize the gravitas of this moment. For a glorious,
astonishing moment, it's as if a whole clutch mourns Adele
properly.

Vel reels with it, stumbling back to brace against a rain-
slick tree. His posture communicates such raw pain that I'm
helpless as to how to help. And then I realize he's shaking,
not from cold, but the Ithtorian equivalent of silent tears. I
pull him to me because that's the human way, and he's lost
a human love. Surely it will offer him some comfort.

He rubs the side of his face against the top of my head. It's
not a kiss like he gave Adele, cheek to cheek, but it's more
than he's ever done before. So I guess I'm doing something
right. His claws dig into my back, hurting me a little, but it's
a pain I'll bear gladly. Endless moments later, he steps away,
composed once more, and now the rain is only rain.

"Better?" I ask.

Vel responds with a quiet inclination of his head. He is
not prone to such emotional displays, but that doesn't mean
he feels nothing. "Shall we continue?"

The rest of the journey passes in silence. As before, I
glimpse the settlement through a tangle of trees. This time,
however, the mounds are not dark and silent. Small lights
are set all around; they look to be some natural-glowing
lichen, and there is movement, the Mareq going about their
daily lives. My stomach coils into a knot, and I touch Baby-Z2
reflexively. The hatchling makes a quiet sound beneath my
hand, a little trill. He's still there, still whole and healthy,
my offering to those from whom I stole. Mary grant it's
enough.

CHAPTER 22

No point in further delay. It won't get easier.

I step out of the jungle and into the village. Immediately, five nearby Mareq surround me. But they don't appear hostile; instead, they seem fascinated. I've only seen images of them, captured by Fugitive scientists, and here I am, up close and personal. *This is it—first contact.* I haven't done this in such a long time . . . and it was never my specialty. I have rudimentary training just in case, but my personality doesn't lend itself to diplomacy and careful interaction.

I expected I might have to do some fast talking, but their chief response appears to be wonder, not fear, anger, or violence—a more human response. The Mareq are innocent souls, then. They haven't been taught that the unfamiliar cannot be trusted. At least, I hope it's experience that causes the difference in our reactions—and that humans aren't naturally more aggressive.

They speak to me all at once, the sounds jumbling together until I can't do anything with it. Just noise. Since I've failed to comprehend their language, at least in this first moment, I don't have much time to make the right impression. Slowly, carefully, I shed my slicker, despite the rain, and a gasp goes up from the Mareq. Widening of the eyes is a universal expression of surprise, it seems, and these bulging frog eyes reveal astonishment that I've peeled off my skin. They all draw back at the pasty flesh beneath, but I'm not done yet.

Carefully, still shielding Baby-Z2, I open my shirt and show them the hatchling. More croaking. The chip still can't differentiate anything about it, so I can only guess what they're saying. *Look, it's a baby Mareq. But how did it get one? Let's call the Elder.*

Whatever they said, one of them does run to get another Mareq, leaving the others to watch Vel and me. A tall male is bold enough to rap on Vel's chitin as if testing to see whether it comes off, too. They seem more fascinated than frightened at this point, which is a good sign. I want a peaceful meeting. So long as we make no sudden moves, it should be fine.

A female Mareq, heavy with eggs, waddles in our direction, and her throat flushes bright red when she sees the infant clinging to my chest. A low, sweet noise trills from her throat, and to my amazement, Baby-Z2 replies. She takes him from me, and he attaches to her with visible shivers of pleasure.

There's no question in my mind. This is his mother. He *knows* her. Even if he's not the son I took away, he's close enough for her to be glad to see him. That brightness on her neck indicates joy. Despite the warm rain on my head, a tremor rolls through me. I don't deserve to be part of such a tremendous moment. Turns from now, anthropologists will study Vel's record of this meeting.

With gestures and sounds, she quiets the Mareq around us; and then the chip has only her voice to process. Which is when the chip provides the first possible Mareq translation, ever.

"You come from the sky," she says. "Above the rains. From the god-place, and you bring my son home."

Frag. How do I answer that with my imperfect chip? But I have to try, so I keep my sentences short and simple.

"I come from the stars. Not a god-place. I took your son by mistake, so I brought him home to you. I'm sorry."

More croaking. My chip kicks in, so long as there's only one Mareq voice. "Things happen. We don't always know the reasons. We don't need to." I have the feeling what she said might be wiser and more profound, but that's close enough.

I translate for Vel, who has no doubt gotten the gist from her delight in being reunited with Baby-Z2. From what I can tell thus far, the Mareq seem to be a peaceful and philosophical race. If they were otherwise, they'd have attacked us right off, before I could show them what I carried. And wouldn't that have been a nightmare?

"I'm Jax," I tell her, and the vocalizer makes a noise of my name.

She offers hers back, a different one, which the chip tells me is Dace. I suspect it just combined some random letters, but it doesn't matter as long as my vocalizer can reproduce the sound. I test it, and it can.

"You must stay for the celebration," she continues.

The other Mareq chime in, croaking in what I take to be agreement. But that bogs my processor down, leaving me to guess what they're saying. She seems to notice this, and quiets them with *anh anh anh* noises. The chip suggests she's saying, *Shut it, shut it.*

"What celebration?" I ask.

"Of the miraculous homecoming. We have a story of the son who disappears, then returns to us unchanged. It is said he carries a great destiny."

Maybe so. I'm just glad I've turned Baby-Z2 over to his mother. She can look after him from this point on. I didn't hurt him this time. I didn't *fail* him. An astonishing lightness spreads through me, as if I've discharged a weight on my soul.

I glance at Vel, then bring him up to speed—and Mary, that's weird, it's a flip of what we did on Ithiss-Tor. He chose not to have his processor upgraded because we don't plan to stay long. Only one of us needs to be able to communicate here.

Then he nods. *Of course we should stay,* his expression tells me. He's right; it would be insulting to drop the kid off and run, and I have plenty of time until Carvati's team comes up with a workable solution to the La'heng situation. Until I keep that last promise, my life is not my own.

"We would be honored," I reply.

It's still a little unnerving to hear my vocalizer making those noises. The other Mareq scatter to spread the word of the miraculous return. I hear them telling the story in snippets as they disperse through the settlement.

"You have cared well for Zeeka. This mother thanks you."

Zeeka? Is it possible he was trying to tell us his name? We never knew why we settled on calling him Baby-Z; it was just right, or the closest we could come. Intrigued, I pose the question to Dace, and she seems delighted.

"Yes, all Mareq are born into the world bearing a true name, and they know it in their souls from the time of their coming-forth. He is a strong son indeed to try and tell his name to strangers."

I think she means strangers in the sense that we are superweird, not unknown, though we're certainly that, too. Vel regards me with curiosity, a welcome distraction from his heavy grief, and I summarize for him with some pleasure.

"Remarkable," he says, when I finish.

"Let us take you to a guest shelter." She leads the way, croaking about preparations.

My chip cuts in and out as we pass other Mareq. I hope over time it learns to compensate, or she will think I'm stupid, unable to process information from more than one source. Otherwise, so far, we're off to a good start.

Inside the hut, it's familiar, similar to the birthing mound where March and I knelt. Compared to the rains outside, it's relatively snug and dry in here. I appreciate that, as there's some risk I'll develop a fungal infection from constantly damp skin—a small price to pay for this buoyancy of spirit, however.

"It will be intriguing to see how the Mareq celebrate," Vel says.

I'm glad to see him taking an interest, though not surprised. For him, intellectual pursuits always offer the most distraction. It will be worth a sojourn on Marakeq if it means surcease from the blow he took on Gehenna.

"Can you understand them at all?" He downloaded the vocabulary, too, but unless it's loaded directly onto the chip, there's some lag time in the learning curve. Which means I might not understand them at all, or at least not as well as I imagine I do. Dace might have invited us to wait in this hut, so we could be cooked and eaten at the feast, but I don't think so.

"Bits of it. If we remain here long enough, I will assimilate the language."

"You've had a lot of experience in that."

"Yes."

Not all of it good. But I don't say that aloud.

Examining the interior, I discover mounded dirt that we can use for sleeping. Soft, green moss grows atop the makeshift mattress, more inviting than you might think. Everything about the Mareq is natural and flows from their world. They exude a certain harmony, and that's why I think they won't hurt us, even if I've misunderstood about the festival.

There's nothing to unpack, so we wait. The village hums with activity and what I take for music. A low but also jubilant sound rumbles forth, harmonies intertwining from a lighter instrument. I'm pretty sure that's what I'm hearing—primitive pipes and flutes, accompanying the Mareq chorus. That's lovely and unnerving because it's so other. It sinks in then that I'm on a class-P world without Corp or Conglomerate sanction. There's no backup here, other than Hit and Dina, no matter what happens.

"Try not to worry," Vel says. "I did not sense harm in them."

He reads me so damn well . . . and without the benefit of Psi powers. Bittersweet memories of March fight to rise to the forefront, but I push them back. This is not the time; countless mysteries await us in the village. I'll turn my thoughts to that instead.

A short time later, Dace comes to fetch us.

CHAPTER 23

*Overhead, the gauzy sun-star that warms Marakeq twin-*kles in the dreamy twilight. Full dark never falls here, just this magical grayness. Fog has set in as well, a cold front pushing against the warm rain. Marveling at the biotech-ture, I follow Dace deeper into the village. There are mounds everywhere, and the glowing lights twinkle brighter against the mist.

We stop in the center; everything is laid out in circular fashion here, rings on rings, forming a larger pattern. Vel glances about with great interest, no doubt his ocular cam recording everything for later scrutiny. Around us, the Mareq celebrate with rhythmic dancing, perfectly in cadence. Each social set appears to have a certain role to play, steps to per-form, and they're all singing. Hatchlings frolic at our feet, splashing in the green-cast water that pools on the ground. One day, Zeeka, the one I stole, will take his place among them. I feel easier knowing that; some of the damage I did has been repaired.

"Come," Dace calls. "Dance!"

It's somewhat ridiculous, but Vel sets down his pack,

and I try to mimic their movements. Their legs bow outward differently than mine or even Vel's for that matter, so
we can't manage a perfect match. Yet there's pleasure in
the shining curtain of rain. The mottled Mareq hides gleam
wet, paler patches making them difficult to spot in the jungle, no doubt. I never thought I'd see the somber bounty
hunter dancing, but in all honesty, he's better than I am.
His limbs are closer to the Mareq's than mine. I can only
lumber along in the line, my feet arched outward. Their
long, webbed toes bend as mine don't, adding layers of
meaning to the dance.

In some ways, I feel like a cripple here, but there's no
judgment, either. The song swells from so many throats
that it begins to sound like one note, endless and beautiful.
As I dance, I realize I have tears in my eyes, and I don't
even know why. I'm sliding in the mud, bumping the Mareq
ahead of me, and he croaks at me, a friendly sound that the
chip attempts to translate:

"You're clumsy. But it can't be helped. You are who
you are."

It feels like the answer to a question I feared asking, like
I've been searching every galaxy for this message. *You are
who you are.* The Mareq accept, and it is the loveliest, most
desirable thing. They should be trying to stab us, rend us
with their primitive weapons, but instead they see our
arrival as a gift. They see me not as the one who stole from
them but who gave back. I want to protect that innocence
from the universe, and I don't think I can. Not once others
learn we've made first contact.

That knowledge grieves me.

The party goes on for ages. They offer us food and
drink, but after Vel scans it, he shakes his head. "We
should decline politely. Toxicity levels indicate it might
make us sick."

Switch to Mareq, I tell the vocalizer.

"We're not hungry, but thank you."

Later, we retire to the hut allotted for our use, exhausted
but content with what we've seen. In the morning, we can

be on our way though I don't know where we're going. Maybe we can explore some uncharted beacons between paying out wrongful-death claims.

My comm beeps. "Everything okay, Jax?"

Though she'd never admit it now that the war's over, Dina cares. We bonded on the *Dauntless* through mutual grief and loneliness. But since that crisis has passed, we're back to sarcasm and ribbing each other endlessly. I'm more used to that dynamic anyway.

"No problems. The Mareq were glad to see Z2. Turns out his name is Zeeka."

"Huh." By her tone, she's surprised at how close we came.

"We're going to sleep at the settlement, then return to the ship."

"Where to from there?" Hit asks.

"I'm not sure. We'll talk about it when we get back."

Dina disconnects then. Vel pulls two packets out of his pack, and I have to smile. This reminds me of the time we were stranded together in an ice cave on the Teresengi Basin. Like the other time, he gets out a chemical cooker and starts making soup out of freeze-dried ingredients edible and palatable to both of us. Fortunately, there is some overlap between Ithtorian and human physiology, though not enough to permit us to eat all the same things. Oranges, for instance, would kill him.

"Hungry?" he asks.

"Yeah." I can't remember the last time I ate, in fact.

A long silence falls as he mixes and stirs. Then he says, "The Mareq have a gift for happiness."

It's a blessing I did not expect. Since it's been that way for as long as I can remember, I expected more punishment and castigation. Instead, there's only this seamless joy. I could almost stay here, despite the mud and muck and the stink of half-rotten vegetation. Except I can't. Not *me*. I always have someplace else I'd rather be, even if I don't know where that is, yet.

"They do," I agree, catching his eye. "We're going to be

all right." I say the words aloud to Vel, testing them, because in the aftermath of the war, Doc's death, my trial, the separation from March, and the loss of Adele, that's the first time I've allowed myself to imagine that anything could ever be *all right* again.

But the world moves on, even when you don't want it to, even when change feels like the end of everything. It never stops. That's harsh and magical and somewhat comforting because nothing is immutable, however much we want it to be. Moments cannot be caught like fossils in amber, ever-perfect, ever-beautiful. They go dark and raw, full of shadows, leaving you with the memories.

And the world moves on.

"Yes," he says quietly in Ithtorian. "As long as we have each other, Sirantha, I believe we will be."

I would follow him anywhere, I realize. Once, I would've only said that about March, but Vel has earned my trust in countless ways. Now we sit together in silence and sip his rough-and-ready soup. It doesn't taste like much, but it contains the energy and nutrients we need to survive.

"Where do *you* want to go?" I ask. "You're still paying dues to the guild, right? I could help you take targets."

"I am done with that life." A flat answer, no explanations.

But I suspect Vel sees his life in chapters. When Adele sent him away, he went back to hunting to distract himself from the sorrow, and her passing marks the end of that version of him. Now he must become somebody new in order to bear the loss. I understand that completely—and whatever I can do to help him, I will.

Once the soup's gone, I lie down on the moss and fall asleep at once. In the morning, which is just a bit brighter than the dark here on Marakeq, Dace is waiting for us. I expect a farewell feast, but instead she has something important to show us. Or . . . that's what the chip's telling me, anyway.

"Hurry," she says. "The others remain in their dreams. If they knew, they would stop me."

"Stop you from doing what?"

Vel grabs his pack, and we follow her. Zeeka pokes his head out, watching over her shoulder. He's already bigger and stronger than our Baby-Z ever became. The synth protein might let him survive, but it wasn't permitting him to thrive as he's doing here, snuggled against his mother's shoulder.

"The secret place," she replies. "The shadow place. All echoes, no silence."

Which tells me precisely nothing. I don't know if we ought to be doing something that the other villagers would disapprove of, but I recognize Vel's look. He's intrigued by forbidden knowledge, so I fall in without protest.

Dace creeps through the village and past, in the opposite direction from the ship. March and I never came this far on our first trip, so I don't know what's out here. It's raining, of course, but I swear there are, like, four days on Marakeq when it isn't. This morning it's only a light drizzle that damps my hair and makes it frizzy.

We walk for several kilometers with Dace gazing over her shoulder periodically, tilting her head as if she can smell something in this swamp besides mold. And maybe she can. Tall brown reeds grow along the river, with small tufts of green spiking from the stalks. She tears one and chews on it like it's a savory treat. The thing oozes a foul, orange sap, and she shares it with Zeeka. Politely, she offers it to us as well. I decline.

And by midday, we reach the ruins.

It looks like the remnants of an ancient civilization, one whose signs I've seen before. The ancients left all kinds of rubble strewn across the galaxy; we found much of it as our slow ships made their way from Old Terra. Here, obsidian obelisks have toppled, chunks of gleaming black rock scattered about the base of a staircase that descends down, down, down. I can't imagine what she wants to show us. *Down there.* My pulse accelerates; I don't like going underground at the best of times, but I can stand it long enough to see this marvel. I'll just grit my teeth, clench my fists, and pretend the weight of the stone doesn't bother me.

"Follow," she orders.

And there's no question she means business. The carefree female we danced with the night before has been replaced with a somber taskmistress. I do as I'm told, though the first steps are slippery with slime. I have the unmistakable sense I'm entering forbidden territory, and that the other Mareq would be really pissed off to find us here.

So be it. I go down into the dark.

CHAPTER 24

Unlike the rest of Marakeq, the ruins are dry. Halfway down the staircase, I can't see much. Vel cracks a torch-tube, and the pale green glow illuminates the path. Dace doesn't seem to have any trouble, however; she can apparently see in the dark. There is no hesitation in her steps as she hurries deeper into the darkness.

From somewhere within comes the steady plink-plink of water dripping from stone. So it's not an airtight seal in here. Whatever's down here may be watermarked and damaged, but it doesn't slow Vel's progress. He stays right with our Mareq guide, and by the shine of his eyes, his ocular cam is recording.

I bring up the rear. At this point, I wish I had a weapon, but they're secured in Vel's pack, as we didn't want the Mareq to think we were a threat, a reasonable assumption if we showed up with shockstick and pistol in hand. But I trust Vel, and if he thinks it's necessary, he'll toss me the means to defend myself.

The tunnel widens as it slopes down, not a sharp angle, but a gradual one. I'm conscious of the stone pressing down on me, but I swallow my instinctive panic. Vel shines the light around, accenting scratches on the walls. Some of them look like they came from animals or natural damage, but others were unmistakably carved by someone's hands. I touch one of the grooves and find it's worn smooth inside.

"This is the way to the dark city," Dace tells us.

City? None of our scans showed anything about an underground city. But then, the readings on Marakeq have never been 100 percent accurate. Fear wars with anticipation at what we're going to find. There could be aliens, another species of Mareq, or who knows what, really. I can't pretend I understand what drives this female, other than that she appears convinced it's vital we bear witness.

Shapes move in the darkness, unnerving me until I realize the shadows belong to us, cast by Vel's light source. Apart from our footsteps and our breath, it's deeply silent. It seems like we walk forever, but that might be my poorly leashed fear. Eventually, the tunnel opens into an enormous room with a domed ceiling.

As I step down into the sunken room, lights flicker on one by one until a complete semicircle illuminates an artifact before me. I've never seen anything like these lights; they appear to be crystals, but there's no external power source, which means they're running on a battery so tiny and long-lasting that there's juice in them still, however long after the ancients placed them here. How astonishing.

Vel kneels to examine one, but by the flare of his mandible, he can't figure out how this technology works, either. I've never run into an unspoiled site before. Other species have usually pillaged anything the ancients left behind, long before humans came on the scene, but the Mareq don't seem to have touched this place at all. It's as pristine as a site so old can be.

"It is a sacred place," Dace tells me, as if in answer to my unspoken thoughts. "Other star-walkers came before. We worship them."

Or at least that's what the chip thinks she's saying. I'd say it's a good guess, based on her rapt expression. I remember she thought we came from the god-place, so maybe that means Dace thinks we're gods, too, akin to the ancients somehow because we travel like they did. With that correlation in mind, I suppose it makes sense she'd want to show us what they left behind if she believes there's a connection.

Above the glowing half circle hangs an impossible inverted arch. I've no idea how they got it to balance like that, but it doesn't seem as though the base has enough stability to support the structure. Yet it remains, a testament to the ones who came before and scattered their secrets to the far corner of the galaxy.

"Why did you want us to see this?" Vel asks in Mareq.

"The god-door will open for you, wayfarers from beyond the rains."

That makes no sense at all. "This doesn't look like any door I ever saw."

She ignores my lack of faith. "You are destined. It is all written."

Now, that's interesting. The Fugitive scientists would pay a fortune for this information. Until now, nobody even knew the Mareq had a written language. I ponder if it's cuneiform, or if they spell words with individual symbols instead. An image of these scrolls, whatever they are, would be worth a fortune.

"Where?" I glance around, looking for a massive stone table.

"In the prophecies of Oonan."

This isn't helping me understand why we're here. I step onto the black tiles that form the flooring between the crystals for a better look at—whatever this is—and it hums to life. Energy crackles between the upraised arms of the arch, a stunning blue-violet, and the crystals wink off and on in hypnotic fashion, like if I watch them long enough, they'll convey some message. It's definitely a pattern, oddly akin to the lights of a nonhumanoid AI processing information. Could this thing be . . . *reading* me?

"Has this ever happened before?" I ask Dace over my shoulder.

Only to find she's already in retreat, as fast her webbed feet will carry her. I can't hear a reply over the rising hum; it's oddly akin to the phase drive, but there are discordant notes as well. Vel steps in and wraps his claw around my arm to tow me to safety, but my feet are stuck fast. The pad upon which we stand is magnetized or something, preventing my escape, and now he's stuck, too. The glow deepens into a true explosion, crackling outward to swallow us whole.

Pain licks along my nerve endings, and I try to scream. No sound. No throat. I've dissolved into inchoate particles that are somehow still Jax. Eons later, I reassemble, but we're not underground anymore. It's bright here, so bright I can't open my eyes all the way right off, and I'm flat on my face. I lie here for endless moments, my pulse pounding inside my skull, and study the stonework because I can't control my central nervous system.

Visceral terror licks through me. Anything could happen now. Anything. I could be eaten. Shot. Set on fire. And I don't fragging know where I am; I'm just positive it *isn't* where I was before. It takes me countless moments before I regain the power of speech.

"Vel?" I rasp.

"Here, Sirantha."

With some effort, I manage to turn my head. He's two meters away, near the edge of the platform. The trip hit him hard; he hunches over, expelling a trickle of yellow fluid. That can't be good; I know I've never seen him do that before. To comfort him with the familiarity of his native tongue, I command my vocalizer, *Switching to Ithtorian.*

"Are you hurt?"

"Just sick," he clicks in reply.

Odd, I can detect his misery when we speak his native tongue. The vocalizer only offers a limited number of normal human inflections, so I wouldn't be able to hear his distress or confusion like I can right now. It's a low thrum that coats each intonation, and I feel it inside my head, more than hear it with my too-human ears.

Pushing up, I find my limbs are shaky. This pad is similar to the one Dace showed us, but the arch has crumbled, and these crystals are broken, unlit. Powdery fragments litter the ground, as if the power has been expelled in a tremendous burst.

"Anything I can do?" Crawling over to him, I check for obvious physical damage and find none.

"It will pass. I think."

At his gesture, I rest beside him and wait for the shakes to abate. I'm a little queasy myself, as if my bits and pieces might not be connected in the same order in which they flew apart. I take stock in our surroundings; it's a mirror of Mareq, only brighter and more colorful. The plants are more vibrant, blooms in rainbow hues sprouting from the canopy.

Eventually, I ask, "Better?" because he's rummaging in his pack. Thank Mary it made the journey with us, or we'd really be fragged.

"Much."

"Any idea where we are?"

"I suspect we activated a gate of some sort."

Yeah, I've been thinking along those lines myself. "Wonder if Dace made up that omen stuff, if she meant to dump us here in revenge?"

"I do not believe so. She seemed sincere."

Which means she thinks there's something on this side of the gate we need to see. I recall she believed we're akin to the ancients and the gods they worship. Maybe the ancients passed through these gates. Maybe we'll *find* them. Despite the lingering sickness, that sends a thrill through me. A discovery like that is almost as awe-inspiring as charting a new beacon. In fact, you could argue there are certain similarities though we're exploring a new world, not grimspace.

But close enough to delight my adrenaline-junkie soul.

"So what now?"

"The logical course would be to attempt to find some means of returning whence we came."

"Too bad this gate's broken." I think maybe our passage overloaded it.

"Indeed."

I push to my feet and offer Vel a hand up. He regards me for a long moment, then accepts my aid. That makes me feel good, despite the generally catastrophic nature of our situation. I can't think when I've ever helped him, except, maybe, for those moments in the swamp where we sang for Adele together. It's always been him saving me . . . and I'm not used to that.

He activates his handheld . . . or tries to. He clicks in disgust as he spins with the device, trying to coax a spark of life. Even I can tell it's not working properly. There's no response at all, just a dead, flat screen.

"That doesn't bode well."

"Check your comm," he says.

I tap it, and nothing happens. No juice. No signal. Wherever we've gone, it's far the hell enough away that our technology can't keep up. Frag me, that's terrifying. This is the farthest I've ever jumped, no question about it, and I didn't even do it on purpose. I guess that sums up my life, when you come right down to it.

"You have to question what she thought this would accomplish," I say, shaking my head.

"We are destined," he repeats with a mocking twitch of his mandible. "It is written."

But Mary, I'm relieved to see him finding humor in anything. He got so cold and distant after Gehenna, pulled back to a place where I couldn't reach him. And that hurt because he's mine. The connection between us makes no sense on the surface; you'd think I would drive him crazy.

"Funny. In the absence of functional technology, I'm thinking we can only guess which way to go. Unless you have some idea?" I eye him hopefully.

Unfortunately, he shakes his head. "This is all new to me though I think it may become quite an adventure. Provided we survive it."

"There is that." I turn in a slow circle, studying the slant of the light, the way the trees are growing, and the tilt of the plants. "If my old science lessons can be believed, then the sun sets that way."

"Your recommendation?"

I shrug. "Hell, I don't know. If anyone was monitoring this gate, they'd have come to see about us by now, wouldn't they?"

"I would think so."

"But there has to be a working gate somewhere, doesn't there? This can't be the only one."

Vel appears thoughtful. "I surmise that they used these gates for transportation, and if that is the case, then it is only logical to deduce that the star-walkers to whom Dace referred required more than one access point."

"Do you have any clue how we might find one?"

"Not without working tech, Sirantha."

Dammit. I feared as much. If we had the capability to scan the area, he could pinpoint energy signatures, and we'd head that way. Unfortunately, our gizmos are fried for the time being. We'll have to be clever.

"Let's look," I say with grim determination. "There has to be way back where we came from."

"If so, we shall find it." His calm, as ever, reassures me and makes it possible for me to take the first step of what might be a thousand-kilometer journey.

Still haven't found him. As I feared, they deleted all references to Svet in the records, which means they're screening male students of appropriate age at all the training academies, a process slowed by the fact that many of these kids still have parents, but they're buried in bureaucratic layers. It takes a ridiculously long time to get a straight answer about a student's status, let alone whether he's a candidate for genetic testing.

I'm telling myself to be patient, but it's hard—and complicated by the fact that people remember me here. I've deflected four attacks now, but I didn't kill any of the hitters. I turned them over to the Nicuan imperial guard. How do you convince people you've changed when they're trying to stick a knife in your neck?

You're not on the bounce anymore, so until I hear from you, I won't know where you are, or what you're doing. I sent this message to your barrister and asked her to forward. I assume you've left your comm code. I'm sorry we're out of touch, but I'm including my new code here. I've taken an apartment in the capital while the officials deal with my request. So strange to find myself living here of all places. It doesn't feel like home, but *you* are home.

Hon and Loras have moved on. I didn't expect them to stick around, though. Hon's got itchy feet, but now I'm very much alone in this. I know I chose this course, but it's odd how alone you can feel, surrounded by people. This is a huge city by any standards, and there's nobody here who gives a damn about me.

I'm afraid of forgetting how you feel in my arms; I'm afraid I dreamed you. I play that message you left before you jumped from Venice Minor sometimes, and I see how much you love me. But unless I'm watching your face, it gets hard to remember how we are together, if it can be as good as I remember.

Reply soon, Jax.

[message ends]

CHAPTER 25

The jungle sprawls around us like a carnivorous plant.
Strange noises, chattering and growling, echo within the
dense undergrowth, making me feel like predators lurk all
around us. I glance back at Vel, braced for the worst.

"Do our weapons work?"

We should've checked that first thing. He digs into his
pack and brings out a shockstick and laser pistol; neither
will power up. I take the former and shove it through my
belt, as we both know it's better than nothing. Without the
shock aspect, it can still be used as a baton or a club, and
I'm trained in its use for close combat. He has his twin,
curved blades, which require no juice at all, and he's deadly
with them. I'm sure we'll be fine. Probably.

"Transport shorted out all our devices."

"Can you fix them?"

He spreads his claws in an *I don't know* gesture. "I would
need a clean, dry place to disassemble them and assess the
damage. If replacement parts or wiring is required to affect
said repairs, then no, not unless we locate salvage."

Glancing around at the impenetrable wall of greenery,

that doesn't seem too likely here, wherever here is. I wish I knew whether we're still on Marakeq or if we've gone elsewhere entirely. That would be the difference between teleportation and a gate between 'verses. The former would be amazing enough, especially discovered on a class-P world. Humans have been unable to perfect that technology, despite finding snippets of ancient schematics. The closest we've come is the disruptor, which scrambles the molecules in the body for a hideous death.

As for the latter, I've speculated that other realities might exist, but it's never been proven. *Until now, maybe.* Of course, delivering that evidence depends on us getting home. Maybe people passed over before; they just never found their way back.

March. Shit. If I don't return, he'll think I left him for good and with no explanations, no good-byes. Surely he'll know I'd never do that of my own free will—just disappear on him. Urgency possesses me, and I quicken my step, bounding over spiky-leafed plants. Vines writhe on the ground, snapping at my ankles, likely attached to some sentient flora.

Running doesn't solve anything, though. It just makes me tired, and when I finally have no more breath, and stop, panting, we're still in the middle of this Mary-forsaken jungle. So far, nothing has attacked us, but I sense things stirring in the undergrowth, circling us to determine our weaknesses. Fear percolating anew, I spin to face Vel. He's already got his twin blades in hand, so I guess he feels it, too.

"Back to back, Sirantha. We are about to meet our first natives."

Without speaking, I ready my weapon and fall in behind him. I'd feel better if I had the live hum for insurance; as it is, we must win this fight on skill and strength. Monsters burst out of the bushes from all sides. I have only seconds to take in an impression of green mottled fur, razor-sharp talons, and long, yellow teeth. There are holes where their ears ought to be, and their eyes are oddly placed. They're also convinced we're their next meal.

Not today.

Four of them, which means taking two at once. My time in prison has left me stronger than ever, even more than when I graduated as a combat jumper, and I haven't forgotten any of my training. In a way, it feels good to have an enemy I can fight instead of the tide of public opinion or a jury's good graces. When the first one lunges at me, I crack it soundly across the skull with my shockstick, a two-handed swing. If I had any juice, the thing would be twitching on the ground, its nervous system blown to hell. Instead, the beast reels back with a high-pitched sound.

Dark fluid trickles from its maw, brown-black, much darker than human blood. The viscosity is different too, stickier, more like tree sap. Could these creatures be evolved from the native flora? Shit, that's not fur. It's . . . moss. I don't have time to ponder as it communicates with its hunting partner, and they both dive at me at once. I counter with another hard swing and a snap kick aimed at the vulnerable throat.

In response to the strike, tentacles flares from the creature's throat and twine around my ankle. I slam to the ground because, despite their slenderness, these tendril-vine things possess a terrible, tensile strength. I wish I had blades like Vel's, but I don't, so I roll, trying to twist them. If these things can move, then they have nerve endings, and I can hurt them.

Vel vaults me, twin blades gleaming, and slices the cords binding me. His monsters follow in unnatural bounds. They don't move like anything I've ever seen; they have too many legs, for one thing, and they *leap*, not run.

Now free, I flip to my feet. I have some sense now of what these creatures are trying to do. Once they get us bound and helpless on the ground, they will devour us while we're still alive. Like the Morgut, they prefer fresh prey; maybe they savor a screaming-terror taste in their meat.

They time another leap, and this time, the lead plant-thing succeeds in biting me. It hurts like a bitch, and the teeth lock on like certain carnivorous fish, so that when I knock it away, it takes a chunk out of my side. Blood streams freely, driving them to greater excitement. I guess I'm tasty.

Vel's not fighting at my back anymore since he broke to cut me loose, but they hunt in pairs, so his flora-beasts take no notice of me. But I still have mine to contend with, and though I've injured the first one, it doesn't show signs of slowing down. But more blood drizzles from its mouth from where Vel severed its tendrils, and it moans as it moves to try to pin me.

Once more, they coordinate a leap; I knock the second one back with a swing of the shockstick. It is *not* sinking those long, curved teeth into my flesh again. *Frag that. Focus, Jax.* I concentrate on the wounded one, aiming a powerful roundhouse kick at what would be its ribs in a normal mammalian creature. Surely this thing has inner organs I can damage. It shrieks then, so high-pitched that I can't hear all the notes, but I can tell by Vel's reaction that it's a horrendous noise.

The scream distracts his opponents, and he disembowels one with a scissor-sweep of his blades. Gray entrails spill out onto the foliage, but it's nothing I've ever seen before—and I've killed some monsters in my day. Instead, it looks like coils of lichens, swimming in that awful black blood, and it stinks of rotting vegetation. His remaining enemy goes mad then, flinging itself at him in a fury and rendering it vulnerable to the grace of his knives.

Mine don't cut and run, though. It's as though these creatures form a family, and they will stand and fall together. I find that oddly touching even as I crush one's throat with a final, lethal kick. That leaves only one, and it becomes quiescent, acknowledging its fate. I almost feel bad as I break its skull wide open with a two-handed swing of the shockstick. More mossy guts splatter everywhere.

"What the hell do you make of that?" I ask, palm to my side.

Red trickles between my fingers. Mary, I need medical attention. I hope Vel has some Nu-Skin. I don't think that has any circuits to be fried in transit, so it should work, even here. My excitement at the adventure dims a bit; when I set out to chart new beacons with Kai, I was generally more prepared than this, and we have precious few resources.

"Cohesive unit, hunting as one. We merely had skills and weapons unfamiliar to them. Our next encounters may not go so smoothly."

"Smoothly?" I show him my wound, and he moves at once for his pack, hurdling the corpses.

You wouldn't expect Vel to be gentle, but his claws are remarkably dexterous as he cleans the wound and then seals it with a fresh pack of Nu-Skin. It bonds at once, relieving my fear. Hopefully, our antiseptic will kill the foreign microbes. The idea of growing that gray moss inside my body nearly makes me throw up—and the smell isn't helping.

"We need to make you some knives."

There's no question cutting worked better on these creatures than blunt-force trauma. I'm not experienced with knives, but I don't want to be eaten, either. I'll work it out, somehow, no matter how steep the learning curve. And the *really* fun part? We don't know this jungle at all, so those creatures might be the nicest things here.

"Do you know how?"

He inclines his head. "Trapper taught me."

Ah, part of his bounty-hunter training.

"We need to move before their friends come looking for them."

"I will look for usable supplies and a defensible place to spend the night."

Now that he's mentioned it, I can see the light is going. This definitely is not Marakeq, with its dreamy twilight. No, this world offers black velvet darkness unbroken by artificial light.

The long night is coming, and only Mary knows whether we'll survive it.

[Vid-mail from Dina, sent on the four-day bounce]

Nola forwarded your message to the ship as soon as she got it, but we'd already put down on Marakeq by then. It sucks like hell to be the one to tell you this, but Jax isn't here. Twelve hours after our arrival, her comm went dark. Hit and I hiked out to the settlement to investigate, but neither of us can understand the natives. They aren't hostile, but Jax and Vel have vanished. No sign of them so far.

I'm so sorry. But we're not giving up hope yet. We're scanning and searching the surrounding swamp. I promise we'll find her if it's humanly possible.

[message ends]

[Vid-mail from March, emergency channel, priority reply]

I'll hop a ship and be there ASAP to help you search.

[message ends]

CHAPTER 26

As night falls, the temperature drops, and I'm dressed for Marakeq weather. For the first time in ages, Vel grows out his camouflage skin, but this time it's for insulation, not to pass as human. But in honor of my aesthetic sensibilities, he takes human form instead of just permitting the faux-skin to shape as it will. This is the first time I've seen him make the transformation, and I am intrigued by the amount of physical sculpting he does.

He did it one other time in my presence—in the cave on the Teresengi Basin, but he was wearing weatherproof gear, and it was dark, so I couldn't see what he was doing. There's just enough light for me to make out the details, and it's fascinating. When given his preferences, he chooses a height that doesn't force him to compact his body or his limbs, so he's tall and slender. Though he can, in order to pass as a specific target, that physical manipulation causes him pain. His features are so average that he'd never draw a second glance. I know for a fact that he's created this identity out of a composite of a hundred male human faces.

When he finishes, he's warmer, but we still haven't found anyplace to spend the night.

It's all jungle, as far as the eye can see. No structures, no signs of sentient life. Well, higher-evolved sentient life, that is. I wonder if Dace sees this as some kind of rite of passage. If we can survive this world and make our way back, then we will prove ourselves worthy. No, that doesn't ring true. I still believe she wants us to discover something here, mentioned in those Oonan prophecies.

I only want to find the way back.

"What do you think?" I ask Vel.

"I have been attempting to locate signs of passage, but this part of the planet appears to be unsettled wilderness."

A sigh slips free. "How the hell do you think we got here? You've traveled even more than me. Ever had anything like this happen?"

He makes a sound in his throat that I recognize as laughter. "Never. Our adventures own the distinction of uniqueness."

"That's small comfort at the moment."

I don't know how long we've been walking, but I'm stumbling with exhaustion. At last, to my vast relief, Vel spots something in the canopy. It looks like an old tree house, a platform that uses the leaves as a roof and has vines leading down from the height so we can check it out.

"Wait here and remain alert. I will signal if it is safe."

I whip out my shockstick and stand ready as he ascends. A few moments later, he calls, "Come up, Sirantha. This will suffice for tonight."

It's a hard climb, but my time in prison left me with serious biceps, and I haul myself up almost as fast as Vel. From here, I can tell the platform has been built with some measure of expertise, free-fall wood lashed together with vines. An old structure, but it appears stable, and we'll be safe from ground-dwelling predators. Of course, there are still fliers and climbers to worry about, but I'm so tired I don't care if a giant bird swoops down to eat me. Besides, its wings wouldn't clear the canopy.

The ledge is also fairly narrow for sleeping. I can't imagine its purpose, except as a lookout post. But if we turn on our sides, we can both manage to lie down, and that's all that matters.

"I will take the outer edge." Vel twines a vine about his arm so he won't fall off if he rolls in his sleep, leaving me the relative safety of the side against the trees.

I don't protest his chivalry. Though I'm by nature a scrapper, I don't mind someone taking care of me—a little, anyway, as long as it doesn't cut into my intrinsic freedoms. And this doesn't. It's just Vel's way of showing affection, I think. He doesn't have the words, so he does practical things instead. Nobody else ever has, not like this. Not Kai. Not March. They both assumed I would reject such gestures because I'm so independent, but Vel doesn't take away my autonomy; he's so matter-of-fact that I can't take umbrage. Maybe *because* he's Ithtorian, I can accept it from him. There are no species-specific snares to avoid.

"Wish I'd packed a thermal blanket," I mutter, trying to get comfortable.

"I have one," he says. "If you are amenable to sharing it."

"Hell yes, I am." It's fragging cold.

But after he digs it out, and we arrange ourselves front to back, it's weirder than I thought it would be. Because he feels human behind me, his chitin covered in two centimeters of skin. So the hardness beneath could be construed as muscle and bone, not what it is, and that's disorienting because he doesn't feel like my old friend. He feels like a human male spooned up against my back.

"It is a practical decision," he says quietly. "The faux-skin is an excellent conductor, so we both benefit from proximity."

I guess he read something of my thoughts, which takes some doing since my back is to him. Then I realize I've tensed against him and make a conscious effort to relax. Of course, I'm being ridiculous; this is Vel, whom I trust as much as anyone in the universe. *And he just lost the woman he loves. Try not to be an idiot, Jax.*

Beneath the blanket, it's delightfully warm, and he offers additional heat at my back. But my side hurts where the creature bit me; it's a heated throb, as if the Nu-Skin and our antibacterial isn't enough to fight the alien microbes.

I shift several times before he says, "Are you in pain?"

"Yeah." Mary, I hate admitting that.

"I can administer a local painkiller."

Ordinarily, I'd say, *No, I can tough it out.* But without it, the only way I'll sleep is if I roll over, and I don't know if I can drop off while curled up against his chest. The alternative is no better; I feel strange about spooning my front to his back.

"Please."

He rummages and comes up with a disposable drug kit. One tiny prick into the skin of my side, and I already feel the delightful numbness spreading. It might not solve the problems my wound is causing, but it makes me care less.

"Is that better?"

"Much, thank you."

Vel sets his pack within easy reach, and I set my shock-stick near my head. This time, it's easier to settle against him. I don't know if it's the drugs, but since it's a local, it shouldn't affect my state of mind. I let myself enjoy the reflected warmth from his faux-skin and the snug protection of the thermal blanket. Wind whispers through the canopy, lulling me, then new noises echo through the jungle: shrill shrieks, raucous calls, gentle chirrups. The sounds blur into a soothing symphony, and I fall asleep faster than I expected.

I wake to a nightmare of teeth and claws scrambling up the tree below me. These creatures are different from the ones on the ground. Smaller, lighter, with talons curved for climbing, and they bear spines on their backs for impaling their prey. I scramble backward, conscious of how far I have to fall. The narrow ledge will make fighting a bitch, and where the hell is Vel?

He drops from above, his twin blades in hand, in the

time it takes me to locate my shockstick. Though I'm hardly awake, I wade in swinging. The movement pulls the bite in my side, but there's enough painkiller left in my system that it's a bearable ache, not a sharp, stabbing pain. Right now, there are only two, though their screams may bring others.

I hit mine hard enough to knock it toward the edge, and I follow up with a side kick, which sends it tumbling off the platform. It tries to control its fall, clawing at branches and vines, but succeeds only in battering against the trunk on the way down. It hits hard and does not get up. In the time it takes me to dispatch mine, Vel has already sliced the other creature's throat. The blood smells different from the other monsters we fought, less rotting vegetation and more mineral in origin. Life on this planet is truly strange.

"Have you slept?" I ask him.

"No. I moved to stand watch after you drifted off."

So he only lay with me long enough to permit me to relax, as I wouldn't have done alone. How well he knows me. That makes me smile despite the fact we haven't survived our first night here yet.

"Then it's my turn. You found a good vantage point above?" At his nod, I ask, "How far up?"

He directs me with an arc of his arm, and then I do something I'm sure he doesn't expect. "Would you like me to stay until you fall asleep?"

Vel hesitates, his posture a clear Ithtorian expression of surprise. Then he simply answers, "Yes."

So I lie down at his back, listening until his breathing steadies. I wonder if Adele suspected even before she saw the truth of him. Because he does not sound human at rest, even clad in faux-skin. His inhalations are too deep, slow and long, hinting at extraordinary lung capacity. I wait until I'm sure he's out, then I slip out from under the thermal blanket and scramble up to the higher lookout position; it's no more than a notch carved in a thick branch, but it offers a stable place to sit.

The rest of the night is quiet. I can only presume that the bodies at the base of the tree offered predators both an alternate food source and a warning. By the time the sun comes up, I'm tired again but glad of the light as well. Vel stirs as the day brightens, and we suck down packets of paste from my pocket. He swore once he'd rather die than eat the stuff, but we can't cook up here, not even on his chemical burner, and we have no idea if we can safely eat any of the native flora and fauna. That problem is complicated by the fact that our technology is fried, so we can't scan for local toxins. I don't know what we'll do when our food runs out.

"How are we for water?"

"We need to find a local source. I have purification tablets in my pack."

"Of course you do. Just in case you get stranded on a class-P world with no functional technology."

His amusement manifests in a quirk of his hidden mandible that almost resembles a smile when it pulls at his face. "Precisely so."

"I'll go down first. Warn me if anything's about to swoop down on me."

"Assuredly."

On the ground, I note that the corpses have been gnawed while we slept. When he joins me, he slices off one of the beast's legs with his knife. I don't know if I can stand to watch him eat it; his people enjoy fresh meat. But instead, he pares the flesh away from the bone.

At my inquiring look, he explains, "I am making you a knife."

After using his own blades to sharpen the bone to a fierce point, he lashes the blade to my shockstick with a thin, tensile vine, and then he cements them with resin seeping from the trees. I take the makeshift weapon and test it with a couple of swings.

"Thank you. We might live through this after all."

"We will," he says quietly. "Never doubt it."

CHAPTER 27

*We've spent seven nights without seeing anything capa*ble of communicating with us. Ten different species have tried to eat us. This is our eighth day.

The jungle thins ahead, opening to a dark plain where nothing grows, all obsidian and basalt. Deep trenches have been cut in the distant land, though I can't tell whether it was nature or machinery. I hope for the latter because that's a sign of civilization.

"Good thing we found the river," I mutter.

Vel's purification tablets rendered the water safe to drink but we're running out of prepackaged meals. Soon, we'll have no choice but to eat local food and hope for the best. That's a hell of a gamble, and not one whose odds I like. Though I haven't said anything, the wound in my side isn't healing like it should, and gray streaks web my skin around the wound. I'm running a low-grade fever constantly, and nothing in his pack can help me; I searched one night during my turn on watch. I'm not worried because I hope, in time, my nanites will work out a way to repair the damage from alien parasites. I just have to sweat and shiver through their learning curve. I hope.

Of course, if they don't, there's nobody to fix them, nobody left who understands how they work. In which case, I'll die a horrible death. Or maybe I'll mutate into some hideous alien monster. That'd be okay, too.

On one hand, it feels good to leave the jungle I've grown to hate so passionately, but I don't feel confident about the land looming ahead. It doesn't much look as if it can support life, but the only alternative is to backtrack to the broken gate, presuming we can find it and set it off in another direction . . . with no guarantee anything better lies ahead. I wish Dace had given us a map or more indication of what the hell we're supposed to see.

But that presumes she knew this would happen. Point in fact, we're sure of nothing—and it's frustrating as hell. For all I know, she only meant to show us a star-walker artifact because she thought we might know something about it.

"Any bright ideas on how to get us home?" I ask him hopefully.

"Working on it."

I glance at Vel, who's studying the terrain ahead. Yesterday, he shed his faux-skin and didn't generate more, as the temperature has been climbing the farther we head . . . well, since I don't know the directions on this world, I'll just call it west. It looks to be hot as hell out on those plains, and geysers of smoke puff up periodically.

"Sulfur springs?" I guess.

"I believe so. The smell indicates volcanic craters."

If we're not careful, we'll get cooked alive out there. I eye the steam and the rugged landscape with more than a little trepidation. At this point, I feel like I have to abdicate judgment, as I'm too sick to think straight. Not that I'm admitting it to Vel. There's nothing he can do, and there's no point in his worrying unless I keel over.

"What do you think? Push on or head back?"

"The jungle is no more hospitable," he answers. "Only dangerous in a different way. Perhaps once we cross these flats, there will be . . . something."

"You lead, then. Your eyes are better than mine."

His olfactory sense will help, too. With any luck—though that's been lacking since we put down on Marakeq—he can find us a way off this world. I won't give up hope that we'll find a gate; there should be another, but there's no telling how far away it might be . . . or what kind of condition it'll be in when we find it. I say *when* because I can't contemplate any other option. I can't leave March wondering what happened to me.

I can't.

I know what he'll think, and I can't let it end like that. Sure, I reacted to his leaving me. *Again.* But I never meant for it to be forever. I didn't intend to punish him like this—with an inexplicable disappearance. Really, I just wanted a little time to come to terms with the way his life would change when he found his sister's kid . . . and my own fear about where it left me. I thought I'd get Carvati working on a cure for the La'heng, take care of my business with Baby-Z, then head to Nicuan to see March. A practical decision, but also to show that I don't dance to his tune—that I still have my own life.

Sure, some life.

These bleak thoughts carry me onward. Three hours into our hike, we've breached the volcanic flats, leaving the jungle far behind us. The sky is a strange blue-violet overhead, but it's definitely daytime. I surmise it must be a gas effect similar to what we see on Gehenna, just with a different chemical composition, but there's enough oxygen that we can breathe.

"What if we can't find a way back?" I ask eventually.

The question has been weighing on me, but I didn't want to voice it because it seems like if I speak my fears out loud, then they gain ground. The unthinkable becomes possible. Before answering, Vel navigates around the edge of a crater within which water boils; I smell it now, and the reek is overpowering.

Once we reach a safe distance, he faces me, imperturbable as always. "Then we build a life here, Sirantha."

"Wherever here is."

I try to hide my horror, but the last thing I ever wanted

was to settle dirtside, and now it looks as though I might be stuck here with no means to contact anyone in the life I left behind. It's not that I don't want Vel to be part of my life—always—just not here. Not like this.

"We cannot give up hope. This world is vast, and it will take time to explore."

"True enough." With a faint sigh, I start moving again.

At what we estimate to be midday, we stop for food and water. The land slopes up to a natural plateau, elevated for us to get a clear view of anything moving to attack us. Here, he can mix up a batch of his soup, a nice change from the paste. But I only have two packets of those left, and he empties his stores for this meal. We eat in silence.

"Have you ever been in a worse spot?" I hope he'll say yes and tell me a story of how he got out of it. He's lived such unimaginable adventures, after all.

"No," Vel answers simply. No elaboration. No false promises.

He and I have seen some troubles since he first tracked me to New Terra, but this caps them all. I can't motivate myself to get up from the makeshift stone table. I'm tired, dirty, and dispirited.

"At what point do we stop walking and start building?"

"I cannot answer that. I only know we will die if we stay here. There is no food to be hunted."

"There were animals in the jungle, but they wouldn't stop trying to eat us." *Not a place to call home.*

"Irrelevant. You will not give up, Sirantha. I have never yet seen you broken." To be honest, he has more confidence in me than I do.

As I stare at the stone surface before me, it registers—these are scratches, and they form a pattern. While I can't be sure about the nature of the trenches, I'm positive about this. Someone engraved these marks, which means there's intelligent life on this planet, somewhere. Or there used to be, at least.

"Look," I say.

Vel kneels to examine the carvings. "It appears to be cuneiform writing, but I do not recognize the language."

"Me, either. But that's a good sign, right?" Hope buoys me up, and I shove to my feet, eager now.

"I would say so." He's cautious in offering an opinion, as always, but I recognize the marks of equal excitement in him. Between the flex of his mandible and the angle of his head, he might as well be whooping with glee.

For the first time since we arrived here, I feel like we're heading somewhere particular instead of wandering blind. "Let's look for more of these markings as we travel. Maybe they're like signposts?"

"An excellent idea."

This give me the energy to move, and I fall in beside Vel. A while later, I spot another stone table, and this time, I suspect it was built on purpose. I climb up to take a look, and, sure enough, this one bears more symbols.

"I think this might be directions."

After a short scrutiny, he inclines his head. "This way."

From here, we angle again west—for lack of true directional—and find four more stone tables before nightfall. Each bear the familiar sigils along with a stylized line crowned in a triangle, something like an arrow, but not exactly. It's close enough to make me think we're on the right track, however.

I trudge on, weariness so deep in my bones that I don't know if I could swing the knife Vel made for me if it came down to it. We cross farther until the grim landscape before us offers something new. At first I can't believe my eyes, so I glance at Vel for confirmation. He's stopped moving, still with shock.

"You see it, too?"

"It is . . . magnificent."

Rising before us are the ruins of an unimaginably immense city, the architecture of which defies description. Even at this distance, I can tell it's ancient, probably dating back to the Makers themselves. Over long turns, we've found artifacts and scattered ruins, but nothing like this, not on this scale.

Anticipation takes hold, then, for I live to blaze new trails. Without waiting for Vel, I break into a run.

I never told you how I wound up on Lachion that first time, did I, Jax? The swamp here on Marakeq reminds me of Nicu Tertius, bringing back all those old memories, and as we search—and find nothing—I'm possessed of that same despair. So I'm going to tell you a story . . . because I need to feel like you're with me. I'm going to pretend you can hear me.

[Muted sounds, rustling, unsteady breath]

The air was thick with clotting blood, the ground a morass of churned mud. Blueflies droned in the distance, laying eggs in the corpses of men I called comrade. This plan had been doomed from the beginning, and if I owned anything like a conscience, I'd have told the soft little Nicuan nobleman where he could stuff his credits because clearly he already had his head wedged up there.

Instead, I checked my account to make sure I received payment, then obeyed his orders, no matter how stupid they were. That was why I—and a handful of my men—lay pinned atop this hill, having failed to take the property our employer wanted sacked. Success or failure; it was all the same to me. I got paid regardless, as I never took a job without money up front.

The only time I worked on down payment was if my employers gave me complete latitude. If they didn't care how I got the job done, then I gave them a little financial leeway. On Nicu Tertius, that didn't happen much. These empire-bred pussies were all convinced they were the next great military genius and only needed one good battle to prove it. They didn't care if they sacrificed real soldiers to test their half-assed theories.

Of the forty men I led to the Ja-Win estate, only five remained: Buzzkill, Ringo, Surge, Vikram, and Franken. Faces smeared with blood and Thermud, they looked to me for guidance, so I took stock of the situation. The mission could only be deemed a complete failure. Ja-Win defenses had proved much more robust than the idiot who hired me had believed. At this point, we could only hope for a successful retreat.

The men's thoughts whirled nearby, shrieked and prodded in my head until I was bombarded with a white-hot noise that crossed the threshold into pain.

Oh, Mary, I may never see Kora again. Should've woken her before I left.

When I get back to town, I'm shoving a shiv through his eye.

If I live through this, it's time to retire.

Fucking March, I'll kill him nice and slow.

I'd lost the ability to tell who was thinking what. It all blurred together in a nauseating ball of fear, pain, and anger. At least I could use the latter.

To the east, we had Ja-Win gunmen. To the north, the compound defense grid. To the west, fuck if I knew what. To the south, jungle. After no more than a few seconds' consideration, I rotated my fingers, giving the silent order to move out. I'd take the dangers of the jungle any day; the terrain would make tracking us a bitch, and it would give us the guerilla advantage when it came to taking greater numbers.

We slithered down the hill on our bellies, staying to the tall grass that yielded to swampy ground heralding thicker undergrowth. Tangled greenery provided much-needed cover as the Ja-Win gunmen charged the hill, only to find their quarry gone. I heard their shouts in the distance. We had to get into the trees before the enemy tracker took a good hard look at all that churned earth. Their trackers would figure it out sooner rather than later, and we needed a head start to survive this brutal game of hide-and-seek.

I motioned to Surge to take the lead. He fell behind the last man, Franken, and aimed toward a distant hill. I only used this as a last resort, but we needed the time. While my men disappeared into the trees, I fired in the opposite direction. When the holo shell hit, it broke wide open and showed the streaky movement of men running covertly. As I'd hoped, it drew the attention of the Ja-Win gunmen. This thing wasn't widely available yet; I bought mine on Gehenna, and I'd be pleased to report its success to the inventor, who'd given me a discount for proving its combat viability.

As I ran, the heat hit me like a closed fist. Nicu Tertius had only two seasons, hot and wet, which made fighting on the ground a bitch. I tried to avoid it whenever possible, but the pay for this job was too good to pass up. *That should've tipped me off.*

I swallowed a curse as I heard the sounds of pursuit, booted feet splashing through the wetlands behind me. The enemy's thoughts assaulted me as well. Outrage, indignation, bloodlust. *Gonna slice up the leader, make him bleed out . . .*

More and more back then, I felt like I was losing my mind. It got harder and harder to push everything back, focus on what came from my own head instead of everywhere else. Pure will let me do it that time, but I didn't know how much longer that would hold.

Dammit, I hoped to buy more time. With no hesitation, I gave another silent signal, telling my men to scatter. Four of them vanished immediately. Only Surge hesitated, then he, too, melted into the thick tangle of undergrowth. We had a greater chance of reaching civilization separately.

Some people might say I abandoned them, sending them off as bait to better my own chances. Well, that would be true, too. I crept through the trees, pausing here and there to listen. Distant laser fire and screams of pain came to me on the wind. I recognized the voice. Franken, down, but it sounded like he'd taken a few Ja-Win with him.

In a way, I wished I hadn't taken credits from Pilatu. The mercenary code prevented me from killing the guy for being an idiot; otherwise, I'd never get work again.

Shit, movement nearby. I dropped to my belly and stilled. The thoughts that filled my head then could scarcely be called that, more impulses, urges. *Hunger. Food. Not food.* I lay there, hardly daring to breathe. A marsh cat. That thing would rake out my intestines and eat them without a second thought. I avoided it narrowly, sensing the animal's fierce hunger moving off, becoming distant, then vanishing as it moved outside my range.

I only encountered one enemy on my way out of Ja-Win territory. Bad luck for him, the merc was facing the other way. I could have shot him in the back, but I didn't want the noise. A mental lance through the guy's frontal lobe solved the problem. The man's expression went slack as he dropped face-first into the mud. Most likely he'd drown before his unit found him. Doubtless it would be kinder to snap his neck, but I wasn't feeling kind, so I stepped over the body and onto the road.

Hours later, I finally reached the place where I'd hidden a rover in case things went bad. On Nicu Tertius, you had to have a backup plan.

Empty.

"Son of a bitch." I stared down the muddy track. In some ways, I preferred being out in the middle of nowhere. It left my mind quiet at least, devoid of the pain that had become a constant companion.

Well, there was no help for it. I'd have to walk.

I stayed to the trees, dodging Ja-Win patrols looking for survivors making their way on foot. More than once, they forced me to my belly and left me wishing I had the mental power to blast them all at once. Their thoughts bombarded me: some banal, some vengeful, some so vapid I was amazed the asshole could hold a weapon.

Damn, but I'd love to see them drop at the same time, drooling and brain-damaged. But if I hit one, they'd snap alert and start looking for their attacker, even if they didn't understand how I'd killed. With a soft sigh, I let them pass unmolested and resumed my journey.

It took me all night to reach a village, where I could hire an autocab to take me to the city. By the time I got to my flat, I was ready to blow the shit out of the entire planet. My head felt like molten metal, searing with the effort of trying to block when I was so tired. I wasn't very good at it at the best of times, and I never hated anything the way I did Nicu Tertius.

With shaking hands, I shot myself full of painkiller. That chemical cocktail balanced the crazy in my head, kept things quiet. The bad news? It was hellishly addictive, and the more I used, the more I wanted. Chem would kill me if this lifestyle didn't. But I couldn't shoot up when I worked. It slowed my reflexes too much.

I leaned my head against the wall, no windows in here where people could get to me. My place was functional, nothing more, a one-room convenience in a high-rise. With a job like mine, I needed the security. It would take a small army to get up here.

The drug kicked in, dropping the blessed veil of silence over the incessant clamor of other people's wants and needs. Exhausted, I took a san-shower, then found a packet of paste. I didn't keep the kitchen-mate stocked, no point.

A quick stop at the comm terminal informed me that everyone but Franken had made it back. Fucking pitiful. Though I'd known these spoiled Imperial types had dead meat between their ears, I'd never lived through anything as egregious and wasteful as the run on the Ja-Win compound. Good men had died out there, soldiers with families, not that Pilatu gave a shit. He'd pay the death benefits, shrug, then come up with some other asinine strategy in the never-ending war games.

In those days, I felt empty in a way that nothing could assuage. Apart from that icy numbness, I mostly felt rage, a growing and nearly ungovernable need to lash out. Svetlana's message made me smile, though. I couldn't wait to see her.

My sister didn't approve of how I made my living, but she also understood why I chased the credits. When I bought my own ship, it would change everything. I could finally achieve my dream of being out there, far beyond the thoughts baying in my head. Blessed quiet.

I planned to hire Svet on as crew, and she could stop working in that crappy secondhand shop on Gehenna. We'd get together next month, like we always did, and argue over my choices and her stubbornness. Nobody meant as much as Svet; nobody could get away with saying the things she did, either. I'd killed for much less.

Out of habit, I sat down at the comm terminal to check my bank account, as I always did after a job. I compared the tally against what the dream ship cost, then took a look at the Imperial postings to see what my next mission would be—and how much closer that would bring me to buying my freedom from this hellhole.

Sure, I could afford passage off Nicuan, but to what end? I wasn't a farmer. I didn't want to go to work programming or overseeing somebody else's bots. All I knew how to do was kill—and fly. So I'd do the former until I could do the latter. I'd be damned if I piloted to put money in the Corp's pocket.

"What the . . ." That couldn't be right. A few taps on the interface and then I spat a curse. The amount I received prior to the Ja-Win job had been transferred out again. Unless he thought I died in the Ja-Win compound, Pilatu was dumber than he looked.

Killing rage boiled up inside me, tinting everything red. I could do this, even under the influence. This job didn't call for speed, just stealth. After tucking a pistol in my belt and a knife in my boot, I went to pay my respects.

Security on Pilatu's city estate was laughable. It was a lush, lavish place full of expensive statuary, gushing fountains, and well-manicured gardens, all hidden away behind heavy, ornate metal gates. Using a grappler, I went over the wall, dropped behind the hedge, and waited.

I had all night.

The droids came first.

After disabling the patrolling bots, I made my way to the guard outpost. Busy watching the innocuous vid feeds I'd provided, they died without making a sound.

Then the place was mine. A heady surge of power lashed through me, akin to lust. I strolled up to the suite where the noble sat pondering his next move. The man didn't know it yet, but he didn't have one.

I closed my hands around Pilatu's throat. If I squeezed hard enough, I'd crush the man's windpipe. A twist would snap his neck. I savored each possibility while Pilatu struggled against my grip, trying vainly to see who had him.

"You cheated me," I whispered into the other man's ear. "I don't work for free. Ever. And my payment isn't contingent on the success of your plan."

"Let me go," the noble tried to demand. "Crazy bastard. If they . . ." Pilatu gasped, struggling to get the words out. "Catch you . . . you'll be . . . executed."

"Weighed against the pleasure of killing you, I'm finding I don't care."

"I have money." Face purple now, the other man wheezed. "I can—"

"No," I said with finality. "You can't."

A little shiver of pleasure went through me as I wrenched Pilatu's neck sideways, then let the body drop. About Mary-sucking time—I was so tired of taking orders from these officious little pricks. Now I needed to get off world fast.

I still didn't have enough cred for my own ship, but what the fuck. There were other worlds, other wars. People always needed killing.

I left the estate quietly and walked a good distance before signaling an autocab. Expedience sent me straight for the spaceport.

Maybe I could buy passage on a vessel departing tonight. It didn't matter where, although Gehenna would be best. Svet would take me in, no questions asked.

But when I got there, the place was very nearly deserted. No surprise, considering it was so late. Droids went about their work in mechanized silence. There was a skeleton crew working the docks and only two ships, neither of which looked ready to go. I stood, hands bunched into fists, considering my options. I really couldn't stay on Nicuan now, but if I didn't have a choice—

"Well, well, if it isn't my least favorite person," came a deep voice behind me.

I spun, ready to fight, then relaxed a little when I recognized Hon, a tall, dark-skinned pirate from the Outskirts. We'd tussled more than once, but in a friendly way most times. The other man still nursed a slight over some trull that had gone with me instead, but nothing like a blood grudge lay between us.

I grinned. "I'd say likewise, but I despise these Nicuan nobles more than you."

The pirate laughed, showing bone white teeth. "You make a good point."

We talked a little while longer before I asked, "So what brings you out so late?"

"Just checking over my new ship." With a lazy gesture, the other man pointed toward a vessel at the far corner of the docking bay.

Envy panged through me. Piracy paid better than killing, obviously, but you had to have a ship to start with in order to make money that way. For a moment, I considered smashing my fist into Hon's face. The urge boiled up, but I checked it with real effort. *Better not to make a scene.*

"It's nice," I said easily, though it cost me. "You heading out soon?"

Hon shook his head. "Need to do a full diagnostic. You know how used ships can be."

Prick. Hon knew perfectly well I didn't. Now he was just taunting me, but surely not over that woman whose name I'd already forgotten. I'd never owned a vessel in my life, just flown simulators to train for pilot certification and gone up once in a real ship at the starport on Gehenna to take the test. Best day of my life.

I made myself smile, though it was getting harder not to lash out. "I don't, but good luck with it."

I started to turn, but Hon's voice stopped me. "What brings you out so late anyway?"

My nerves prickled to life. "Why?"

Hon's smile became predatory. "You have the look of a hunted man, March. Maybe you're worth something to me now? Your whereabouts, anyway."

Before I knew I meant to act, I slammed my fist into the pirate's face, hard enough that I heard cartilage crunch. Blood spewed from Hon's broken nose, and while he swayed, I slammed his head against the pylon behind him. I wanted to stay and finish the job, but people would come soon. I couldn't be here when they arrived.

Instead, I bent and pocketed the remote to Hon's ship. If it had a jumper on board, we were going to Gehenna. Casually, I made my way across the bay and keyed the boarding ramp down. I strolled on board like I owned it.

Luck spun my way. There was a Rodeisian on board, the foremost source of jumpers outside Farwan. Large and furry with powerful haunches, they didn't like to work with humans—said they were pink and stinky. This one had apparently made an exception for Hon.

The alien froze when it saw the pistol in my hand. I could kill it as easily without moving a muscle, but there was no reason to brag. I kept my gaze steady.

"Here's how this is going to go," I told it. "We're going to Gehenna. I pilot, you navigate. You get me there safely, you walk away. If anything happens to me, I guarantee you go with me. You can keep this ship for your trouble." The Rodeisian's ears perked at that. "Or bounce a message to Hon telling him where you are. Once I walk away, I don't care what you do. Are we clear?"

"Indeed." For such a big creature, the Rodeisian had a surprisingly light, sweet voice. This one might be female, which explained a lot. Hon always had a way with the ladies. "You want a ride to Gehenna. So let's go."

I had to smile. "As easy as that?"

"I make it a policy never to argue with armed, desperate men."

The Rodeisian led the way to the cockpit. She took her seat in the nav chair while I contacted ground control and relayed our plan to depart. Without her full cooperation, it wouldn't have worked. She showed me where Hon kept the registration numbers so I could file the flight plan officially. In fact, she guided me through the process, as if she knew I'd never done this for real before.

She confirmed that with a glance from dark, long-lashed eyes. "I can tell this is your first time. I'll be gentle."

I didn't know if I wanted to hit her or touch her fur to see if it was as soft as it looked. A confusing knot of unfamiliar emotions stirred. It had been a long time since anybody but Svet was nice to me—most people feared me back then—and this Rodeisian had more reason than most. I'd all but taken her hostage, for Mary's sake.

"Thanks," I muttered.

Waiting seemed interminable. If Hon regained consciousness before we got out, it would ruin everything. Maybe I should have just killed him. The bastard was talking about turning me in, after all.

"You have clearance," came the response from the tower, and the hangar above began to open.

I fingered the shunt in my wrist, knowing I'd have to jack in once we were clear of the planet's gravitational pull. That was how a jump worked, but damn, I was nervous. My hands trembled as I set them on the control panels. The ship twitched in response.

Taking a few deep breaths, I centered myself and tried to remember my lessons. *Like that. Yeah.* An unsteady thrust got us out of the hangar, then I felt like I'd been doing this all my life. *What a fucking rush.*

"You're doing great," she told me softly.

We pushed upward through the atmosphere, safe at last. My smile felt strange and tremulous as I glanced away from the sensors briefly. The night sky bloomed, stars sparking all around us with a cold, fierce light that made me feel clean in ways I'd almost forgotten—or never known.

"I could die up here," I breathed, hardly remembering she was there.

I could, too. Happily, even. That's something we have in common, Jax.

"People have," she murmured. "People do."

The silent accord between us felt perfect; I ached with the beauty of flying. And I thought the Rodeisian female felt it, too—

that quiet shiver of light refracted from the sensor screens, inter-
preted by my nervous system as pure pleasure. I'd never known
anything like it. The ship felt natural in my hands, an appendage I
should have been born with.

"Ready for jump?" I asked eventually.

Her reply sounded suggestive, somehow. "Since the moment
you came aboard."

[Narration pauses, time lapse of six hours and twelve minutes]

When we jacked in, the wetware amplified my power, laying the
navigator open. I could sift through her memories as if they were
jewels in a treasure box. She knew—and she didn't seem to mind.
More startling, the female wanted me. She liked my anger and bru-
tality, the scent of blood that lingered about me.

Well, if she wanted rage and savagery, she came to the right man.
That much, I could offer. It was, in fact, all I had left. That was the
first time I became part of a woman, Jax. There in the cockpit, and
I think it prepared me for you.

The ship shivered as the phase drive hummed. I knew how it
worked, opening a small wormhole through which we would access
grimspace. I'd seen the charts and numbers. And even so, I wasn't
remotely prepared for that first jump.

I flew with her, became part of her. But our link exposed me, too,
showing more than I ever wanted anyone to see. I sensed no judgment in her, but it was enough that she'd seen the darkness roiling.
Nausea rose in my throat even as my hands responded to her silent
directives.

"Here," she said. "Jump here."

And I had to trust her. I hit the panel, signaling the ship we were
ready to return to straight space. Shaky and queasy from the after-
effects, it took me three tries to unplug. By that time, the Rodeisian
was already out of her seat.

I glanced at the star charts, trying to place where we'd come out.
Jumps had to take place well away from planetary pull, so some-
times it was a matter of hours before reaching the final destination.
But what I saw on the screen didn't match.

"This isn't the way to Gehenna."

"It isn't," she agreed. Her huge fist slammed into my temple before I could brace for impact.

The lights went out.

[Narration pauses, time lapse of five hours and twenty-nine minutes]

Distant voices reached me before my brain came fully back online. My head throbbed with a low, dull pain, reminding me of the score I had to settle. Right then, I made up my mind—I'd kill that treacherous jumper if it was the last thing I did.

I should have known her sexual impulses didn't necessarily predicate her true thoughts. Should have realized she had been too helpful, agreed too easily. Desperation made me stupid, careless, and now I'd pay the price. *If they knew how much people on Nicuan would pay to get me just like this . . .* Mary, it didn't bear thinking about.

I always thought I would die on my feet. I lay with my eyes closed, trying to make sense of what I was hearing, but my heart thudded in my ears, making that difficult.

Two females, nearby. I couldn't pick anything up from them, so either they'd sedated me, or a Rodeisian fist worked wonders at shutting down my ability.

"What in Mary's name have you done, Tanze?" A woman with a low, rasping voice sounded exasperated. "I wanted Hon, along with his ship. Half those diggers he delivered for the mine don't work!"

I opened my eyes a slit, risking a look to assess how much trouble I was in. They'd bound my hands and feet, with a filament that would slice my skin if I struggled. They weren't screwing around, then.

Two females, one human, and one Rodeisian, the same one who tricked me, then knocked me out. Rage almost overwhelmed me, but it wouldn't do any good to struggle when they had me tied. No, I had to figure out what was going on here—and what they intended to do with me. Maybe I could play along, offer whatever they wanted. They probably wouldn't be fool enough to trust me, though.

Tanze didn't appear overly concerned. "Plans change. This guy came on board instead of Hon, and I figured you'd take what you could get. We can keep the ship in recompense for the busted units. You don't need trouble with offworlders, Mair. Bringing Hon to Lachion would complicate the whole plan."

What plan? Where was Lachion anyway? I fumbled through my galactic geography and came up blank. It couldn't be an important tier world; I'd killed on most of those. That would limit my escape options.

But Mair must be the old woman. I stole another glance. She was small, but wiry, still strong-looking despite her age. I didn't make the mistake of counting her out. Her white hair stood up around her face like a cloudy nimbus, as if she hadn't combed it in weeks, and she'd caked altogether too many cosmetics on her wrinkled face.

"That's true enough," she agreed with a sigh.

"And this one needs you," Tanze went on. "He'll die if you don't help him. I don't know how he's made it this long without going mad or being scooped up by the Corp, but he's on the brink, now."

Every muscle stiffened. *What the frag's the Rodeisian on about? Does she know? How could she?* Being discovered was my worst nightmare, and here I lay tied, listening to it happen. It was bad enough when I thought they just might sell me back to the Nicuan nobles, but if Farwan found out that I made it through adolescence without being chipped, it would be exponentially worse. I knew all about what they did to people who violated their rules. After all, they did it to my father first, leaving me with a stepmother who hated me, and a half sister who needed me to provide for her.

Crazed with the voices in my head, I started fighting in the streets, and unscrupulous people noticed my way with knives. They hired me to do what they didn't want to, Jax. Quiet jobs, dirty ones. I didn't care as long as it paid. And that's how I got started as a merc.

I didn't know then if it'd ever see Svet again. I feared most that she'd think I had run off without a word, like I promised I would never do, no matter how many times I shipped out. When she was a kid, I did it time and again, joining whatever private war paid best to keep her in school. And now I wonder if you're suffering that same fear—that I think you chose to go wherever you are. This is my answer: I know you couldn't help it, and I'm trying my damnedest to bring you home, love.

Anyway, about Svet . . . I'd taken to buying her a little gift from wherever I traveled, something she could look forward to, and hold in her hands when I went away again. She liked shiny things, rings and necklaces that sparkled, no matter how cheap. If I hadn't long ago lost the ability to weep, I would have. But I had no tears then. I hadn't met an angry, gray-eyed woman yet who could save my soul.

"Brain scrambled, is he?" Somehow, the hag made the cold words seem almost kind.

"Not quite." I heard a shrug in Tanze's voice. "I'm not even sure he's salvageable. But you might have a go before we put him down."

They would, too. And maybe they'd be right. A hard shudder rolled through me. It was no use pretending I wasn't awake, listening. The old woman knelt beside me, peering into my face. I couldn't move.

"What do you say?" she asked, running her fingernail down my jaw. "Shall we try to make something out of you, you pretty, doomed thing?"

I'd never been called pretty before. Somehow, that only added to my silent horror. I knew I wasn't. Even then, I had a strong, ugly face, and a strong, scarred body.

Finally, I managed to rasp out a question. "What are you going to do with me?"

"I'm going to break you into tiny pieces," the old woman said with an awful smile. "And then put you back together again."

When her mind touched mine, I screamed.

You know the rest. How she saved me and taught me to block. How she awoke my conscience and turned me into something more than a monster. But Mair's the reason I won't give up on you now, the reason I can love you so fiercely that it has no end and no limits.

We'll keep looking. And I'll play this for you when I find you, as proof that I always knew you were coming back to me.

[message ends]

CHAPTER 28

The distance is deceptive. Eventually I stop running because I've covered only half the measure to the ruins, and a stitch crimps my side. I'm stronger, but I haven't had the freedom to run in longer than I can recall. Vel doesn't chide me, though he has to know I was foolish and impetuous. He merely matches his pace to mine, and we continue on while I hold my side.

It's not just the cramp. The bite hurts as well, and I shouldn't have exacerbated it, but Mary, the idea that we might finally make some progress? Irresistible.

"When do you plan on telling me the truth?" he asks quietly.

Shit.

"About what?"

"Your injury."

Busted.

"I didn't want you to worry."

"I have heightened olfactory sense, Sirantha. You smell worse than usual, quite apart from our hygienic challenges."

Trust Vel to cut to the heart of it like that. "Sorry. But I don't think there's anything you can do."

"You are correct, sadly. But I should examine you nonetheless and sterilize the site, if nothing more."

I'm so dirty that when he peels away the Nu-Skin, it leaves a clean spot, but the wound itself is hideous. Worse than it was when I peeked at it . . . shit, I've lost track of time. It's been two weeks since we arrived. I think. The gray webs all the way to my ribs, nearly to my breast, and it feels hot, sore, when he brushes a claw against it.

Wordlessly, he tends to the problem as best he can, spraying with antibacterial, then he applies fresh Nu-Skin, which is supposed to promote healing. Something in the creature's saliva is prohibiting that bond, however, and not allowing my flesh to heal.

"Let's go." I set out without further discussion of my infirmities.

The remnants of these structures defy my sense of reality in the same way the underground gate did. Some of the towers have fallen, but others remain in impossible spirals, as though the ancients understood secret laws of physics. Unquestionably, these buildings came from an advanced culture. Even now, they gleam, the metal alloy shining silver, untarnished after all these turns.

There is no sound save the wind whistling through the broken spaces, no movement except our own. We've found another dead, lost place, but maybe there's some technology that can help us here, provided Vel can figure it out. And my credits say he can.

"Are you taking footage?" This is another occasion that ought to be logged for posterity.

"Of course."

We enter the ruined city cautiously, keeping an eye out for monsters like the ones from the jungles, but this place is abandoned. Or so we think, until we pass between two fallen buildings, and hear a rumble ahead.

"It sounds big."

He tilts his head, listening. "Not organic life, I think."

The noise grows closer, and I hear what he means; the hum of motorized parts is unmistakable. A bot whirs into view, quite unlike our own. This one is smooth and sleek, fashioned after the number eight with a narrow head and waist. I can't tell its purpose just by looking at it.

The bot stops when it detects us, and a green ray of light beams up. I freeze, thinking it's a weapon, but instead the machine appears to be scanning us. Then it speaks, but I've never heard the language before. If I had to guess, it's a verbal version of the signs we've been seeing cut into the stone tables along the way.

"Can your chip make any sense of that?" Vel asks.

I shake my head. "It's just noise. Yours?"

"My linguistic chip includes a complete database of all human languages, including the dead ones, and this is unfamiliar."

"Try Ithtorian?" That makes sense. The Makers are so old, and the Ithtorians were one of the first races to travel the star lanes; therefore, their paths might have crossed at some point, long before the nuclear winter that changed the face of their planet. But I'm not sure how much the language has evolved.

In response, he switches to his native tongue, and asks, "What is your purpose?"

A green light flashes on the thing's head. Well, what *would* be a head if it was remotely human. It's very other; I can tell an alien intelligence designed it. The twinkling continues for a good several minutes. And then it answers in what sounds a language similar to Ithtorian, but my chip can't process it. So I glance at Vel for clarification.

"An archaic form not included in your language set. There would be no purpose to it, as it has not be spoken in over five thousand turns."

"So how old is this bot, then?" I ask in wonder. "And what did it say?"

"I have no means of ascertaining that without functional

equipment. And 'I safeguard the truth.'" After translating for me, he converses with the bot for a few minutes, then says, "We are to follow it."

"Where?"

"To the truth, of course."

I flash him a dark look, but he's already turned. The machine reverses, and it leads us through the ruins, through twists and turns. It hovers when necessary, avoiding obstacles far easier than we do. Then it leaves us entirely, zipping up to a floor to which all staircases have collapsed.

"Shit."

"We must find a way up. It spoke of Maker archives." He hesitates. "It called them the Sha-Fen."

The words mean nothing to me, which means they're so old as to have been lost from all records. Except, possibly, the ones up there, out of reach.

"Build a scaffold?" It will take time, of course, but without working technology or a gate back to Marakeq, we have nothing more pressing to attend.

It takes two days to pile enough rubble in such a way that we don't die trying to climb it. In that time, we finish the last of my paste. If we don't find food or civilization soon, we might find ourselves wishing we'd stayed in the jungle, where we could, at least, eat what we killed, even if my stomach churns at the prospect.

I ascend first. Vel says it's so he can catch me, but if it were me, I'd want someone else to test the integrity of the structure. He's like me in that respect. I don't argue because I'm dying to see what's up there, and tired of sleeping on the hard ground. At least this place has a roof, and it appears to be mostly intact. Not that it's rained since we've been here.

With care, I manage to scramble over the broken lip of the wall and into the tilting floor. The bot is waiting for us patiently, as if it has no concept of time. Most likely, it doesn't, or at least, not in the same way that we do. It knows time has passed, but it's irrelevant to something that can keep going for thousands of turns. While I wonder how that's even possible, Vel resumes his discussion with it.

At the conclusion, it takes us through two solid double doors, which it unseals as it goes. Air hisses out as if it hasn't been opened for a long, long time. Behind Vel, I enter a vault of some kind, filled with unfamiliar technology. Panels with rows of colored lights, silver coils twined around a flat disc with notched edges.

"Can you use any of this to repair our gear?"

"Perhaps," he answers. "Or to replace it."

Devices whir to life in our presence, and the bot circles the room, performing what I take to be maintenance. I'm already bored, in addition to tired, beyond filthy, and hungry, so I sit down on the pristine floor while Vel communes with the machines. At some point, I doze off because the next thing I know, he's waking me.

"There are terabytes of data here, Sirantha, a treasure trove of immense and unbelievable proportions."

"Did you fix your handheld?" While I'm happy that we've discovered the mother lode of Maker data, I must focus on practical concerns first.

"I did."

"Learn anything about the bot?"

"It is ten thousand turns old."

That leaves me wide-eyed in astonishment. "How?"

"It is self-maintaining, self-sustaining. Its power core appears to be solar-powered, and it can generate replacement parts here."

"Which is how you fixed your tech?"

"Precisely."

"I don't suppose there's a kitchen-mate." Damn, I'm hungry.

"Not here, but I have not explored the whole complex by any means."

"There's more?"

"The vault has a back egress, accessible only from within. I believe we have only discovered the tip of their marvels."

"Why is it helping us?"

"It is programmed to assist friendly sentients and to

share knowledge with those who possess the wherewithal to ask for it."

"The Makers figured if anyone showed up and was able to ask, they should be served." I ponder that, pushing to my feet. "But what happened to them? Where *are* they now?"

"From the best of what I have been able to decipher with the bot's help, there was a cataclysmic event. Global weather patterns were disrupted, solar flares went wild, and only a few ships made it off the homeworld."

Chills ripple through me. "This is the Maker home-world?"

They might've called themselves the Sha-Fen, but that means nothing to me. I imagine a handful of vessels setting out from here, and seeding their technology along the way. *Nobody* else in the galaxy knows this.

CHAPTER 29

The bot unlocks the door for us at the back of the vault.
It swings open, a seamless exit, and I never would've known it was there.

After talking to the machine a little more, Vel turns to me. "It will not accompany us. Its task is to guard this room, not explore what lies beyond."

That bodes well. Still, he cracks a torch-tube, and we set off into the darkness. There are no artificial lights here. This appears to be an underground tunnel, not dissimilar to the one Dace led us through. If there was some cataclysmic event, there may have been a time when the surface of this planet wasn't safe to travel on. The Makers would've gotten in the habit of building down, which explains their ruins on other worlds. By that point, it was custom, not necessity.

These walls are, unquestionably, ancient, but the stonework is anything but primitive. Even by the pale green gleam, the construction reveals real sophistication; this place was built to last—and it has. A chill rolls through me at the idea that we're the first in a thousand turns . . . or

more . . . to see what lies before us. I get the same feeling I
do just before a jump, full of anticipation.

"It's humbling," I say softly.

"You take my words. I do not feel worthy to be here."

I shake my head at that. "If *anyone* is, you are."

With his enhanced senses, Vel leads the way deeper into
the labyrinth, and the vault door closes behind us, leaving
us with only the glow of his shockstick. I follow for countless moments in silence, trying not to freak about the
weight of the stone. Are we still inside the building or has
this led down into the ground itself?

My heart races as I fight irrational fear. This reminds
me of being trapped in the *Sargasso*, though there's no
accompanying stench of burning meat. The last time I had
one of these trips, Doc talked me down, but he's gone now.
The wave of memory hits me like a tide, and the pain is
blinding.

*"Jax?" I can't see him, but I hear sympathy and under-
standing in his voice. "One step at a time. Closing your
eyes might help. Forget about the dark."*

*How embarrassing. He knows. Sirantha Jax, afraid of
the dark. Nonetheless I take his advice and squeeze my
eyelids shut. Feel my way down.*

*Somewhere along the way, I miss a rung, but I don't fall
far. Solid as a brick wall, Doc's placed to catch me. I think
he could hold a baby elephant. He holds me for a moment,
effortlessly, while we listen to the sky falling above us.*

*I'm sure it's just my imagination, but I swear I can hear
the rustle of wings. "Is this a good idea? I mean, don't the
Teras live underground?"*

*"Clan Dahlgren dug the bunkers," he assures me. "And
secured them. They don't connect to the natural caverns
where the Teras make their home."*

"If you say so."

*I remember what he said about magnesium mines. You
couldn't pay me enough to work down there. Or maybe it
was all automated, like some of the moon's mining facilities, just a skeleton crew to oversee and repair the droids.*

Doc sets me on my own feet and cracks a torch-tube. I've never been so glad to see chemicals mixing. Soon, the ambient light bathes our faces in a sickly yellow-green glow.

"I'm afraid your tests will have to wait."

Really? I thought you'd produce a pocket lab and cure me right now. *Somehow I manage not to snap at him. He's the only thing standing between me and madness down here.*

"Yeah, I gathered that. Where do these tunnels lead?"

"To the main bunker. It's a honeycomb down here, and unless you know the way, you could wander for days and never find the way in."

"I guess that's the idea." *I fall behind him, keeping one hand on his shoulder. I don't care if he thinks I'm touchy-feely, overly familiar, or just scared shitless. The latter is true, and he's seen me melt down before.*

"Exactly. This is our final fallback. They can reduce the compound to rubble, but they'll never find us." *He sounds so calm at the prospect of living for an undisclosed period of time belowground.*

The very idea makes me sweat. I can smell my fear, sour and sickly. My fingers trail along the sides of the tunnel as we move, puffs of powder drifting into the wan light. I fall quiet, listening to our footsteps scrape over the dry stone. Time slows, becomes impossible to measure.

Just Doc and me, surrounded by an island of night. I want to hide my face against his broad back. Instead, I walk on, trying to think of this as a test. If I come out of it unscathed, I'll be stronger.

At least there are no Morgut down here.

I come back to myself with some effort. That's the only thing the two occasions have in common—the dark and my irrational response to it.

I'm so sorry, Saul.

To distract myself from the guilt, I say, "I don't suppose you asked the bot if there's any food around here?"

"Of course. And there is not."

That makes sense, however grim the news. Machines don't eat. Unfortunately, the diversion doesn't last long, and my chest tightens painfully. Vel slows his pace and takes my hand. His claws are longer than my fingers and cool to the touch. The skin between the chitin feels rough, leathery, but the underside is thinner and softer. I don't remember if we've ever held hands like this before. His touches have been rare and guarded, but this is more; this is him offering a lifeline in the dark.

"Thank you."

He acknowledges my gratitude with a dismissive lift of one shoulder, a very human gesture, one he learned from Adele, I think. But I don't bring her up because we're in too scary a place, all the way around, to want to add emotional weight. The tunnel slants downward sharply, becoming more of a slide, and I balk.

He tugs. "I will protect you, Sirantha."

I'm touched, though I know he can't save me from my own fears: the darkness, the pressure of the stone over-head, or wherever the hell this ends. Though it feels like a bad idea, I follow, because there's no hope for survival behind us. All of the information in the world won't keep our bodies alive, and not even my nanites can repair dehy-dration and starvation. Shit, they have enough work on their hands trying to heal this bite.

"Good enough for me. I'm going." After all, there's no turning back.

As soon as I hit the top of the ramp, there's a peculiar lack of friction, as if this surface has been greased, and I can't control my descent at all. I slide into a fall, careening wildly into the darkness, tearing away from Vel. He calls out, but my speed has already put me ahead of him, and there's no way he can catch up. Whatever awaits us at the bottom, I'll face it first.

I slam into the wall and then there's a sharp turn before I spill onto level ground. The impact tears the wound in my side; warm blood trickles down my hip. *That's just what I need, an invitation to any predators lurking.* With some effort, I remind myself that there are no Morgut here. We're Mary knows how far from any known life, and that knowledge allows me to swallow the scream building in my throat.

"Vel?" I call.

Then I hear the noise of him slipping down after me. I try to scramble to the side, but he hits me full on, knocking me to the ground. *Shit*. His chitin really packs a punch. I whimper a little, and he rolls away with an apologetic click.

"Have I injured you?"

"No worse than I was. Where the hell are we?"

"Let me scan the area."

Thank Mary, we have functional tech again. After trying the primitive lifestyle, I've got to say that I prefer modern conveniences. His handheld hums in powering up, then glows; we have to be careful with the charge, so he can't keep it on constantly. Once it's gone, who knows when we can juice it up again? There are no charging stations around here, and the solar pack was fried when we went through the gate. I don't think he was able to replace that in the vault.

"It appears to be a system of catacombs."

"Isn't that where people buried their dead?"

"Some cultures," he admits.

Lovely. We walked away from a high-tech area for a tomb. I've been feeling like we made a mistake ever since we left the jungle, but there's no fixing it now. Sometimes, you have to push through the terrible stuff in order to find something better. I'll cling to the hope that's what we're doing.

CHAPTER 30

It's miserable down here.

The oppressive weight of stone is bad enough. I feel like I can't breathe, and the sensation only intensifies as we creep through dark stone passageways filled with bones. Oh, they're carefully tended and stowed in niches cut into the wall, but that doesn't help in the least, particularly when I note the distinct lack of humanity in their physiology. They aren't Mareq. Nothing I've ever seen before.

Right now, I'm passing through the dead heart of the Maker civilization. Nobody's been here since they left this world, however long ago that might have been. I can tell the truth of that from the thick dust on the ground.

After setting his pack down, Vel stops before one of the open tombs, studying the skeletal structure by the faint glow of his torch-tube. I have no words for how alien they are, but they took great care with their dead, as the remains have been arrayed with kingly care.

"I do not believe they were bipedal."

I've no idea how he discerns that, but I'm not arguing. I just want out of here before exhaustion, hunger, and sheer panic overwhelm me. My pulse pounds in my skull, and each new breath feels as though the oxygen has thinned.

"Let's keep moving," I say, my voice thready with fear.

He cuts me a sharp look, as if trying to determine what ails me, then turns back to the bones in abject fascination. "We cannot leave just yet," he says. "Think of what scientists can learn if they can extract a suitable DNA sample."

Before I can name any one of the hundred reasons I think this is a terrible idea, he reaches into the niche and plucks out a small, curved bone. The response is immediate; beneath our feet, the ground gives way. Desperately, I dive for the far side and catch hold of the stone lip, dangling with one hand as Vel disappears. The torch-tube bounces away into the darkness, leaving me alone with my ragged breathing and the fear of falling.

Inevitably, I think of Kai—and our last moments together—how I teased him.

Are you afraid of falling, baby?

No, I'm afraid of landing.

Oh, Mary, so am I. *Get to solid ground, Jax, and then look for Vel. He can't be dead. Not Vel. Oh, please, don't leave me alone.*

Each movement tears at the wound in my side, but I pull myself up, conscious of fresh blood dripping down my hip. Blindly, I feel for his pack and locate another torch-tube. Our last. I crack it without hesitation and shine it into the pit. At first, I see only the razor-sharp spikes that line the bottom. *The Makers hated grave robbers.* And then I spot Vel, clinging to the side about halfway down, his claws dug into the soft, crumbling stone.

"Sirantha," he says calmly, "I cannot support my weight in this fashion for long. Already my talons have begun to tear."

That sounds unimaginably painful. With a shuddering breath, I dig into his pack. I don't need to be told to look for a means to haul him up before he's crippled by loss of his claws, then impaled. Even my long-lived, damn-near-indestructible Ithtorian bounty hunter cannot survive that.

I must save him.

My hands are shaking, but at least I have something other than my fear of confined spaces to focus on. Now I'm terrified of losing him. I locate a thin, tensile cord that should be long enough to reach him, but I will need to anchor him and pull him up. I loop the rope around my waist and drop it down; once I do that, I inch backward until I can brace my feet solidly. There's nothing for me to hold on to down here, just stone walls and bones, so I have to be strong enough to bear his weight. No other options—failure isn't in my vocabulary.

"Can you climb?" I ask.

"Yes. Don't move, Sirantha."

When he grasps the cord, I stumble forward two steps, and Vel tumbles down farther, terrifyingly close to the spikes. His low curse, clicked in Ithtorian, shames me.

"I won't let you fall," I promise. "Give me a second."

The passage is narrow, so I throw my arms open, using the stone to brace. I won't let go this time. I won't budge. Slowly, I widen my stance.

"Ready?"

"Come up."

He crawls upward, using his claws as well as the cord. I hold steady, despite the unbearable strain. I'm bleeding profusely now, but I don't shift. Not even a millimeter. When I glimpse the top of his head and his arms above the pit, I lie down on my stomach and slide forward, reaching to pull him up.

By the time I get him on solid ground again, I'm shaking from head to toe. I wrap my arms around him and rest my head against the side of his face. He leans into me, and I feel tremors rocking him, too. Despite his constant composure, he's not immune to fear. He just puts on a good show to reassure me. Struck by this revelation, I wonder if this misadventure has been as frightening for him as it has me; he just didn't want to burden me with it. Conversely, the possibility that he's not utterly self-reliant bolsters me. I can be strong for someone else when the situation calls for it.

"How badly are you hurt?" I ask.

"I lost a claw."

"Will it grow back?"

"No. But when we return to civilization, I can acquire a prosthetic."

When, not if. I love him for saying that, even now. I love him, period. And I almost lost him. Shaking sets in. In a different way from March, different, yes, but not less. I love him.

"Don't scare me like that again," I say.

"I will do my best not to."

With the gaping hole behind us, we must go forward. Since I'd already decided that was the best course, I'm okay with that. I'm just glad I was on Vel's right when the pit opened up; that allowed me to scramble to the other side, which means we're not trapped down here.

"Will Nu-Skin seal your wound?"

"Yes."

"Then I'll treat you now if you patch up my side again."

"Gladly."

That exchange of care uses up the last of our medical supplies, however. I never thought I'd see him out of necessary goods, but we've reached the bottom. If we don't get out of here soon, we'll die. That's not histrionics or me being dramatic. It's a fact.

"I'm thinking maybe we don't want to touch anything else, if we can help it," I say with a hint of a smile.

"Agreed. But I still have the sample," Vel adds, as if that validates our near-death experience.

"You've no idea how relieved I am." My dry tone elicits a staccato series of clicks from him that I recognize as laughter. And that ability in him—to laugh in the face of certain death—prompts me to speak words I couldn't have imagined, turns before. "When we get out of here"—I, too, cling to *when*, not *if*—"I want you to wear my colors."

I carry his colors on my throat, a beautiful vine-and-thorn pattern he designed himself. He did it on Ithiss-Tor to protect me from repercussions in diplomatic circles. There, I overheard whispers of speculation from his people, wondering whether he had taken me as his partner in every sense. So I have an inkling what my acceptance meant—and what my request will mean to him.

I go on, bravely, considering his unresponsive stance. "You said once that we'd discuss it further if we both survived the war."

"I did. And we did."

"We're going to beat this, too," I say firmly. "So will you?"

His weighty silence makes me wonder if I should've asked questions first. Maybe I'm leaping without looking again, and being stupid or offensive. Mary knows I don't want to hurt Vel.

"Do you understand what it means?" he asks at last.

"It's a statement of partnership and trust." That much, I heard from the merchants on Ithiss-Tor. I know it can't be a romantic thing because the Ithtorians don't bond in that way. They act for dynastic value, so I'm honestly not sure what connotation it would have between Vel and me.

"It is also a promise that we will be together always. And . . . rare for an Ithtorian, to take colors for a single person instead of honors granted by his house."

"I'm willing to pledge that. After all we've been through together, I can't imagine my life otherwise."

He considers for long moments, his face illuminated by the pale green glow. "Nor can I."

This means he's willing to watch me age and die. That will be unspeakably painful for him, but I won't send him away as Adele did. I'm too selfish for that.

Vel seals the bargain by brushing the side of his face against mine, first time he's done that. I touch the hinge of his mandible in the dark, wondering how I can feel so safe down here among the ancient dead.

The answer's simple. He is with me.

I push to my feet. "Come on, let's get out of here. There's got to be food and water somewhere on this Mary-forsaken world."

"And an end to our journey."

I nod. We'll find that damn gate soon.

Jax,

I have no idea if you'll ever get this message, but I couldn't leave without any word at all. I don't know if the Mareq female I left this with will give it to you or if she'll throw it away as soon as my back is turned. We're doing a little better at communicating with them, but it's slow going.

I just heard from the authorities on Nicu Tertius. They've found my nephew. He's in a state-run home, but he's become a problem, and they're discussing the possibility of neutralizing him. It's an advanced form of lobotomy that takes away all Psi ability. I can't let that happen.

So I've had to choose between searching for you and going to help Sasha. That's his name, by the way. It was the one request of Svet's that they honored; they kept the name she gave him.

The fact that I'm writing this probably tells you all you need to know. I looked for six months, Jax, nonstop. Six months, I spent on Marakeq, slogging through the swamp looking for you. I found no sign. I wish I could say it makes me feel better knowing you're with Vel, wherever you are, but I'm small enough that it doesn't. All I know is that you aren't with me, and I'm losing my mind, wondering if you're safe. I know you'd send word if you could, so the situation must be dire. Anyway, I'm leaving Marakeq today. You have my comm code . . . I still have the same flat. I've been paying the rent while I was here, looking for you. If you come back, that's where you can find me.

Love and miss you, always.
March

CHAPTER 31

Light.

Just when I can't walk another step, I see it glimmering ahead. Our final torch-tube burned out long ago, but this glow is different. It's sweet and pale, like the first glimmer at dawn. I increase my pace until I'm running, only vaguely noticing that the incline slopes upward, as if we're going aboveground at last.

The tunnel opens in a hillside covered with verdant growth. This is a different aspect of the planet—neither the hungry jungle nor the dry wasteland—but a gentler clime that permits more familiar flora to thrive. If Mary is kind, we'll find a gate somewhere nearby, and we can end this exile. I've lost all certainty of how long we've been gone. Days and nights have blurred together, and privation takes its toll, but if I haven't lost count entirely, it's been three weeks to a month.

I inhale deeply through my nose, delighting in the fresh air. Beside me, Vel scans the surrounding area, looking for toxins and large predators. He lowers his handheld and points off into the distance.

"There is a settlement that way. And I detect a power source similar to the gate we used on Marakeq."

That's the best news I've heard in forever. But things get better still when we climb down the hill and find a narrow stream running among the rocks. My throat is so dry at this point that it hurts to talk. Without waiting for Vel to scan, I kneel and drink from my cupped palms. I'll take my chances with local parasites over a painful death from dehydration. He's a little more cautious and takes some readings before doing likewise.

"It's safe?" I ask.

"You had better hope so." Amusement threads his words.

"Yeah, yeah."

After further exploration, he finds some fruit and roots that should be safe for us both to eat. The former is bitter and green, but it's so much better than nothing that I don't complain about the taste. It takes me fifteen minutes to chew down a root; it's clearly not meant for human teeth. Vel has no such trouble, grinding it with his mandible. I feel better almost immediately.

"To the settlement?"

I nod. Sleep sounds divine, but maybe we can rest in a more comfortable locale. Excitement pounds in my veins. These might be descendants of the Makers. How amazing would that be? I quicken my step, trusting Vel to keep pace, and soon we close the distance. I'm shocked to see familiar moss-covered mounds in the distance. This looks quite a bit like the Mareq village.

"Perhaps a few Mareq activated the gate, as we did," Vel offers.

That seems most likely. But—

"If there was a return gate nearby, wouldn't they have figured out how to get back?" *And not still be here*.

"One problem at a time, Sirantha."

Yeah, he's right. At least we have food and water now, and we're out of that hellish hole. And overall, it's a lucky break for us. Unless their language has evolved beyond all recognition, we should be able to communicate with them.

The trek passes in near silence, and it's all downhill, another mercy. Just as I'm thinking things have shifted for the better, two creatures come up the hill toward us. They bear some resemblance to the Mareq we know, but they've lost the oversized heads and the bulging eyes. These alt-Mareq are more streamlined and muscular, as if they've had to fight to survive here. That doesn't bode well for us.

One of them speaks in quick, rhythmic croaks, but my chip can't interpret it. Not yet anyway. *Shit*. Their language *has* changed.

There's no mistaking their meaning when they draw weapons on us. Not primitive ones, either. It must be salvaged Maker technology because it looks like a pistol of some kind, but I can only imagine the kind of death it deals. We could fight, but that would guarantee hostility from the rest of the village, and there are only two of us. We can't fight a war on our own. I exchange a glance with Vel, who inclines his head, silently counseling surrender.

The smaller one approaches to bind our wrists with a thin razor cord; struggling against this would slit my wrists. They confiscate Vel's pack though there isn't much in it anymore. I'm sorry to lose the handheld, and, by his expression, he is, too.

Then the other gestures down the hill toward the settlement. We are, unquestionably, being taken hostage. I suppose I should be grateful that they didn't shoot us on sight, but maybe they're used to beings wandering through the gates and turning up here. Their town may be more diverse than we expect.

A hard shove gets me moving, as if I doubt their intentions. But even with the language barrier, I understand what I'm meant to do; I start walking.

It isn't far to the village proper, and once we reach it, they drag us through an interested crowd of onlookers to a mound that has clearly been designated as a prison. It's smaller than the others, and the door is different—well, the fact that it has a door. The others offer freedom and open space instead.

Our captors push us within, where it reeks of bodily waste and old food. There isn't enough room for us to stand upright, so I drop down and lean back against the dirt wall. This time, there is no cozy bed to sleep on, just mud and a whisper of white that could be bone, but I hope it's not. It would be kinder to kill intruders than leave them here to a slow death.

"On a scale of one to ten, how fragged are we?" I ask tiredly.

"That depends on their intentions."

I offer a wry smile. "Let's pretend they're planning us a party."

"Will there be choclaste?"

"You're so cruel." My mouth waters.

Though it seems unlikely under the circumstances, I'm so exhausted and weakened from the journey that I pass out as much as fall asleep. I wake with Vel's injured claw atop my head. At first I don't know why he's bothering me until I hear the footsteps drawing closer. Someone is coming to check on us. Or execute us. Either way, it means a change.

This time, it's a different alt-Mareq, a female I think, by her size and markings. She's heavy with eggs, and she croaks at us in inquiry. Unfortunately, my chip offers gibberish in place of a true translation: *Want run fly target hope fall off?*

No, not really. *Switching to Mareq,* I tell my chip, and then answer without any hope of being understood. "We came through a gate. We just want to go home."

To my astonishment, she cocks her smooth, green head, and studies me. *Hm. I wonder if she got any of that.*

She replies, "Come portal?"

"Yes."

"From Faraway Broken," she tells me.

I have no idea if we're actually communicating, but I'm encouraged to keep at it. My chip is the advanced kind, which learns, the more it hears of a new language. It doesn't offer immediate perfect comprehension, but if I can keep the natives from killing us while it trains to local nuance, we may have a shot, here.

"Yes. Need near gate, not broken. Know one?" It seems best to keep my sentences short and simple, less chance of the vocalizer going insanely awry.

She makes an angry, negative sound. "Only Close Broken."

Shit. None of the return gates work? We are so fragged.

She leaves then, but a short while later, a packet of food is shoved in through a slot at the bottom of the door. The roots have worn off by this point, so I unwrap it to look at what they've given us. Some kind of meat, it looks like, so these creatures are not herbivores like the ones on Mara-keq. There are also tubers, greens, and some gray pasty stuff, along with simple water.

"It seems unlikely they intend to kill us," Vel says. "Or they would not bother feeding us."

He takes up some of the meat and downs it without visible difficulty. I haven't eaten real meat often—only that time on Venice Minor—and I don't know the nutritional value of these others foods. A protein deficit at this point could be disastrous, so I hold my nose and force the flesh down. It sits uneasily in my stomach, and I whimper, trying not to picture what I've just eaten.

Time passes. I'd lose track, except they give us a new packet of food each morning, and I note the arrival on the wall beside me. On the fourth day, a small alt-Mareq male steps into the hut with us. He bears some interesting implements, which look like a knife, a scanner, and something I've never seen before.

He explains, "Fix smelly female," before setting to work.

That's more sense than I've gotten from any of them yet. He uses all three tools on me, and I scream while he burns the infection out. It requires Vel holding me for the Mareq healer to finish the job, and I'm weeping by the time the wound seals. Afterward, Vel pets my hair with his claws until the shaking stops.

We wait more. Ten meals. And marks. If my poor count holds true, we've been stranded here six weeks. Dina and

Hit must be petrified. Now I bear a nasty, puckered scar in the shape of the creature's teeth, and since the Mareq worked on me, I've shaken the fever that's plagued me since the attack in the jungle.

"How's your hand?" I ask Vel.

He peels off the dirty Nu-Skin to show me the blunt tip, where his claw once grew. But the gouge where it ripped free has sealed over cleanly.

"On Ithiss-Tor, I would be cut in caste for such a disfigurement," he says quietly.

"Even with a prosthesis?"

He nods, but before he can say more, I hear footsteps, and it's not mealtime. Hopefully, this means they've come to some decision about what to do with us. If they haven't, Mary help them.

Because I'm Sirantha Jax, and I have had enough.

CHAPTER 32

We're escorted to the town hall, though it's just a large mound. The alt-Mareq eye us as we enter, but I can't interpret their expressions. I wasn't among the regular Mareq long enough to learn their body language, as I can read Vel's, and these aren't the same peaceable creatures we left on Marakeq.

There are too many of them talking at once for my chip to distinguish any words. Consequently, I hear only croaking en masse, no distinct meanings. This appears to be a judgment of some kind, though, as I'm brought to stand before a committee of seven: three males, four females. Their colors are all lighter than the others, which makes me think they're older—that and the baggy skin around the throat. Some signs of aging are universal.

They motion the others to silence with wide, sweeping gestures from their webbed hands. Soon it's quiet enough in here that I can hear my own breathing. That's not a good sign, especially the way I'm laboring; I sound nervous even to my own ears. Not surprising, that, given they hold our lives in their hands.

The female who visited us has laid her eggs since we last saw her. She's leaner now, and more vicious-looking. In one hand, she bears a weapon similar to the one they trained on us before. She comes to a halt before Vel and me, surveying us from head to toe. I know we're filthy, and we smell disgusting. Mary, we did *before* they locked us up.

"Talk," she says. Or at least, that's what my translation chip claims. "Not killing, it might know some useful thing."

Hard to say if that's a statement or a question, but I'll try to know some useful thing if it keeps us alive a little longer. "About what?"

"Close Broken gate."

"Take us to it. Maybe we can fix it." That's quite a gamble. But honestly, we can't worsen our plight at this juncture.

More rumbles and croaks, so that I lose the meaning. Vel doesn't seem to be having any better luck processing the group discussion. Eventually, I make out one word from the elders:

Go.

Please let that mean we're going to the gate.

"Follow," the warrior female orders.

I comply, not only because she's jabbing her weapon between my shoulder blades. From here, I move out of the assembly mound and out of the village. It's a forced march, probably less than two kilometers from the village. The gate sits atop a hill like some kind of ancient temple, and unlike the pad where we came through, the structure's intact, including arch and crystals. The bottom is paved in the same black stones I noticed on Marakeq.

"Near Broken gate," she says, pointing at it with a flourish.

But it doesn't look busted like the first one we saw here. Keeping an eye on her weapon, I edge a little closer for a better look. Yeah, it's the same in every respect, and I cast back to when we fell through. What the hell happened, exactly?

"Do you remember how we activated it?" I ask Vel, low.

Depressingly enough, he shakes his head. To the best of

my recollection, I just stepped on the pad while Vel was examining the crystals. Which we haven't done yet. The lights in the crystals are still dim, so I guess that means we're not close enough. The lights came on first, before anything more interesting happened.

If this gate works like its twin, then our proximity and weight on the pad should activate the mechanism. I'm guessing it recognizes something in our DNA. Big if. The question is, will she-with-the-gun shoot us if we step onto it? I motion Vel toward the crystals, and he gets it at once.

After taking a deep breath, I step forward as he moves into the position, and the crystals click to life, one by one, a dazzling glow even in daylight. The Mareq warrior behind us croaks out a protest:

"Broken!" she insists, even as the lightning kindles between the upthrust arms of the arch. She seems to have forgotten her weapon, wide mouth hanging open.

"Not for us," I say.

Violet energy ebbs and flows madly, creating the pocket maelstrom that sucked us through before. I hope to Mary these gates don't have multiple stops. *Come on, right back where we came from. Come* on.

The universe grants my wish in a violent twist, dissolving my being in a fashion that's now familiar to me. Sickness swirls through me, though I lack any sort of a body to encompass it. I can't feel my hands anymore, and the last thing I see with eyes that aren't eyes any longer is the strange Mareq female fighting not to be pulled into the vortex. But she falls, as we do, into the endless darkness.

Numbness ripens into pain when I land, hard, on the other pad. I recognize this one. We came from here. *Thank Mary. Oh, thank you. We made it back.*

The crystals flicker on our arrival, but they don't power up. I guess they know the difference between coming and going. Just to be safe, I crawl off the pad as soon as I can control my arms and legs again, then collapse against the wall. The way out is pretty simple, and I think I can find the Mareq village. This time, Vel shakes it off faster than I do, bless his adaptive Ithtorian physiology, but the alt-Mareq female makes a noise that sounds like weeping, low and hopeless and without end.

I try to comfort her, but she slaps me away and shoots me in the face. Or, at least, she tries to. She doesn't realize that the gate fries technology, a serious drawback in any transportation system. So it leaves her weapon clicking in her hand instead of killing me like it's supposed to. In absolute rage, she hurls the thing at my head, and I slide sideways.

Soon enough, I climb to my feet. Just a little farther, and we'll be done with this fragging planet. I've spent enough time here to last a lifetime. Vel's already waiting by the far end of the sunken room, ready to put this disaster behind us.

When it becomes clear to her that we're heading out, she staggers upright and pleads, "Not to leave behind."

With a faint sigh, I motion her onward. She can live among the native Mareq, from whom her people come; I have no doubt. Right now I don't care, either. I just want off this rock. Once more, doing the right thing had unforeseen consequences. Still, despite the hardship and fear, I'm not sorry I brought Baby-Z2—Zeeka—home.

The return journey passes quickly because I'm running. This swamp holds no horror for me, compared to where we've been. The other two follow close behind.

At first, I don't notice the changes because I'm in such a hurry, but as we get closer to the village, I can see that the undergrowth has been cut back, creating a definite road that wasn't here before. I cast a glance at Vel, who's noticed it, too. There are score marks on the trees from laser fire, as if someone was determined to burn a path.

"How long were we gone?" I ask softly.

He lifts one shoulder in a mute shrug. *Hard to say.* I don't stop to ponder the number of trees that have been removed, however. I keep moving toward the settlement, which has changed as much as the surrounding swamp.

There's a definite modern presence here now, bits of technology that might've come from our ship. A metal shard stands in the middle of the green, a comm tower, if I don't mistake its purpose. Unease crawls through me, but I'm sure Dina's been out to look for us. It may have been as long as a month or two; she's gonna be so mad when we finally see her again. I don't know whether she'll punch me or hug me. Probably both in quick succession. Before I can decide whether to hike to the ship right away, the natives take the choice from me.

The villagers greet us with a glad hue and cry, Dace leading them. Somehow, she doesn't seem surprised to see us. She greets us with open arms and a bump of her chest. I gather that's something like a hug. I stumble a few steps in answer to her exuberance.

"The door to otherness is unlocked," she proclaims. "The prophecy of Oonan has come to pass. Long live Jax Oonan!"

What the hell?

"Explain," I demand.

"The star-walkers own the otherness doors. We walk them only with our masters."

So the Mareq were, long ago, enslaved to the Makers? That's my best guess.

"Will they work for you now?"

"It is promised."

A cheer goes through the village, terrifying our alt-Mareq companion. The warrior cringes behind us, much as I would if confronted with a specter from mankind's evolutionary past. Others push closer, touching her skin to see if it's sleeker than theirs. They gasp and marvel while she whimpers with discomfort.

"I don't think she likes that," I warn them.

To my surprise, the Mareq back off immediately, and the female quivers, taking a step farther away. I understand her culture shock; this has to seem so surreal. One minute she's in her own place, minding her business, and the next, she's *here*. I get that displacement from the ground up.

"Dace, I have a ton of questions for you, but right now, Vel and I need something to eat and a place to sleep. We'll head for the ship tomorrow."

"The flying boat is gone," Dace tells me.

A cold shock runs down my spine. "Gone where?"

"For many turns now," she answers. "Gone up above the rains. But I knew you would return, for it is written."

Many turns? Surely she doesn't mean turns in the way I do. This must be the chip screwing with me.

"Just how many 'turns' were we missing?"

A puzzled silence falls in response. They don't count as we do. They just do "few" or "many" and in conjunction with the simplicity of their lives, it works for them just fine. For Vel and me, this could be catastrophic. I really need to know how long we've been gone.

Dace hands me a dirty, crumpled piece of paper. Curiously, I unfold it and see March's handwriting. I read the message and dread curls through me. *He searched for six months. How long has it been? Mother Mary of Anabolic Grace.* As if in answer to my silent horror, the female warrior we brought from the other world drops to her knees and weeps.

CHAPTER 33

In the morning, once all my physical needs are tended, I fire up the comm tower. It looks like our exit won't be instantaneous, but that's fine. Now that we're back in the village, I can muster a little more patience. Our ride should be arriving in the next week, once Dina gets the emergency signal on the bounce.

"Do you still have the bone?" I ask Vel.

I'd hate like hell for our trip to be pointless. Bringing back proof of the ancients and the ruins we found renders our journey invaluable.

He inclines his head. "I also have a substantial amount of data I downloaded from the vault."

"It didn't fry on the return trip?"

"I have an internal data spike. The technology in our bodies was protected in passage."

Yeah, that's true, but I didn't know about that piece of hardware. So flesh provides a protective cushion. Good to know . . . not that I plan on making that trip again anytime soon. If I did, I'd look for a way to pad our gizmos so they worked from the start, but that's a disturbing mental image, a handheld cushioned in a meat pocket. I shudder a little.

"What do you plan to do with it?"

"After I take the first look, I shall auction it off to the highest bidder."

That surprises a chuckle out of me. I shouldn't be shocked. I mean, how else did he build a vast personal fortune? He's not an altruist.

"So what do you make of the Mareq response to all this?" I ask.

He considers. "I believe they had a legend, and you fit the profile."

"You mean I'm *not* Jax Oonan?" I clutch my chest in feigned disappointment.

"I suspect any sentient being that activated the gates would do."

"About that . . ."

He knows me well enough to guess the unfinished question. "This is pure conjecture, but I think the Makers locked the gate so their servants would not be able to travel as they did."

"But they respond to any other signature?" It's a simple answer, and maybe the only one we'll ever get. It's not like the Makers can pop out of extinction and explain their ten-thousand-turn-old plans.

"Or perhaps one of us carries traces of Maker DNA," he says.

"It must be you. Humans are the new kids on the block in galactic terms."

Vel lifts one shoulder. "It is possible."

"So you're actually Vel Oonan. I'll tell Dace."

A little click of laughter. "Do not dare, Sirantha."

Later, I check the comm tower to make sure it's giving off a strong emergency beacon. As the days pass, I keep an eye on the heavens with every bit as much anticipation as the natives. I use my time to help the alt-Mareq warrior integrate with the others. It helps that she doesn't have

more advanced weapons to assert her will, so like us, on
her turf, she has little choice but to make nice and learn
their language. I facilitate that as best I can, though it's an
imperfect process.

In time, I bet they'll figure out how to pass back and forth,
open lines of trade, somehow. But that's not my worry. I just
want off this mudhole and to find March.

The fourth morning after our return, a young male
Mareq approaches. He is slim and tall, with bold markings
to proclaim his youth, a handsome specimen of their people, at least so far as I can tell. He holds his hands in a
warm greeting, as if I should know him, and he bumps his
chest gently against mine. Such familiarity startles me, but
I almost feel as if I should recognize him.

Switching to Mareq, I tell the chip.

"Good day," I say cautiously.

"You do not know me." It's not a question.

Mary knows I don't want to offend him. Maybe we
danced with him at the celebration, so long ago now,
though I'm *still* not sure how long exactly. "I feel as though
I should."

"I am Zeeka."

I puff out a surprised breath, and for long moments, I
can't process it. We were gone long enough for him to *grow
up,* though to Vel and me, it only seemed like a few months,
at most. I don't know how long it takes for a Mareq to reach
maturity; maybe they have a short life cycle. I can hardly
accept the idea that I'm talking to Baby-Z2. Wonder and
gratitude spill through me.

He takes my silence for encouragement and goes on,
"You took me out into the singing stars, where I fell into
the void. And then you brought me back again, carried me
home to my mother's arms. You are Jax Oonan, of whom
much has been sung, and I am destined to leave with you.
My destiny lies out there."

Zeeka glances up at the eternal twilight of the Marakeq
sky, but he sees the star-studded darkness above—or
maybe it's more accurate to say he remembers, although I

don't understand how that's possible. The Mareq are wondrous beings.

"You want to leave with us?" I ask, astonished. "Will Dace allow it?"

"I am a sovereign creature now." I get the sense that my chip didn't translate perfectly, but I get the gist. It's *My mom can't say no because I'm a big boy.*

"What will you do out there?" I can't take him on as a dependent. I just can't.

"Learn your trade."

The first Mareq jumper? I don't even know if he's got the J-gene. From Fugitive scientist data, Doc posited that the Mareq owned a genetic quality that could aid in longevity for navigators, but I have no clue whether they have the potential themselves. It's not like you can tell with one look, either, as you can in humans. Like the Rodeisians, Mareq eye color tends to be uniform, a muddy brown, and it will require some tests in order to determine whether Zeeka can realize his dream.

I make a swift decision. "You can come with me as far as Gehenna. I can get you tested there. If you don't have the J-gene, then I'm sending you home."

My vocalizer has some trouble with those concepts because Zeeka cocks his head, trying to decipher what I've said. "You will test me? If I fail, I must go home."

Close enough. "Does that sound fair?"

"Yes, Jax Oonan."

I really must read these writings about Oonan. When Dace said the prophecies of Oonan, I guessed that was some old Mareq prophet, but it appears they think *I* am Oonan, and the person who wrote all this stuff down didn't get remembered by name. For a moment, I'm tempted to set the record straight; as a member of the older starfaring race, it's probably Vel who triggered the gate, but he asked me not to, and I have more pressing matters to attend to right now, such as breaking up a fight between our gate-traveling alt-Mareq and the throat-flushed male who finds her fascinating.

On the eighth day, lights appear in the sky. It can mean only one thing.

Rescue.

Quickly, I speak my farewells and thank Dace for everything. She responds with a regal nod. "Protect my son."

Then she gives him a bundle of items that will do him little good where we're going; the Mareq youngling vibrates with excitement. Vel and I gather our things, slight though our belongings may be, and hike toward the landing site. Halfway there, I pause. Hit is a skilled pilot, but if we're standing where she's trying to put the ship, that won't end well. Vel monitors their progress, and when he gives me the all clear, I take off again at a dead run.

As we break from the swamp into the clearing, I recognize the *Big Bad Sue*, even from fifty meters away. The hatch opens, and Dina steps out. Her hair is a lot longer, spilling nearly to her waist, and as I draw closer, I see the signs of time on her face: new lines framing her eyes and mouth. The question haunts me anew: *How long were we gone?*

"What the frag happened?" she demands, sweeping me into a fierce hug. "Where *were* you?"

"It's a long story. Could we get off this rock before I tell it?"

"Sure." She pauses, angling her head to study me. "You don't look any different, bitch. How's that possible?"

"Has it been so long?" Vel asks.

"Five turns." She glances at the Mareq. "And who's this?"

She's not going to believe it. "Baby-Z2. But he prefers to be called Zeeka."

For once, the blond mechanic is speechless. And then she manages, "No shit. Well, let's get inside. Hit and Argus are waiting in the cockpit. They didn't figure you'd want to linger on world, after being lost so long."

"You got that right," I mutter, still reeling from her revelation.

Five turns. March must've given me up for dead and

moved on by now. There's a cold dread building in my stomach. For the last five turns, he's been settled and raising his sister's son. Sasha, the note said. *Oh, Mary. What a fragging mess.*

"Dace didn't tell you where she sent us?" I ask.

Dina shakes her head. "It took us ages to communicate with them at all. I had a chip put in, but it was slow going. And then she would only say *Jax Oonan is destined to open the door and return in her own time.* I wanted to pound her, but Hit said that wouldn't help anything."

We head inside the ship with our would-be Mareq jumper craning his neck to examine all of the technological marvels. He's seen it all before, and I wonder how much of that he remembers. Vel follows quietly, probably processing the idea that it's been so long since Adele died, even though it has to feel fresh for him. We're out of step with the normal world now, and I don't know what to do about that. But there are practical concerns to address now; I head for the hub and show Zeeka how to strap in.

"Where to?" Dina asks.

"Gehenna. Zeeka here wants to become a jumper, but I don't know if he has the J-gene."

"So you want Carvati to check him out," she guesses, buckling in across the way. Once she's done so, she touches the comm unit on her wrist. "All passengers aboard, love. We're clear to depart, destination Gehenna."

Hit's voice comes through loud and clear. "Glad to hear it. Welcome back, Jax. I thought you might've died down there."

"I knew you didn't," Argus puts in. "You're going to die in some memorable, glorious fashion, many turns from now."

I wish I had his confidence.

Dina adds, "I'll let March know where we'll be. He made me promise."

I don't know if I'm up to facing him. Mary knows I've longed for him, but I've been gone so long. It seems wrong now to turn up like an unlucky specter, reminding him of the life he left behind. The irony doesn't escape me that I once tried to build a life without him—and now he's done that without me, away from the stars, away from grim-space. Some would say this is karma biting me in the ass.

The rumble of the engines comes first, then the sweet lift that carries us far from the endless green swamp that is Marakeq, but I don't know if it's possible to get back to where I was before, and furthermore, I don't know if I should try.

Maybe he's better off without me.

CHAPTER 34

Gehenna hasn't changed.

Five turns isn't a long time for the dome city, I suppose. Part of its charm is that it doesn't shift. There are no gorgeous sunsets or sunrises, only the endless titian swirl of the gases in the sky above. Today they are especially dramatic with bursts of red and orange, mingled with paler cream. Zeeka stares up, mute with wonder.

I have to translate any conversation that occurs for him, which means he needs a chip and a vocalizer, as soon as possible, if he qualifies as a jumper according to Carvati's tests.

Mentally I switch to Mareq, and say, "Pretty amazing, isn't it?"

"I was reborn here," he answers.

True enough. But how remarkable he knows that.

The *Big Bad Sue* passes all the locks without difficulty, and soon we disembark at the spaceport. I watch Zeeka to make sure he's not overwhelmed by it all, but he appears entranced rather than terrified. Hit leads us through the customary searches with a minimum of fuss, then we look for a place to stay near the market, which is colorful, as always, full of diaphanous fabrics and belly jewels, totemic carvings and sacred kirpan. That much has not changed, but the air is smoky today, full of burning kosh. It makes my eyes water. I remember when I lived here before, how I would come to the market to shop before I began my shift at Hidden Rue. Old thoughts fill my head.

It's like penance. There's a reason I ended up here. I didn't do right by Baby-Z, so I'll make it up as best I can. It's not what I'd choose to do, but I don't even know what that would be. The most important thing is that I'm accomplishing it by myself.

As I turn to leave the market, an old woman catches me by the arm. "Your shadow troubles you."

I expect to find a fortune-teller soliciting me, reading cards or bones or peering into a cup to glimpse my future in sodden leaves. But this woman is simply garbed in black; she might be a cook or a housekeeper, certainly someone's grandmother, for her back is bent and her face withered.

"My shadow's fine," I reply with a frown.

"She is not," the stranger insists. "She has gone away and dreams another dream. You shift what lives inside your skin until she does not know you. And without her, I do not know how you will face this destiny hanging on you. So many ghosts walk behind you, so many ghosts . . ." She shakes her head and sighs. "I will light a candle for you at Mary's shrine."

At that she releases my arm, and I expect her to ask me to pay for her blessing or insight, but she merely wraps her black shawl around her head and hurries on, as if she's tarried too long.

This feels as if things have come full circle. In guilt over what happened to Baby-Z, I fled to Gehenna to seek my own path, and now, here Zeeka stands, gazing around at all the marvels. Aliens are common enough in the dome that he's not drawing undue attention. I suspect people don't realize he's the first Mareq to travel thus, or he'd be bombarded with attention from the paparazzi.

Then I realize why I've got that old woman in my head; she's watching me from across the market. She's even more stooped and wizened than she was when she accosted me, a black shawl wound around her slight body. I murmur an excuse and cut across to meet her. She stands patiently, as if she expected me.

"Good day," I say, for that's the accepted greeting on Gehenna, where there are neither nights nor mornings. "Do you remember me?"

"Should I?" Maybe my mind's playing tricks on me. I mutter an apology and turn, but her voice stops me. "You found your shadow, and you faced your destiny, and came out stronger on the other side. But at what cost, Sirantha Jax? At what cost? Yet you are nearly to the end of your road, so have no fear."

Nearly at the end of my road. What does that mean? I wonder if she's saying I'm going to die soon. It would almost be a respite at this point. I don't know if I'm ready, but I am *so* fragging tired.

I spin to question her, but there's only a vendor selling lovely, hand-painted fans. She raises a brow at me, but I shake my head and return to the others. After chiding me for wandering off, Hit finds us a berth for the night, a hostel with a club attached; their musicians are paid to provide an appealing background, not make conversation impossible. Mikhail's is a sophisticated establishment, known for good food, expensive wine, and quiet entertainment, making it a rarity in Gehenna; dark faux-wood and wine red upholstery adds to the upscale ambience.

In the warm amber light, I study my companions. Hit shows the least signs of aging; her dark skin looks much the same, her features strong and elegant. I realize I have no idea how old she is. Argus, too, has changed since I saw him on New Terra; he's a man now, not an eager boy. His shoulders are broad, and he's lost the hint of gangly youth. From what he said on the way from the port, he spent the last five turns working with Dina and Hit as their navigator, and he wears that experience in the form of a little swagger in his stride that makes women turn as he passes.

"Is there anyone special?" I ask him, over drinks.

Argus shakes his head. "Not since Esme."

He's not as carefree as he seems, then. The memory of the girl he lost haunts him still. First love can hit you like that, though for me it's the loves who came after Sebastian that have caused me the most pain.

For the first time, I understand something of what it must be like for Vel, watching everything change around you while you remain the same. It isn't a blessing as some people would imply; it's a curse. Anyone who wished for immortality is out of his head, as it means constant loss.

"So you just vanished," Dina says eventually. "You want to tell me how that happened? We searched for ages before leaving the beacon in case you found your way back to the village."

If they hadn't, Vel and I would've been stranded on Marakeq until the next ship arrived, which could've been a hundred turns. I might've died there. A cold shudder works through me.

"Thanks for that. You saved our asses."

Dina smirks. "Like usual."

After the food arrives, I tell our story. That carries us through until the desserts. The others listen with silent astonishment, interjecting only the occasional question. I don't think Zeeka is paying any attention at all; he's too busy soaking everything in.

"The Makers," Argus says, shaking his head in wonder. "You're going to be famous. Well. *More* famous."

Just what I need.

"Bidding on the Maker sample is up to ten million credits," Vel puts in.

Hit shakes her head. "You're gonna want find somewhere safe to put that stuff. It's not worth your life, and collectors would absolutely kill for it."

I grin at her. "You'd know."

Later, as we're all mellow from the drinks, of course, Dina asks, "Can I see your scar?"

In answer, I pull my shirt up and show her the bite mark. "Satisfied?"

"I can't believe you survived," Argus says softly.

"I have Vel to thank for that."

"And I would not be here if not for Sirantha."

The mechanic glances between us, a frown building, but she doesn't speak of whatever conclusions she draws. Instead, she says, "In the morning, we'll go see Carvati." After a moment, she adds, "You should expect March in the next few days, as soon as he can hop a ship."

"He hasn't moved on?" I ask softly.

Her eyes widen. "Did you think he ever would?"

Hurt and gladness tangle together, until I don't know what I feel or what I want. At this point, I might as well wait to see him in person. I need to send him a message, but if he's already en route, my vid-mail will bounce past him. Frag, I have no idea what to say to him. I've missed him, but it hasn't been turns in my head, so we're coming at this separation from different perspectives. For me, it felt like longer while he was fighting on Lachion, but my perception isn't the truth. On the other side of that gate, Vel and I parted company from the world we knew.

"So how's everyone else?" By that, I encompass a number of mutual friends.

"Surge and Kora aren't on Emry anymore," Dina says.

"Oh?" That's right; they were staying for Siri, but the kid must be pretty old by now.

"You missed her vision quest. I had to do it without you." Her tone grows somber. "That, more than anything, made me think you must be dead."

Shit. We were named godmothers of the child we helped deliver on board ship on the way to Emry Station. I had been on the docket to take Sirina into the wilderness with Dina in some Rodeisian cultural tradition. Instead, I had been trapped on the other side of the gate while life went on without me.

"What was it like?" I ignore what she said about my premature death.

Smiling faintly, Dina explains how she spent three days roughing it while the girl chanted and danced. It didn't seem spiritual to her, I guess, but I'm sure she was properly respectful of the tradition. I wonder if she thought of me through those days, if she thought, *Mary curse it, Jax is supposed to* be *here for this.* By the shadow in her green eyes, she missed me. Mourned me. And I don't know what to say.

"I have something for you," she adds.

"Oh?"

In reply, she hands me a data spike. I stare at it with a question in my eyes. "Research?"

Dina shakes her head. "It's Constance. When Surge and Kora left Emry, her duties ended. No more troops to train. So she asked them to download her, and they brought her to me."

"Why didn't you install her in the *Big Bad Sue* or get her a new body?"

"Because she's *yours*, Jax."

Huh. So Constance will be going with me to La'heng. Maybe I can find a body for her there. Surely there will be some Pretty Robotics salvage.

"Thank you. This means a lot."

"Anytime."

From there, we talk a little more about people we know. Share stories about some of the missions that Hit, Argus, and Dina have run.

"It's fragging weird without March," the mechanic says. "But he can't be budged from Nicuan. I tried to tempt him with a big job not long ago."

Hit nods. "He laughed. Said he was done with that life."

I'm left with a knot in my throat as I wonder what else he's done with. Despite Dina's reassurance, I won't believe there's anything left between us until I see him. Idle conversation carries us along for another hour, and then it's beyond time for me to crash. The others speak their good nights, and I see Zeeka to his room.

The bed puzzles him. "No moss?" he asks.

"Nope. Make the best of it."

"This is part of the test," he croaks.

"Sure. G'day, Z."

I have a hard time believing we're back, and I'm not used to being alone. For that entire ordeal, Vel stood beside me, and I feel like I need to see him before I can fall asleep. My steps carry me to his door, then I wonder if this is a dumb idea.

He opens it before I signal. "The bot told me you were here."

Not a psychic connection, then. Just as well—I can only handle one of those. "May I come in?"

"Certainly." He steps back so I can.

"It's weird, isn't it?"

"It does not feel altogether real," he admits.

"Have you yielded to the temptation to peek at the data yet?"

"What do you think?"

"I'd bet a million credits that you're already working on it, so you can see what you got."

"Correct."

"Anything interesting? Something that could help Carvati?" Maybe he doesn't need assistance, though. For all I know, he's figured out the La'heng cure and we're ready to move.

"There is so much unfamiliar technology and scientific data that I am dizzy." That's a huge admission for him. "I may ask Carvati to examine it tomorrow."

"I think you could trust him to a point. He certainly isn't hurting for credits."

"My thoughts precisely."

There's no reason to linger. I can't ask to curl up beside him or to sleep on his floor. I want to, but what was normal while we were stranded isn't anymore.

So I murmur, "I suppose I'd better clean up and get some rest."

There's a long silence, as if he's considering his options. Maybe he feels the same way—and he's gotten used to having me close by. But he only says, "Dream well, Sirantha."

As I'm leaving, I think he's going to ask me to stay. But he doesn't.

In my room, I reflect that it's good to take a proper san-shower; I'd almost forgotten the pleasure. For the first time in ages, I face myself in the mirror, but I don't see any of the changes I noted in Dina. My face looks the same as it did after my trial. Turning away with a muttered curse, I find a comb. It's been turns since I got the tangles out, and this could take the rest of the night.

Just as well. I probably won't be able to relax. I'm lonely without Vel, and I'm not sure I can sleep without him. I miss the slow, deep exhalations that mean I'm safe. Except the toll on me has been considerable—I can't help it. I abandon my hair and lie down just for a moment.

And when I wake, March is with me.

CHAPTER 35

"Jax," he breathes.

March cups my face in his hands and kisses me as if he's dying, and only my breath can save him. I draw him down onto the bed beside me. At first I'm not sure if I'm awake or dreaming, but he's always welcome beside me.

Oh, my love, my love.

It seems as if we've never been together as Kai and I were, sharing normal occasions, daily joys. Instead, it feels as though we have only these stolen moments caught between the crises. He's tougher to be with than Kai, more unwilling to follow my lead, and honestly, I don't like letting others choose my course, no matter how much I love them. Those things don't matter now, as his lips claim mine. Sweetness. Heat. Oh, Mary, how I ache. If this is a dream, I will die when I wake.

"Are you here?" I ask, long moments later. "Are you real?"

March spills into my mind in a hot rush, and the silence is filled at last. Nobody else makes me feel this way. I've missed him so, though I didn't allow myself to feel the full force of it before, or I couldn't have functioned. It was more of my self-defense mechanism—that compartmentalization—at work.

I'm here, Jax. I can't believe you're alive.

Then he shows me his absolute devastation; I see the long months on Marakeq, where he lived in squalor and spent his days in the swamp, painstakingly trying to track us. But the rains and the native mud made that all but impossible, even for an experienced merc like him. He spares nothing, not a single second of his grief, fear, and loss. Tears well in my eyes at his devotion; I am not worthy of his steadfast love, but I cherish it.

Once I draw back a little to study him, I see the marks of time in his face. Before, no more than ten turns separated us, but now it looks more like fifteen. A fine web of worry lines surrounds his eyes, and there's a touch of gray in his dark hair. He wears it well; in my absence, March has become downright distinguished.

"Do you still love me?" he asks.

Mary, how can he? Can't he feel the truth? That used to be my question . . . and my doubt, but it's been so much longer for him. No wonder he isn't sure whether our status has changed. I can't believe he *waited* for me. I open myself to him and let him examine my memories, so much faster—and more intimate—than telling the story verbally.

But I answer him aloud so there can be no doubt. "Always. I will *always* love you."

"I never gave up on you." He turns onto his side and draws me into his arms. During my long exile, I tried to imagine what it would be like between us, whether it would be torrid or fierce, but he's gentle in his desperation, my head resting on his heart.

I breathe him in, savoring his familiar scent. "I never stopped trying to get back to you. I just had no idea it would take so long. And it wasn't, for me."

"I want you to hear something," he says then.

Rising, he motions me to silence and pops a data spike into the comm unit beside the bed. To my surprise, it's his voice, telling me the story of how he left Nicu Tertius and wound up on Lachion. Until the end, I don't understand the purpose, but then, in the final words, it becomes clear. He was talking to me on the vid when I was gone, as proof he expected me to come home.

My tears fall then, and he kisses them away, one by one. I want him so much; it's been forever since he touched me. He kisses me again, this time with the passion he's suppressed beneath layers of fear and doubt.

I can't blame him.

A normal man would've found someone else by now, but he isn't that guy. He's a hero, all the way down to the bone, and he's mine, still. I don't know how I got so lucky.

We twine together, hands stroking. Silent sparks, desire beyond all bearing, flood me. His touch comes like sunrise on all worlds but Gehenna and Marakeq, sweetly inevitable but also delicious for those who have waited patiently for the darkness to end. That same golden glow spills through me at the brush of his hands over my skin. My clothes have gone, and his, too, a pool of fabric on the floor.

March runs his lips down my throat; I caress the curve of his ear. Despite the long separation, we are easy in our coming together for fear the other will vanish in a smoky illusion, no more than a vision. He kisses me again and again, his mouth hot on my skin. I run my fingers down his back, digging in as I recall he likes a little edge, and it spurs him on. Lowering his head to my breast, he nips and nuzzles, reminding me how good it can be. I come to life beneath his touch, writhing and moaning.

"Now," I whisper.

He covers me smoothly, his body hard as ever. The turns have not changed him that much. In a single thrust, he takes me and holds with such delicious intensity. I feel his heartbeat inside me. Unable to resist, I move beneath him, little curls of my hips that make his ugly-beautiful face tighten with bliss. Oh, how I've missed that broken nose and his shot-amber eyes. Right now, they're molten with desire, long lashes sweeping down to shield his expression, as if I can't feel what he does.

It's all heat, all perfect promise, and I can't get enough of him. I kiss his throat, his shoulders, his chest, my movements grown jerky with relentless need. Normally, he would flip now to give me femme dominant and let me ride him to completion. This time, he doesn't. March studies my face as if memorizing my features as he moves, and each shift, each lift of my hips, spurs a half smile from him.

He pins my wrists over my head as if my submission can expiate those long, lonely turns, and so I yield, this one time. By his faint smile, he knows it will not become a habit.

Mary, it's good. His thought? Mine? It's all the same right now. I have his leashed desire in my head, so I thrum with heat inside and out; his arousal drives my own. He tastes the sweetness of his hard length rocking inside me, just as I know the delicious feel of my slick heat. I've never been able to finish this way, so I struggle as the sensations become overwhelming.

March lets himself down on his arms, shifting his angle inside me, and claims my mouth in a scorching kiss. It's too much after such a long drought, and I arch beneath him, quaking through a relentless orgasm. He comes with me a few beats later, his body tightening in long, inexorable strokes.

Afterward, he rolls to the side and wraps me in his arms, face nuzzling my coarse curls. "I'm so glad you're back. Now you can come home."

Home. What does that even mean for someone like me? I have wanderlust in equal measure to grimspace cations in my veins.

"You mean Nicuan?"

"The flat is more than big enough for all of us," he says, assuming I will go where he leads, even now.

In times of war, I would. No question. He is a great general, willing to sacrifice his own pleasure for the good of the Armada. I remember that very clearly. And I agreed with that decision. I don't regret it, however painful it was then. Any other course would've been selfish. Our continued cohabitation would've had a deleterious effect on morale, no doubt. Because how could the rank and file trust a commander who was shacking up with his second in command? His decisions would be questioned, particularly in regard to his orders to me.

But this isn't wartime, and I'm not a follower. He has to know that deep down. March is the other half of my heart, but I don't know if I can do this, even for him. I have promises to keep. Torment twists my face, and he sees it. Doubtless he feels it, too.

"March . . . I have business to finish here."

He seals a finger against my mouth, stilling my instinctive protest. "Don't make up your mind now."

"Did you bring your nephew?" I ask.

He nods. "He's with Dina and Hit tonight. You can meet him tomorrow."

I'm not sure about that, either. Mary, he's been raising this kid for the last five turns, while I was fighting monsters and slogging through ruins. It's mind-boggling. For the first time, I fear we've taken such divergent paths that they may not meet up again. But this isn't a night to think such thoughts. For now, he's here, and I'm in his arms. If there's a good-bye looming, I won't face it now, coward that I am.

.UNCLASSIFIED-TRANSMISSION.
.AFTER LONG SILENCE.
.FROM-SUNI_TARN.
.TO-EDUN_LEVITER.

My dear Edun, it has been such a long time. I have thought of you often over the turns, wondered if you were well. We live in such interesting times, do we not? I am seeing claims that the Maker homeworld has been located and in some other 'verse as well through a gate on Marakeq. I will need to send a delegation to explain to them their rights, as they shall soon be overrun with scientists and research teams. Somehow, I was not surprised at all to discover Ms. Jax at the heart of the whirlwind. She carries chaos like an overcoat.

But I speak of her only because she is a name to us both. That is not the reason I have contacted you, as I am sure you well know. You may have seen on the bounce; I finished my final term as chancellor. I am a free citizen now, and at liberty to pursue friendship with whomever I so choose, regardless of past allegiances and/or political affiliations. If I did not imagine the fondness between us, I should like to accept your invitation at this time and develop a more personal relationship.

You need only convey your location, and I will come to you. If your feelings have changed, or I misinterpreted them, let me know, and I will trouble you no further.

Yours,
Suni

CHAPTER 36

Sasha March is a beautiful child, with Svetlana's faintly elfin features and her pale hair. The father must be fair also to produce such offspring. I know; that's a fairly clinical word for a person March loves so much. But I don't know this kid, and I have no experience to draw on, apart from those six weeks in the crèche at Hidden Rue. Even then, it didn't matter so much whether I related to the children, only that I kept them from harm while their mothers performed.

At the best of times, I don't like children. They're messy, noisy, and they're always poking around where they don't belong. I was just like that, once, but I grew out of it, and I prefer dealing with people who've completed their neurological development.

Zeeka is with Hit and Dina, exploring the wonders of the dome, and later they'll take him to Carvati for testing. Vel has gone to meet with scientists, scholars, and collectors, so they can examine his Maker sample in order to decide how high they're willing to bid. He doesn't need the credits, but he's too much a businessman to take less than the best possible offer.

He's promised me half the amount from the sale, which I intend to use to keep my promise to Loras, and the La'hengrin. *No more servitude, no more shinai bond.* I have a gift for wrecking the status quo, and I intend to aim that capacity at the infrastructure on La'heng.

Once he concludes his business, Vel intends to get his talon replaced with a prosthetic. Afterward, I'll meet him at Carvati's to talk about the cure I commissioned five turns ago and have the good doctor check out that terabyte of data.

With the others engaged this morning—intentionally, I suspect—that leaves me to breakfast with March and Sasha at a café near Mikhail's. As always, the weather is temperate on Gehenna because they regulate it with a complex computer algorithm dedicated to giving the denizens of the dome some variety, but no extremes.

And I've been lost in thought too long, letting Sasha gaze at me worriedly. Right now, the silence is awkward, and I can't let it stand, seeing the sadness dawning in March's eyes. He wanted us to bond, I think, but the child is scared of me, or maybe it's more accurate to say he's afraid his world is about to change for the worse.

"So how old are you?" I ask the kid.

"Ten," he whispers.

Frag. I'd rather be back in the jungle, fighting those plant-tentacle monsters or trudging through that Maker catacomb, than trying to make conversation with a child. Adele would argue he senses my discomfort, and I should try to relax. Mary, that makes me miss her even more. The world lost a bright, bright spark in her.

In her honor, I keep trying, though this ship is sinking fast. "And you go to school on Nicuan. How do you like it?"

A quiet shrug comes in reply. Shit, how do you talk to kids? Asking about friends and hobbies doesn't seem likely to yield fruit, so I wrack my brain for other topics. I glance at March for help, and he slides into my head.

Mmm. Missed you.

I missed you, too, Jax. Try asking him what he likes to

study. He'll open up. There's no way he won't love you like I do. When he draws back, he does so with a slow reluctance that leaves me warm and tingly.

"What's your favorite subject?"

"Maths." He picks at his breakfast, eyes wide and sad.

I hate math. *Well, that went nowhere.* At this point I give up and finish my breakfast. This isn't how I imagined things would go; March and I should still be making love.

He's never been off world before, March explains. *He needs the reassurance of routine.*

"I can't keep him out of school long," he says out loud. "So we need to leave soon, much as I hate to."

Sasha brightens. "We're going home?"

"I'll come to Nicuan after I wrap things up here," I promise.

To what end, I don't know. But I want to spend more time with March, and it's clear he can't take off with me as he once would have. He's not free to roam the stars with me anymore. That bothers me more than I'd admit out loud.

I admire his commitment, of course. I just don't share it. This child isn't blood of my blood, bone of my bone. Mary forfend. I've no doubt I'd be a worse mother than Ramona. Some females should not breed, and I am one of them.

"Why?" The kid's voice rises with pure fear. "She doesn't work for Psi-Corp, does she? I'm not allowed to leave Nicuan. I'm not fully trained."

That's not a logical question, but kids aren't. I sure wasn't, as I recall.

Before March can respond, our table quakes in response to Sasha's state of mind. This isn't just an ordinary, run-of-the-mill scared child. He's a TK 8, a powerful telekinetic, and his emotions have significant consequences. Those tremors fling me out of my chair, and I slam my head on the side of the table going down. It's a solid hit; blood trickles from my temple. I lie there a minute, listening to the breaking dishes while March tries to calm Sasha down. Other patrons scream in terror because Gehenna does not suffer earthquakes, at least *not* inside the dome, where everything is artificially stabilized. Eventually I climb to my feet.

Amber eyes frantic, March signals for the bill, his hand fast in his nephew's. "I have to get him off world before they figure out who did this. They'll detain him if we stay. He's not supposed to be away from the Psi academy right now."

I grab his hand, keeping him a moment longer. "Come with me," I say on impulse. "If you expect trouble, wait for me in orbit . . . I won't be on Gehenna that long. You can train Sasha yourself, right? Teach him not to lose control. And then, once I finish on La'heng, I can do whatever you'd like. We can see the galaxy. That'd be a great education for a kid." My tone turns coaxing, and I hate myself for it.

"I wanna go home," Sasha whispers, his tone thick with tears. "Please take me home, Dad."

The word eviscerates me. It represents a bond I can't touch, nor would I want to. It's immutable. Forever.

His expression tight with regret, March shakes his head. "He needs stability, Jax. I can't." He pauses, assessing the wound on my head. "Are you all right, though? Do you need me to take you to the clinic?"

Since Sasha's only here because March couldn't wait to see me, this knock on the head is practically my fault. I don't blame him, or the kid. "It's not as bad as it looks."

"Are you sure?" He'll do it, I know. Put this child in danger to get medical care for me.

I won't let him make that choice. Psi-Corp is run by Farwan personnel, and I know what they do to people who break their rules. March and Sasha need to scramble off world before they get caught.

So I nod. "I'm fine. You're leaving, then?"

It's too soon. Things aren't supposed to *be* like this. I want to believe we can take up where we left off, but I don't know if it's that simple, and my heart aches.

Our love consists of stolen moments, but maybe I should cherish them instead of fighting for the impossible. We've ever been out of step, a beat ahead or a beat behind; I long for the day when our lives synchronize as our hearts and minds did long ago. March leans over and kisses me soundly, passionately even, but I can't focus on pleasure with a child crying silently beside me. Even I'm not that selfish.

With obvious reluctance, I pull back, searching for a napkin. Head wounds bleed like a bitch. A spreading red stain covers the white cloth, and March regards me with quiet despair. I know just how he feels that it's come to this. Sometimes, love isn't enough, even when it's all you have.

"I'm sorry." He drops a credit spike on the table and takes Sasha's hand. "I hope to see you soon, Jax."

"You will." As if I could stay away.

I just don't know whether I can stay for good. By his bittersweet smile as he leads his nephew out of the café and onto the sidewalk, March knows that. He doesn't look back, but I watch them go, a tall, strong, dark-haired man with a slight blond boy clinging to his hand. There was no other choice this time, as there wasn't before. Things never align the way I want them to, but as I've learned to my cost, I'm not the center of the universe.

All around me, they're trying to set the café to rights, servo-bots sweeping up the wreckage. I wish I could be fixed so easily. New flowers are placed on the tables, and the remaining patrons resume their meals. My hot choc-laste has spilled across the remainder of my sweet sliced kavi, leaving a pink and brown mess on my plate.

The manager or owner touches my shoulder, likely worried that I intend to blame his establishment. "Are you injured?"

How funny. It's been long enough that they no longer remember my face. I'm not famous or infamous any longer. I'm not the Butcher of Venice Minor or the legendary Sirantha Jax. I'm just a wounded woman in a random café on Gehenna. I marvel at the anonymity of it. There's a clean and lovely symmetry in it. I feared Vel's discovery would put me center stage again, but at my request, he has managed to keep all but a few whispers of my involvement from all but the most dogged bounce stations, and even then it's just speculation. On one feed, I was amused as hell to hear them refer to Vel as my "longtime Ithtorian companion." Idiots. He's so much more to me than that. There are no words for it.

"Not badly." Answering him belatedly—and I'm sure he now thinks I'm concussed—I pull the cloth from my temple and check it with my fingertips; the cut has already clotted, thanks to the nanites that render me not-quite-human.

"Your son's adorable," a woman says as I pass by. "But he doesn't look much like you or your husband."

It's on the tip of my tongue to deny the connection; instead, I merely accept the compliment with a mute nod and join the throng. Today, I face an unpleasant truth; March has family, and I do not. I am adrift, cut free from my moorings. I walk aimlessly, needing to get my emotions under control before I face the others.

My path takes me through the market and into the poor quarter, where I spent so many peaceful hours with Adele. I wish she were here; Gehenna is painful now that she's gone, but I come to stand outside her building anyway and gaze up at the window that used to be hers. Did she live here when she was with Vel? It's so hard to imagine him settled, spending quiet evenings with her when she was young. Even *he* has his secrets. Boiling with pain, I move on.

Eventually, I make the meeting at Carvati's, where I find my "longtime Ithtorian companion" waiting on the platform. It's an amazing view from the aerie, breathtaking even.

Vel knows me too well to accept the assurance that I'm fine. "He hurt you?"

He's not talking about the wound on my head, either. "No more than he had to. His nephew comes first."

He offers a mute nod, then changes the subject, more of his quiet perception. "The implant went well."

I watch as he flexes his claws. "It doesn't show."

"Carvati is good. And it appears that Zeeka does, indeed, possess the J-gene."

I wonder if the fact that we jumped while he was a tiny hatchling has anything to do with his yen for grimspace. If he'd been a human child, we wouldn't have done it. Long ago, I discriminated against Loras because he's not human. Frag, I hope I don't do that to Vel.

"That's good news for Z. He'd be crushed to fail his test."

Vel tilts his head toward the clinic. "Shall we go talk to the man?"

The bot in reception is different from the one Carvati used the last time we visited. Not surprising, I suppose, that he would upgrade in five turns, but it's another reminder of how long we were gone. Vel shares a look with me that tells me he feels it, too, that sense of being unconnected to the right time stream. Maybe it's a side effect of gate travel and will wear off soon. I hope.

Once he hears we've arrived, Carvati comes to greet us personally. "So good to see both of you. I'd heard you were lost."

"It's a long story," I say, not that I'm eager to tell it again.

But he's a businessman and respects my reticence. "Understandable, and we have more important issues at hand."

"Right. How's the cure coming along?"

Carvati sighs. "Stalled, I'm afraid. I'm missing some vital link. I've tried 285 different formulations, and so far the results in the simulations have varied from awful to catastrophic. Our knowledge at this time is insufficient to fix what we broke in the La'heng."

Dammit.

"It's not your fault," I say, heavy with disappointment. I'd hoped this quest could distract me from the wreckage of my personal life. "If it can't be done with current data, it can't. I never expected the impossible."

Except from me, Doc says in my head. *Ten times before breakfast.*

"Do you have time to evaluate the Maker data we retrieved?" Vel asks. "There might be something that could illuminate your work on the cure."

"That would be nice," Carvati mutters.

I decide not to badger him. That never helps. "Then we'll talk about it after you check the Maker archives."

"I'm honored you're permitting me a look, but you understand it will take some time for me to sort and analyze. Do you trust me not to retain a copy and attempt to undercut you?"

Vel's mandible flares. "I will trust you as soon as we work out a contract with suitably severe penalties if such an unfortunate incursion of my intellectual property should occur."

Carvati laughs, unoffended by this caution. "I would act the same. Shall we meet with my solicitors?"

"Will you excuse us, Sirantha? This could take hours."

CHAPTER 37

With a nod, I return to Mikhail's, where I avoid the oth-
ers. I'm not ready to do a play-by-play on how it went with
March. Or anything else, really. I should be excited about
training the first Mareq jumper, but right now I hurt too much.

So I send Dina a message, asking her to watch out for
Zeeka in my absence. For the next few days, I hibernate. I
tell myself the quiet is good for me, and I won't let my door
admit anyone. Even Vel respects my need to hole up after a
couple of attempts to talk to me.

It's been a while since we landed on Gehenna when my
comm beeps. Because I'm starting to get bored with my
isolation, I answer, and Carvati's excited face pops up on
the vid. "I have phenomenal news. *Amazing*, truly."

That perks me right up. "What?"

"Remember how I said we didn't know enough to make
the cure work?"

I nod.

"Well, I finished analyzing the Maker data . . . and we
do now. What I've learned from their records about genetic
manipulation is *astonishing*. Over the last four days, I've

run eight hundred tests in the simulation, and the new vaccine has a ninety-eight percent success rate."

Mary, that's a lot. So he's done it, and he's sure. My heart lightens a little. Our journey to the other 'verse mattered. It will set the La'heng free. *Frag me.* This makes the long trial worthwhile. Though it's screwed my personal life beyond hope for redemption, at least I can push forward now. Relief floods through me. It means I can finish what I've started at long last.

"What do you need from me?"

"Ideally, a volunteer of pure La'heng stock willing to undergo an experimental procedure."

I know just the person for this job. "Let me make a few calls and get back to you."

"Very well, Ms. Jax. Let me know when you're ready to proceed." Visibly exhausted, he cuts the call.

After cleaning up, I sit down at the comm station, my hair pulled back into my lieutenant's twist, professional and contained. That's the image I want to convey now. After inputting the only comm code I have for Hon, I say:

"Carvati has devised a cure, but we need someone to test it. That means you, Loras. We can't move forward without you. Come to Gehenna, as soon as you can, if you were serious about wanting to set your people free. Send." The voice command activates the vid-mail protocol, and my message bounces out. Where they are will determine how long the vid takes to arrive.

There are a ton of old messages for me to sort through after my long retreat from the world, including one from Nola Hale. That one I play, because I'm interested in what became of Pandora. My former barrister appears on-screen, looking competent and attractive, as ever. "Since you paid for her legal counsel, I thought you'd want to know Pandora's verdict. I got her acquitted, Ms. Jax. I believe she intends to track you down and thank you personally."

Now, that's good news. I ignore a couple of messages from Tarn and delete them. The rest of my messages are from March and Dina, kind of a log of their search. From the tone they take toward the end, I suspect they didn't think they'd see me again. I watch the ones from March four times before deciding I'm being maudlin.

It's funny.

I was missing five turns, and March never reported me dead to claim my assets. My ex-husband, Simon, did so within a matter of days, and I had far fewer credits in the bank then. But in my absence, the wrongful-death claims have been piling up. Vel pays them while we're waiting for Hon and Loras to arrive on world.

A wicked melancholy has fallen on him since we returned, and I know why. He has such memories here, a whole other life within the dome, and it is over now, that chapter closed for all time. And I am not Adele; I lack her patience, her kindness, and her sweetness.

For so long, I focused on getting back to our world, only to return and find it's reshaped itself in my absence. I don't doubt March still loves me, but I fear there might not be room for me in the new life he's built. Fortunately, after I emerge from my room, the others don't give me time to dwell on my fears. Hit and Dina keep me busy showing Zeeka the sights. I'll take him with me to La'heng and start training him as I did Argus. I've learned from my mistakes, though, and I'm not doing it without having Carvati run a complete medical panel on him to see where he stands on the longevity chart.

We do that while we're waiting for the *Dauntless*.

Fortunately, Zeeka is a good candidate. "Maybe one of the best I've ever seen," Carvati says.

The young Mareq swells with pride. Literally. His chest and throat puff with air, and his wide mouth gapes in his version of a smile. Yeah, he's happy to hear it.

"I will sail the stars, just like Jax Oonan," he croaks.

"Just Jax is fine." I prefer he doesn't call me that. Vel and I know I haven't earned that title, and I'd like to forget everything we went through.

Well, maybe not everything. I wouldn't rescind my request for Vel to wear my colors. Odd that he hasn't brought it up. We could probably get it taken care of here. Gehenna offers just about every vice known to man.

Zeeka stays with Dr. Carvati to get his universal chip and the vocalizer to utilize it. He's such a bold, bright spirit that he doesn't even seem afraid although the technology seems magical to him. Deep down, I have some doubts about him as a jumper because he doesn't understand this life. He's just constantly amazed by everything. But maybe a jolt of his wonder and innocence is just what this jaded galaxy needs. I'm done trying to decide what's best for other people; if his mother acknowledged him as a "sovereign being" and let him go off into the unknown, then who I am to deny his dream?

A week after my bounce, I get a reply from Loras. "We'll be there in two days."

Of course, this message is already two days old. Which means I can expect them anytime now . . . and I'm excited. I haven't seen either Hon or Loras since before my incarceration—frag, not since the Battle of Venice Minor. Even then, I didn't see them on the way to my trial.

Four hours later, my personal comm beeps. "Jax."

Hon's dark, smiling face appears on my wrist. He's grown his pirate braids back but replaced his gold teeth with circumspect white. "I brought you a willing La'heng test subject. Where should I deliver him?"

"Frag you," I hear Loras mutter.

"We're staying at a place called Mikhail's, near the market. If you want to drop your things here, we can proceed directly to Carvati's clinic. I know he's eager to get going."

"As am I," Loras says.

At last, everything feels like it's coming together. Zeeka should be recovered from his minor elective surgery when we present ourselves for Loras's treatment. This means we're about ready to leave Gehenna and head for La'heng, provided this treatment works. *Please, please let it work.* If it doesn't, I have no further options, as the only person who might've achieved this, other than Carvati, died on Venice Minor. Guilt accompanies that thought, but there are no amends I can make.

An hour later, I meet Hon and Loras downstairs in the lounge. Hon grabs me up in a bone-crushing hug and twirls me around; the war hasn't crushed his big, big spirit. And even Loras looks stronger than he did when I first saw him on Emry Station; apparently working with Hon has been good for him. Loras offers a hand, and I use it to pull him into an embrace.

"Told you I'd work on the problem for you."

"You mean contract it out," Hon corrects with a roguish grin.

"Close enough. I know Loras didn't expect me to handle the science stuff on my own."

"I thought Doc would do it," he says quietly.

I sober instantly. "I'm so sorry."

"Why?" Hon asks. "You weren't bombing Venice Minor."

Mary help me, but I can't bring myself to explain how Doc and Evie came to die. Only Vel knows that they were likely responding to our comm chatter when we warned the fleet overhead. They were coming to help us—save us—and probably show us their hiding place . . . and I got them killed. I chose March over any other. And maybe that's why this separation fills me with such anguish . . . because what I did spikes a needle of shame straight through my heart every time I think of March.

"Survivor's guilt," Loras suggests.

And I let that explanation stand. "Why don't you get a room and run your bags up? Then we can head to Carvati's."

Hon nods. "Be right back."

While I wait, I nurse a drink. Mikhail's is pretty laid-back, which is why we chose it for our headquarters, but you can't hang around the lounge if you don't buy something. As I sit, Vel joins me, and shortly thereafter, Hit, Dina, and Argus as well.

That raises my brows. "We're all going?"

Dina nods. "We all have a vested interest at this point."

"But I wanted to chat with you." This, from Hit. She has a glass of something red and sweet-looking in one hand.

"Go."

"We've been talking . . ." That has to mean her, Dina, and Argus. Together, they've been running missions on the *Big Bad Sue* for turns now.

"What about?" I ask.

"We'll take you as far as La'heng, but after that, we need to get back to business. We didn't agree to sit around while you lobby for approval, bribe officials, or whatever you're going to need to do in order to finish this for Loras. "

Hit sounds harsh, but I know she doesn't mean it that way. And she's right. This is my personal quest. I don't want anyone sitting dirtside if they'd rather be out on the Star Road. Frag, *I'd* rather be out there, too, but I have to keep this promise, or I won't enjoy my freedom later.

This is the final price for everything I've done. I realize no amount of goodwill bring back the people who died because of my actions, but nothing less can assuage my conscience. If I can succeed in this, then I may experience some measure of peace. I can go out into the beauty of red dwarves, gas giants, asteroid fields, and uncharted wonders with an unfettered spirit.

I glance between Dina and Argus. "You both agree?"

Neither hesitates to meet my gaze as they nod. I get it. I was gone a long-ass time, and they have a new life. One I'm not part of. They have their own jumper, even, one I trained. I know I'm leaving Hit and Dina in good hands with him.

"If you're all right with it, I have one stop before La'heng. Then once you drop us off on world, I won't expect anything more. If not, I can find another ship." I don't mean to sound terse, but I guess I do. Despite my intellectual understanding, I'm a little hurt. Dina's my best pal, or she was, but I was gone, and she moved on.

"Don't take it like that," Dina says with a faint sigh. "We'll always be your friends, dumb-ass. But we just can't stay dirtside."

"I know." And I do. I wish *I* didn't have to. But it's the last link in the chain holding me to my former life. When I finish this quest, I'll be free to fly.

CHAPTER 38

Zeeka comes through the surgery with his natural exu-
berance intact. The upshot of that is that he can now question everyone else without need for translation. Just now,
he's badgering Hit about why she's a different color from
everyone else.

"What is the purpose of your darkness?" he asks.

She eyes him. "It makes me pretty."

"You are painted for beauty?"

Hit grins, flashing white teeth. "I like to think so."

"Me, too," Hon puts in.

Zeeka looks as though he cannot decide whether they're
telling him the truth. "The others are ugly?"

I suspect to Zeeka, much like Vel, we're all ugly. Sup-
pressing a grin, I wait to see how Hit will handle this question. Dina's tapping a foot, one brow raised.

"Beauty comes in many shades," Loras offers. "And it is
made dearer by attachment between sentient beings."

"Love makes the ugly beautiful?" Poor Zeeka is really
confused now.

"It does," Vel says. And he's looking at me when he says it.

Maybe he's thinking of Adele. I remember in the story he told me that day before we visited her, he mentioned that he didn't find her attractive at first—that none of her features appealed to him. But he came to see past it in time because she had so many other lovely qualities. There's such sweetness in that.

This is typical of how we spend an afternoon while Loras completes his treatments. He's receiving a series of injections, one a day for seven days. This incremental approach permits his adaptive physiology to process the chemical neurological change at a safe rate. At the end of that time, he'll either be cured, or insane with bloodlust. His people, before humanity rendered them docile, had more than their share of aggression. They were insanely fierce and completely xenophobic, so it's not a stretch to imagine the manner in which this could turn bad. Since he told Carvati he'd rather die this way than in servitude, I figure it's a good risk.

Still, I can't help fear for my friend. I've only just got him back in my life. I'm not ready to lose him again so soon.

This is the seventh day, and we're killing time before his last treatment. Vel reprogrammed the servo-bots at Mikhail's to offer selections more savory for him and Zeeka. While we can eat some of the same things, our palates are a bit different.

"It's time," Hit says.

As one, we rise and head for the hover cab. I love flying in Gehenna because there's relatively little traffic. It takes three tries to find a vehicle large enough for all of us, but we squeeze in, and the bot asks us our destination.

"Carvati's clinic."

"Thank you. Enjoy the ride."

Shortly, the hover cab deposits us on the platform outside. Loras leads the way, coldly determined to find out whether he'll die a monster or become a free man. The receptionist waves us back to Carvati's private lab. As always, he evokes echoes of Doc, but I push down the sorrow. It's not the time.

"Loras?" In that one word, Carvati asks if he's ready to proceed.

He responds with a slow nod. The doctor turns to the rest of us. "If you could wait in the next room?"

This is standard. The lot of us exit into an open space that appears to be used for training. I can't imagine what Carvati does in here, but it's part of his lab complex. Maybe it's to test certain cybernetic upgrades, as he does a wide range of procedures.

"Nervous?" I ask Hon. If this works, he's losing his status as *shinai*.

"This is what he wants." Deep down, he's not as mean as his reputation suggests—and maybe that's the secret. If gossip does most of the heavy lifting, he doesn't actually have to rape and maim his way through the galaxy.

We wait an hour before Carvati and Loras join us. He doesn't look any different, so that's a good sign. If he'd been overwhelmed by bloodlust, he would be snarling and trying to kill us all. Instead, he looks much as he ever does, blue-eyed and fair-haired, with a beautiful face, faintly etched with lines earned by hard experience.

"I need a volunteer," Carvati says.

"Hon." Loras doesn't wait to see who will speak.

The pirate steps forward. "Aye?"

Loras smiles. "Hit me."

He doesn't argue, but he doesn't hit him like a man, either. Instead, it's an open-faced slap, which feels like an insult. Loras responds immediately, his grin widening; he unloads a flurry of punches on the bigger man's upper body. Hon tries to block, and though he's bigger, he's nowhere near fast enough. Loras has been saving this rage for turns, and there's no denying it. He kicks the living shit out of Hon before Carvati grabs him. The pirate staggers back, bracing on the wall, with genuine surprise. This is *why* we pacified the La'hengrin, but we didn't have that right.

"How do you feel?" Carvati asks.

Loras bends over, breathing hard. "Free, like something unlocked in my head. Before, no matter how furious I was, I couldn't do that. It felt like I had strings attached. But they've been cut, and I'm a puppet no longer."

I cheer and give him a big hug. He shoves me back . . . mostly because he can, I suspect. "I didn't say you could touch me."

"Sorry." But I'm smiling, and so is he. "So what do you think? Should we carry Carvati's Cure to La'heng and free your people?"

Loras nods. "Absolutely. Today, this is my independence day. And I dream that eventually, all La'hengrin will know this joy. If you help me achieve this, you will be the best friend I've ever known."

I feel like that's expiation, and a goal worth striving for, because he doesn't offer friendship lightly. I once left him to die, and if he can forgive me that, then maybe I'm not beyond all saving. *Mary, please, let me succeed in this.* I'm not selfless enough to want to do it for the sake of all the enslaved La'heng. I want to do this for Loras to prove I'm not a selfish ass. And there's some self-serving agenda tangled up in it, but doesn't it matter more what you do rather than why?

"I'll go get the ship ready," Dina says. "I guess we'll be leaving soon."

Hit nods in agreement. They take Argus and Zeeka when they go; both males are eager to get into grimspace, Argus because he's a junkie, and Zeeka because he aspires to Argus's status as a veteran jumper. I find it adorable the way Zeeka dogs Argus, trying to imitate him. Which leaves Hon regarding Loras with one hand pressed to his injured side. I'd bet he has broken ribs, based on his ginger movements.

"This is good-bye, I think. No hard feelin's?"

"If I see you again," Loras says, smiling, "I'll probably kill you. You treated me like a pet, one you expected to forage for its own food."

Hon shrugs. "It made you stronger, didn't it?"

Loras doesn't answer, letting the man go. His ship waits for him, along with the rest of his crew, at least the ones who survived Venice Minor. He's still running under Armada colors, and he has a galaxy to patrol. To my vast amusement, they promoted him when March stepped down, and now he carries the title of commander, along with all the privileges of rank.

Vel, Loras, and I walk out of the training room together. Loras holds himself differently, his shoulders straighter. I see a glimmer of the fierce warriors that my people could not conquer, and so chose to defeat in a bloodless coup. The knowledge makes me sick. But I'm trying to right the wrong even if I had nothing to do with it personally. That's kind of the point—to fix something I didn't break. I don't kid myself it will change any of the harm I've inflicted, but it will comfort the soul Adele taught me to believe in, the quiet, smoky thing that lives at the heart of me and occasionally whispers at me that I can do better.

Carvati catches my arm. "If you have a moment, Ms. Jax, I'd like to speak with you."

I tell the other two, "Head back to Mikhail's. I'll catch up with you."

Vel agrees with a nod, then departs with Loras. I follow Carvati back to his lab, wondering what he wants. *Maybe more credits?* Mary knows he's earned them. I won't argue if he asks for the project-completion bonus. Even though I'm running low on Ramona's bequest from the wave of wrongful-death payments, I still have the promise of half the credits from Vel's auction of the Maker artifacts. The bids are flying fast and furious; a real war's broken out.

"From your records, I understand you have a great deal of experimental tech implanted. How long has it been since you've had a checkup?"

Five turns, at least. In this world, anyway. In the Maker 'verse, it only felt like weeks. Maybe months. Hard to say how gate travel will affect my implants down the line. At this point, however, almost everything about my future remains unknown. I'm not human; I'm . . . other. For the first time, I get how Jael must have felt—and I can almost see how he ended up a merc, willing to do anything for a credit, because there was nobody else like him in the universe, no one who understood.

"Not since before Doc died." The words hurt my throat.

"I'd like to run some tests before you leave Gehenna, if you don't mind. I'm concerned about your well-being."

"How long will it take?" I don't figure he'll have good news for me. Doctors never do. So I'm understandably reluctant.

"Half an hour."

That's not long enough for me to make the excuse of being pressed for time. I sigh and hop onto the table. "Go for it."

He scans me, pokes me with needles, and examines his findings with a curious expression; I don't know how to interpret it. Finally, I can't stand the suspense.

"Well?"

Carvati glances up, as if surprised that I can talk. "Some very interesting results, here. Apparently, thanks to your nanites, you're no longer aging as normal people do."

Shit. I'm like Vel now, doomed to watch the people I love die. That hits me like a ton of bricks. "What does that mean, exactly?"

"It means this is proprietary, unknown technology, and with its creator dead, there is no telling what your life span may be. Regular aging will kick in if the nanites ever go inert, but they appear to be self-maintaining and show no signs of breakdown five turns after their implantation."

This isn't news I wanted. Maybe other people would be thrilled to learn this, but not me. I'm shaking my head. "Can you take them out? I know there was some way to turn them off."

"I can only surmise there was a signal device, but it was doubtless destroyed on Venice Minor."

Along with Doc and Evelyn. Dammit.

"Is the rest of my tech playing nice?" I ask, quietly despondent.

"The nanites have repaired any deterioration, so yes. But I thought you would be happy to learn this . . . It's better than Rejuvenex. In time, they may even repair the burn scars."

Not my scars. Frag. I feel like punching something. I don't want to be this less-than-human thing anymore. I miss the woman I was.

There's no point in trying to articulate my point of view. "It's complicated. Thanks for all your help, Dr. Carvati."

"Feel free to look me up again if you ever have a lot of credits to spend and some impossible project to complete."

At that, I smile ruefully. "Mary, but you remind me of Doc sometimes."

He etches a salute. "I've started a foundation in his name, you know. Researching a cure for Jenner's Retrovirus. If we ever beat it, I'm calling it Solaith's Solution."

Right now I want to hug him, as that was Doc's favorite impossible disease; it's so tough because it adapts to all treatments. It's the smartest virus modern science has ever encountered. Mentally, I flash back to all the times I asked him to tackle some tough problem, and he would say with such asperity, *Shall I cure Jenner's Retrovirus while I'm at it, Jax?*

What the hell. I do hug Carvati. "Thank you again. I'll send a sizable donation if you give me the account particulars."

In answer, he beams the details to my handheld, then I'm off.

CHAPTER 39

"What troubles you, Sirantha?" It's Vel, of course. Even though he can't wait to get off Gehenna, he still noticed my mood when I returned from the clinic.

We've made all the plans to depart in the morning: Hit, Loras, Argus, Vel, Zeeka, and me. For however long it takes for me to convince the bureaucrats on La'heng to embrace the cure, I will no longer be Jax the Jumper. Over the turns, I've been an ambassador, a navigator, a survivor, a prisoner, a traitor, a deserter, and a lover, but I've never before been a lobbyist. I have a feeling it may be my most difficult task yet.

With a faint sigh, I turn to him. He's rung for entry to my quarters. Mikhail's does not offer luxury accommodations, but that's fine. Right now I just want privacy. Not from Vel, of course. We've shared too much for me to shut him out. So I summarize what Carvati told me.

"You feel apart," he guesses. "Something other."

I nod. "No longer human."

"I know what that is like."

I suppose he does. Not Ithtorian, but instead he's the deadly, terrifying Slider of legend. Maybe he's the only one who can even approach understanding how I feel. It's time, before we leave, to close the circle. So I do the one thing I can think of to make sure Vel understands he's not alone. He hasn't been himself since our arrival on Gehenna, probably haunted with memories of Adele, and I hate seeing him this way. Though I know nothing can assuage her loss, I'm still going to make a tangible effort.

"During the war, you said that you'd wear my colors if I asked."

"I remember."

"And I *did* ask." After I saved him from impalement, I asked as a promise and an affirmation that we'd survive. I'm not sorry, either. I haven't had a chance to reiterate the request, but this seems like the time.

It's not like a marriage; that much, I know for sure. But it's a promise, and though Kai might not understand because he was opposed to promises—he was all about personal freedom, and usually, so am I—but I know this is the right thing. Vel needs to know he's not alone, and he never will be. And honestly, right now, I need that, too. It feels as though all familiar things have fallen away while I glanced over my shoulder for the briefest instant, and I need someone to swear he'll stand by me.

Maybe I've *always* known it'd be Vel since that day in the Teresengi Basin.

"I wondered if you would mention it, once we returned to civilization. This is permanent," he adds softly. "I will never have these marks removed."

"Neither will I." I touch my throat, tracing with one fingertip the pattern he designed, and his aspect gentles.

To formalize my intentions, I bend with my arms tucked against my body in the most eloquent *wa* I can offer. *Brown bird flies for white wave, always. Take my heart as your colors.*

Vel freezes, studying me, as though wondering if I

understand, if I mean it. And then slowly, he returns the bow. *White wave knows no greater honor, no greater joy. Your colors are my heart.*

"Are you certain?" He asks because he must. Vel is nothing if not cautious.

"I'm sure. Is it something we can have done here?" Gehenna is a place of wonders, contraband, vice, and unexpected beauty. But I don't know if the tattooists on world are conversant with this type of marking. I wouldn't have his chitin marred by someone inexperienced in the art.

"I know a place," he says.

"Then let's go."

He leads me down from my room to the street, where we hail a hover cab; Vel keys the destination on the pad, and it takes us deep into the heart of the market. A few meters below, the passersby swarm along the walkways. Gehenna has limited air traffic inside the dome, only public vehicles and those who can afford the exorbitant license fees, which leaves most of the populace afoot.

The automated vehicle lets us off outside a one-story building; it's built of some dark alloy. No windows and not even a sign to tell what kind of business goes on within. I certainly wouldn't approach on my own, but Vel seems sure as he moves toward the door.

He presses the arrival button on the comm, and momentarily, a face appears on the vid screen. "Tat or piercing?"

"Exotic ink," he replies.

"You have payment in full?" I can see why that would be a concern in a business like this one. You don't want to produce a lovely work, then discover the client can't afford it. Repo is tricky in this particular market.

"Of course."

"I'll buzz you in."

It's brighter and cleaner inside than I expected, given the general dreariness of the exterior. I follow Vel down a well-lit hallway covered in abstract art to a waiting room with white walls and sleek, lime green chairs. A couple of others are seated ahead of us in the queue; most already possess interesting body alterations. One man has pointed ears and a blue pattern running down one side of his face. He smiles at me, revealing sharply filed teeth.

"Will it hurt you?" I ask.

He shakes his head. "There is no feeling in the carapace."

It takes an hour before the others are served. Eventually, it's just Vel and me, watching the Friendly Robotics model receptionist. She's one of the efficient-looking Jane units with a no-nonsense hairstyle and a plain face. The Lila—like the form we found for Constance—had the disadvantage of looking too sexy; it didn't serve well in business. That's part of why they retired the model; the other reason was that people often bought it as a sexual surrogate, due to its extreme attractiveness, and the licensed sex workers protested, saying such technology cut into their ability to earn a living. If a client can purchase a partner for the equivalent of five visits to a professional, it pays for itself in no time. So they implemented the Jane, and we've seen her all across the galaxy over the course of our travels.

At last, the artist calls us back. She is a slight woman whose skin shows no sign of the interesting patterns she puts on other people, but perhaps she prefers to keep such designs private. I can understand that. Despite signs of Rejuvenex treatments, probably to keep her hands steady, she's also older than I expected, and I wonder if she knew him when he was with Adele. Her warm greeting indicates that may be the case.

"I'm glad to see you as yourself, my friend. It was a shame you had to hide for all those turns."

"Different times," Vel says.

She nods at that. "Truer words were never spoken. How things have changed."

She glances at me then. "You must be Jax."

I don't know why I'm surprised; people have been recognizing me for turns. "Nice to meet you."

The artist shakes my hand. "I'm Colette. Do you know what you want?"

Though I haven't discussed it with Vel, I do. "The Ithto-rian symbol for grimspace in black, red, and silver."

"Black for the outline, red for accent, silver for fill?"

I am *impressed*. "Exactly. How did you know?"

"That's how I'd choose to do it."

Turning to Vel, I ask, "Is that all right with you? I know it's not the color of Ithtorian honor marks."

Those are kind of a mustard yellow, and they don't do designs. Those are just slashes of rank. If we go forward, this will separate him from his peers in yet another way, but this is a personal pledge between us, not a promotion. I've worn his mark for turns, apparently; it's time to complete the circle.

"I like it," he says. "It represents you well."

Colette busies herself with the supplies. "I'll get prepped, then."

The bell rings, but she ignores it. I gather we'll be her last clients of the day. A chemical smells wafts from the con-tainer she's mixing in; this must be the acid wash that tex-tures the chitin so it will hold the ink. I confess I find the process fascinating. I sit quiet as she finishes and turns to Vel. Unlike the Ithtorians, she doesn't treat a wide area. They assume the subject will want a large patch prepared, thus stating the intent to work toward greater honor. Instead, the artist draws the pattern I want with a delicate brush, painting it on first with the base treatment, thus readying the carapace for a very specific pattern. Mine.

Until this moment, I didn't know exactly how I'd feel about this step. I was sure, but you can't know how a moment will feel until it arrives. Everything else is just guesswork and anticipation. But right now, I'm so proud, I can't stand it. He's willing to proclaim to the world that he's my partner; I wonder if he feels that way about his pat-tern on my throat. And even if nobody else in the galaxy knows what this ink exchange means, it matters to him. I can tell by the cant of his head.

"Just hold still," she tells him, as she finishes the first step. "We need to give this time to set."

He complies, claws resting on his legs. There's a somber air about him, as if this is a ceremony of great weight. But I already knew that. It's not marriage, but for him, it's every bit as profound. In all honesty, it is for *me*, too. I don't undertake this commitment lightly. It's more than I've promised another person since before my ill-fated marriage to Simon.

"This needs to dry before I can continue, and I have another client. Let me go check on her." Colette leaves us alone in the studio, and I turn to admire the images of her work that line the otherwise pristine walls.

"How do you know her?" I ask, once the door swishes shut.

I already suspect, of course, but his life with Adele fascinates me. She loved him freely and openly, no boundaries, no judgment. From what I knew of her, that doesn't surprise me at all, but it also makes me wonder at his secrets. What was Vel like with her, and did she know him better than I do? This feeling isn't quite jealousy, but I wouldn't know what to call it, either.

"Adele liked tattoos. She added a new pattern, a small one, each turn that I knew her."

"And you came with her?" I'm guessing.

"Sometimes, if the shop was closed."

I imagine them going about their lives beneath the titian sky, quiet lives, normal ones. He must have been content with that. He's like a chameleon, then—able to stay or go, with no preference to hold him hostage. Unlike me. I'll always be a junkie. Grimspace blazes in my veins, boils in my cells. I can't give it up, nor do I want to. Asking me to stay dirtside? Well, it would be kinder to shoot me.

Colette returns shortly thereafter. She goes about the rest of her work in silence, inking the pattern in lines of color, and when she finishes, it's both elegant and artful. The other Itthorians will find it shocking—maybe even offensive. I hope I'm around for that. When they realize he's chosen a human partner, they will be even more shocked. Or maybe not. They were speculating it was the case on Ithiss-Tor, and they're calling him my longtime companion on the bounce. Soon, they'll be making smut vids about how we make the physiological differences work. Since there are so many niche fetishes, it wouldn't surprise me in the least to discover it's true.

"Do you want me to seal it?" Colette asks.

Vel glances at me, the light refracting on his side-set eyes, and answers, "Yes."

So as a final step, she paints a clear lacquer over the symbol. The Ithtorians don't do that; they leave the carapace unbonded because it shows ambition: the intention to gain more honor marks as they ascend the political ladder. This seal indicates Vel has no higher aspirations than the mark I've given him—and I could hardly be prouder than I am at this moment.

"Do you like it?" I ask, as we leave Colette's shop, stepping into the warm orange twilight.

"You chose it." For him, that is an answer.

Now our business on this world is ended. I am fast approaching a fork in my journey, and that choice—whether I bear left or right—will decide everything in the turns to come.

.UNCLASSIFIED-TRANSMISSION.
.RE: AFTER LONG SILENCE.
.FROM-EDUN_LEVITER.
.TO-SUNI_TARN.

My dear Suni,

You imagined nothing, and my regard remains unchanged. I understood your decision of expedience then, as I welcome your return now. Please journey posthaste to La'heng, where I am embroiled in my latest intrigue. Trust I will put your vast political experience, your impressive brain, and your treasured company to good use.

Do not keep me waiting. I've waited long enough.

Yours,
Edun

CHAPTER 40

Leaving Gehenna feels like a permanent good-bye. Before,
I always knew Adele was waiting for me—and that the
little garret I once occupied, I could claim again, should I
have the need. But she didn't own that building, and they've
already rented her apartment. Yet however much I mourn
her loss, for Vel it's worse.

I remember the framed image, sitting beside her bed
even these many turns later. She loved him, no matter their
differences, and held him in her heart until the end. The
way he held that picture, studied it, with such intensity,
breaks my heart. She is lost to him, but he must go on. I'll
help him deal with the pain however he lets me, and I hope
my colors on his chitin offer some measure of solace. It is
a pledge between us of continuity and companionship—in
a universe where chaos consumes all it touches, this one
thing shall never change.

Titian skies blaze all around us as Hit receives clearance from the spaceport. I have a decision to make before
we can plot our course. It is, at base, a significant one, and
the echoes will follow me through the turns. Do I keep my

promise to March, though it will probably be hard and painful?

I said to him, *I'll come.* But part of me wants to get on with my mission. I don't want to see the new life he's built, in which I have no part. Yet avoidance offers the coward's path, I think. With a faint sigh, I angle my steps toward the lounge, so I can see the atmosphere yield to darkness and stars. The ship is idle, as I ponder our path—straight to La'heng . . . or not. I wanted to get off the ground, but now I am possessed of an unusual uncertainty. For once, my heart and head are completely opposed, as I stand by the screen, watching the stars. They twinkle with unusual brilliance, as if tempting me to travel.

Sometimes I wish I could fly away from everything, leave behind my promises and my failures, and just leave the universe wondering what became of me. They can replay the old bounce stories and speculate, and in time, forget I ever existed. I'm to the point where I'm ready for eternal anonymity. Though some people spend their whole lives chasing notoriety, I feel like I've spent mine fleeing from it . . . and trying to live down a reputation I gained through grief and desperation.

But before I disappear off the galactic radar, I have one final piece of business. Loras thought he didn't matter to me because of the way I treated him—the way everyone treated him. I left him to die, and the fact that he survived doesn't let me off the hook. I have to make things up to him, the only way that matters: by figuring out a way to set his people free. Maybe it's too grand a scheme, but I'm not alone in it. Vel comes with me, always. I touch my throat and smile. Zeeka, too, will stay by my side, a grace I undoubtedly do not deserve. It strikes me then—as I've become less human, so have my companions. I suppose that's fitting.

Hit pings my comm. "Should I sit tight?"

The unspoken question is, though: *Are we jumping soon?*

"Yeah."

As soon as I make up my mind whether I'm going to be brave.

We'll be grounded on La'heng for a long while, no doubt, while we try to get the necessary permissions to start the trials. It will take time to gain trust and gather allies. La'heng isn't a good place, for obvious reasons. Their inability to defend themselves have left them open to an endless parade of armed invaders, ostensibly present on planet for altruistic reasons and who instead rape the resources. Once they've taken what they wanted, the soldiers disappear until the next wave arrives. Hostile forces have occupied La'heng more often than any other world since the Axis Wars, and nobody cares enough to change things.

But I do. Not because of the plight of La'heng itself, though that's unforgivable. I'm doing this for my friend.

Vel joins me a few minutes later. We gaze in silence for a few moments before he says, "You cannot decide what to do."

I let out a sigh. "No. It's not that. I've made up my mind. I'm just debating whether I have the wherewithal to handle it in person."

"It would be unkind to act otherwise," he notes.

"I guess that's my answer, then." I pause, gazing up at him.

"Indeed."

He is so familiar to me now that he doesn't look strange. I can read his moods as I would a human male's: cant of head, positioning of limbs, flare of mandible, how he holds his claws. They also tell me a story about his state of mind. And right now, he seems troubled.

"Does it bother you that I love him, too?" That's the first time I've used that word aloud for what's between us, but it fits. Nothing else is big enough. When he almost died in the Maker 'verse, it hit me like a payload of magnetized iron how lost I'd be without him. And that, too, is why I asked him to wear my colors.

"No. There are many types, some of which are beyond any human ability to experience. Can you imagine what it is to 'love' a thousand clutchmates, as humans would a sibling?"

It's not the same, of course. Ithtorians don't bond as

humans do. Familial loyalty offers the closest facsimile, but otherwise, they lack emotions as we know them. Vel was an anomaly on his homeworld, and since his exile, he's learned emotional behaviors that take him even further from the standard. He's a hybrid now, much as I am.

"No, I honestly can't."

"And does it bother you that I will always love Adele and that her passing grieves me? It does not seem so long to me since I was happy with her. Does that injure you in some fashion, Sirantha?"

"No."

I see his point. We're not like other people. Long life span gives us a different perspective on love and the nature of time. I've had a chance to process what Carvati told me, and I accept I'm different. Over the turns to come, my ideas will shift even more, I suspect, and that's the nature of existence. Life without change is stagnation.

His mandible flares, telling me he's being honest with me right now. "To my mind, one thing does not lessen another. The heart is not a glass of water, but more like an endlessly pumping spring."

That makes sense. He's saying that what I feel for him doesn't reduce what I can feel for March. Love isn't finite; it's not miserly and small. I don't know if March would feel the same, but he's not like us. I certainly don't want to hurt him more than I already have, so I won't mention this when I see him. It's not infidelity when it's so different. Is it? I don't know, but I don't feel as though I'm doing wrong right now, standing in the lounge with Vel.

"No, it's not. Thanks for being . . . you."

"I am constant, Jax. Right now, your presence is enough. I have been alone for a long time, and I am content to know I will have a companion down the turns."

"I'm sorry you were lonely." The idea hurts me.

"I will not be anymore."

"That much, I do promise." I'm not sure even if March was out of the picture—and he's not—whether I can be as open-minded as Adele. I love Vel, but I'm not positive where my limits lie, and at this juncture, I'm not free to find out. At least, not in that way. If we crossed that line, then it *would* be infidelity.

He goes on, "If there is ever more between us, then I will take pleasure in that as well when the time comes, even knowing that day may never arrive."

I couldn't ask for more than such patience and unconditional acceptance.

"So you're happy to wander with me, after La'heng."

"I am."

"Sometimes I try to imagine what I'll do, after we finish on La'heng. The possibilities are endless."

"What do *you* want, Sirantha?"

Nobody ever asks me that—and it's part of the reason Vel is so special to me. "I'm not sure yet. But I always loved finding new beacons and charting the territory."

"Blazing new paths in the Star Road."

Oh yeah, he gets it. "Does that sound like something you'd enjoy?"

"As it is something I have never done, I believe I would."

"Would you consider getting a pilot's license?"

Hit and Dina have formed their own crew, and they have dreams that don't include us. It hurts to think of all of us fragmenting, but March has already embarked on his own path, and Doc is dead. Loras is free. It stands to reason I need a pilot willing to commit to me, and one with Vel's longevity would be an added bonus.

"I am."

"You can take the training on La'heng. That way, we'll be ready to go together when it's time."

Vel nods. "I will make the arrangements."

Pleased, I rest my head against his arm, and he touches a claw lightly to my hair. Then he leans down and brushes the side of his face against mine. An ache springs up because I know what it means. He loves me, too. His devotion is not loud or demanding, but quiet and steadfast, a deep tidal pool that never runs dry. The contact is not repugnant, though his face feels hard and smooth. There are gaps in his chitin, where he can appreciate a touch. I can't go down that road with him. Not now. But like Adele, I find too much to admire in his fine spirit to be horrified by the body Mary gave him.

One day, we'll be self-sufficient. His knack with machines and my knowledge of gunnery make us a complementary team. I can see us turns from now, charting new beacons—with nobody ordering us around or sending us to do boring jumps. That sounds like the closest I'll ever get to paradise.

"I always loved first contact, too. Like with the Mareq."

No telling how long we'll be on La'heng, but afterward—freedom. I live for the moment when we're obligated no longer, and I've discharged all my debts.

"Always with the risks." But there's a fondness in his words, echoed by my colors on his carapace.

We are bonded through camaraderie and shared experience that few would understand. But it doesn't matter whether others find our relationship comprehensible; it's enough that we know the reasons why. I only know that it works, and I never want to be without him. We've been through too much together.

I make up my mind then, pressing my comm. "Hit, get Argus in the nav chair. We have one stop to make before La'heng."

CHAPTER 41

Nicu Tertius isn't what I expected. Given the torment March harbored due to his experiences with the place, I expected a world of burning brimstone, black volcanic rock steaming sulfur into the atmosphere. Instead, it's actually quite lovely as we make our final approach. Not on the level of Venice Minor, of course, before the bombing, but there's an old-world charm in the lines of the buildings and the way the city is laid out to follow the river.

We're putting down in Tyre, where March lives. When I saw him last, he asked me to move here, and I told him I would think about it. There could be no other answer besides the one I've come to give, but I figured I owed it to him to say it in person; it's not the sort of thing that should be left to the bounce. Still, I'm not looking forward to the conversation, and I toy with the idea.

If Kai had asked, would I have been willing to give up flying for him? The answer comes immediately—no. And he wouldn't ask, either. He understood it meant everything to me, and that all my loves come second to that great one. Maybe it's wrong to love a thing like grimspace more than any single person in your life; I don't know. But I can't be other than who I am, and I hope March gets that. Mary knows, I don't want to hurt him any more than I want to wind up heartbroken.

"Are you sure you wish to do this alone?" Vel asks.

"I have to."

He nods, and the others head out to explore the city while I hail a hover cab and input March's address on the pad. I'm beyond nervous as the lights zoom past; at the speed we travel, the colors become lines in the sky, streaks of red, white, and green keeping pace with the vehicle. The cab puts down outside a ten-story structure, constructed of a pale material that gleams in the moonlight. It's a lovely place, echoes of palatial style. But then, all architects want to invoke the idea that the emperor—or one of the hundred hopefuls vying for the title—would be glad to live in his building.

At the front door, the bot scans me, then says, toneless, "What is the purpose of your visit?"

"I'm here to see March in 1002."

"One moment, please."

Excellent security. Naturally he would want to be sure Sasha is safe here. He's all that's left of his sister. A couple of minutes later, the vid-cam scans the street to make sure nobody is trying to enter behind me, no suspicious movement in the perimeter, and the door kicks open for exactly ten seconds—long enough for me to step through and nobody else.

The bot tells me, "I will unlock the lift to transport you to the tenth floor."

I don't need to respond to that, so I simply get on and let it take me up. March's flat occupies the whole tenth story, which tells me the Conglomerate did well by him in the severance package. He sure didn't use my money for this. Not that I would've minded.

When I approach the door, it swings open, and there's March. He steals my breath. I always think I've forgotten something about his rough appeal; his strong-ugly face epitomizes the masculine ideal in my eyes—with his crooked nose, square jaw, sensual mouth, and amber-laced eyes. His face bristles with a couple days' worth of beard. No military dress code anymore, but he's still wearing soldier's pants with all their pockets in a drab green. His white shirt is a little wrinkled, but he's broad at the shoulders, strong across the chest. It hurts me all over again that he looks older. I can see the turns I missed in his face, creases at mouth, lines at the eyes.

Oh, March.

He wraps his arms around me before I can say a single word. The pressure of his arms feels so good, so right, that for a moment, I wonder if I'm crazy. *Why not just stay?* He kisses me with heat and longing, his hands in my hair, until I can't think.

But a small person nudges forward and between us. Sasha looks so much like the still I once saw of Svetlana, with his fair hair and sea-green eyes. I remember the TK scare on Gehenna, and my ardor cools. March lets go of me.

"Sasha, you remember Jax."

By his expression, he does, but he's afraid I'll take away the one person who's solely his, and I'm not eloquent enough to convince him that if it came down to a choice, March would pick flesh and blood every time. That surety might hurt another woman, but I understand him, and I'd never put him in that position. That's part of the reason why I've come.

"So glad to see you. You're just in time for dinner." In a polite, small voice, Sasha continues, "We're having pasta. It's my favorite."

"What kind of sauce?"

"I like it with cheese," he volunteers.

"Sounds good." I feel so awkward talking with him. Some people have the instinctive knack, but I'm not one of them. So I try to treat him like a normal grown human. "What kind?"

"White," he answers.

"Me, too." Hey, we have a little common ground. "With cream?"

"Yeah, it's good that way. We have to eat vegetables, too, though."

"Green and crunchy?"

Sasha nods. "Always."

Sounds like March is doing a good job. He knows how to raise a kid.

"It's almost ready," he says, ushering me in.

Lovely place. The first room is enormous, furnished with good synth-wood that shines almost like the real thing. Everything is comfortable but spacious, with plenty of room for a kid to run without tripping or breaking something. At the far end of the main room is the kitchen-mate, then a hall that leads down to what must be the san-facilities and bedrooms. It's so strange to feel March's imprint here; this is where he's lived for turns . . . without me. A pang goes through me at how thoroughly he's settled. There's art on the walls, for Mary's sake—some of it drawn by Sasha's hand. *This* is his home, for all he once recorded in a vid message that I was his home. That's not true anymore, if it ever was.

For long moments, I study the pictures. In prints, he favors black and white with bursts of red. In a rare intuitive flash, I realize that for him, I *am* those flashes of color . . . the irresistible brightness in each frame. It's both humbling and lovely, that revelation, but the color is always running toward the edge of the picture, always going away, whereas the other images in the picture are solid and show no signs of motion. That's March and me, beautifully illustrated, and my heart breaks a little.

But if he were the portraits on my walls, he would be the one going away. He left me twice, and I never tried to stop him from doing what he thought was right. A tiny hope I didn't realize I'd been nurturing shrivels up and puffs away in my next breath. I'm not going to convince him to come with me. I recall what he said before, and nothing's changed; Sasha needs to attend school. He's not an average kid who can be raised in the haphazard way I was. When I was thirteen, my parents took to traveling, mostly because the gallery wasn't doing well, and I suspect my mother was getting involved in shady matters, even then, maybe even for the reason she claimed—that my father had no head for business, and they were drowning in debt.

From that point on, my attendance at school was sporadic at best. I didn't mind; I loved ships, and I loved the freedom. Even dealing with an AI for lessons didn't deter my determination to join the academy, as soon as I realized I met the criteria to be a jumper. But what worked for me wouldn't suffice for Sasha.

Time to forget that idea and resign yourself to what's possible.

"Out here." March leads the way to a table out on the balcony.

The servo-bot is already setting the food out; this rectangular model with food-prep capacity inside reminds me of the ones on Ithiss-Tor. I wonder if they're already in wide commercial production off world. Well. Maybe "already" isn't the right word. I keep forgetting how long it seems like it's been, and how long it's *actually* been. Different time streams, different 'verses.

We sit down to eat, and Sasha has to be coaxed to speak. He's shy with me, still, worried that I'll prove more important to his uncle, whom he calls Dad. I don't blame the kid for feeling insecure. He's never had anybody who belonged to him before; he went straight into crèche-rearing because of his unusual gift, and he was five turns old before March found him. So he's pretty scared right now. What if March stops loving him because of me?

"Tell her your good news," March prompts him.

"I took top marks in the control competition."

"What's that?" I ask.

Without meeting my eyes, he explains, "It's a program at school that tests how well we can manage our abilities."

"Good job." With TK like his, it's imperative he can handle the pressure of the gift, and for his sake, I'm glad he doesn't have to deal with the constant influx of people's thoughts, like March.

"My teacher says kids in the state homes don't have as much support as me, so that's why I won."

"She's probably right."

"How long will you be here?" Sasha asks, after the food is gone. Then, with a nervous glance at March, he adds, desperate for approval, "You can stay as long as you want."

Anything, as long as you don't ask Dad to go away with you again.

"That's kind of you," I reply.

My heart breaks a little more.

As we leave the table, the bot clears the dishes, and March takes Sasha off for their bedtime ritual. On the balcony, I stand and stare at the stars, trying to imagine what it would be like, living here, seeing the same constellations in the night sky. But I can only think of what waits beyond the atmosphere, all the wonders I've yet to see.

As I'd known when he asked me to join him, I can't imagine this life, the one he's chosen, as mine. And it's time to tell him so.

CHAPTER 42

"He's a beautiful kid," I say. *"You've done a great job* with him."

Sasha has been asleep for about an hour, after three stories and two drinks of water, and now March and I stand on his balcony overlooking the lights of Tyre, the jewel in the newly crowned emperor's throne. Maybe this one will last longer than six months in the cutthroat Nicuan political climate. I never dreamed he would settle here when this world drove him crazy—nearly cost him everything—but Sasha's school is here, and he'd do anything for the boy.

"Thanks. I love him more than anything."

That's not news. I can see it in their interactions. All kids should have that, and it's wrong that they don't. I wouldn't alter the situation for a billion creds. Would things be different now if I'd gone to Nicuan as soon as I was acquitted? Impossible to say or know.

Five fragging turns. I still can't get over that. I'm standing with March, seeing the echoes, and he's lived a lot in that time—resigned his military commission, given up flying, and become responsible for another human being.

Thing is, we always knew I wasn't meant to settle down, and that's exactly what he's done. Granted, I wasn't around to give him an alternative, so he had to do what was best for Sasha. Special Psi school, a nice penthouse overlooking the river. I watch the flat-bottom boats cruise along; white lights rim the edges, giving them a jolly air. They're celebrating something down there, some local festival. The music and laughter make mc feel even more melancholy.

There's no point in dragging this out. I came here, hoping I could salvage something, but he's settled. Sasha calls him Dad, and I can't compete. Nor do I want to. It's crystal clear to me that March needs this even though it breaks my heart.

"I'm going to La'heng," I tell him. "The cure worked on Loras, so we're ready to try and get the necessary permissions to start trials on a larger scale."

"I knew you were. It'll take time, but I have no doubt you can do it."

I don't deserve his faith—not after everything I've put him through—but it still lights me up. "Thanks." I pause, hating the awkwardness. "Do you want me to head out? I don't know your policy on overnight guests."

Knowing March, he errs on the side of caution and doesn't indulge in behavior that could hurt his nephew. I don't expect he's been faithful to me all this time, half suspecting I was dead. I'm sure there have been women. I just don't want to hear about them. Not when I still love him, and I am walking away from him, even if it's not forever. Mary grant it's not.

"I don't ever want you to leave," he says softly. "But you will. The morning is soon enough." My comm beeps, and I check it.

When we were stranded on the other side of the Maker's gate, the thought of him kept me going. Day after day, I pushed on, even where I was tired and half-starved, when the cold felt like it would kill me, then the heat. But I can't be bitter when I see how happy March is and how much Sasha loves him.

He touches my cheek, catching a tear that got away.

Mary knows, that's how I feel about March. Then I feel him inside my head, as I haven't in so long. I'd gotten used to the silence. This time, since it isn't so fleeting as it was on Gehenna, I notice that he's pure warmth, different now that he's known a child's unconditional devotion. The old March had rough edges and dark places; this one streams light. I catch my breath at the difference, and he flinches at my secret pain.

"Do you really think I haven't been true to you?" he asks.

More tears fall . . . and I hate them. I'm not this person. I'm *not*.

"I don't expect it."

"Jax . . . you know how I said . . . before your trial—that I'd be there waiting? I always will be. Five turns. Ten. Twenty. There's no one else for me. I live in hope that there will come a time when you'll need no more wandering, and you'll come home to me."

I wish I could. I wish I were wired that way. But I'm not. As March said once before, I'd wither on the ground and come to hate the person who tied me down. I was born to jump, to tag new beacons and keep moving. There's so much out there, and after I keep my promise to Loras, I intend to see it all.

"And *I* live in hope that you'll still want me when Sasha's grown. I hope someday you'll be ready to captain a ship again and join me out there."

I tip my head back and gaze at the stars, crystal and diamond on black s-silk. It's a lovely view, but it can't compare with grimspace—or even the beauty of the constellations in straight space. Even if he asked, I can't stay. The promise to Loras gives me a compelling reason to leave, but even without it, I don't want to remain here. Though I want March—and I always will—I can't do it if it comes with this life.

"Someday," he says softly. "What're you doing in eight turns?"

"Dunno, but I'll keep my calendar clear."

He braces his hands on the balustrade, not looking at me anymore. "I can't make love to you again. Not when you're leaving. That last time, before you jumped, before the beacons changed . . ." He trails off and shakes his. His hair is long now, past his shoulders. Once more, he has the piratical look that I always loved. "For the longest time, that was all I had of you. First the trial . . . and then you were just gone. Before that, I had that memory. Of making love to you . . . and then waking up alone. Finding your message. That felt like death. But I kept moving. And then the Morgut—I just can't, that's all."

"It's fine." I'm not in the mood for sex. Too much sadness, paired with the knowledge that I have countless turns ahead of me, and he won't be there to share them, even if we manage to get our timing right. Someday.

I intend to try. He's worth fighting for, but I won't change who I am for any man. No more than he should alter himself to suit me.

"A kiss?" He's asking me.

"Please."

I have had passionate kisses and fierce ones, kisses so sweet they tasted like pure honey and kisses that cut like knives, but until this moment, I've never had one that said both *hello* and *good-bye*. Much as I love him, I can't take more than the butterfly brush of his mouth, before I draw back, a tremor rocking through me. How I wish I could throw myself into his arms and stay there forever, but I must keep my word to Loras, and for me, life isn't about where you come to rest; it's the journey.

A deep, shuddering breath helps to restore my equilibrium. "How can love be so magnificent and still hurt this much?"

"I don't know. Over the turns, I've asked myself the same thing."

No doubt. I'm not the same woman he fell in love with, turns ago, but love is delightfully tensile—and the best kind pulls and stretches to accommodate new growth. He's not the same man, either, but I adore him for his steadfast care and his fidelity to family. Which makes what I'm about to do even more absurd. It's also the *only* course for a woman like me.

"I don't think I can stay the night. The parting won't be easier by daylight."

Vel and the rest are waiting on the ship, anyway; they signaled me that they're back from sightseeing and won't mind taking off tonight. The sooner we leave Nicuan, the sooner we can begin on La'heng—the sooner we can liberate Loras's people. That's not a trivial task.

His smile flashes bittersweet humor. "At least this time I get to see you go."

Farewell for now, my love. I say it in the silence of my head, but he hears.

For now, he replies. *And don't think I'll go those eight turns without seeing you. I will come for you. Always.*

That sounds like a promise, but one unasked. We can't be sure what the future holds. *I understand if you need to find a . . . partner. Someone to help you raise Sasha. I understand.* I do, I *do,* even if that generous offer threatens to break me.

Tender warmth streams through me. *That's why I love you. Thank you, Jax.* But in him I sense the resolve not to. Sasha doesn't need anyone else, he thinks, and might only be unsettled. He'll wait, like he promised. And as Sasha gets older and more secure, he'll come to La'heng, or I can visit here. It's not impossible, just . . . hard. But things always are with us. "Always" is a word that carries both magic and despair. I clutch it to my heart like a bladed fan.

I run then; I can't bear anymore. Blindly, I seek the door, navigating his finely furnished living room through a field of tears. The door recognizes me and lets me out, and I weep silently in the lift, which takes me to the ground, unasked. March stays with me, and I feel his pain as well. The anguish amplifies in my head until I know he's crying, too.

Not for me, I tell him. *Don't let Sasha see you sad. We'll be fine. I'll comm.*

Me, too, love.

The tenuous connection breaks as I stop on the first floor. I'm too far away from him now. Too far, too far. *Oh, March.* Squaring my shoulders, I exit his building and walk backward until I can see his apartment. He's still on the balcony, watching me go, as he promised. I stop and lift a hand to him, a dark silhouette against the starry sky. He puts his palm up, and I feel the heat of his touch across the distance. I am not the woman to raise a child with him, but I *am* the one he loves.

There will *be a someday.*

Then I turn and hurry toward the hover-cab stand. I am not born to be an earthbound thing. Even as I step into the cab and it lifts, so does my heart. I believe in a future where all things are possible, promises are kept, and you can, indeed, go home again. And he will be waiting. Always.

From national bestselling author Ann Aguirre

SHADY LADY

A Corine Solomon Novel

I'd spent my whole life settling, trying not to attract attention, doing what it took to keep other people happy. I didn't want to do that again. Not when I was finally comfortable in my own skin. Sure, there were challenges, like a drug lord who wanted me dead, and the fact that I owed a demon a debt that he could call due at any moment. But everybody's got problems, right?

When Corine Solomon touches an object, she knows its history. But her own future concerns her more and more. Now back in Mexico, she's running her pawnshop and trying to get a handle on her strange new powers, for she might need them. And soon.

Then former ally Kel Ferguson walks through her door. Muscled and tattooed, Kel looks like a convict but calls himself a holy warrior. He carries a warning for Corine: The Montoya cartel is coming for her—but they don't pack just automatic weapons. The Montoyas use warlocks, shamans, voodoo priests—anything to terminate trouble. And Corine has become enemy number one. . . .

penguin.com

She shoots first.
And never asks questions.

From national bestselling author Ann Aguirre

KILLBOX

A Sirantha Jax Novel

Talk is cheap when lives are in jeopardy.

Sirantha Jax is a "jumper," a woman who possesses the unique genetic makeup needed to navigate faster-than-light ships through grimspace. With no tolerance for political diplomacy, she quits her ambassador post so she can get back to saving the universe the way she does best—by mouthing off and kicking butt.

And her tactics are needed more than ever. Flesh-eating aliens are attacking stations on the outskirts of space, and for many people, the Conglomerate's forces are arriving too late to serve and protect them.

Now Jax must take matters into her own hands by recruiting a militia to defend the frontiers—out of the worst criminals, mercenaries, and raiders who ever traveled through grimspace . . .

"Sirantha Jax doesn't just leap off the page—she storms out, kicking, cursing, and mouthing off."
—Sharon Shinn, national bestselling author of *Troubled Waters*

M861T0411